"One morning this chap came into my coffee shop and ordered a coffee. He sat down at one of the tables with his laptop and began to type. I thought nothing of it, until he turned up most mornings over the next couple of months with the same routine. One day I asked him what he was doing. 'Writing a book,' he said. I asked if I might read it, and he agreed. I thought it was going to be at best dull, but found to my delight it was a really good book. When I read it I had no religion. Now I'm a Christian! Funny how life works."

Peter Morrissey

"Robert gave me 'Dysmas' to read a month or two before I started doing so. I picked it up as Easter week was approaching, and soon found myself engrossed. I read it over that week. Though I know it is a fictional work, it made Easter come alive for me. I told Robert it was the best Easter I have had. I recommend it to everyone."

Elizabeth Roki

Robert M Smith is a Catholic father of seven children and ten grandchildren.

Asked one day to explain the apparent discrepancy in the Bible with regard two thieves insulting Jesus in one Gospel, and one seeking redemption in another, he wrote this book as a response...

Cana Press
www.notredamemonastery.org/canapress
ISBN: 978-0-6450285-8-4

Cover design by Dominic de Souza
www.dominicdesouza.com

Printed in Australia

The Thief Who Stole Heaven: A Tale of Dysmas

Robert M Smith

Contents

A Journey Conceived

"No!" she screamed as she struck the bedding with her fist. "It cannot end this way. No, please not like this." She was lathered in sweat and crying.

"Muriam, Muriam! Wake woman," called her husband who had woken startled by the commotion beside him, but it was to no avail. This state that gripped her held her tight in desperate fear and remorse. She began to wail and thrash about uncontrollably. A large pitcher of sweet-smelling oils kept on a small table beside the bed was too close and thereby, inevitably upended over the bed and all therein.

Her husband left her, and managed to light a lantern from a coal left in the fire used to prepare the meal the evening before. What the light revealed was a woman desperate, yet still sleeping. It had been a very hot day and the night air was still muggy, especially within the confines of their little home. This added to her husband's concern as her face was so red.

"Muriam!" he screamed.

He grabbed her by the shoulders and shook her so violently as to snap her head back and her eyes open. She stared dumbstruck at her husband who was clearly shaking, and not realising her state, threw herself around his neck and held him so tightly, he had to pry her loose. All the while the tears ran freely.

"Azel," she said, "Azel. Oh my lovely Azel. What have they done to you, husband? What have they done to you?"

"Nothing, Muriam, I am here. I am here with you. You were dreaming, wake up and be still, woman."

She stopped then and became aware of her surroundings, and indeed her state, and was completely perplexed.

"But it was so real. Azel, it was real," cried Muriam.

"Well, it was real enough," he said as he held her now, quite shocked himself. He held her at arms-length and looked into her eyes.

"You had me so worried," he said, and could not help but hold her close once more.

"Well," he continued at last, "this won't do. Strip the bed and yourself while I see if I can't fetch water to bathe both of us," and he smiled that reassuring smile that had swept her off her feet twelve years before. He changed his clothing and was gone in moments to be about his task, as she quickly set about her own.

She was still shaken, but now felt more than a little foolish about all that had just taken place. So real it had seemed to her that even now she felt the restriction in her chest that so often accompanies great fear.

With all the soiled clothing bundled at the door, she sat now wrapped in a blanket on the one good chair they owned, waiting for her husband to return from the well. Moments later he pushed open the door and brought forth two large pitchers of water.

"How are you feeling?"

"A little silly," she said.

A reassuring smile was the only reply.

The water was soon poured into a very large crater hewn out of a rock they had built their home around. It was the nearest thing to a Roman bath in the area, and they were the envy of their friends, who often playfully scoffed at their scandalous flamboyance.

"I'll be back with more in a moment," and he was gone again.

Immediately she climbed the little stair Azel had made to make bathing a more lady-like affair, sat in the water and began the ritual.

Presently, Azel was back with another two pitchers of water, and poured them this time over the head of his wife.

"I think you enjoyed that," she quipped.

"It wasn't bad," he smiled. "Would you like some more?"

"Oh no, that is perfect. Really," she replied.

"While you're taking care of things here, I'll go and wash by the river, I'll be back soon. By the way, perhaps we can find a more suitable place to stand our fragrant oils," he said, laughing as he disappeared through the door once again.

She bathed and pondered what had just happened, and shuddered at the thought of the dream she had just had.

"It was so real," she kept saying to herself. "So real."

She climbed out and dried herself. She found fresh clothes for herself and linen for the bed.

"What a good man I have been blessed with," she thought as the bed was once again fresh.

She stopped then and went to her clothing chest and began to rummage through.

"Ah ha!" she exclaimed as she lifted out a beautiful silk night dress her parents had given her as a wedding gift. The very one she had worn on her wedding night. She smiled to herself as she removed her normal night attire, and replaced it with silk. No sooner was she ready than Azel returned to find his wife as beautiful as the day they were wed.

"Oh," was all he could manage as she stole the breath right out of him. "Ah, how are you feeling?"

"Much better. I thought I might try on this old thing to see if it still fits," she said mischievously.

"Oh, it fits just fine I think!" he replied with a smile.

He often marvelled at the beauty of Muriam, though in younger years his friends had been puzzled by his choice of what they had considered a rather plain woman. Homely I believe they called her. Azel himself was a handsome and solid man, a little over six feet in height, who had some of the young ladies hopeful of his attention. He was broad across the shoulders and carried himself with dignity, though rarely with pride, unless he was in public with his wife.

"I should smack your bottom for frightening me half out of my wits," he said at last as he took her in his arms.

"I have a better idea, why don't we ask the Most High once again to hear our plea for a child?"

"I love you so," he said, "why don't we?"

He kissed her then with a tenderness that bespoke such great affection, that she forgot all about her earlier trauma. They knelt down at the bed's edge and sought together the Hebrew God's blessing. That He might consent to grant them a child from their union of love.

They had no way of knowing, nine months later to the very day, they would welcome a son. Their first born and only son, Dysmas.

Morning found Muriam awake as the first rays of light were cutting through the darkness. Very gently she slipped from the bed, was dressed and gone in moments. She gathered up the bundle of linen at the door and was on her way to the river, when a dog barked from the lane just past their humble home.

"Be still," she said and hurried on.

The bundle unwrapped, the contents were soon in the water being scrubbed. This was hard work, but a light and lively heart made it a pleasure indeed. She loved to wash early before the chatter started. She could just let her thoughts rest on the call of the birds and the cool of the morning breeze. Soon however her thoughts turned to the night before.

"What could it mean?" she asked herself.

"Don't be silly," she chided now, "it was but a dream. A silly dream."

A dream nonetheless that left a dread in her heart.

Just then a duck with nine little ducklings splashed into the water on the opposite bank.

"How lovely," she thought, and thanked God for these little blessings. "Each small weight I carry, you lift, O God, with such tenderness."

"How is it you pay any attention to one such as I?" she prayed.

In what seemed no time, all was washed and placed in the basket. She sat on the bank and prayed while watching God's little creations splashing and playing together. One would disappear under the water only to pop up a good distance away. Muriam couldn't help but wonder at the miracles all around her.

"What a marvellous and holy God. How He cares for us, we who are so little; and He so great. Who could know the wonders of God?" she thought.

"So how are we this morning?" came the familiar voice of Azel as he sat down beside her.

"I am so much better, thanks to you. Oh and the Lord's gifts as you can see," she answered, motioning to the ducklings.

"So, are you up to telling me what last night was all about?"

"It was just a bad dream," she said.

"It was a little more than just a bad dream. I was really worried if I couldn't wake you, I might even have lost you. What was the dream about?"

She looked at the ducklings for a long time, tears welling in her eyes.

"Look Muriam, it's alright, if you don't..."

"No," she said, "it's just that it frightened me so. It was so very real, I felt like it was really happening. I love you more than anything; I couldn't bear to lose you."

"So it was about me then?"

"Yes. You were being dragged through the streets of Jerusalem with two other men to be crucified. There was nothing I could do Azel, nothing. There was a huge crowd who were screaming hateful things. One of the men was being beaten and flogged from every side. He was covered in blood. It is impossible to explain to you how terrible it all was, and in all of it was you, my beautiful husband. I saw you as clear as I see you now, hanging on the cross, your life's blood draining from your body. It was too much Azel. I just couldn't bear it," and she paused, transported back to the terrible image, yet there seemed a need to be rid of it.

"Go on," said Azel, "it's alright."

"It was strange," she said, now remembering the details, "but the man who was being abused so violently was the only one who seemed calm, even peaceful. Even the people standing at his cross seemed oddly peaceful. For me it was the most frightful thing I have ever experienced. Then they came and broke your legs and," she broke down then, sobbing as Azel put his arms around her.

"It was just a bad dream, Muriam. Why would the Romans want to crucify a lowly thresher? They wouldn't waste their time."

"I know it's all just silly. I'm sorry, I can't help loving you."

"Never be sorry for that. Rest assured, I'm not interested in upsetting the Romans, and I'm sure they are even less interested in me. Now, let's dry those tears, get this basket back and have something to eat."

"You are so good to me, thank you," she smiled.

"It's not hard to be good to the one you love," he smiled. "You are very easy to love. I thank the Most High for you every day."

"You love our Lord very much, don't you?"

"Is there anything else to love?" he said, drifting away as if overcome with peace. "He that gives us every good gift, who prepares our goods in due season and delivers them in ways for our best outcome. What more could one do that might win our wayward hearts that He has not done? I love Him most of all because He has ordained that you might be my wife. And I know that He will grant us the blossom of our love, for this too I love Him with a gratitude that I fear will burst my very heart."

Muriam couldn't hide her joy. She loved to hear him speak of the Most High. It set her own faith alight with hope, and confirmed more and more how great a gift Azel was to her life. They were very much in love. Though they had little, they had everything.

On his feet now he held out his hand and helped her up. Taking up the basket he started running and she knew at once the race was on.

"You are cheating me," she said as she scrambled after him.

"Not at all. I have the basket you know," he laughed.

They ran through the little village, the sun now flooding all with its grandeur. All creation responded to the call. The dew ran down the leaves, the birds darting through the trees singing as if songs of praise. It seemed all creation was awake to give thanks and watch the dawning of the new miracle before them. All, that is, except man. The people of the village were still sleeping.

They stopped at the door, breathing hard.

"It is only man who seems to ignore the glory around him," said Azel as he cast his eyes about sadly. "What a terrible shame."

Muriam put her face right up to his and said with a smile, "We didn't," and burst through their little door.

While Muriam prepared their simple fare, Azel set about transferring his thoughts to parchment. In due course the food prepared, Muriam was at his side.

"Are you going to share your thoughts with me?" she asked, sitting down now.

"I love the mornings, especially with you," he smiled.

"Read to me," she said.

So he began:

"The crisp of the morning, the dew drops are forming,
They roll down the leaves and fall to the ground.
Horizons are born as the sun meets the sky,
Warms the earth and I feel alive.

The snap of a twig felt beneath my feet,
The crisp of the breeze the birds flock to meet.
The gift of life going on everywhere,
Just my love for you to compare.

I thank God for the time I've had be sure,
Shed a tear for the time I haven't got anymore.
Let's take a brief moment of every morning to share,
The gifts going on everywhere."

"That you notice is why I love you," she said, her eyes dancing. "Come, it's time we ate."

The contents of their dwelling were spartan to say the least. With the exception of their valued Roman bath, there was precious little else to speak of. The poor table was pushed up on one side of the rock that formed their envied bath, so that it doubled as a chair, with their single chair on the other side. The stove was a fire on the floor with a bar of iron bent to hold the pots for cooking. The bed stood concealed with a small bedside table in the other room.

There was but one room in reality, separated in two by a large sheet of canvas Azel had procured from a grateful caravan guide and owner, by way of thanks for having nursed his best camel back to health. Upon the caravan's return, the man was astounded to find his camel well and in fine condition. This was to become a firm friendship cherished by both, and Petmar would become a familiar guest as the years passed. His caravan visited four times a year.

From that time, Azel and Muriam joined him and his wife each year to make the trip to Jerusalem for the Passover. His wife Arlett was so taken with the young lovers and their zest for things beautiful, that she soon started mothering Muriam to Azel's delight. Muriam, he thought, needed an older woman to talk to, having lost her mother just after they married. It was truly a blessing to all concerned, as it became evident that Muriam was with child.

"You will not be with us next year when we go up for the Passover I think," said Petmar. "It will likely be the time for the child to come."

"Yes I think that is so," replied Azel.

"You must go Azel," said Muriam. "Take our prayer to the Most High for our child."

"Yes Azel, why don't you travel with Petmar. I will stay with Muriam to help her. After all, what good would a man be then?" laughed Arlett.

"Are you sure, Muriam?" asked Azel.

"I am sure. I will be in good hands, and the Lord will hear your prayers. We will all be in good hands."

"So it is settled then," said Petmar in a buoyant mood, "no women to drive us crazy next year," and he laughed with a roar that he was somewhat famous for, sparking a smile from all at the table.

"We have another announcement I'm afraid," said Petmar. "Come."

Leading them out to their tent, he and Arlett motioned them to enter. Azel looked with puzzlement, but she motioned again.

Upon entering they were confronted with a most beautiful child's cradle, complete with linen and wraps of the finest quality. They turned to their hosts with genuine surprise.

"These are those things that we purchased for our child so long ago, explained a resigned Arlett, while Petmar was uncharacteristically pensive.

"We thought you had no children," replied Muriam.

"It's a bit of a painful story I suppose and we have not spoken of it. Perhaps it's time we did. Will you tell them Petmar?" asked Arlett.

"I am sorry my love, but could you?" he replied with a sad smile.

"Eighteen years ago," she began, "We were elated when we found I was with child. Petmar was like a child himself. We travel a great deal and so started gathering baby clothes and cradles and the like. It was a very exciting time. In the Lord's own time we were given a son."

"I thought I would lose Petmar to an explosion," she laughed. "He was so proud I thought he would burst!"

"Three weeks of joy we had before the Lord took him back. It was clear he was not well. The doctor could do little, and so we resigned ourselves to cherishing every moment that the Most High gave us with our little boy. They were wonderful weeks," she sighed. She smiled at Petmar who smiled back, nodding.

"We kept everything all these past eighteen years. We kept the cradle and baby clothes in our home where we could see them always and remember our joy. In all these long years it has never occurred to either one of us, that we would meet a couple so special that we would like to share our joy with, until we met you," and she started to weep.

Muriam went to her and held her and they both wept. Arlett, composing herself, continued. "Our time is some years past. We no longer have future prospects for such things as children. We look forward with joy to your time. It is our deepest desire that you accept these gifts, that you might always know how we both treasure you, and what place you have in our hearts."

Azel began to weep then. "We never even suspected," he said, and they all embraced.

"Come," said Petmar, a most practical man. "We shall help you in with these simple items that say so much more than we are able," and he picked up the cradle while Arlett gathered up some of the linen and blankets.

Azel and Muriam looked one to another. "We have family we knew nothing of for much of our lives," Azel said at last.

"How is it we are blessed so?" replied Muriam as they both gathered up the rest of the clothing and followed after the others.

Azel noted with a smile as he entered the house, "We may have to extend."

"You keep having children and I think that's inevitable," laughed Petmar as he looked around for the best place to locate the cradle.

"In that corner I think," said Muriam, pointing. "If we move the table to the left, that'll work fine."

"Oh, we have a cupboard that will hold most of the clothes and linen that we can drop in on our next trip through. The trip after that I'll drop in a wife and pick up a son, to take with me to Passover," said Petmar, and they all smiled.

"We are truly a family," thought Muriam to herself. "What a great blessing."

No sooner had Petmar and Arlett left than Azel was talking about making some mud bricks and perhaps extending at the back of their little cottage. To this end he started whenever he had any free time, to gather wood of as uniform a size as he was able to find. The plan was to bind together the wood to form a uniform hollow on the flat stone that formed the ground beside the cottage. With this done, he would travel to the creek some distance away and carry the mud back from there, because it was far superior mud for building than that from the river.

Muriam sometimes worried about how hard he was working, but he assured her that God had given him a strong body, perhaps for this very task. "Surely," he would say, "you would not have me ignore God's gifts?"

So the work continued. Mud was mixed with hay and any other binding agent he could afford or barter for. Slowly as bricks dried, they were stacked neatly at the opposite side of the cottage, and the process begun again.

It was a slow process, but a willing and patient worker with a goal to aim for and the determination to reach it, had more and more bricks appearing over time, to the astonishment of others in the village.

It seemed to Azel that no time had passed when Petmar was calling on him one day late in the afternoon. It was a time of great joy and Muriam sprang to her feet to rush to greet them.

"You are early, surely," cried Azel as he strode toward Petmar smiling broadly. "And what is this I see?" he continued marvelling at the four-wheeled carriage upon which Petmar had made his entrance.

"Ah, you have noticed my fine carriage," replied Petmar. "And you are right," said Petmar, "it is early."

"Where is the caravan?" asked Azel as Muriam joined them.

"It is on its way to Masada, but I find myself with another difficulty that I was hoping you could help me with, so I broke off as you were not so far, and brought my problem with me."

"So I see. Another camel problem," said Azel.

"I'm afraid so. He has become lethargic, just as before, and he is not eating. However, he is not as bad as before I think. Can I leave him with you?"

"Only if you share our table and tell us of your news, and of this carriage," said Azel.

"Oh yes, your table," said Petmar, returning to the small wagon the camel was lashed to. They both followed, a little puzzled.

"I believe these will be of some use at your table this night. What do you think?" he said as he lifted two chairs from the back. "We are never home these days anyhow, and we have too many."

"You are too kind to us Petmar. Both of you are," said Muriam, hugging him.

"The wagon, Petmar," pressed Azel, intrigued.

"Ah, yes, the wagon," replied Petmar. "Who would have thought one such as I would ever own a wagon?"

"Those wheels would have cost you a small fortune surely," said Azel.

"Indeed they did, but one need consider also what they have saved attached to this wagon. So often have I had need of swift conveyance for more than could be borne by a camel, and so often it has cost much in man power and camels. I am not getting any younger and yes, though I agree that the cost of a wagon is absurdly extravagant, I concede also it to be the only extravagance of my many years as a caravan guide. This one luxury I have provided myself," he smiled. "You would not deny me this surely?" he said, throwing his arm around Azel's shoulders.

"Not at all," smiled Azel, "not at all!" still marvelling at this rare treasure before him.

"Come then, let's see if these chairs still work," continued Petmar. So they were quickly transported to their new home and tested while supper was arranged.

"She is looking radiant and very happy, Azel," said Petmar as Muriam prepared supper.

"Motherhood certainly agrees with her, Petmar. Can I ask you something?"

"Of course. You seem troubled my friend."

"We have spoken often about the difficulties you and Arlett suffered, and, well, I suppose we are worried."

"I see. You are worried that something similar may befall you both. I cannot say with certainty that it will not. No one can. You are swimming in the ocean of God's mercy, Azel, and there is but one guarantee. He ordains all that it may work for your greater good. You may not always know it at the time, but it is inevitable that time itself will show you its truth eventually."

"One must concern oneself with what is to be, only in so far as prudence dictates with regard one's state in life. You know for example of your duties providing for Muriam, and now your child. These things are ordered that you might consider prudently how best to achieve this in union with God. It is He who provides, it is for you to cooperate. However, never worry about what is to be and what the future holds. You know not, and your worrying about it will not reveal anything. Is there not far too much to consider in the present?"

"It is enough to know with certainty that He has ordered all, and with far greater resolve for our good than we could ever hope to ask for or even dream of ourselves."

"How does one live that? Though I know it to be true, is it not hard to live?" asked Azel.

"I have a deeply comforting thought," replied Petmar, "that I return to often and will share with you. The great God created man for himself. He created everything else for man, so that he might be holy. It is a wonderful thought that our God has ordered all things for our good."

"Consider for example, Arlett and I. We thought our lives were over and could see no hope. For many months we avoided each other, in truth we were avoiding ourselves. Then we started to realise the blessing God had bestowed upon us, and were too foolish to notice because we were focused on ourselves. It never occurred to us that greater things were at play."

"One day we discovered each other, having each walked a very lonely track, and fell in love more deeply than we had previously known. We realised we had experienced the divine miracle of becoming parents. We had basked in the wonder that so many never know, albeit briefly. We are truly blessed. Had none of this happened, had not God tested us with suffering, would we be who we are? Would we love as we do?"

"Be at ease Azel, and put your beautiful wife at ease. The one guarantee you have as a certainty, is that one from whence every peace comes. God has ordained all creation to conspire for your greater good, and that of your family. You may well rest easy, my friend."

"Thank you Petmar," said Muriam, overhearing the last part of the conversation. "I really did need to hear that. We have been so worried, but you are right of course. It is but our lack of faith," she said, smiling at Azel.

"And your natural love and concern for one another, I dare say. We are weak creatures, sometimes we just need to be reminded.

Don't think for a moment that I don't need to be reminded, and often. I truly don't know what I would do without Arlett to keep me on my toes."

"She is a joy to us," said Muriam. "How did you two meet?"

"Ah, like all good love stories, it was love at first sight. I was just a young man of twenty-two, and she a slip of a girl at seventeen. She was magnificent, truly," he said, looking up and smiling as if they didn't believe him, or he was not doing her justice.

"I was captivated when I saw her," he said. His eyes seemed to glaze as he stared into nothing with the softest smile, as if he could see her just as she had been. "How could one describe her eyes? Stunningly innocent, truly filled with life. Youthful yet mature and wise, and so she proved to be."

"You're drifting," whispered Azel with a wide grin. "Look at you, the love sick boy," and they all laughed.

"It's true, I have always loved her," continued Petmar. "She has always captivated me. We were both attending a wedding. My father was very close to her father. They were firm friends and had been for many years, though strangely, as children we had never met him."

"My father travelled as a merchant and apparently had had many business dealings with hers. The bride of the wedding was in fact his eldest daughter Bethal. I suppose it became obvious I was looking at Arlett, as my father asked if I should like to meet her." Laughing, he went on, "I must have looked like a lovestruck child. I can honestly say I have never felt so awkward in my entire life. We first went to her father and sought permission that we should speak with her. He was very warm, a most generous man, and has remained so all these many years. He has been like a father to me."

"Well, I found myself in her presence at last, and promptly tripped over the carpet's edge and fell face first at her feet. I have remained there ever since," he said as he roared laughing and little could be done but to follow him. "Oh truly it was very funny. I was fumbling and didn't know what to say. My father was surprised and bemused as I had always been a confident young man, but not this time."

"She was very gracious as she is wont to be, so I grew in confidence by the moment. When introductions and conversation were over, I turned briskly around with the intention of striding away holding myself as a man. I hadn't noticed we were standing near the wine jars and I ran straight into one of them. We danced together for a moment, the jar and I, before we both crashed to the floor. I tell you truly there was wine everywhere!" Petmar was finding it difficult to speak as he was laughing so much with tears rolling down his cheeks. "I have never been so embarrassed in all my life! It was very good for my humility."

"Why have we not heard this story before?" asked Azel. "It's a wonderful story," he laughed.

"Surely it's not true?" enquired Muriam.

"Every word of it, I'm afraid. My father was waving his arms around apologising for me and trying to pick me up. It all might seem funny now," he said, catching his breath, "but at the time I was devastated. It has of course become the old chestnut story wheeled out to amuse all at the family gatherings, but that's alright, I tend to see the funny side of it these days."

They all had tears in their eyes. Petmar had a wonderful way of telling a story, gesticulating and laughing. It was all very infectious.

"So?" Muriam said at last.

"So what?" he replied.

"What happened? You must have been brought together somehow."

"Oh that! Well, once I had pulled myself together I didn't even look back. I just excused myself and left the wedding, but who do you think was waiting at the gate with her eldest brother? Yes, Arlett. She was very gracious and politely asked if I had had enough wine. Then with the tenderest of smiles asked whether I might perhaps come back soon to visit. I was genuinely stunned, and I think it was at that moment that she stole my heart. I looked into her eyes, and there was someone in there that captivated me and has done ever since. All the fumbles left me, and I believe that was also the moment I became a man. We spoke briefly and I sought a suitable time from her to return. I assure you, I was not late."

"I spoke to my embarrassed father about the entire affair, and he agreed to speak with her father. He was pleased with the possibility of a union between us, under the condition of course that I stayed away from the wine, and so the courtship began."

"I have loved her with devotion all our life together, she is a blessing from God to a most unworthy servant. I often wonder if there's been some mistake made, but if so I am grateful for it. I certainly have the best of it all."

"Arlett might argue with you on that," said Muriam.

"Arlett could argue on anything, and win every time whether she's right or wrong. She has my heart," laughed Petmar. "Speaking of Arlett, I should be getting back to her. I will pay you for your efforts with my camel. He is one of the best I have ever had."

"Don't be silly," replied Azel.

"No, I insist. No one else seems able to treat them when they get like this. It is a gift and you should be rewarded for it. Now I must be on my journey. We will return in two weeks' time."

"We will look forward to that," said Muriam.

"And no jokes about wine," he laughed as he climbed aboard the wagon he had driven in.

Azel quickly untied the camel and stood with Muriam as they watched their friend out of sight.

"We have been so blessed, Azel," she said and kissed him.

"You look beautiful!"

"I feel enormous," she said rolling her eyes.

"You are beautiful," he said again as he took her in his arms. "And soon we will hold our love in our very hands if it pleases God, and you will feel enormous no more, just joy," and she kissed him once more.

"I will take this one around to the stable and see if we can't cheer him up a little," he smiled. It seemed to Azel that Petmar was as a father to him, and he was grateful for his friendship. He was very much looking forward to their trip to Jerusalem for the Passover.

A Journey Begun

"What is it?" cried an exhausted Muriam with delight. "It's a little boy!" replied Arlett, as she placed him on the breast of his mother.

"Oh Arlett. Look at him. Just look at him. Is he not the most beautiful thing?"

Arlett smiled and then burst into laughter. It was as if the great strain of watching her beloved Muriam suffering had been lifted from her shoulders and replaced with utter joy.

The little one rested after his great ordeal, safely on the breast of what was to become his great lifelong love.

"How do you feel?" asked Arlett.

"Wonderful. Oh yes, wonderful!" was the enthusiastic reply.

"Good. I'll be back in a moment. We need water."

Arlett left the little cottage and went to the stable where she slumped to the corner of the stall and wept. She had not before realised how deeply the strain of the birth would affect her. She was moved with such pride seeing the great courage of her beloved Muriam. Since early yesterday morning she had been watching over her little daughter and hadn't left her side. As the pain increased she had encouraged her and comforted her. She had been stern with her when she had reached the point as all women do, and claimed she could not do this.

"You are a woman. None but you can do this, and you will do this," she had said, squeezing her hand tightly. "I am here with you. We will do this together. I won't leave you."

Many hours had passed with many contractions and much anxiety. Muriam greatly feared her frailty in facing such a challenge as childbirth, but Arlett had assured her many times of her hidden strength.

"God has created women with such strength as we are unable to grasp, lest our pride overtake us. From the side of Adam he drew forth from so near the heart of man, the very bone protecting it, and women from that moment on have protected the very heart of man," she had said.

"But it is man who is strong," Muriam had protested. "Surely it is he who protects us."

"In the physical world, yes, and in so doing he releases woman from the burden of concern that she might concern herself with what is truly important, the very heart of man, his eternal soul. Do you not storm heaven for the constant good of Azel?" she had asked. "And what good do you seek? What is the greatest good you could imagine?"

"To be with God, as we were once with God. To be one in thought and love."

"And as Azel busies himself with the care of his family, do you not seek for him the greater part?"

"Yes," smiled Muriam, "I see what you mean. His love for God is so beautiful that it draws me closer to our God just to be near him. When I am not near him I plead constantly for his love of our God to ever grow."

"Your prayer has been heard by all accounts, as the simple, humble, selfless prayer of a wife is always heard. Yet soon you will be a mother, and your prayer will be manyfold more powerful," Arlett continued. "You have cooperated with God's plan. You have given your very self in the unbridled gift of life. You will have done what only God Himself could do before. You have formed within your body life itself. God has deemed you worthy to share in His creative power, and from this day until He takes you to Himself, your prayers will resonate to the heights and the very ends of heaven. Such is the power the Most High grants with His singular gift of life. You must never forget how precious you are. You must never forget the profound station you hold."

Arlett had tears in her eyes now. "It is the most beautiful joy that God has granted woman. One cannot help but be swept up and overcome in the wonder of such gifts."

So the night had progressed, with much pain and as much joy, until the great moment when the mother finally met her son.

A few minutes and Arlett had regained her composure and rose from the stall dusting off the straw that clung to her clothing. She quickly collected the water needed and made her way back to the cottage.

She found a sight within that moved her to tears yet again. Muriam was sitting up in the bed asleep cradling her newborn son, who himself was asleep yet still suckling his mother's breast. She sat on the small stool next to the bed and just watched until she lost complete track of time.

There was no way of knowing how much time had passed when Muriam started to stir to find a smiling Arlett gazing at her.

"How long have I been asleep?"

"Oh I don't know," said Arlett smiling. "How do you feel?"

"I feel wonderful," said Muriam. "Really, it's amazing. I feel my old self, only better. It is a wonder how completely my wellbeing has returned so quickly. I feel like I could get up and get back to my normal life."

"Well you won't be doing that! You wouldn't deny me the chance to mother you now I'm here would you?"

"No, no. Mother away," smiled Muriam.

"Good," said Arlett. "You enjoy your little treasure and I'll see to a meal fit for a new mother."

Soon all was prepared and they were eating and admiring the fruits of their labours for the past thirty hours.

Finally Muriam spoke. "I don't know what I would have done without you. I could feel just toward the end that I could not go another moment, I was so weak. You were my strength."

"No Muriam, all women in childbirth arrive at that very moment. It is only in the impossible that the miracle becomes obvious. It is no weakness that women arrive at that moment. It is in fact that very moment more than any other that sets them apart. That moment defines them as the great masterpiece of the Creator. To find the courage to trust and the strength to go beyond your limits in the service of love, against what seems impossible, defines womanhood. There is no weakness there."

"And what would I have done without your wisdom?"

"Well, in truth it is Petmar's wisdom, so much has he taught me. He is like your Azel, burning with love for our God. When we are home it is a joy to listen in on the conversations he has with Joachim. They talk for hours about the mysteries of God and how our people have been blessed, and of course how poorly we respond."

"Who is Joachim?" asked Muriam.

"Oh, Joachim and his wife Anna are great friends of ours. Truly wonderful people. We have known them for many years. They have a daughter Mary, who is such a beautiful soul. You would be fast friends. I hope you can meet her one day."

"Where do they live?"

"Nazareth, not so very far from our home. Now you should get some rest; Azel and Petmar should be returning from Jerusalem soon, and I'll be in trouble if you are not well looked after," she smiled.

Three days had passed when Arlett could hear a wagon approaching at about the third hour, and she rushed out to meet it. She smiled to herself as the two men returned. She knew there would be elation upon the news, and she was not disappointed.

Azel was beside himself with joy and rushed to his beloved Muriam's side, who was feeding their little boy when he arrived. They simply looked at each other without a sound and yet, so much was exchanged. Finally, he knelt beside the bed, kissed his wife and laid his head on her shoulder watching his little boy and the miracle of life. It was overwhelming to him as tears of joy flowed down his cheeks.

"What have I done to deserve such joy?" he said finally and kissed her once more.

"He is finished feeding," she said. "Would you like to hold your son?"

"Oh, but, I, well... I..."

"You'll be fine Azel. Cradle your arms. That's it," and she placed the little one gently in his father's arms.

Azel was a big strong man, and truly awkward holding this tiny little body. Muriam smiled at the delicate beauty she had not seen before in her only love.

"I feel like he will break," said Azel nervously. "Glory to God, what miracle is this I hold in my arms?"

"It is the miracle of love, Azel, God's great love for us," smiled Muriam.

"I love you so much. How could I tell you how much?" and he wept.

Muriam climbed out of bed and put her arms around her husband. "You already have. You're holding your love for me in your arms," and she kissed him.

"You have chosen a name, I expect?" she asked, smiling.

"Sunset" he said simply. "The peace and joy of our love is as the sunset. We shall call him Dysmas!"

Never before had Azel understood the remarkable beauty of this woman as he did now. Never before had Muriam felt so utterly joined to her husband as she did at that moment. Truly they were one.

"So are we going to share our little man?" she said at last.

"Oh! Petmar!"

"Yes. Petmar. He must be past waiting by now," she smiled.

"Well I thought you had forgotten me," said Petmar, as he strode to see the little wonder in the arms of Azel.

"My goodness," he said. "Are you not afraid he will break?"

"There is nothing of him, Petmar, but I have it under control as you can see. Here, it's time you held him," said Azel smiling.

"But well, I... but..."

"Oh, really, Petmar!" said Azel. "It's only a baby."

"You are such a naughty boy," said Muriam smiling. "He was terrified, Petmar, don't you believe a word."

"Ah, you have sold me out," said Azel laughing.

"He is beautiful," said Petmar with a great tear in his eye. "Truly he is beautiful."

Arlett had by now started the dinner arrangements, happy to have her man back once more.

"Thank you Petmar," said Muriam.

"What on earth for?"

"For Arlett. I could not have done it without her. She is a marvel."

"She is indeed," said Petmar. "I had to bring her, it was more than my life was worth had I left her behind," he laughed.

That night was one of the happiest they shared together. There was great rejoicing over the birth of a healthy baby boy, and much good humour provided by Azel as he played with Petmar. They had become very great friends indeed.

As the night aged, the men organised the wagon for Petmar and Arlett to start their journey home in the morning, while the women had leave to just talk of their joys and loves.

First Contact

Nine years later, almost to the day, Joseph reached the crest of the hill behind their little home. He could see the entire village below. Carefully he surveyed the surrounding area for signs of Herod's guard. Though all appeared clear he wanted to be certain.

Word had travelled fast of the senseless slaughter of the infants of Bethlehem, and they had therefore had a close call while travelling with the caravan. Had it not been for the wisdom and quick action of Petmar, they would have themselves been in real peril.

Having discovered a caravan had passed through Bethlehem earlier, Herod's guard suspected some parents may have joined it with their children. Hasshim had ordered his troop to form immediately after the ghastly deed was done. They had left not a single male infant alive, and indeed two of their own lay dead. They who would not carry out the dreadful order were slain with those that were its target.

The troop had set out at once in pursuit of the caravan.

Petmar however had been at his trade for many years, and was recognised as the most experienced and astute caravan leader, which is why people deliberately chose to travel with his caravan. In these days of robbers and thieves he always had scouts out in all directions ensuring none could ambush his charge. His senses were more strained given the news from a rider of the happenings of Bethlehem. When word came that a troop of soldiers were approaching from some distance at speed, he anticipated their intent and was quick to act.

He sought out Joseph immediately. "Gather your belongings quickly, do not waste a moment." He literally bundled Mary and the child into the wagon, while Joseph threw what he could carry in with them. They were then despatched at full speed to the base of the mountains that could be seen in the distance, where caves were plentiful. Petmar had packed some supplies and had given Joseph directions and instructions to ensure they would be cared for until his return. "We will get you to Egypt Joseph," he had said, "but there will be a short delay. Azel and Muriam are wonderful people. They will see to your wellbeing."

"Full speed," he had instructed the driver, "and return at once. Waste no time, we will keep moving."

So the wagon had sped off on a dangerous trek to the mountain. No time was wasted unloading its complement or on farewells, before it was returning faster than it had left, allowing it to catch the caravan thirty minutes before Herod's guard managed it.

It was clear they were moving quickly and with purpose as Joseph and Mary observed the troop pass from their makeshift hideout. Mary held Jesus close to feed just in case a cry carried, though it was unlikely they would hear. The soldiers themselves seemed so intent on their mission, their gaze never faltered from the path before them.

Having finally found the caravan they first flanked it, and at once descended from all sides, making it quite impossible for anyone to escape.

"Who leads this caravan?" demanded Hasshim, who was in charge of the troop.

"I do," replied Petmar, "how can I assist you?"

"You passed through Bethlehem yesterday did you not?"

"Yes of course."

"I require you to gather here immediately all those that joined your caravan in Bethlehem."

"Perhaps I can help," said Petmar. "Who are you seeking?"

"Never mind," he snapped. "Bring them."

There were only two old women and a trader brought before him.

"These are the only people from Bethlehem?" demanded Hasshim.

"I assure you sir, of all those here, these are the only people who joined us from Bethlehem," replied Petmar.

"Search every tent," snapped Hasshim.

An hour later the search was completed with nothing found. Without a single word Hasshim reined his horse to open country and rode off, his men following closely behind, leaving the caravan to proceed on its way.

Joseph had been concerned not to be found in open territory accidentally by a returning troop of soldiers, so had decided to remain in the cave for the rest of that day, and all of the next.

"We will sleep here tonight and tomorrow night," he told Mary. "It should be safe to move then."

So it had been an uneventful couple of days. On the morning of the third day they had set out for the town Petmar had assured Joseph was on the other side of the mountain they were on.

Joseph found himself surveying the town now.

"No sign of any soldiers," he said at last. "Going by Petmar's instructions, that little place there is where we are headed," he continued to Mary, pointing.

They made their way down the hill into the little village. They soon found the door they were seeking. There came from within the sound of the cries of a young child. Joseph knocked and was shortly faced by a man in his thirties with a gentle demeanour and a ready smile.

"Hello," he said. "Can I help you?"

"Hello," said Joseph. "This is a little awkward, but Petmar told us to seek you out."

"Did he now? Well then there is nothing awkward at all, you are most welcome here. Come in."

"My name is Azel and this is my wife Muriam, and that little fellow is our son Dysmas."

"I am Joseph son of Jacob, this is my wife Mary, and our Jesus."

"Please come sit," said Azel. "Tell me how Petmar came to send you to us."

"Well, we joined his caravan four days ago..."

"At Bethlehem," Azel had finished the sentence, his face ashen.

"Yes," confirmed Joseph.

"The soldiers, they came for the caravan?" continued Azel.

"Yes."

"I understand. God's blessings were upon you that you joined Petmar's caravan. He is wise and shrewd. We have had word of Bethlehem. All of Judea has had word of Bethlehem. You were, it seems, the only ones to escape, thank the Most High," said Azel. "You are welcome to stay as long as you will."

There was a knock at the door and all froze.

Azel rose and opened it to find a familiar face.

"Baslar, my old friend, Petmar has sent you no doubt."

"He has indeed," replied the dusty visitor.

"Baslar is one of Petmar's most trusted confidants," he explained to Joseph.

"Mary," said Muriam, "Would you like to come outside and sit in the sun."

"Thank you," smiled Mary. "That would be delightful."

When the women were gone, Baslar continued. "I did not wish to alarm your wife Joseph. Petmar sends me here to assist you both on your journey back to the caravan. Some in the town told of a young couple with child who had left Bethlehem the day of the slaughter. They were unable to tell them by what means you had departed, or the direction you took. The soldiers have been in search of you. Petmar has had scouts following their movements and estimates they will arrive here in two days. It is almost night; we should leave in the morning. I have a wagon and we could make good time. Petmar has camped two days from here and is awaiting your return. He has been stalling the travellers with sick camels and the like. He does not think they will bother the caravan again given they have already searched it and found nothing, so it is probably the safest place for you to be just now."

Joseph nodded thoughtfully.

"A hearty meal then and a good night sleep for all will make the journey less tiresome," said Azel. "We have room for you too, Balsar."

"How would I sleep in a house? No thanks. You married types have to do such things, I'm still free to sleep under the stars," and he smiled broadly.

Joseph and Azel were smiling and looking at each other when Azel said, "He doesn't know what he's missing. You will share a meal with us though."

"Of course, who in their right mind would miss out on Muriam's cooking?"

In the garden Dysmas was crying from the pain of the welts all over his body.

"Has he been like this for long?" asked Mary.

"About two weeks ago it started," replied Muriam. "He is normally such an active boy, but for the past week he has been almost crippled with this dreadful rash. He is not eating and has lost so much weight it frightens me. Nothing seems to work. The poor little love is almost always crying now. We believe he has had some kind of allergic reaction to something, given no one else has caught it in that time, but we have no idea what. It is getting worse, I'm beginning to fear I will lose my little boy. I can't help him."

"There is one who can," said Mary, "Why don't we ask Him together?"

Mary took her hand and closed her eyes and began to pray. All at once Muriam felt a calm and confidence she had not known for two weeks. The worry left her and was replaced with a genuine peace. The prayer of this woman was unlike her own. It was not so much what she said as the utter simplicity of her confidence, and what seemed like a familiarity that somehow swept Muriam up and along in a manner she had not experienced before.

When Mary had finished they sat in silence for what seemed like a few moments, but was in fact almost fifteen minutes. Muriam found her face wet with tears, but tears of relief for some reason.

"How old is Dysmas?" asked Mary.

"He was nine years old, two weeks ago."

Azel appeared with Joseph, "Muriam, Balsar brings word from Petmar. Joseph and Mary will return to the caravan in the morning to continue their journey. They will share our hospitality tonight."

"Thank you, Muriam," said Mary. "Can I help you with the meal?"

She handed Jesus into Joseph's care who bounced him on his knee while the women set about the eating arrangements, and Azel set about getting the fire started.

Soon a humble meal was prepared and all at table were sharing their stories of Petmar and his travels with much laughter. "He is a wonderful man and a fine friend," said Azel. "He has brought nothing but good tidings to this house. You can trust him with your life Joseph, he will not let you down."

"He has for many years been a great friend to Mary's family," said Joseph. "I know I have the right man watching over us."

"Who are your parents, Mary?" asked Muriam.

"Joachim, son of David, and Anna of Nazareth."

"Oh, it's you that Arlett was speaking of."

"Arlett? Petmar's wife?"

"Yes."

"My father and mother have been great friends with them since before I was born. They were family in our home when I was growing up," replied Mary.

"I think they are family in many homes," said Azel, smiling. "Are there better people to be found?"

"When Dysmas was born, Arlett was my midwife. She spoke of your parents with such love and affection, and of their little girl that was the joy of their lives. That was you," she said smiling. "She did say that she hoped we would meet one day and here you are. What a joy to meet you at last. Perhaps, that is why you are so familiar to me."

"Thank you," said Mary.

The evening passed quickly. "I think," said Azel at last, "it best if Joseph and I go with Balsar tonight, so that you ladies and the children have some room." So it was agreed.

As it was a warm night, not much was needed by way of blankets, so the men settled down quickly around the wagon and were all asleep in little time.

Inside the house however, Muriam was trying to make Dysmas more comfortable with little success. She was clearly very tired herself. The last two weeks had taken their toll.

"Why don't you hold Jesus for me Muriam," said Mary. "Let me comfort Dysmas for you while you rest a little."

She handed Jesus to Muriam who sat on the chair.

Mary sat on the bed and put her arms around Dysmas, holding him close to her heart, and she began to sing a gentle song, rocking him back and forth as she did. Soon he began to calm, and very soon after, was fast asleep. He was exhausted, for he had found little sleep in the past week himself.

Mary lifted him and laid him down, and thanked the Lord he didn't stir.

"Thank God," breathed Muriam. "He has suffered so much."

"You could use some sleep yourself," said Mary as she took Jesus back with a smile.

"Could I ever," replied Muriam.

"Don't feel you have to sit with me, Muriam. You may not get another chance."

"Thank you, Mary, I would dearly love to sleep." She went to bed immediately. As she lay there she couldn't help but wonder where she had seen Mary before. Her face was so familiar, and the memory seemed at the edge of her mind, but she could not match a place to it.

"I just know I have seen her somewhere," she thought as she dozed into slumber. She woke sometime in the night and could see a dim light through the curtain, and the silhouette of Mary sitting up rocking Jesus, and she dozed off once more for the rest of the night.

When she woke the next morning much had been prepared for the journey, and she realised she had overslept.

"Ah, sleepy head," Azel said when she appeared. "That's great to see."

"I can't believe how soundly I slept. I feel really good."

"You needed a good night's sleep," said Azel. "I wasn't going to wake you."

"Where is Dysmas?" she said.

"He is still sleeping, can you believe it?"

"Oh, what a blessing Azel," she said, relieved. "He was desperate for sleep."

Mary had been to the well, collected water, and had bathed Jesus in the great Roman bath. Breakfast was already prepared and Muriam apologised to Mary for sleeping in.

Mary laughed, "You have nothing to apologise for, you were very tired."

Joseph came in then with Balsar. "All is ready," he said.

"We are ready, too," said Mary as she handed Jesus to Joseph. She turned to Muriam and took her hands in her own. "So little time we have shared and yet what joy you have brought to my heart. Thank you."

"It is I who should thank you," said Muriam. "I haven't had any sleep since Dysmas fell ill."

"Nonsense," said Mary with a smile as she hugged Muriam. "I do have a small task for you though, if you would humour me."

"Of course, what would you have me do?"

"I have left the water in the bath; when Dysmas wakes, bathe him. It will save you getting more from the well. You have enough to do."

"Alright," said Muriam smiling, "thank you."

"Will we see you again?" asked Azel of Joseph.

"I genuinely hope so Azel. I can't tell you how grateful I am to you."

"Balsar will get you there safely, have no fear."

The farewells over, the wagon began to roll and was soon out of sight.

"Well, that was a whirlwind visit. He is a very fine man," said Azel.

"He is," replied Muriam, "and he is wed to a remarkable woman. What a beautiful soul she is."

Just then Dysmas could be heard and Muriam went to him. He was already getting upset and, as most mornings, the welts seemed worse.

Muriam tried to make jokes with him but he was in no mood for jokes. "A sponge bath will soothe you," she said at last with a smile. Soon she had him sitting beside the bath of water and began sponging the water over his little body. In no time he became calm and even smiled up at her for the first time in what seemed a lifetime. When she had finished and dried him, he hugged her tight and ran back to his bed and climbed in between the covers.

"What on earth?" she thought to herself.

He was soon asleep and she was delighted. She went outside to Azel.

"Where is Dysmas?" he asked.

"He has gone back to bed. He is already asleep."

"You're joking?"

"No. I can hardly believe it myself. While I have the time, I think I have much to catch up on," smiled Muriam, and went back inside to gather the washing that needed doing.

Three hours passed, the washing was drying on the makeshift line, and the house was swept and cleaned. Muriam was feeling like she was on top of things once more. She was putting water on to boil when Dysmas appeared and hugged her leg.

She turned to him, then swept him up in her arms and began to run to Azel yelling his name.

Azel wondered what she was so excited about. She was running to him carrying Dysmas.

"Look at him Azel, he is healed!"

Azel took him up and examined him closely. Truly there was not a single welt to be seen. "What has happened?" asked Azel of Muriam. "This cannot be."

Muriam fell to the ground weeping, holding Azel's leg. The strain of the past two weeks lifted from her as if by magic. "Oh, Azel, I feared we were going to lose him," she sobbed.

Dysmas was smiling at his father who himself had tears in his eyes.

"We must thank God, Azel, it is He who has done this for us."

Azel knelt down then and held his wife, "I think we shall have the rest of the day off," he said at last. "Come," and they made their way inside.

It was not long before Jillian and Enzar were knocking at their door. They had been helping Muriam with a healing cream that Jillian's mother had used on her as a child for such ailments as Dysmas was suffering. It had done no good whatever over the past two weeks, yet they were good people who meant well, so Muriam was content to consent to their kind offer of help. And it was true to say that the cream from goat's milk, did provide some soothing for the welted skin.

When Muriam opened the door, she was beaming with joy.

"Well you look happy," said Jillian smiling.

"I am happy, come in, come in," cried Muriam.

"How is Dysmas?" asked Enzar.

"Wonderful," said Azel entering the room with Dysmas in his arms.

A gasp left the lips of Jillian when she saw he was completely cured.

"It worked," she cried. "See Enzar, I told you it would work!"

Muriam and Azel looked at each other and smiled, but neither let on.

"I am so grateful to you both," said Muriam. "You are great friends."

"I can't tell you how happy we are for you," said Jillian. We have prayed and prayed for healing. I know how it was breaking your heart Muriam, we both do. What a wonderful day."

"We were just about to have lunch, would you care to join us?" asked Azel.

"We'd love to."

"Where is Gestus?" enquired Muriam.

"Gestus is with my mother for the afternoon. She loves to have him visit."

The afternoon passed swiftly. Azel and Muriam smiled to each other as they listened to the entrepreneurial plans Jillian was making for greatly expanding her market of herbal creams and balms.

As night was falling and visitors had been farewelled, Azel and Muriam prepared for an early night. They had both been sleep-deprived for the past two weeks, and an early night was just what they needed.

Dysmas was no trouble to settle as he was still catching up on his sleep too.

As Muriam lay in bed waiting for Azel to dress she seemed very distant.

"Something on your mind?" asked Azel.

"Well, yes. Mary."

"Mary?"

"Have we met her before?"

"Not that I recall. Why do you ask?"

"I know this is going to sound odd, but I know her from somewhere."

"You can't know her, surely. She comes from the other side of Palestine. You have never been there, nor she here."

"I know all that is true, but Azel, I just know we have met somewhere; I just can't quite put a place to it. She is so familiar to me somehow."

"Perhaps because you two were so much alike. You are a beautiful soul too. I can attest to that."

"Oh, come to bed," she laughed.

He took her in his arms and they fell asleep at once.

44

Worlds Collide

"**P**lease Father, come with us," said Dysmas. "It won't be the same without you, and you know Jerusalem so well."

Muriam smiled at Azel. Dysmas had never been to Jerusalem, but had been promised for years that at the age of twelve, he would be allowed to join Petmar's caravan and go. However, Azel had announced he had too much to do to get away just now.

Dysmas tried everything a young boy could to no avail.

"I promised I would study the Torah and have I not, Father?"

"You have, Dysmas, you have learned much. None are your equal in the village," Azel had replied.

"However, is this not your duty before God?" he had continued with a smile.

Dysmas was outfoxed and knew it, and downcast, went to bed, unable to persuade his father to join them come morning on their trek to Jerusalem for the Passover.

"I didn't want to disappoint him, Muriam," said Azel.

"You are the man of the house, so you must do what you believe best for us, but, you are his father, and he adores you. He was looking forward to seeing the great city with you."

"I hope he doesn't resent me for not going," Azel winced as he began to second guess his decision.

"Resent you? He wouldn't know how. None in the village enjoy the love of their son as you do. There is always talk of it."

"What do you mean?" asked Azel.

"Never you mind," she said with a mischievous smile as she packed her things for the morning.

"What would I do without you," said Azel taking her in his arms. "What a woman you are and a wonderful wife. You always know what to say to lift me."

"You're not so heavy," she smiled and kissed him.

Azel had a sleepless night, and decided at about three in the morning that he would put his tasks on hold and do them upon his return. He lay there for some time planning the trip now, and felt much more at ease the decision was made as he drifted into a sound sleep at last.

Dysmas was overjoyed when he woke to the news.

All but Azel were packed, so he set about gathering his things quickly as Petmar would be close at hand.

"Did you hear, Mamma? Did you hear?" asked Dysmas excitedly.

"Yes darling, I heard," she replied smiling. She too was very pleased Azel had changed his mind.

Azel had no sooner finished packing when there was a knock at the door.

Dysmas ran to open it with a beaming Petmar to be found on the other side.

"Uncle Petmar," he cried and threw himself around the neck of his beloved uncle.

"Dysmas, Dysmas you've grown," laughed Petmar. "Just these few months and look at you!"

"Mother," cried Dysmas. "Uncle Petmar is here."

Muriam returned from outside to find an excited Dysmas in the arms of his beloved Petmar.

"Well, you're very welcome," she said.

"So it seems," smiled Petmar.

"Azel is just tidying up some loose ends in the barn, he'll be here in just a moment," she said as she kissed him on the cheek. "Come now Dysmas," she continued, "gather up your things and load them into the wagon."

Dysmas did not need any more encouragement and was gone in an instant.

"We have a little time," said Petmar as he pulled a beautifully carved camel from beneath his tunic.

"Dysmas," he called.

Dysmas came running back.

"I thought you might like this as my gift to you for your birthday."

"Where did you get this from?" asked Dysmas. "It's perfect. Mother, look! It's perfect."

"It really is beautiful, Petmar," said Muriam. "I don't think I have seen better."

"Yes, it truly is excellent. On our last trip to Samaria, a Persian carver travelled with us. His work was the best I have ever seen. I remembered Dysmas would soon be turning twelve, so I asked him to carve a camel for him."

"Oh, it really is perfect in every way," said Dysmas. "Look at the detail."

Just then Azel arrived. "Petmar my old friend," he said as they hugged. "Good to see you at last."

"Are you joining us?" asked Petmar.

"Yes, it is settled. I will be coming," smiled Azel.

"Ah, my prayers have been answered yet again, Dysmas. You see, trust in God, He is always listening."

"So, it was you!" said Azel. "As if I could resist these two, but you as well!" and they all laughed.

Azel gathered the belongings they were to take, and placed them in the wagon Petmar had brought. Dysmas had already taken his place on the driver's seat.

"He is well ready to start his adventure," quipped Petmar.

Azel and Muriam smiled and nodded.

The little cottage secured, with final instructions given to Enzar, who would care for the stock in their absence, and they were on their way.

The caravan was camped two miles from Hebron, and Dysmas was already excited by this short journey. Both Azel and Petmar were kept ever busy answering the many expectant questions of a boy excited at the prospect of new discovery, as well as time with his two favourite men. Muriam gazed on with delight enjoying greatly the unbridled enthusiasm of her son.

"Is it true the temple reaches the sky?" asked Dysmas.

"Of course not," said Petmar. "It reaches way past the sky!"

Azel laughed and hugged his son.

The trek to Jerusalem was a joy to the heart of Azel. He lay watching Dysmas and Petmar talking one evening with Muriam. "I am so glad I came," he said. "It has been a very great joy to be with you both. I am the happiest of men."

"He is so excited," said Muriam. "In just a few days he will see Jerusalem for himself for the first time, with the two men he loves more than any other thing on earth. I am with the three men I love more than any other thing on earth. I am the happiest of women," and she reclined on the breast of her husband, smiling.

As the sun rose revealing the new day, Dysmas was already up and dressed. The caravan was stirring as its inhabitants slowly began packing their belongings up for the next segment of their journey to Jerusalem. Dysmas was impatient to be underway.

"Ah, Dysmas," said Petmar catching sight of him. "This night we camp at Bethany, behind the Mount of Olives. Be quick now and help your mother pack."

So it was, an hour from dusk they made camp. Azel was seeing to the family's bedding arrangements for the night, while Muriam set about organising the evening meal.

Dysmas as usual was very excited. "How long will it take to get there tomorrow?"

"Not long. You will be eating figs in the market before noon," replied Petmar.

The questions had been constant from the first day, yet Petmar never tired of hearing them. He had found in this trip a genuine delight, in the enthusiasm of this boy he had grown to love as his own son. He and Dysmas were very close, and Dysmas never missed an opportunity to spend time with his beloved Petmar. They had become very great friends indeed.

Night was upon the camp site, and those who had built fires were busy with meal preparation and preparing the young for bed. A small troop of travelling musicians, who had been travelling with the caravan, were in the habit of practicing immediately the day of travel concluded, and so the soft rhythm of music was heard wafting over the camp site, much to the delight of the many weary travellers.

Petmar lifted Dysmas upon his great shoulders and started to make his way to where Azel had staked out a patch of ground for his family.

"He will not sleep much tonight I think," he said to Azel, smiling.

"In that case, perhaps he should sleep in your tent tonight."

"Oh, can I?" asked Dysmas.

"Very clever," said Petmar. "You're at it again. I have been trapped once more."

"You have indeed," replied Azel laughing just as Muriam returned with the evening meal.

"Dysmas is sleeping in Petmar's tent tonight," announced Azel smiling broadly. "He's very excited."

"Have you been at it again?" asked Muriam.

"At what?" said Azel, smiling mischievously.

"Yes, he has," said Petmar. "He won't fool you as he does me so easily I think."

Muriam smiled to herself as she dished out their meals. She loved watching these two banter. Azel was always setting poor Petmar in a corner he could not wriggle from. It was always wonderful to watch as she was unsure which of them enjoyed it most.

"Alright," said Petmar finally, and it was done.

"Thank you, Uncle Petmar," said Dysmas smiling.

Petmar looked to a beaming Azel who burst out laughing, and simply shook his head smiling.

The evening meal was as usual, filled with questions from Dysmas and much good humour from the rest. They were indeed a happy group.

Others nearby would often visit their humble little patch to spend some time and join the good humoured merriment that was always on offer.

Others in the camp often spoke of this little group with great fondness; they were very popular.

Soon Dysmas was yawning and was told to go off to bed, and so after farewells and good nights, he was quickly on his way to Petmar's tent.

"He will be asleep before you go to bed," said Azel.

"Don't you start making out that he will sleep. It will make no difference anyhow, he will be asking questions in his sleep," laughed Petmar. "You have outsmarted me once more. I concede, I have been beaten," he said as he rose to retire for the night.

Azel and Muriam smiled as they watched Petmar saunter off to his tent.

"How could one not love him, Muriam?"

"He is a joy, that is true," she smiled and kissed her husband. "And so are you, though a rascal."

The night seemed to drag on for Dysmas, although he had uninterrupted slumber almost until dawn.

When the sun finally splashed its brilliance across the horizon, the day revealed was a marvel. High clouds reflecting pinks and reds back to earth, for the pleasure of any and all who would watch the show that was beaming across the sky.

The camp was already abuzz with activity, with food being prepared, tents and possessions being packed. Children were waking and wagons were loading.

The morning meal was always a short affair and the caravan was soon underway.

Dysmas sat up front with Petmar and was the first to see the great walls of the city.

"There it is!" he cried as more and more of the city became visible. Soon he was quite silent as the wonder of what was spreading before him was revealed. The massive ramp leading to one great entrance, with what seemed to Dysmas to be millions of people going up and down.

"There are so many people, Uncle Petmar," he said finally.

"There are indeed," Petmar replied.

The caravan secured outside the city, soon it was Dysmas himself making up their number, as he climbed the great ramp in wonder and awe. Muriam was basking in the joy of watching Dysmas as each new corner revealed the next surprise.

So close to the Passover there were many more than usual visiting Jerusalem.

They found their way to the marketplace and as promised, Petmar gave two figs to Dysmas. "It is almost noon," he said with a smile. "Enjoy!"

Dysmas ate his first fig in Jerusalem.

They had been in the marketplace for almost an hour when Azel said to Petmar, "There are many people this year."

"Yes," replied Petmar with a frown, "too many I think."

"What's the matter?"

"I don't know, I am uneasy. Where is Dysmas?"

"He is with Muriam, watching the tent maker."

"I see him. Let's go to them now," he said as he started toward their position.

Just then there was a very loud crashing sound just beyond the market, with much noise and commotion following it. People started to disperse in all directions at once as Petmar started running now with Azel toward Muriam and Dysmas.

Dysmas, hearing the commotion, was drawn to the shouting and noise. Steel was clashing on steel and it all seemed exciting to an innocent boy who was unfamiliar with such things.

"Dysmas," cried Azel, as he saw his son start to run toward the commotion, but Dysmas could not hear his father over the din of the crowd, who were now running in all directions.

Azel looked to Petmar as he ran off after Dysmas. Muriam had seen all of these things from the opposite side of the tent makers stall, but was well aware of the danger and sought to fight her way through the crowd.

As Dysmas ran through the crowd the noise became louder until finally he came to the corner of the small lane he was running upon and burst into the middle of the fray. He realised instantly his mistake as severe fighting was well underway.

Gaius, a Roman centurion in command of this small detail of Roman soldiers under attack, at once saw Dysmas and, grabbing him by the front of his tunic, flung him across the lane under a nearby bench laden with vegetables on sale, so as to get him clear of the fighting and out of harm's way.

As he turned back to face his attacker, he saw a blur of movement in his peripheral vision and instinctively raised his sword. Azel ran straight into the blade impaling himself as Gaius sought unsuccessfully to drop the sword in time. Azel collapsed to the ground as Gaius withdrew his blade, having received the wound directly through the heart.

Gaius had little time to grieve his mistake as two men were on him in a moment.

Though three of his men lay dead, the rest of them had by now taken control of this skirmish. However, as his sword found its mark and one of his assailants fell, the other whose sword had been broken hit Gaius over the head with a small faggot, knocking him senseless to the ground. Swooning and all but unconscious, he barely perceived the extra soldiers arriving to take control of the situation. They had been dispatched immediately upon notice of the attack.

The small attacking band led by Barabbas began to flee.

By this time Dysmas, enraged now by his father's death, had himself retrieved a sword from one of the dead and was standing over Gaius, about to drive it through his heart.

Barabbas, whose escape route took him past Dysmas, heard the order to the archer to kill the boy, and immediately saw what Dysmas was about to do. Quickly he scooped Dysmas up as he ran past, but as he lifted him, the arrow that was meant for Dysmas' heart, found his leg instead.

Dysmas screamed in pain and was unconscious in a few moments, as Barabbas fought his way through an ever-thickening crowd with Roman soldiers in close pursuit.

Muriam had been held back by the crowd, yet what seemed an eternity was but a few moments. When she finally found her way through, the full horror of the carnage lay before her. Azel lay dead, with others, both solider and Jew, all around, dead or dying.

Muriam threw herself on her husband searching for any life, hoping for a sign as she kissed him, pleading with him not to leave her, but he was gone.

Gaius staggered to his feet, and was joined quickly by a fellow centurion, Capious, who held him steady. "You are very lucky Gaius, you were a moment from death."

Gaius was quickly regaining his wits. "What happened?" he asked.

"A young boy no less, was about to run you through. He took an arrow to the leg. He will not be hard to find, if he survives."

"A young boy," cried Muriam. "A young boy, where is he?"

"He's gone with the rest of the rabble he was with," spat back Capious.

"You've killed his father," cried Muriam heartbroken and crying.

"His father should have kept better company," he retorted, as Muriam slumped in despair over the lifeless body of her beloved.

"He wasn't with them," said Gaius. "He was innocent. His death was an accident."

"He's only a Jew," said Capious.

Gaius swung around and caught Capious a heavy blow knocking him to the ground.

"He was an innocent man," cried Gaius. "Has Rome lost sight of the difference between innocence and guilt on account of an accident of birth?"

Capious was silent for he knew Gaius to be his better.

Gaius leaned over Muriam. "It was an accident, a split second within the heat of battle. It is little comfort I know, but I am deeply sorry."

Muriam looked up into his eyes, and he was moved by her terrible pain. "What of my son?" she cried.

"I promise you, I will try to locate him and return him to you safely."

"Capious," he snapped, "return to the prefect and report what has happened here. I will take command of the garrison."

"I want that boy found and returned safely," he continued. "See to it."

The garrison dispersed in teams of four in search of Dysmas.

Petmar arrived then in time to hear this last order, and found Muriam slumped over the lifeless body of her dear Azel.

Tears welled in his eyes at once. Gaius perceiving him to be connected to this family asked him, "Do you know these people?"

"Yes," replied Petmar now crying. "What has happened here?"

"A tragic accident," replied Gaius, and then as if to himself, "a tragic accident."

"Please, if you could, take this woman to my home that she might be cared for while we seek her son who is missing, lost in the melee. It is but two lanes away."

"I will," replied Petmar, collecting himself.

"Follow this path. Two lanes down you will find a house with two large pitchers to the left of the door. Jelrah is my trusted servant; tell him Gaius has sent you and he will see to her wellbeing. I will have her husband taken there immediately, and see to the safe return of her son if I can. I will explain what has happened here upon my return." With that Gaius disappeared into the crowd alone.

Gaius was in much turmoil. He knew well he had killed an innocent man, even as the blow was struck. It was of great personal importance to him that he at least put right what he could, so finding the boy for his mother became central to his thinking, blocking out years of training and discipline. His judgement was compromised by his valour, and desire to right a tragic wrong. He realised this as he came upon four dead soldiers, and a disinterested crowd of Jews. Instinctively he drew his sword and searched the crowd for those responsible, but could find only disinterest.

"What manner of people are these that are so numb to life?" he thought to himself.

He dragged the four together in a group and waited. Soon four soldiers emerged from the crowd to discover him protecting the dead bodies of their comrades. There were stares of disbelief and anger from the group. They knew well that they should not have been on patrol looking for a Jewish boy in groups of four so soon after the attack in the market.

What was on their minds was clear to Gaius but it was all too late now.

He dispatched two of the soldiers to the Praetorian guard to procure assistance.

Presently more soldiers arrived and the dead were quickly gathered and returned to the garrison.

As Gaius was about to depart on his quest for Dysmas, a messenger arrived from the prefect requiring his immediate return.

Gaius knew at once Capious had related more than was necessary to the prefect.

As Gaius directed his steps to the prefect, Barabbas was now on the outskirts of the city with an unconscious Dysmas over his shoulder.

The soldiers following him were those that Gaius had come upon, his followers ensuring the escape of their leader.

"He is still unconscious," Eleazar called. "Perhaps it is best we do it now."

Barabbas stopped and quickly looked about.

"Good idea," he said.

He laid Dysmas down on the ground and, seeing he was clearly unconscious, sought to pull the arrow from its seat, but it was caught behind the bone.

"Nothing for it," he said, "We don't have time."

With that he pushed with his whole might and forced the arrow through the leg. Grabbing the arrow head, he pulled it through and quickly wrapped the wound to stem the flow of blood.

"Let's go!" he cried with a grunt as he flung Dysmas over his shoulder once more and continued running.

Soon they were at the gates. They could hear only commotion and shouting in the distance. They gazed through the gate opening and the path that lay ahead. There was a vast expanse of open territory before them.

"There is no cover," said Eleazar.

"We will have to chance it," cried Barabbas as he rushed past and began the trek that could be his last.

"Hurry," cried Eleazar to the rest. "If we're quick we may yet escape undetected, and they will think we are still in the city somewhere."

With every ounce of speed they could muster they all strove for the nearest dune just before the tree line. They were soon upon it as they cast themselves down behind a small outcrop of boulders, sucking in air and trying to listen as to whether they had been detected or not.

Barabbas cast Dysmas aside and rolled on his stomach, carefully looking around the boulder that was his cover.

"Nothing," he said. "Wait."

Just then six soldiers burst through the gate. There was about two hundred metres between them.

"Quiet," whispered Barabbas.

The soldiers looked in all directions. One said to another, "They could not have covered that much ground, they must still be in the city somewhere."

With that they posted two guards at the gate and returned within to start searching premises nearby.

"We will find them, they could not have gone far."

"It's clear," said Barabbas. "Keep your heads down, they have left two guards. If we can make the tree line, we're clear."

Remaining low and using the boulders as cover for their retreat, they found the safety of the tree line easily and were soon on their way.

"He is bleeding too much, Barabbas," said Eleazar, who was following behind and observing the blood trail issuing from Dysmas. "If we don't cauterise the wound he will likely die."

"There," cried Barabbas pointing to a small hut nearby which had smoke issuing from its chimney. They burst through the door without warning, startling the woman within who screamed in fright.

"Silence woman, we mean you no harm."

There was no time for ceremony. Dysmas was laid roughly beside the hearth while Eleazar quickly pulled the red hot poker from the fire and applied it first to the wound on the underside of the leg, rolling it across the wound. He returned it to the fire for a time, and repeated the action to the opposite wound.

"That seems to have done the job," said Eleazar, "but he has lost a great deal of blood. He may not survive, still."

The woman knelt down beside Dysmas with some cloths and bandaged his wounds. "That should keep them clean at least," she said.

"Thank you," said Eleazar as Barabbas again picked Dysmas up. "We must go," and with that they re-joined their companions outside and were again on their way.

"Murasa," called Barabbas, and Murasa ran to answer.

"Scout to the rear and keep a sharp eye, they will know by now that we have escaped the city."

They travelled off the main roads and paths until nightfall, taking turns to carry the still unconscious Dysmas.

"Will we make camp Barabbas?" asked Eleazar.

"No, the moon is all but full and visibility good. Better to carry on."

Murasa caught up with them just at that moment.

"Nothing to report," he declared. "Not a sign of anyone following."

"Well then, the night will be our haven until we are well hidden."

So the small troop continued for twenty-four more uneventful hours, until they entered the enclosure Barabbas had claimed in blood as his own, some four years before.

It was, to be exact, a mini-fortress, formed naturally by the mountain that surrounded it.

The previous owner had been a thief of some renown by the name of Macario, and had taken painstaking steps to ensure the entrance was not only not visible, but most difficult to find indeed, even if one knew it existed. There was in fact a massive rut of rock protruding from the side of the mountain, and Macario had hewn an entry well back in it, large enough for a man on a laden camel to pass. As far back behind the rock as was possible he had started, turning into the cavern in a slight 'U' shape in the hope of providing further cover from internal sound and light. A small cave then led to the main body of the cavern within, where Barabbas and his cohort now rested.

The cavern was some thirty metres across and one hundred metres in length. Two great pillars of rock rose from the centre of the cavern twenty metres apart climbing to the very top, providing support for the naturally domed ceiling above. There were also three smaller caverns that joined the main area. Four penetrations in the roof at various points led to the top of the very inhospitable mountain that contained it. These let air circulate within the cavern and removed any smoke, allowing fires to be lit. It was one of these penetrations that had in fact been the means by which Macario discovered this isolated cavern in the first place.

Some years earlier he had been running to escape Herod's guard, who came upon him quite by chance in the act of stealing a number of Herod's prize camels. The trouble was, although he had put good distance between himself and the relentless guard, they were indeed relentless.

He knew of the mountain and how inhospitable it was, and so had made for it. Leaving his horse, and indeed everything he owned, at the base of the mountain, he quickly grabbed for his only rope and ran for his life.

He had almost reached the top when he misjudged the landscape and ran off a large overhanging boulder, somersaulting and landing flat on his stomach. It was at this precise moment that he saw under the boulder something that could only be seen if one was on one's belly. He could see a hole, easily large enough for a man to hide in, and completely covered from view.

Hearing voices farther down the mountain he squeezed under the outcrop. It was clear to him immediately that the hole was too deep to just jump into, so he quickly tied his rope through a large opening that had formed in the rock and lowered himself quietly, as the sound of shouting and footsteps went pounding past and simply faded away. They had completely missed him.

His eyes were quickly adjusting to the light and he realised, though at the extremity of the rope, a little more and he would be on solid ground once more.

He climbed down the boulders and rocks that formed a natural ladder to where his rope had reached, and started looking for an exit from the massive cavern within which he found himself, only to find the one way out was the way he had entered.

He could see light from three other areas above, but it was a sheer rock face that led to all of them.

It had instantly occurred to Macario that he had stumbled on the greatest hideout he had ever heard of, let alone seen. He then spent the next two days investigating every inch of his newfound paradise, entirely sustained by excitement. He climbed the rocky ladder to his rope then and, with much effort, hauled himself up and out.

Some days passed while he re-entered and exited the cave many times, making his calculations for the perfect place to hew a more accessible yet entirely hidden entry. By the time the work had begun, he had had no idea how far into the rock he would have to tunnel; he knew only that it would be worth every minute of labour. Eight months later and his dream was realised as he finally broke through to the cavern. It was perfect. It even had a secondary escape route through the roof. Who could ask for more? Indeed it was truly perfect, but it was his for only two more years.

He had made the terrible mistake of stealing from one of the most ruthless men in all of Judea. Very much unknown at that time, yet one who would become very well-known indeed: Barabbas.

Caught red-handed and dragged before Barabbas who had drawn his sword and was about to strike, this thief begged a bargain to trade his life, for the only thing he had of value: his secret hideout.

Babbling on with descriptions Barabbas became intrigued, and agreed to spare his life in exchange for this extraordinary hideout, if indeed it was all he claimed.

Arrangements were made immediately to view the cave and they had set off within the hour. Barabbas was very impressed indeed, amazed at how remarkably well-concealed the entry was. Truly it was impossible to make out that there was anything that could possibly lie beyond what was visible.

"Up there, can you see the rocks leading up? They lead to the secret exit at the top of the mountain."

While the thief had been looking up, Barabbas had drawn his sword and slayed him where he stood.

"No point in having a secret hideout if you know where it is," he had said to the dead man at his feet.

And so it was that four years later Dysmas was being dumped on the ground beside a fire by an exhausted Eleazar, who promptly dropped beside him and was himself asleep almost instantly.

Jews and Romans

"Gaius!" screamed the prefect. "Just what possessed you to send a troop after a Jewish child in a hostile crowd?"

Capious was enjoying himself greatly. It was he who had ensured the prefect had every detail of what had transpired.

"Seven dead!" he screamed. "Do you hear, seven dead Romans! Seven dead Romans, and many of the assailants escaping. Get out of my sight, I'll deal with you tomorrow when I can bear to look at you. Get out!"

Gaius saluted and left. He knew well he had not heard the last of this. Those scouring the city for Barabbas and his band had been reinforced to groups of six men, yet it was now clear they had escaped the city.

Gaius found two of the groups and enquired after the boy, with no sighting being reported.

"Have you heard from any of the others?" he asked.

"They have all reported no sighting."

"Damn," said Gaius.

He made his way to his house where he found both Petmar and Muriam anxiously awaiting his return.

"Please," she said, "is there any word?"

"I'm sorry," he replied, "I have no news yet."

It was clear that the entire event had taken a very great toll on Muriam, who was truly faint with worry. Petmar held her and became aware that he was indeed holding her up.

Gaius called to Jelrah when he realised Muriam was in real trouble.

"Take this woman to the guest room. Take care of her, Jelrah. She has been through much today and the day is not yet over."

Jelrah helped Petmar take Muriam to more comfortable surroundings while Gaius went to the door in answer to loud knocking.

Upon opening it a guardsman reported to him that his attackers had indeed escaped the city and there was no sign of the boy. It had, however, been confirmed that the boy had been pierced by an arrow, but more information as to his condition could not be ascertained.

"By the gods," thought Gaius. "What can be said to this poor woman?"

"Thank you," he said at last and closed the door. He stood there for a few moments when he realised someone was behind him. He turned to face Petmar.

"It is not good news, I think," said Petmar.

"No, it is not good news."

Just then there was another knock at the door. Gaius opened it to find six soldiers carrying the body of Azel.

"Place him in the great hall," said Gaius. He manned the door until they had left.

Petmar had now regained his composure.

"What happened?" he said finally.

Gaius explained that while he and his small troop of soldiers were marching through the city completing the rounds as required by the prefect, they had been ambushed by a number of men.

"The first I knew of it myself was when I saw a sword spear through the stomach of the soldier beside me. He had been run through from behind as had two others. It could have been me, he just didn't choose me."

"Training had the rest of us reacting quickly and we drew swords and started to defend ourselves when I saw a young boy run headlong into the midst of the fighting. I grabbed him quickly and threw him under a vendor's table to get him clear when all of a sudden I could see another running at me from the side. As I turned I realised instantly he was not with the attackers, but by then he had run into my sword before I had time to move. I was hit on the head with something and the next thing I knew they were gone as more soldiers arrived. There was nothing I could have done to save him. He was dead instantly. I truly am sorry. What was his name?"

"Azel," said Petmar. "His name was Azel. He was chasing his son Dysmas, trying to stop him from running into danger. The noise from the crowd made Dysmas unable to hear his father calling. It is a tragedy. Such a fine man, a wonderful husband and father. It is too much," said Petmar as he broke down sobbing.

Gaius was at a loss to know what to say to this man before him.

Finally it was Petmar who spoke. "What can we do to find Dysmas?"

Gaius related to him then the information he had been given regarding the arrow. "This could well be a double tragedy, Petmar, I'm sorry to say."

Petmar slumped to the ground. It was as if every nightmare he had ever had, played together to crush him. His beloved Azel, and now Dysmas. And what was to become of Muriam? The nightmare played out in his mind and he was numb.

"What will we do?" he said to himself. "How are we to tell her?" as tears streamed down his cheeks.

"You will both rest here as long as you will. I will see to the burial according to your customs. At least she may be spared that. I have friends among the Jews who will make the proper arrangements on her behalf."

Jelrah had returned now to hear this last statement. "Jelrah," he continued, "see to it."

Jelrah nodded and was gone in moments.

"Come," Gaius said to Petmar. "I need some wine, and you could use some too."

Gaius led Petmar to a balcony at the rear of his more than palatial house and poured a wine for each of them. Both consumed the entirety of their goblets instantly and refilled.

"I know," said Gaius at last, "if Rome was not in your city with its legions patrolling, this would not have happened. I know how Jews think."

"Not all Jews think as one," replied Petmar. "It is true that if Rome were not in Jerusalem patrolling our streets the skirmish would likely not have happened, Azel and Dysmas would be alive. It is also true that Israel has betrayed its God for false gods and human respect, and God Himself foretold the consequences of this act. It is further true, that if it had not been you, it would have been another who would perhaps have been indifferent to the life of a Jewish child and may not have tried to save him in the first instant, or care that his father was killed. Nor indeed do anything to assist his distressed wife and so on. This man that has this day died at the end of your blade was like a son to me, yet even now I know with joy that, because he was who he was, and what he stood for, he is residing in the bosom of Abraham. I know this to be true."

"The Most High God has a plan, and it was no accident He ordained you, of all Romans, to be at hand at this moment to care for His children." Petmar was intense now. "These that you have encountered today are truly Jews. They did not speak of it, they lived it. Nor were they distant and condescending, but generous and kind, regardless of rights of birth. These are the salt of the earth, little in the eyes of men, but great in the family of God. You and Azel would have been close friends I think. It is sad that you never met, and sadder still that you have most likely met very few Jews if any."

Gaius was moved very deeply by these words, and stood silent looking over the street below, unsure of just how to reply. Clearly there was something profound and startling about this insight that had taken him completely by surprise. Finally he said, "I thought you would be angry."

Petmar turned to him now, "Angry? I am enraged beyond your ability to understand, but not with you. Israel has brought this injustice upon that poor woman in there, not you. You were just the hapless instrument."

"How can I help her?" asked Gaius.

"I truly don't know," replied Petmar. "How can you restore a beating heart? For hers beats as one with his. As much as I love my Arlett, never have I seen two more inseparable creatures than these. In their presence truly one could feel the love between them." He turned to the street, "It is the saddest of days," and he wept.

Gaius, truly moved and feeling himself very low in spirit, withdrew then to be alone. He found himself soon upon the porch on the east side of the house, overlooking a small garden. He was greatly surprised to see the woman kneeling on the ground leaning on the stone seat sobbing quietly and pleading with one unseen. He watched her with much curiosity. He had many times seen Jewish women mourning their dead, and been desperate to flee their presence to escape the incessant screaming. Yet here before him was one like none he had encountered before. A truly gentle soul, of great faith and deportment. Perhaps Petmar had been right, he thought, these were the true Jews. Peaceful, gentle and filled with faith and trust in their God.

Just then Muriam perceived his presence and collected herself.

"I'm sorry to have disturbed you," he said. "If I may, I will bring Petmar to you, to explain all that we know at this time."

"Thank you, yes," was her simple reply, as she wiped tears from her eyes, and he left her.

Soon Petmar joined her and explained all that had been conveyed to him.

"Oh Petmar, what am I to do?" she cried as she threw her arms around his neck and wept bitterly.

"Truly I do not know," he replied holding her, "I can barely take it all in myself," and he joined her once more in tears. Never had Petmar known such heartbreak in his life. He knew now for the first time, the short time shared with his own son and his loss was heartbreaking, but this, this was debilitating. This had crushed his spirit. He had never known such pain.

Night was upon Jerusalem, the day had taken a great toll on all of them, and all had retired early.

Gaius could not sleep, though he spent some hours trying. At about midnight he found himself too restless and rose. As he made his way quietly through the house he perceived a very faint murmuring. He quietly followed the sound to the great hall where he found Muriam sitting beside the body of her husband, holding his hand and again speaking gently with one unseen. He could not help but admire this woman and her great dignity. He quietly withdrew and returned to his room to seek the elusive sleep he needed. Three in the morning found him once more walking the night, and once more he found this woman holding the hand of her husband. She had not moved, and he found his own heart was breaking.

Muriam sensed him, and without looking up said, "I understand it was an accident."

Gaius was taken aback by her candour.

"I am truly sorry for all that has happened."

"I know," replied Muriam. "But it is not you who are to blame, circumstance often provides fate her chance. I am just lost for now."

Gaius slid down the wall sitting on the floor with his back to the wall staring into nothing. "I will do what I can to find your son if he is alive, but I, like you, are lost just now, and know not where to look if I were not." And they both sat in silence for the following hour with their own sad thoughts.

"What made you become a soldier?" Muriam asked then quite unexpectedly.

"I am of an aristocratic family in Rome, and my father had ambitions for a place in the Senate for me. It was expected of one such as I to earn his place as it were, and so he obtained a commission for me. Our family fortune was lost, and the commission was all I was left with, so here I am."

"But how is it you are in Jerusalem?" continued Muriam, "I understand that Jerusalem is considered a punishment among Roman soldiers."

"And you would be right. I have angered my superiors in and out of battle, wherever they have sent me."

"Why?"

"They always claimed the same charge, giving comfort to the enemy. I always claimed the same defence. Thus far my defence has won the day each time, but that did not stop the generals from spitting on me and having me transferred. I have seen almost every front line known to the legions, so often have I been moved. That is until one general who had been here himself, decided the only place for me was the pit known as Jerusalem. So here I am. I shall never see the senate with so many who now hate me there, and my father would be shamed should I return. They have been unable to strip me of my commission, given I have been found innocent each time, so I have resigned myself to living out my days in this place, never to see Rome again."

After a very long silence Muriam asked, "What was your defence?"

"I simply claimed I was a Roman, and Rome has conquered the world. It was not to terrorise other nations, but to bring to them the wealth of knowledge and culture that is Rome. We as Romans must then respect that those we conquer are worthy of the gifts we claim to bring. If they are not and but chattel to be used, we are simply conquerers, slaughtering all before us, hiding behind a lie. We would be no better than those we claim are barbarians. I struck Capious yesterday because he had no respect for your people. He like so many others are drunk with power and have forgotten what Rome was meant to be. The innocence or guilt of one can never be determined by his race. The pain that one experiences at the end of a sword is no less for a Jew than a Roman. The pain of loss is no less for a Jew than a Roman. I believe that there is no pressing need often to treat people with cruelty. Or to deny them relief in battle. Once my commander claimed that they would not afford Roman soldiers such relief, to which I responded we are Romans, we are leading the way are we not? He had no response. My defence is that Rome claims its legions are bringing progress to the world. It is incumbent upon Rome to lead the way."

"And you believe this?" said Muriam.

"With all my heart," replied Gaius.

"My husband would have disagreed with you that Rome had more knowledge or culture than Judea, but in all else, you would have been very close friends indeed. Very close."

"I have to admit that my faith in Rome's all-knowing approach has been shaken more than once since my arrival here. There are mysteries here I have found nowhere else."

"What will happen today?" asked Muriam staring into nothing.

"I have alerted my Jewish friends here of what has transpired, and they have agreed to assist your preparations for the proper burial of your husband. It is all taken care of, your personal wishes are the only area of which I could not enlighten them. They will join you here soon after dawn. I have need to provide defence to the prefect at dawn for my conduct yesterday, so I will be leaving soon."

"A defence for?"

"Sending soldiers in search of your son. Three were killed in that endeavour."

"What will happen?" she asked.

"There is little he can do really I suppose, other than appeal to Rome to reduce my rank. And he will not do that as I am acting as his Tribune here, given he cannot get one to actually come to Jerusalem. They always seem to have some great catastrophe detain them, or make appeal to Caesar through friends in the Senate. By whatever means they do not come. I am and have been by necessity for some time the acting Tribune. There would be some generals who would be greatly angered if they knew, but the prefect has little choice. There is nowhere else they can send me, no one else wants me. I am a thorn in his side on one hand, but my experience has saved him many times on the other. He knows full well he can rely on no other under his command as he can me. He will view it as a mistake in judgement, of course, but he will likely consider it a rare mistake in judgment and let it pass, once he has put on a show for the gallery."

"As to yourself and Petmar, you are both welcome to stay here as long as you will. I will move into the garrison, it will be more comfortable for you both if I were not here."

"That is not necessary," said Muriam. "We have no fear of you, nor do we blame you. Azel himself would not blame you, God rest him. It is God Himself who called him home, you were simply the instrument. A great reward awaited him, and he is watching over me even now. Who knows why God wanted him at that moment, but I know he did. The Lord hath given me, and the Lord hath taken back, blessed be the Lord."

Gaius thought to himself, "Just when I think I have this people worked out as backward fools, I find wisdom and understanding beyond that of Rome." He was very puzzled.

"I must take my leave," he said at last, "I will see you then upon my return," and he left her still holding the hand of Azel.

Gaius did not see Petmar as he left for his required meeting with the prefect. He found himself somewhat disinterested in this meeting now as he walked along, his thoughts entirely cast back to the conversations he had had with both Petmar and Muriam.

They were unlike any Jews he had met. Even his Jewish friends he understood were so, because he had shown himself to be fair and even friendly toward Jews. In truth he had no doubt that if it came to it, they would betray his innocent blood in place of a guilty Jew. He was well aware that he was always a foreigner in their midst.

Yet these two were not like this. They who had reason to hate him most had no taste for it. These who had reason to blame him found forgiveness in place of anger. Gaius knew well men to be shown in the darkest moments of life, not the lightest. These had traversed the darkest moment before his eyes and at his hand, yet felt for his plight. Their humanity surpassed his Roman idealism before his eyes, while the fire was still searing their hearts. Though darkness had fallen upon them, still they were guided by a light that seemingly could not be quenched. He found himself at once confused and envious.

He collected his thoughts as he approached the Pretorian palace, and his required meeting with the prefect.

The truth was, the assessment Gaius had earlier made regarding the thoughts of the prefect were entirely accurate. The prefect had himself been awake much of the night considering what he would do. As Gaius entered the main gate, the door to the right which was standing ajar opened.

"In here, quickly." It was the prefect.

Gaius obeyed and soon found himself in the palatial private residence of the prefect, Valerius Gratus.

"What are we to do, Gaius?" he asked. "Capious is baying for blood, and he has cause."

"Capious is an ambitious fool with a thirst for innocent blood. He is unworthy of Rome. He came to you yesterday because he was put in his place publicly, and it was well past time."

"I am aware of all this, but that does not solve my dilemma."

"What would you have me do?" asked Gaius.

"You tell me. What can you do?"

"Capious has been caught breaking every regulation known to the Roman Legion."

"Can you prove that?"

"Instantly."

"Then do it, and get it on my desk. Now, what of these others? Atop the four you lost in battle, there are three further dead. What explanation can be given?"

"Well, sir, even had I not sent them for the boy, I would have sent them in pursuit regardless. We could not just let them escape without making some effort to capture them. Yes, the loss of life is outrageous, that is true, but the only difference to the outcome is that they were sent after the same group for a different reason. I was concussed and may have inadvertently called the right action with the wrong order."

"Brilliant," replied the prefect rubbing his jaw while considering the statement. "Yes, indeed, brilliant. Provide the report thus, and get that material on Capious to me at the same time. Do it today."

Gaius saluted and left.

Much of the day was taken up writing the report required by the prefect and the dossier on Capious. Capious had few friends within the ranks. He was a very coarse man with little regard for others, who had treated the men very poorly, so it was little effort gaining witnesses to his many indiscretions.

It was late afternoon by the time Gaius had completed his task and delivered the material to the prefect.

"I believe you have visitors in your home. Would you care to explain why?"

"It is the wife of the man I killed yesterday, and the mother of the child missing," replied Gaius.

"I know this already," replied the prefect. "The question is why?"

"Passover is upon us and the city is full, these people are headstrong and given to impetuous acts of rebellion. By showing her compassion I hoped to dampen their rage and confirm it as an accident. It was my hope that we might be spared an uprising and possible further loss of Roman lives, and thus far it would seem the mob are appeased."

"I see," said the prefect. "There are times, Gaius, I could ring your neck, but there is no arguing with your logic. You won't be needed tonight," the prefect said, "and short of the uprising you seek to avoid, attend to your guests until Monday; we will speak then."

Gaius saluted and left.

By the time he had arrived home the body of Azel had been removed. He had been careful to ensure a tomb was provided and all expenses with regard to the proper burial according to the customs of the Jews. Jelrah informed him that Muriam and Petmar had not returned. He left then destined for the burial site, and found them both praying beside the tomb.

Gaius stood there for some time watching these two gentle souls, bidding farewell to what was in all probability another such soul.

Soon they were rising, then, turning, realised his presence.

Muriam stopped in front of him as she was passing. Gaius thought she looked very unwell. The terrible events were taking their toll.

"I am grateful to you for your assistance," she said, "I know it was not easy arranging all this during Passover, but please, is there any word of my son?"

"I'm sorry," he replied, "there is no word. The prefect has restored my command, so I will make it a priority to seek him out, I promise you that, but I cannot promise I will be able to find him. I will do my best."

Tears welled in her eyes as she nodded gravely. She turned then to leave and took a single step before she collapsed.

Gaius had anticipated her state and caught her as she fell.

Petmar swept her up in his arms.

"This way," said Gaius as he took a path that led them through the back of the garrison headquarters that provided a substantial shortcut to his house.

They laid Muriam on her bed and Gaius called for Jelrah.

"Go to the house of Simon," he said. "Tell him what has happened here, and ask if he could provide a nurse. Tell him I will make good any expense." Jelrah was on his way in a moment.

"She does not look well, Petmar."

"I know, I am worried for her. If only we had word of Dysmas to cheer her."

"I can do nothing until Monday. I have been relieved until then. However, my first duty will be to dispatch a spy to enquire into his whereabouts. That's if he still lives."

Simon's house was but two doors away, and Jelrah returned almost immediately.

"He is making the arrangements," he said, and went about his duties.

Soon after, the nurse employed by Simon's wife was at the door, complete with her belongings for a short stay. She was taken to Muriam and reported immediately that Muriam had contracted the fever. "She is burning up," the nurse reported.

"Given what she has been through," said Gaius, "it is more likely shock. I have seen it before. After what she has endured, it is little wonder."

"I will tend her," said the nurse.

Gaius found Petmar deep in thought on the porch. Quietly he said to Jelrah, "Fetch a skin of wine."

"How are you holding up?" said Gaius as he came up behind Petmar who had tears in his eyes.

"I honestly don't know," he replied. "I have lost one who was as a son to me, possibly another who was as a son to me, and my dearest daughter lay in there with the fever. I have never felt so broken in my lifetime."

Jelrah returned then and wine was poured.

"I am lost," said Petmar at last as he stared into his wine, "What am I to do?"

Gaius was silent for a time and said, "What are you supposed to be doing?"

"What?" replied Petmar.

"Well, if none of this had happened, what is it you would be doing now?"

Petmar thought for a moment. "I would be arranging the Passover meal for those in the caravan, who must be wondering what has become of me."

"Why don't you start there, Petmar? You are welcome to stay, but I think it best if you busy yourself with familiar tasks. Muriam has a nurse and she will be well cared for, I will see to it. I will send you word immediately of any change."

"Perhaps you are right," said Petmar after a long silence. "Yes, you are right. I will return after Passover, or if needed, earlier."

"You may return whenever you wish," said Gaius, "now or in the future, this house is and will remain a friendly house to you. I am aware that it is much to take in, but know this: in other circumstances, this house would still have been a friendly house to you."

"Thank you, Gaius. I will gather my belongings and get about my duties," and soon Petmar was on his way back to the caravan.

For two days Muriam slipped in and out of consciousness with her nurse ever present and Gaius keeping a close eye on her progress. By Monday noon she was awake once more and able to get up.

"Ah, you are awake!" said Gaius as she walked out onto the porch. "How do you feel?"

"Weak," she replied.

"Here, sit," said Gaius motioning her to the vacant couch.

"Where is Petmar?" she enquired.

"He is with the caravan, I expect. He was quite beside himself and lost. He thought it best he organise the Passover for his travellers. Keep busy, you know."

Muriam nodded to herself.

"I have sent word to him moments ago that you are awake. He asked to be kept abreast of your condition. I have no doubt he will be joining us quite soon. He loves you very much."

"I will be returning to my duties shortly. I will set about the location of your son upon my return. You are welcome to stay as you will, and recover. If you think it best to leave, I will get word to you of our progress."

"I think it probably best if I leave with the caravan."

"As you wish." Gaius found himself genuinely disappointed to be losing her company, and was puzzled by his feelings.

Lies and Recruitment

There was the smell of smoke in the air when Dysmas awoke two days later, and a searing pain in his leg. Though tempted to cry out in pain, he checked himself, confused and frightened by these strange surroundings in which he found himself.

"Excellent," said Barabbas who had been watching him, "You have strength, and wisdom."

"Who are you?" asked Dysmas.

"I, my young warrior, am the man that saved your life."

Dysmas was very weak and slumped back to his bedding. "Saved my life," he said to himself as he tried to get his bearings.

"You have lost a great deal of blood, and you are very weak. I suggest you rest. We can talk when you are strong enough."

Even then, Dysmas felt himself lapsing back into sleep, and was indeed unconscious once more in a few moments.

As he started to come to his senses later, Dysmas slowly took in his very strange surroundings. He could smell smoke and could see a number of fires burning at various locations, around what appeared to be a cave. The smoke from these various fires climbed to the darkened roof above, disappearing through some unseen vents. There were perhaps thirty men he perceived scattered throughout the cave.

All at once he remembered his father, and it stabbed through his heart as sure as the blade that had killed his father. Tears welled in his eyes then, but Azel had taught him well. There was no sound, no obvious sign that he was awake.

Barabbas, however, was close at hand and had again been watching.

"You are awake at last," he said. "How do you feel?"

"Tired. Where am I?"

"You are in our hide out. My home, I suppose," replied Barabbas.

"How did I get here?"

"Well, we all took turns carrying you," Barabbas said smiling. "Do you remember what happened?"

"Yes," he said as tears started to flow, "my father was killed."

"Your father?" said Barabbas. "Oh yes, of course, that explains it. I did not know it was your father that Gaius killed. That explains a great deal."

"Gaius?"

"The centurion that killed your father. A murderous Roman centurion. A feared warrior. He has been responsible for our losing many battles. We had hoped to be rid of him that day, but it was not to be. You, my young warrior, almost did the job for us. However, had I not snatched you up when I did, that arrow through your leg would have found your heart instead. You are an outlaw now. All of Rome is looking for you."

"Why?"

"For the same reason they tried to kill you; you took up sword and almost killed their centurion. You don't think they will let that go, do you?"

"But he killed my father."

"Rome has no interest in your father or any other Jew. They hate us."

"What of my mother?" asked Dysmas.

"I don't know," said Barabbas. "I saw no woman. You had better hope they didn't connect you to her."

Dysmas was thoughtful, trying to stay calm.

"Don't worry, they will never find you here," said Barabbas.

"What about my mother?" said Dysmas.

"Where are you from?" asked Barabbas.

"Hebron."

"Todras," yelled Barabbas, and Todras came running immediately.

"I want you to go to Hebron and seek out the house, oh." He turned to Dysmas then. "What was your father's name?"

"Azel, son of Micah."

"Seek out the house of Azel, son of Micah. Find out what you can of his widow. Go now and report back as soon as possible."

Todras was on his way without question. It was clear to Dysmas that Barabbas' commands were unquestioned in this place.

"What is your name?" asked Dysmas.

"Barabbas. Perhaps you have heard of me?"

"No," replied Dysmas.

"And what is your name?" asked Barabbas.

"Dysmas, son of Azel of the house of Micah."

"Very good," said Barabbas nodding to himself. "Very good indeed, young Dysmas."

He motioned to one of the younger men who came quickly.

"Arrange some broth for young Dysmas, and some meat. Let's see if we can't get him back on his feet," and Barabbas left them and the cave.

Eleazar was outside on watch when Barabbas joined him.

"How is the boy?" he asked.

"Awake, and impressive for such a young boy. Very impressive."

"I sense an idea," said Eleazar, smiling.

"He would make a fine soldier trained properly, but we will have to be careful how we go about it. Yes indeed," Barabbas said, almost to himself as he rubbed his jaw.

"You know it was his father that Gaius killed?"

"That explains a lot," said Eleazar.

"I have sent Todras to Hebron to find out about the family, and what has become of the widow. I want you to go back to Jerusalem and find out what happened after we left."

"You think he's worth this much effort?" asked Eleazar.

"There is something about this boy, Eleazar. He has determination; no fear or self-interest. He is wise beyond his years, yet has retained his innocence. He's already tall for his age, has a big build and is agile despite it. Oh yes, I think he is well worth it. If he joins us now, imagine the asset he would be!"

"I'll leave first thing in the morning."

"Go alone, you'll draw less attention alone. Find out if Gaius was injured or not, and report to me privately upon your return."

Barabbas returned to the cave once more deep in thought. A plan was hatching.

Dysmas was sitting up eating his broth, and it was clear for the first time that he would recover.

Days turned into weeks without a word from either Todras or Eleazar.

Dysmas was improving each day, and it was now barely noticeable that he was limping.

Barabbas had included him over the past week in the daily drills and exercises of the men, and found to his delight, though not his surprise, that he was a natural with a sword in his hand. Even though the sword was heavy for him just now, he was still quite fast.

During one such drill, Todras returned.

"What news?" asked Barabbas as Dysmas joined them, having observed the arrival of Todras.

"There is no news, I'm afraid. A very popular family in the town. The home is still deserted, none have returned. I'm sorry young man, I had hoped to have better news."

Dysmas was silent as he returned to his exercises.

"I stayed for a few days," Todras continued to Barabbas, "but no one returned."

"That is actually good for us," said Barabbas. "He will make a fine soldier."

"He is staying?" said Todras a little bewildered.

"We will see," replied Barabbas smiling.

Eleazar returned three days later and sent word to Barabbas of his return through the watch.

"I was starting to worry about you," said Barabbas as he joined him. "What did you find out?"

"A great deal. His father is dead but his mother lives. She is still at the house of Gaius."

"She is where?" replied a stunned Barabbas. "Are you serious?"

"Oh yes," replied Eleazar.

"How can that be?"

Eleazar then unfolded all the events he had been able to learn, and they were in fact, remarkably close to the truth.

Barabbas was deep in thought now. "And what of Capious?"

"Valerius Gratus has banished him to Rome, for trial no less. Our incursion has inadvertently served only to strengthen the position of Gaius."

"How can that be!" screamed Barabbas, infuriated. "The very one we seek to destroy is somehow more secure than ever."

He was livid with rage.

"I'm only the messenger," said Eleazar lifting his arm, a little afraid now.

Barabbas checked himself.

"I'm sorry," he said at last, and drew in a couple of breaths to calm himself. "By what treachery has Gaius managed to convince this boy's mother that he himself is the victim here?"

"Honestly, Barabbas, I myself have been baffled by everything I have observed. I deliberately stayed and observed everything I have relayed to you. She seems not only unconcerned with the fact that Gaius is the murderer of her husband, and as far as she knows her son, but is a gracious guest of his house."

"That makes no sense at all," said Barabbas totally astounded. "The report from Todras said these people were to all extents and purposes, very much in love. What happened between Hebron and Jerusalem that changed all that? I just don't get it," said Barabbas, now quite perplexed.

"Truly," said Eleazar, "as God is my judge, the account I render to you is the truth."

"And this Petmar you speak of, what of him?"

"From what I could understand, the boy's mother was very ill for a time, and Gaius agreed to see to her wellbeing until Petmar's return two months hence, at which time he has plans to return her to his home near Nazareth I think."

"So he just left her with Gaius? How extraordinary," said Barabbas, truly astounded by the entire story.

"Well, then," he said at last, "what is to be done?"

"Are you going to tell the boy?" asked Eleazar.

"Of course not! You will tell him that his father is indeed dead. Tell him that you had two reports that a woman attacked a Roman soldier who was turning his father over at the incident. Tell him one report had said she was killed, while the other said she had been taken prisoner. You were unable to confirm which of the stories were true. What you can confirm is that she is not being held in any jails. Tell him that Rome has issued an order for her capture for trying to kill the centurion. I'll take it from there."

"And should he find out at some time in the future that his mother lives?" asked Eleazar.

"We have not claimed she doesn't," said Barabbas smiling. "Leave it to me."

So it was that the story was told most convincingly by Eleazar, even though he himself had grave reservations about all of it.

Dysmas was visibly distraught upon hearing all this, and left for the solitude of a dark corner of the cave.

After a few hours Barabbas made his way to Dysmas who was simply staring at his feet quite stunned.

"Look," said Barabbas, "all is not lost. I have an idea that might be worthwhile. This is what we will do. We will wait a full cycle of the moon, and then you and I will travel to Hebron. If your mother is still alive she will be there by then. The Romans don't jail wives for trying to protect their husbands. If they did that, everyone would be in jail. No, if she is alive, she will be home by then in the hope you have gone there. Does that make sense?"

Dysmas brightened then. "Yes, it does."

"Between now and then, you are welcome here," said Barabbas.

Barabbas well knew that his mother would remain in Jerusalem for two months. It was in his view a fool-proof plan.

Over the following month Barabbas spent much time with Dysmas, and made him especially welcome. Dysmas kept training with the men and continued to improve, much to the delight of Barabbas.

There were two raids conducted by the men which were necessary to relieve weary travellers from Egypt and Samaria of their wealth, to "fund the cause" as Barabbas would say. Dysmas was left to guard the cave on the first occasion, but Barabbas considered it wise to get him out of the cave on the second, and so included him.

"You are too hot just yet," Barabbas had assured him. "Should the Romans see you, who knows what would happen? You will need to be well-disguised to travel." To this end Dysmas joined them, but always had his face covered.

The group spent the next two weeks in the open country between Hebron and the border with Egypt, surprising unsuspecting travellers travelling in either direction.

They would pounce on their victims, for the most part without causing any injury, while intent on being as threatening as possible. Often they were held overnight to allow them to properly consider the precarious nature of their positions, frightening them half out of their wits. Dysmas was surprised by this, but thought it best to simply observe. He was certain Barabbas was just in his decisions.

On the fourth night late in the evening, the men returned with a couple who had with them a young child. They were as the rest had been, held in a makeshift prison. Dysmas was, as always, charged with delivering food and drink to the new 'benefactors'. This couple, however, were not like the others Dysmas had encountered when he brought food.

They did not appear wealthy. They were neither angry with regard to their plight, nor seemingly in any way afraid. They simply made up bedding and put their young son down to sleep. They thanked Dysmas with genuine kindness assuring him that they understood that this was not his fault, and that all would be well. Dysmas was greatly disturbed by their kindness to him in the circumstances.

This was apart from the unshakable feeling that he knew them from somewhere.

This uneasiness grew through the night as he slept a broken sleep. Some hours before the cock was due to herald the new day he found himself shaking Barabbas awake.

"What is it?" he snapped, calming when he realised it was Dysmas.

"It is that couple we have," said Dysmas.

Barabbas sat up then wiping sleep from his eyes. "The couple? What about them?"

"Can we let them go?" asked Dysmas. "Please?"

"Why?" asked Barabbas.

"Because they remind me of my parents. They will have nothing of value but each other. They are poor."

Barabbas stared at Dysmas, amazed. This boy had not only compassion but real wisdom, and a keen eye. Apart from that he considered it an opportunity to show deference when it would cost him nothing, but may come in handy when dealing with Dysmas later on some other matter. So after some faint protests he agreed that Dysmas could release them.

Dysmas was overjoyed. "Thank you Barabbas," he stammered as he leapt to his feet bound to bring the news to them immediately.

He found the man awake and standing guard while his wife and child were sleeping when he arrived at their makeshift prison.

"You may leave when you will," said Dysmas a little too loudly, waking the man's wife.

"And you know this, how?" asked the man.

"I have just spoken to Barabbas and he has agreed to let you go."

"Joseph?" asked the woman.

The man turned to her and said simply, "We are free to leave. We should collect our things and be on our way." Turning back to Dysmas he said, "Thank you, young man."

They collected their belongings and strapped them to a small donkey that they had procured for the long trip from Egypt to Nazareth.

Dysmas felt greatly relieved for some reason that this couple at least were on their way safely.

The child was placed upon the donkey as his father began to lead it from the enclosure. The woman stopped in front of Dysmas before she followed.

"Thank you for interceding for us, young man. I promise from the depth of my heart, that I will never cease interceding for you." She knelt then and kissed his cheek.

Dysmas was baffled as to what she had meant as he watched them until they were out of sight. He was at last at ease once more and returned to his bedding to claim what sleep the night would provide him.

This and many other personality traits of Dysmas had truly had an impact on Barabbas. He announced to his men that after further consideration, he had decided to wrap up the entire operation and return to the cave. "It is perhaps time we started targeting the Romans to fund us rather than our own," he had conceded.

Dysmas was very pleased to be heading back.

After their return, with the rising of the crescent moon once more, Barabbas organised the trip to Hebron promised to Dysmas the month before.

Dysmas was at once excited and afraid.

"Don't be concerned," Barabbas had told him. "The future will unfold as it must. Let us discover it together, yes?"

Dysmas smiled, "Yes." Dysmas had grown to like Barabbas very much. He was more at ease now as they set out, and resigned to whatever outcome fate would decree, unaware that Barabbas already knew what the outcome would be.

It was a nine-day journey, and uneventful by all accounts.

Each night Barabbas would speak of Israel and the chosen people, how God had decreed the Jews would rule, and the great privilege of being a Jew. He would regale Dysmas with tales of conquest and adventure, weaving and knitting the glories of Israel into a tapestry of awe and wonder. Though not formally spoken of until now, it was understood that the Roman presence in Israel was as a pestilence upon the very ground on which they stood.

"You have seen it for yourself," he said finally. "Your beautiful father, full of the truth of the God of Israel, slain senselessly with no regard for the great truths of life and reason. I cannot stand by and allow other young men, such as yourself, to be orphaned by the callous indifference of Rome," he had concluded. It was a most moving oration that had Dysmas quite on the edge of his seat.

They had arrived as Barabbas had planned, early on the tenth day. He was able then to observe the town from the same ridge Joseph had used those years ago. He was hoping that his calculations were indeed accurate, that the mother of Dysmas had not returned.

He called Dysmas to his vantage point. "We will stay here out of sight today. Can you point out for me your house?"

"There," he said indicating his home.

"Ah, yes," said Barabbas. "I will watch today and we will go down tonight under cover of darkness. I have no doubt the Romans will know where you live and will be watching. If your mother is back she will be keeping a low profile so she may not show herself. That is most proper, so don't be alarmed. You get some sleep if you can."

There was no sleep for Dysmas. He was like a coiled spring waiting to be released. Never had he experienced desperation before, but he was now at the edge of desperation for the first time, and it was not a welcome experience.

Barabbas had a great deal at stake in this little venture, so he was most vigilant all afternoon. As night fell, he called Dysmas.

"None have come or gone," he said simply. "It is time. Do you want to come with me?"

"Of course," said Dysmas.

They made their way to the house, and met none on the way.

As they entered into the darkness of the house the heart of Dysmas sank. He could already make out much of the space. However, Barabbas lit three candles and the interior was exposed more clearly.

Dysmas looked around stonyfaced and said finally, "It is exactly as we left it. None have been here since we left."

He bowed his head then and said through trembling lips. "She is dead." He had steeled himself from what he had somehow known was the inevitable, but in the end to little profit.

"Is there anything you wish to claim while we are here?" asked Barabbas.

"Only that Roman bath," said Dysmas with a smile as he fought to hold back tears.

Barabbas had by now been a little overcome himself with emotion and hugged him. "It's alright," he said. "Everything will work out. Come, we had better not stay in case someone saw you enter."

They closed the door and were almost across the yard when they heard.

"Dysmas!"

Dysmas turned to see Gestus running toward him.

"Hello, Gestus," he replied.

"Where have you been?" he asked. "The whole town has been wondering."

"Ah," he began.

"Better not say too much," counselled Barabbas.

"I can't really say, Gestus, sorry."

"Who are you?" asked Gestus of Barabbas.

"My name is Barabbas, boy," Barabbas replied testily.

"Not The Barabbas?" said Gestus. "The freedom fighter?"

Barabbas lightened immediately, "So you've heard of me?"

"Oh, yes, all Israel has heard of you. I hope to join you in the fight against the Romans one day, but mother says I am just a foolish boy."

"Well, if no one fights for Israel, how can she win?" asked Barabbas.

"Exactly," replied Gestus.

"We have to be away," said Barabbas, "but we will meet again Gestus, and maybe you will join us one day. In the meantime can you keep a secret?"

"Of course."

"Let no one know that you have seen us here this night."

"I won't, I promise."

"Come, Dysmas, we must go," said Barabbas.

"Goodbye Gestus," said Dysmas, "I'll be back one day."

With that they were gone quickly under cover of darkness.

As they travelled, Barabbas asked Dysmas of Gestus and Hebron. He had been surprised that he was so well-known so far from Jerusalem.

Dysmas explained that they had grown up together. Gestus was two years older than him, and had always been talking of freeing Israel from Roman hands. "We used to play soldiers as children, ridding Israel of the scourge of Rome," he said. "My father used to caution me against such games."

"Well, he would likely have a different view now," said Barabbas and silence fell between them.

The return trip was a sombre one for Dysmas. Memories of so many events of his childhood played over in his mind.

As he walked alongside Barabbas now many emotions were surfacing. His state moved from smiles to tears and at one point he burst out laughing before checking himself.

He found himself wondering as to why God would allow these events to happen in his life. What possible purpose?

He was angry with himself for running off on that day, and had great personal guilt when he considered his parents would still be alive if he hadn't. It was a theme in this young boy's life that was destined to visit him often throughout the rest of it. As he grew, so too did the bitterness of this terrible regret.

Then there was Gaius, this Roman centurion. That he was seeking only to survive a vicious attack seemed lost on this young man, whose hatred of the man who killed his parents would consume him. Such anger and outrage Dysmas had not known before. He was unaware that the delicate innocence of his humanity had been desecrated. Not from without, but within.

Dysmas had not even considered the contribution Barabbas had made to the death of his parents. It seemed entirely lost on his young mind that seemed so intent on hatred.

Had his father been alive he would have provided the guidance needed to spare Dysmas the years of agony ahead, but where guidance is absent or spurned, providence is a sure but harsh replacement.

Barabbas for the most part left him to contemplate his thoughts alone through the travel of the day, contributing self-propagation over the camp fire at night.

There was much said of the Romans and their incursion into Israel, the suppression of the people under Roman law and so on. Dysmas listened intently, and his young, impressionable mind was much impressed by this new world view. His father had instructed him in the ways of the God of Israel as he understood them. He had instructed Dysmas of forbearance and humility. "Trust in the God of Israel," he would say, and the certainty was that these events were the fault of Israel for ignoring God's call to repentance. "Your first concern," he said often, "is the love of God. The joy of loving God is so great; you will find little taste for the poison of the world."

All these words now seemed so far distant to a young boy who had seen it was action that took the life of his father, and who now had what appeared to be a man of action before him. He knew that action had changed his life forever, and could not see the point in the pleasantries of inaction.

"It had been inaction that had been the death of his family, was it not?" Barabbas insisted.

"I would love to believe that what your father taught you was possible, but I see every day the oppression of our people. Until we drive these Romans from our country, we will remain prisoners in our own country, making the dreams your father hoped you would dream impossible. Something must be done," said Barabbas finally.

To a young half-formed mind it was a strong argument for which he had no reply. These things had a great impression on Dysmas. He thought of little more than of the loss of his parents and of killing Gaius. Azel had instructed him well in the Torah; however, the "thou shalt not kill" of the Decalogue was quickly put aside for "an eye for an eye". For a young man with only biased guidance, it was not a dilemma that could be easily reconciled.

"And what of Petmar?" thought Dysmas. "Given what Barabbas had told him of their narrow escape, the blood trail of a small boy that must have been the report, he must think me dead," he concluded.

"Poor Petmar," he thought to himself. How heartbroken he must be, believing he had lost the whole family.

Dysmas had no idea where Petmar lived or how to find him.

"We will make camp here tonight," Barabbas said suddenly.

Dysmas had spent much of the day considering what he would do, where he would go. As they settled down around the fire some time later, all of the considerations over the past several days were working themselves out.

"Are the Romans still looking for me?" Dysmas asked.

Barabbas stared at him for a moment. "In truth, they probably think you're dead, but if they saw you, they would soon arrest you. Why do you ask?"

"I'm trying to work out what to do," replied Dysmas watching the fire.

"You can stay with us if you wish," said Barabbas.

"I was thinking more of joining you."

Barabbas was thrilled but showed nothing. "Well," he said finally. "You are too young to join us on raids just yet, but there is much to be done in the cave until you are old enough. You will be expected to train and train hard."

"Oh, yes, I want to train. I want you to make me a great soldier. It is my only chance to kill Gaius."

"Gaius?" said Barabbas. "You will need to be a very good soldier to defeat Gaius."

"I will train," said Dysmas with determination etched into his eyes.

"Well then," said Barabbas, "it is settled."

Dysmas slept well that night for the first time in many weeks. He had purpose once more. Revenge. He would deceive himself for many years that it was justice, but it was certainly revenge. Given his tender age, it would be six years before Dysmas joined Barabbas on his first raid, but he was dertimined to be ready.

When they arrived back at about the sixth hour, Eleazar was placed over Dysmas to train him, and to assign various duties.

At first it was the mundane preparation of food, cleaning and the like; however, it became apparent quickly that Dysmas was wasted on the mundane. Soon he was reporting to Barabbas the various shortfalls in supplies, and was in effect the quartermaster of supplies soon after. He organised better systems to procure supplies and store them, better methods to streamline production of weapons.

He noted, for example, the smoke in the north end of the cave where the small smelter stood, making it hard to breathe for those working on weapon production. To this end, while Barabbas was away on a raid, he organised those left behind to move the furnace box so that it was positioned directly below the penetration at the far end of the cave. A great hood was fashioned from stone and limestone, dust and clay. The furnace was lit quickly drying the material, hardening the hood as a strong and permanent feature. Next, together they built a funnel almost to the penetration itself, using the same method, bracing the structure from the walls wherever possible. When the furnace was finally lit, there were cheers with roars of laughter and congratulations for young Dysmas. The result was a spectacular difference in air quality, and an ever-growing esteem the men held for this remarkable young man, who was quickly proving himself to be an invaluable asset.

Barabbas had been both amazed and thrilled upon his return. The ingenuity of the design coupled with the organisation of its construction, was discussed at length for weeks after.

At training also, none were more focused than Dysmas. He learned his lessons well, deliberately placing himself in harm's way, to both test his skills and learn new ones. He was true to his word to Barabbas with regard to enthusiasm.

By the time he was sixteen, he was clearly the best swordsman among the men, whose only advantage lay in their superior strength. Yet even this was on the brink of being lost, as this young boy was rapidly becoming a man.

His stature among the men grew daily, as did his place in the heart of Barabbas.

Barabbas had been close to no one. As an orphaned boy, those opportunities that presented themselves when he had, at some point, let someone in, had inevitably been used against him. Though he had found his mother years later, even this relationship had remained a little distant. He was bitter with personal relationships, and so had seen to it for much of his life that none were allowed a place in his heart. He believed it clouded his judgement anyway. Dysmas however had a place there that had taken Barabbas quite by surprise. He was loyal and prudent, fearless in training and always ready to assist.

He had been pestering Barabbas for some time to join the raids, but Barabbas had thus far manufactured excuses to shield him from the battlefield. He had come to realise some time ago that it was because he feared losing him. The reality, however, was catching up with him.

Dysmas still had Gaius uppermost in his mind, and the fact that he had all but never left the cave in the past four years, concentrating only on his skills for a single purpose, did not dampen his enthusiasm for hunting Gaius down.

Barabbas, however, had convinced Dysmas that the greater cause of ridding Israel of Roman oppression was more important than personal vendettas. "You would not like to think that other families suffered what yours did, would you?" This had been a very effective argument. Dysmas saw the point and had agreed. For now.

Barabbas had argued that they needed to build up their numbers, and manufacture a cache of weapons large enough to arm at least one hundred men.

Dysmas had set about transforming the area of the cave set aside for forging weapons, into what was to become a seamless system of manufacture that could produce almost twice the number of swords and arrows, in half of the time previously needed. Eighteen months later the transformation was truly extraordinary. During this period he never allowed himself to miss a training session, and in general trained harder than all the other men.

Six months from his nineteenth birthday, he was truly a force to be reckoned with. A strapping, strong young man, none could best him, not even Barabbas.

The difficulty for Barabbas was that he had become an enormous admirer of Dysmas and a proud father figure. He was himself having issues with his own emotions as it had become clear to him, and indeed all others over the past two years, that Dysmas was much more than just a wonderful discovery or an opportunity to be taken advantage of. He had become like a son to him.

Dysmas too had grown close to Barabbas over the years, in particular as Barabbas had greatly softened his attitude toward him.

Dysmas however had never let Barabbas forget that he was ready for battle, more than ready, and even the men were wondering why he had not yet joined them in the raiding parties.

Clearly this was creating for Barabbas a dilemma that he did not need to get out of hand.

So it was that Dysmas found himself laying on his stomach behind a boulder overlooking a pass south of Jerusalem, waiting for a Roman company of about sixty soldiers to hopefully trap them in an ambush.

Barabbas had for many years tried to confirm information about the wages delivery for the garrison stationed at Jerusalem. Many times he had been given information that had been found incorrect, but for reasons known only to himself, Barabbas had assured everyone this time the information was accurate.

So he had assembled every available man to ensure success. Everyone who could lift a sword was lying in wait, including Dysmas.

The day unfolded without the slightest incident until just after noon, when they could hear the approach of what sounded like a whole Roman legion, but was in fact only thirty-five weary Roman soldiers leading a wagon, laden presumably with gold or silver.

Dysmas was well past ready for battle, but the hairs stood up on the back of his neck all the same, as he realised this would be for real.

"This is it," said Barabbas, excited that finally his information was correct.

The soldiers marched toward the pass seemingly unconcerned that it was a perfect place for an ambush.

Dysmas watched in disbelief.

"Watch and learn a valuable lesson," whispered Barabbas as he lay still beside Dysmas. "They believe they are invincible. They believe none will challenge, they believe they are safe, because they are so great, and all others weak. We will send them a message this day. A message they will not forget in many years. Cover your faces," he commanded.

So the march continued to the entry of the pass, where a halt was called. There was a small commotion at the head of the company as two scouts were dispatched to investigate the pass.

"Ah, not so stupid after all," said Eleazar.

"Now is the time," said Dysmas.

"We are not in position," said Barabbas.

"Look at them," continued Dysmas, "they are sitting down, and see, some even lay while they await their orders. We could move quietly doubling back while their scouts go forward. They would not know what hit them."

Barabbas saw it now. "You're right," he said. "If we could attack while they were getting to their feet, we would have the advantage." He thought for a moment, "Spread the word. Quiet, and move now."

As the scouts moved forward on either side of the pass, Barabbas and his men were moving in the opposite direction just over the crest and out of sight. The pass swept in on both sides at the entry, and so, as they approached, Barabbas did not allow time to settle. They were within metres of the company, many of whom were now laying on the ground taking what rest they could before the return of the scouts.

He gave the signal, and without a word being spoken, his thirty-two men started running at the Roman troops, swords drawn.

It took a few moments for the Roman soldiers to realise what was happening, but that was all Barabbas needed to give his men a chance.

The younger ones scrambled to their feet first but were still slow, and these drew the first attention of Barabbas and his men.

Many of them were run through before they could even draw their swords. The odds had, in the first few moments of the battle, fallen in favour of Barabbas, but the older soldiers were the experienced soldiers. These quickly formed for battle as best they could, and very quickly Barabbas had a fight on his hands. The odds were now better with eighteen Romans dead on the ground, but there were now seventeen seasoned experienced soldiers and it showed in battle.

Barabbas lost two men in succession to the centurion leading the company and was about to engage him when Dysmas ran into the centurion knocking him off his feet. He used the momentum of his fall to continue rolling to his feet and was facing Dysmas who was bearing down on him.

Barabbas' heart went to his throat and he was about to engage the centurion himself, but was set upon by another soldier.

Although the centurion was seasoned, he was no match for this young titan before him, who fought with the ferociousness of a lion and the skill of a swordsman twice his years. As the centurion thrust, Dysmas easily evaded his sword, and in an unbroken motion brought the hilt of his sword down on the back of his head. The centurion lay unconscious at his feet.

Barabbas had defeated and killed his foe and by now many of the soldiers were facing two, and some three, of Barabbas' men as one by one they fell.

Barabbas had observed the ease with which Dysmas had dispensed with his foe, and even he was surprised. "All that training paid off," he said as he approached him now. "That is no small feat, Dysmas, to best a Roman centurion." He raised his sword then to finish the task, but Dysmas held his hand.

"No," he said.

"What do you mean?" asked Barabbas both surprised and annoyed.

"I mean no. I will kill if I must," said Dysmas, "but not if I am not forced, and never an unarmed man on the ground. Never."

Barabbas was struck by this masculine determination in such a young man. "Alright," he said and sheathed his sword. "Probably best. He will have much to explain as to why he was the sole survivor, lost his company and his cargo of wealth. Good enough Dysmas, you are right of course," he said now cheerful.

Barabbas ordered Jeremiah to the wagon. "Turn it around and head back to the cave. We will be right behind you."

"Barabbas," said Dysmas.

He turned to see Dysmas shaking his head slightly. "A word," was all he said.

"Hold, Jeremiah," called Barabbas, and they paired off out of ear shot.

"What?" asked Barabbas.

"We must leave the wagon here. If we take it back they will simply follow the ruts it leaves and find us. Even covering them up will not hide all trace. They will track it to us if we use it."

"There is too much gold to carry," said Barabbas.

"Yes that is probably true, but we still have twenty-five men."

"What do you suggest?"

"Give each man what he can carry. Pair him with another and send them in a different direction to the rest, with instructions to walk until dusk. We all meet back at the cave over the next few days. What we can't carry we hide among the crags in the pass. It is unlikely the Romans will even bother looking. They will think we took it all, but even if they do find it, we will have most of it, and be untraceable. Better that than get all of it and run the risk of being found. This is the first time we have been able to hit their payroll, Barabbas, you said so yourself. Let it not be for nothing."

"You are right," said Barabbas thoughtful now. Calling the men together he ordered them to break open the chests. There were four in all.

"Gather what you can carry."

"Not too much," yelled Dysmas. "Take only what you can carry easily."

Barabbas looked around nodding, and looked back to the men. "That's right, we don't need you failing halfway back."

After the distribution was complete there was one full chest, and a small amount in a second chest left over. These were carried into the pass some hundred metres, and hidden within an outcrop of boulders.

Barabbas instructed the men on the plan and set them on their way two to a group, while Barabbas, Eleazar and Dysmas all travelled together.

Warfare and Loyalty

Horses could be heard at a distance approaching from the North the next morning, as the three lone travellers walked along the dusty road.

"That is Roman cavalry by the sound of it," said Barabbas, "and we in the middle of nowhere."

Dysmas ran off the road to drop his sword and gold in a large divot he had seen.

"Quickly," he said, and the others did the same.

They threw what stones and rocks they could readily find on top to cover the cache, then returning to the road they picked up their pace. By the time the soldiers came into view they had travelled a good two hundred metres.

"We are travellers on our way to Jerusalem," said Dysmas, "unarmed travellers."

Barabbas felt very vulnerable but it was their best chance.

As the soldiers approached, Dysmas started to laugh and pushed Eleazar's shoulder who followed by laughing himself.

Gallious was the centurion in charge of this troop in search of the company that was now overdue. As he approached these men he quickly noted they carried no swords and were only lightly attired for travel. He ordered his troop to a halt.

"Hail Caesar," he said.

"Where are you travelling to?" he demanded.

"Jerusalem," replied Eleazar. "Is there a problem?"

"Have you men seen a Roman company?" he asked.

"We have seen only a merchant going to Jericho," replied Eleazar. "We have seen none other."

"What business have you in Jerusalem?"

"We go to the temple," replied Eleazar, shrugging his shoulders.

Without a further word Gallious turned to his troop and motioned them forward, they kicked their horses to a gallop once more.

Barabbas looked at Eleazar and smiled. "I even believed you," and he slapped him on the back. "Well done Dysmas," he continued.

"That was almost too easy," Dysmas said. "A few minutes more, and we will be able to retrieve our cargo." And so they did, as the sound of horses faded in the distance.

"We need to find a more secure place to hide the gold," said Dysmas, "and we had better continue to Jerusalem."

"Why?" asked Eleazar.

"Because," replied Barabbas who had understood immediately what Dysmas was getting at, "we are still two days from the cave. On horseback they are hours from discovering the dead. That gives them plenty of time to reach us on their return journey. If they discover us heading away from Jerusalem, that would be unfortunate, given we said we were going there."

"We need to change our clothes," said Dysmas. "If the centurion is with them he will not recognise us, but may recognise our clothes. Best if we change them. We take some of the gold, go to Jerusalem, buy three horses, come back, pick up the rest of the gold and head home. And we have then three horses."

"And where do we keep three horses upon our return?" asked Barabbas.

"You leave that to me," said Dysmas with a smile, "I have an idea."

"It makes sense," said Eleazar.

"Well then, there is a village ahead, we can get clothing there," said Barabbas.

So they did and continued on to Jerusalem.

The following day with Jerusalem in sight, half of the troops they saw previously came thundering toward them, indeed with the one survivor of the raid.

Gallious heeled his horse and the troop stopped, but as soon as he saw Eleazar with the other two, he spurred his horse forward without a word as the troop continued on its way.

Eleazar just smiled at Barabbas and they continued on.

The plan was a simple one, and like all things simple, fool-proof, and they found themselves in sight of the cave the following afternoon.

"Now what do we do with the horses?" asked Barabbas.

"Ahh," said Dysmas with a smile. "I thought I would take Hazmar and Gushion with me, and retrieve the rest of our gold. If it is still there, it's almost certain the Romans are not."

Eleazar smiled at Barabbas, "Now I understand the horses."

"Go on," said Barabbas, as he turned away shaking his head and smiling to himself.

Dysmas gathered the supplies he needed for the trip and was underway within the hour.

"We will be back in two days," he said as he rode off.

"It wears me out just watching him," said Eleazar with a smile, as Barabbas shook his head once more enjoying very much the enthusiasm of his youngest charge.

The journey was a quick one indeed thanks to the horses, and just as Dysmas had predicted, the site was clear of bodies, and the Romans were gone.

"Hazmar," said Dysmas. "Get to the top of that ridge and scan the surrounds. Gushion, take the other one."

They both ascended their respective hills and scoured the surrounding countryside, but there was nothing to be seen and they returned to Dysmas.

"Nothing," they both reported.

"Good," said Dysmas. "Better to be safe than sorry. Now let's see if our gold is safe."

Just as suspected, the gold had remained undetected by the Romans, and they quickly divided it up into three equal portions, placing each in the saddle bags they had brought.

"Tie them behind you in front of the flanks" said Dysmas. "Now listen carefully. The reason we are carrying it this way is but one. Should we be stopped by the Romans we could never outrun them with all this weight. Don't hesitate, cut it free and save yourselves. Let them have the gold. With the Romans' armour weighing so much, you will have an advantage in a race, so use it. This gold is only a bonus, you are far more important than it is. Do you understand?"

They both nodded.

As they started out, both these men were glad of Dysmas. The men in general had become used to taking orders from Dysmas. He was a cautious man and an excellent tactician. They knew how genuinely valuable they were to him and felt safe with his decisions, sometimes more so than the more hot-headed Barabbas.

The return trip was as uneventful as the first. Dysmas deliberately avoided any contact with towns or villages, and made stops only for water. When one of the men suggested they detour to acquire some skins of wine, he simply shook his head and kept riding.

Their return was greeted with great jubilation when Barabbas found the gold had been found untouched. "We break out the skins tonight," he had announced to a very happy group of men.

Sometime later, Dysmas asked Barabbas, "Where is Tallious?"

"He has not returned?" he asked, a little surprised. "If I find he has stolen the gold, I will kill him myself!"

"Tallious would not abscond," said Dysmas. "He is no thief, something has befallen him. Let me take Hazmar tomorrow, and see if we can find out what".

"Agreed," said Barabbas.

So it was. In the morning, Dysmas and Hazmar rode toward Herodium, the direction in which everyone seemed to think

Tallious had been sent. No sign of him was forthcoming, and no news of him could be found. On a hunch, Dysmas rode on to Bethzaith which was the home town of Tallious.

They approached the town at about the ninth hour. As they rode in on the main road a dust storm was blowing in, and of necessity they were forced to cover their faces from the storm. Through the dusty distance, Dysmas could make out a group of people at the edge of the town, and something larger. As they got closer, the very distinct shape of a cross, and a man hung on it became all too clear. It was indeed Tallious, dead, his body mutilated by scourges. Those who from a distance had been at the base of the cross were now gone, as the storm had driven them indoors. Dysmas and Hazmar stopped in front of the cross both silent.

The storm was now increasing and visibility was fading quickly. "We must take him down Hazmar," said Dysmas at last. "I will not leave him here to be mocked."

"We have no tools," replied Hazmar.

"Use your knife and cut him free, before the storm passes. Quickly."

Within minutes his brutalised body was lying over Hazmar's horse and was tied secure. Hazmar climbed up behind Dysmas and they rode into the storm, which did not let up until nightfall.

The Romans realised within an hour of the storm's end that their prize was missing and proceeded to search the town but found nothing.

Meanwhile Dysmas had decided that they would make their way overnight to Etam. "They will likely search the town. That will give us the time we need to make arrangements for his proper burial." So it was that they arrived before morning and sought out the undertaker.

The undertaker immediately perceived the work of the Romans. "He is a Jew, and a good one," said Dysmas, handing over more than enough to cover the costs of the burial. "I'm sorry we cannot stay, for that may bring unwanted attention to you." The undertaker nodded. "Leave it to me," he said. "It is an outrage, but at least he will have a proper burial."

"Thank you," said Dysmas taking him by the shoulders. "Thank you."

They mounted then and were leaving Etam as the sun was rising.

"Best we don't stay," said Dysmas. "We don't know who is here or who is watching. We have done what we should, now we must report back." They rode back to the cave in all but silence, both immersed in his own thoughts.

The mood at the cave was sober upon the news carried by its new arrivals. Barabbas was livid. Eleazar was in tears, as he and Tallious had been like brothers for many years.

Dysmas had had the presence of mind to procure some skins of wine on the return journey. "It is right that we should toast him, Barabbas," he said, and the gathered men nodded silently. So it was they drank to their fallen friend and comrade.

Barabbas took Dysmas aside quietly. "Could you say something to the men?" he asked. "Losing a man in battle is not the same. Say something, would you?"

Barabbas called the men together. "Dysmas has something to say in honour of Tallious," and so they gathered to listen.

"Tallious was more than a comrade in arms," began Dysmas, "he was a true hero and friend. The very reason we are here now, alive to toast him, is his doing. They tortured him unmercifully, yet he did not give us up. Had he done so, they would have been here by now. Tallious has sacrificed himself for us and the cause he believed in. Let none of us forget what he has done for us. Ever."

He raised his cup, "Let us resign ourselves to finish what he died for," and they all drank.

Life around the cave was a little sober for the next few days, but there was no mistaking the men's growing esteem for Dysmas. Much had been said by Hazmar upon his return with regard the care Dysmas had for Tallious. Truly he held a place in the hearts of all the men at many levels. They both respected and loved him. Though many years their junior, they were willing to follow his orders as he had shown himself to be not only wise but shrewd.

Barabbas too had come to realise that Dysmas was a thoughtful soldier. His tactical ability and clear thinking had made him a most valued confidant, while in battle none could best him, yet he was improving still. Barabbas was now far more confident with taking Dysmas into battle, and had in fact made a mental note to stay close to him. It was probably the safest place to be.

Dysmas for his part seemed unaware of much of this. He had become accustomed to giving orders since Barabbas had some years earlier invested authority in him, while he was organising and designing the cave space to be more efficient. Authority was something that rested very gently in his hands; consequently, there were never tirades or reports to Barabbas for laziness or mistakes; he had his own unique manner of dealing with such things.

As days became weeks, things returned to normal. Production of swords and arrows had now ceased as the stores were full.

Barabbas then turned his thoughts to recruitment of new members. "We will always be little more than a raiding party and a thorn in the side of Rome if we don't grow. If we want to have any chance of pushing them out of Israel, we must become a rallying point that Israel will gather to as a nation. We will never be that with only twenty-seven men," he had said.

"I propose we all go our separate ways for the cycle of one moon, and each man returns with a new recruit. Surely we could all find one."

The men thought this an excellent proposal for a number of reasons, not least of which that they had the chance to return to their homes for a time. Most had the thought that it was the best location for prospecting anyhow; they knew who they could talk to, and who to avoid. And so it was decided.

The trip to Hebron was one of emotion and mixed feelings for Dysmas. Though he believed within himself that that part of his life was gone and forgotten, it was becoming clear to him with each step that this was not the case.

He arrived just after the ninth hour when many were taking their afternoon rest. Much of the town was empty but for some children playing and a few dogs.

Dysmas opened the door to the house of his childhood and entered the darkened room.

As tears began to stain his cheeks, the great Roman bath brought back memories of tears and laughter, as he stood beside it now smiling to himself.

Some children had observed him entering the house and knew it to be empty, and so ran to tell their parents. A few moments after Dysmas had finished surveying the little house the front door burst open, and he was faced with a hulking young man with a familiar face.

"Is that you Gestus?" he said.

Gestus was startled. "Who are you?" he said.

"It's me. Dysmas."

"Dysmas? But, but you're dead."

"Really?" smiled Dysmas. "Who told you I was dead? You saw me with Barabbas years ago, remember?"

"Yes, but I thought you were killed at the raid in Jericho, and when your mother returned she was certain you were dead."

"What?" cried Dysmas as he leapt upon Gestus and held his shoulders. "She lives?"

"Oh, yes," said Gestus. "You didn't know?"

"Where is she?" asked Dysmas, his mind racing.

"Well, she moved away about two years ago. I think she went to Nazareth."

"Nazareth? What's in Nazareth?" Dysmas was now confused. As a young boy he had no idea that Petmar and Arlett lived in Nazareth.

"I don't know," said Gestus, "I just heard my father mention it to a friend. Where have you been all this time?" he asked.

"I've been with Barabbas fighting the Romans."

"Barabbas!" exclaimed Gestus. "You fight with Barabbas now?"

Dysmas smiled, "Among other tasks," he nodded.

"I have often thought of joining him," said Gestus, "but had no idea how to find him."

"Well then," said Dysmas, "if you want to join Barabbas you had better come with me."

"What? Now?" asked Gestus.

"Yes, now," replied Dysmas.

"Where are we going?" asked Gestus.

"Nazareth of course," replied Dysmas with a smile. "You have much to tell me on the way. I will wait for you until dawn in the old cave we used to play in, but I will be gone soon after dawn. If you want to join Barabbas, I'll see you there."

"I'll be there," said Gestus and returned home to ready his things.

The cave was much smaller than Dysmas recalled and served to remind him that he was no longer a boy. Still it was large enough to be comfortable.

Sleep eluded him as he lay awake considering the news Gestus had brought him. Could it be true, he asked himself. Yet he still had his doubts.

True to his word Gestus called out just before the sun rose the following morning.

Dysmas was already packed and ready to leave. "You are sure my mother is alive?" asked Dysmas.

"Yes," said Gestus. "She returned to Hebron about four months after you all left for Jerusalem and lived here for a few years. I know she is alive, I have seen her with my own eyes, but she thinks you are dead. What happened?" asked Gestus.

"It's a very long story," replied Dysmas, "but given we have a long journey ahead of us, I suppose we have time to tell it. Best we were on our way." They gathered their belongings and were soon underway.

Dysmas recounted the events of the day his father died, and his own escape as best he could remember it. He spoke of his time with Barabbas and the importance of secrecy. He assured Gestus that Barabbas was recruiting. As was his way, he left much of his own importance within the group unsaid.

Gestus was greatly pleased that he would be welcome to join the freedom fighters of Barabbas. He had heard much of their exploits.

He recalled for Dysmas the return of his mother, and how lonely she had been. How the joy seemed to be missing in her when she returned. She wasn't the light-hearted, happy woman Gestus had remembered as a child. "I never saw her smile in the time she lived here before she left for Nazareth," said Gestus, very pensive now, as Dysmas stared off into the distance.

The journey was indeed a long one, even on horseback. As many years had passed since Dysmas had apparently died, there was much to talk of: how Hebron had changed; who had moved into and out of town. Dysmas was much surprised that Gestus had no maiden in mind for courtship, but Gestus assured him that he wanted a bit of adventure before settling down to a family. "You will be delighted to know then that Ishmar has already taken a bride."

"Ishmar? Really? Who would have thought he would be first?" said Dysmas. "He would go green if a girl said hello," he laughed.

"Oh, he figured it out pretty quickly early on. Grew into a fine young man in the end."

"Isn't that great," said Dysmas as he smiled to himself.

"Where are we going?" asked Gestus. "Nazareth is by way of Jerusalem is it not?"

"We go via Bethzaith," replied Dysmas. "I need to pay my respects to a family there. Then we go on to Etam that I may pay my respects to one who is laid there. I must ensure all went well. Then we travel to Nazareth."

"Who is it laid in Etam?" asked Gestus.

"Tallious. He was killed by the Romans last month. He was one of us."

A silence fell upon them now as Gestus digested this last piece of information.

Seeking Truth

So it was that they called on the kin of Tallious and the undertaker of Etam. Dysmas was greeted with great pomp and had many times to decline the offer to be their guest. Word had found the family of Tallious, that had explained the mystery of the disappearance of his body from the cross. They were, as one would expect, most grateful to Dysmas.

The undertaker of Etam too was most gracious to him, and assured him that all had gone well with regard the interment of Tallious.

It was then that Dysmas became quite determined to make his way to Nazareth. "It is nearing Passover," he said. "We must be swift if we are to return in time."

They made their way across to Jericho and through the rough trails to Ephraim. On to Sychor where they stayed with Hazmar, who was honoured and delighted to have Dysmas visit. Gestus was surprised to see Dysmas treated like royalty by his fellow soldier, who was obviously many years his senior.

"You seem to have made an impression," he said later on the road.

"They are too kind," was his only reply as he smiled and rode on, leaving Gestus wondering.

Dusk was closing in as they approached Nain, and Dysmas chose to spend the night there. "Best to have an easy ride to Nazareth in the morning," he told Gestus, but in reality, he was torn in many directions with the thought of finding his mother alive after all these many years.

The night was one of memories and dreams of times past. He recalled his father's great love for his mother, how he used to laugh when he played with Dysmas, his poetry, and how his mother would sit and listen with real joy. They were so in love, he thought to himself.

He couldn't imagine how destroyed she must have been to have lost the husband she adored and the son that was the apple of his eye on the same day. How she must have suffered, pondered Dysmas.

Sleep was patchy at best as his memories took over much of the night, and he gravitated from smiles to tears and back once more. His emotions were so much centred upon his mother's loss, that it never occurred to him that he himself had been faced with a similar dilemma with his belief that he had lost both his parents on the same day.

The sun was rising too soon and Dysmas was watching its ascent when a bleary-eyed Gestus revealed himself with a grunt as he shuffled through his things in search of something to eat.

"Didn't sleep much," he said at last.

"No, neither did I," replied Dysmas, still pondering the day ahead. "Best if we get an early start," he continued as he rose and started packing his gear for the day's journey.

He was still puzzled as to why his mother would have chosen Nazareth of all places to live.

They were soon on their way in silence, Gestus still waking while Dysmas was deep in thought.

As they approached Nazareth, it struck Dysmas that it was a solitary place, remarkably quiet even for this time of the day. It was the third hour.

There were only two children to be seen at the village well, but neither could help with information regarding his mother.

"It appears they are late risers here," smiled Gestus.

"Yes. I might take the opportunity to look around," was Dysmas' only reply, and he was gone. There was not much to Nazareth but a very few short roads that would qualify more as lanes, a small marketplace and houses scattered about its epicentre and beyond the village perimeter. There was something strangely peaceful about the place, which was not lost even on Gestus.

As Dysmas walked, people slowly began to appear. He noticed an unusual disinterest with regard to strangers in town. Though polite and friendly, people seemed less inquisitive than was usual in small towns he had often visited in Israel. This became so evident that he for a time found himself an observer rather than a seeker.

After a time he asked one woman if she knew of Muriam of Hebron?

"Muriam," she said to herself thinking out loud. After a time she recalled that there had been a woman who had stayed with Arlett for some time. "I'm almost certain her name was Muriam. She did not leave the house much or indeed have any real social interaction with the town, just Arlett. I'm not even sure if she is still here," she went on.

"Arlett, you say?"

"Yes, Arlett of the house of Petmar."

"Petmar," cried Dysmas as he unconsciously grabbed the woman by the shoulders. "Petmar lives?"

The woman was quite taken aback with fear at first until she realised the excitement of her enquirer. "I'm so sorry," she said then, "but Petmar is dead. He has been for almost a year."

This brought Dysmas back to earth instantly. "Oh," he said as he released the poor woman.

"Arlett will be home I am sure, and Muriam may well still be there, I truly don't know. She ventured out so infrequently; no one in the village would be able to tell you with certainty."

"Where might I find the house of Petmar?" asked Dysmas.

"It is not in the village proper," she replied, pointing to a ridge to the west. "It is just on the other side of that ridge. It is not a journey of more than a few minutes," she assured him.

"Thank you," said Dysmas as he started to move away. She caught his arm then, and looking up into his sad eyes said. "Trust in God's providence. What you learned as a child will stand you well as a man if you don't forget it," and she turned and left him somewhat puzzled.

He returned to Gestus then and told him to remain in town while he investigated the woman's information, and set out immediately for the house of Petmar.

The woman's information was indeed correct and the journey took but twenty minutes on foot, the horses being left to water and rest in Nazareth.

Dysmas found himself surveying much disused equipment scattered about the property as he sat on a boulder atop the ridge he had just climbed, leaving the road access to collect his thoughts.

As a man's logic began to unfold the child's story, he realised why his mother had found her way to Nazareth. It had never occurred to him that Petmar and Arlett had lived anywhere. As a child he knew only that they travelled about Israel perpetually.

Muriam had in fact made the journey at the request of Petmar, who had sent word some two years earlier that he was dying. He had asked Muriam if she would consider assisting Arlett, who as yet knew nothing of his true condition, over this difficult time. He had been greatly saddened that he could not assist her with travel, as he himself was unable to travel. To this end she had in fact turned to Gaius for assistance once more, and he had gladly organised transport and escort for the journey.

Over the years since the death of Azel, Gaius had indeed proven himself a man of his word. He had personally seen to her wellbeing wherever it was within his power, and was prudent about it. Whenever he was near to Hebron he would call and ensure she was adequately provided for. Had he any senior officers under his command that he trusted in the vicinity of Hebron, they were always instructed to call and assess her needs. His conduct was always that of a true gentleman, and they had formed a deep respect and affection for one another.

Muriam had some years past understood that he and Azel would have been fast friends in other circumstances, while Gaius had formed a very different view of the Jewish people. Indeed a dangerous thing for a man in his position.

Petmar had been very cautious with regard this somewhat unusual relationship; however, it became clear over time that this Roman centurion was a man with honour in his veins. It became equally clear that the demeanour of his beloved Muriam was lifted in his presence. That she herself was unaware of this, showed the innocence of their friendship. He was surprised when he found himself hopeful that more would someday come of their relationship. It had indeed become habit for Petmar to stay at least one night at the house of Gaius whenever he was visiting Jerusalem. He had always been impressed with the genuine concern for Muriam's wellbeing, which had over time turned into a concern for that of the Jewish people in general.

Gaius was an excellent student, and Petmar a prudent and truthful teacher of Jewish history. Gaius had come to understand the God of Israel and the Torah. He now understood the various arguments and philosophies, the suffering and the promises. The anger he had felt upon his arrival in Israel with regard the arrogance of the Jews, had given way to a genuine sadness, as he now understood their ill-begotten pride in light of the gifts clearly provided them.

Petmar and Gaius had in fact become fast friends over time, with their common concern for Muriam being the catalyst of charity that had initially bound them together. This had inevitably grown into great respect and fondness for the other on both sides.

For his part, Gaius had fallen in love with Muriam. He had never had any illusions however that anything more could come of it, and had been particularly careful not to let on for fear of destroying the friendship that had blossomed between them, and that he treasured so much.

Over the years Muriam had taken to an annual pilgrimage to Jerusalem for Passover, to both honour the memory of her beloved Azel, and pray for his soul. Gaius from year to year grew ever more anxious of these visits. The first year she returned after the death of Azel, she had sought refuge in one of the many inns with no success. Gaius had heard of it and provided her his home while he moved to the garrison for the entire period of her stay. When he had come to understand this was to be an annual event, he had made it clear to her that his home was at her disposal for all future visits. He would simply move to the garrison in case he made her uncomfortable by his presence. She had agreed, however, was most insistent that his presence did not make her uncomfortable, but rather she was uncomfortable with the inconvenience she was causing him.

So it was that each year hence, Gaius looked forward to receive this guest that had become a delight to his heart.

Muriam herself had, after her initial visit, found this arrangement oddly attractive. The conversation was always light yet engaging. Initially it had revolved around what had been the fruitless search for her son. Over time she had come to accept as Gaius had some time earlier, that Dysmas had died of his injuries. Though this was a source of great sadness for her, the passage of time, the support of dear friends such as Petmar and Arlett, and indeed Gaius himself, had brought her to a point of acceptance of God's holy will for her. A peace began to settle over her heart.

As the years had passed, she herself had found to her surprise that she looked forward to these visits also. This should not have come as such a surprise given the great sadness and loneliness that beset her while in Hebron, surrounded as she was by the many reminders of those so dear to her heart now lost to her forever.

She had at first been reticent to allow the kindness of Gaius to intrude upon her grief, but there had been much grief, and a heart could only bear so much pain. She had found solace in the humility it had required to simply allow herself to be treated with deference. Also the genuine gallantry and compassion of this man who had set his own comfort aside to accommodate her needs, and had continued to do so over these many years with no strings attached was no small matter. It bespoke of genuine virtue. Though entirely innocent, she found herself admiring qualities she first found attractive in her dearest Azel. Who could not be attracted to virtue?

It was a relationship not considered by any, yet one that lingered in shadows from all.

Dysmas finally found himself making his way toward the house down the rocky ridge beneath him. The house though humble of itself was surrounded by a number of outlying structures which truly made it as a whole, a most impressive property. There were empty yards and stables where no doubt camels were once kept. There was substantial shedding, and still parked in time at the side of the tack room, was of course, Petmar's famous wagon. He recognised it immediately as his conveyance to Jerusalem on that fateful day. There were also outlying houses, loosely attached to the main house by proximity rather than design.

"Halt!" was the call as Dysmas approached the main house. He turned to see an old man that he recognised immediately, and a smile burst upon his face with a tear forming in his eye.

"Baslar," he cried. "It really is you." Baslar stopped bewildered.

"You know me?" he asked.

"Yes, I know you," smiled Dysmas holding back tears. "You are the first familiar face I have seen in many years."

Baslar was completely at a loss. "I'm sorry but I have no idea who you are, nor how you come to know me."

"That is not surprising," replied Dysmas. "I was but a boy when you used to visit with Uncle Petmar."

Uncle Petmar, thought Baslar to himself, now completely puzzled.

"I am Dysmas, son of Azel."

Balsar was dumbstruck and the colour drained from his face. Fearing he might faint, Dysmas ran forward and held him up.

"That can't be," he said.

"Oh, I assure you I am," said Dysmas. "Is my mother here?"

Baslar was exasperated and disorientated, and it was clear to Dysmas that this revelation had been a little too much for him to process.

"Come, Baslar," he said. "Sit." He assisted him to a nearby water trough to gather his thoughts, but he kept shaking his head repeating to himself, "Dysmas, alive, praise God."

Just then a woman appeared at the door of the house. "Baslar?" she called.

Dysmas turned to see Arlett who looked concerned, but the moment she saw him she knew who he was.

"Dysmas," she said, "is it truly you?"

Dysmas went to her now as she sat on a chair outside the door she had come through. "Yes, Auntie, it is me."

"How? Where have you been? Look at you, you're a man, a grown man."

"Yes," said Dysmas smiling, tears streaming down his cheeks. "I never thought I would ever see any of you again."

"We thought you were dead, Dysmas. Everyone thought you were dead."

"Is my mother here?" Dysmas asked now kneeling before the seated woman.

"No, Dysmas, I'm sorry. She makes the pilgrimage to Jerusalem each year for the Passover now, in honour of the husband and son she lost all those years ago. It may be that she will be away longer this trip, as she was to arrange the sale of her home in Hebron. Come," she continued, "eat with us."

Baslar had by now collected himself and joined them, still shaking his head. A humble table was arranged and they were seated in short order. Arlett couldn't take her eyes from Dysmas. "Well," she said at last. "We know what happened on that terrible day, but what happened to you after?"

Dysmas again recounted all that he remembered, while Arlett and Baslar were at times incredulous, yet the truth of it all was before them. Dysmas sought to complete the tale where the decision was made that he would remain with Barabbas and his men, but Arlett pressed him to continue. As he did so, it became increasingly clear that Dysmas had cemented himself as an important feature within the dynamic of this band of freedom fighters. This gave Arlett cause for some concern, though she showed nothing.

Some two hours passed before the entire story could be told.

"I am an old man now," said Baslar smiling. "Just hearing of your adventure wears me out. Petmar would have loved this day," he continued as he chose a fig from a dish on the table. "We often spoke of you. It broke everyone's heart to think you dead, but

Petmar, he had a heart bigger than most men, with a special place in it for you and your parents. It killed him to see what your mother suffered."

"It did indeed," joined Arlett. "He loved you all dearly. Your mother and father were as his own children. He was crushed, yet he was a man with responsibilities. I watched him somehow pull himself together, just so the rest of us could come to terms with what had happened. He was a wonderful man, a blessed man. He would have been very concerned to hear you have been in the hands of Barabbas and his teaching."

"Why?" asked Dysmas. "Is it not true that the Romans are foreign combatants in our land? A land that is our right to occupy under God? A land..."

"Enough," said Arlett gently, while Baslar looked a little uncomfortable.

"All that you have said is true, and no doubt you could say much more. Much that you have learned from Barabbas no doubt. What is missing is our response."

"I don't understand," said Dysmas. "Our response is to fight back and rid our lands of the Romans."

"No," said Arlett. "That is not a response, that is a reaction. A reaction born of fear and pride. If Petmar were alive he would guide you wisely. I am not so wise as he, but I know enough to know 'thou shalt not kill' has meaning that restores balance."

Dysmas fell silent now, thoughtful.

"I know for a young man, strong and able, it seems the right thing to do to cleanse our land of the tyrant. We must stop to consider, however, though they are here, they are not slaughtering our people."

"That is not true," cried Dysmas, "they killed my father."

"They were themselves under attack, and their lives were threatened. They were not the aggressors. You are claiming your right to defend yourself while you see it just to deny them the right you claim for yourself."

"They killed my father."

"Yes, you said, but did they really?" asked Arlett. "Or was it a combination of an unprovoked attack and a terrible accident?"

Dysmas was getting agitated, but was trying to remain calm. These people don't understand at all, he thought. They are so far removed from Jerusalem, how could they know? "Well" he said at last, "I was there, I saw what happened."

"Yes, Dysmas," replied Arlett. "You were there. That's why your father was there."

Dysmas started. "Are you blaming me?" he cried.

"No, Dysmas. I'm showing you that there were many factors involved that day that were not in the control of anyone, be it Barabbas who attacked or the Romans that defended themselves, the inquisitive boy drawn to the commotion, or the father who sought the safety of the son he loved. It may well have been, had Petmar been as fast as your father, I might have lost him that day also. God spared him, just as He spared you, and indeed your mother. I held you in my arms at the moment of your birth, Dysmas. Short of God and your mother, none love you as I. It's because I love you that I cannot allow you to deceive yourself. You are a man now. What you perceive through the eyes of a child needs to be understood by the man, in the light of truth, not the emotions and construct of a child."

Dysmas had tears in his eyes as the memory of that terrible day played out once more in his mind. He was struggling between many emotions, but he knew in his heart that Arlett was right. "What of my mother?" he asked finally.

"She is well. She has been staying here for just over two years now. She no sooner arrived than she was leaving again as the Passover was upon us. This is the third pilgrimage she has made to Jerusalem since her arrival here. When Petmar died last year, she was so grateful that she had arrived back in time. Strangely, his passing and his gentle words to her before, seemed to bring her great peace. It has been many years of journey for her, but the smile has returned at last."

"I remember her," said Dysmas, "always smiling and laughing. I must myself be going if I am to arrive in Jerusalem in time for the Passover. Do you know where I might find her?" he asked.

"She will be at the house of Gaius," said Arlett.

Dysmas lept to his feet at once. "Gaius? The centurion?" he shouted startling Arlett and Baslar. "He is the murderer of my father. Does she not know? He has deceived her."

"No, Dysmas. It is well-known what happened. And much has happened since then that you do not know."

Dysmas was now in complete emotional turmoil. "I won't hear anymore," he cried and stormed from the little cottage, leaving Arlett and Baslar staring after him in silence.

"If only Petmar were here," said Baslar quietly.

Dysmas stormed over the ridge and walked for ten full minutes before realising he was walking in the wrong direction. Stopping abruptly he found himself torn between more emotions than he was even aware he possessed. He started this way and that only to turn once more. "What could she be thinking?" he kept asking himself.

Dysmas found himself for the first time in many years unsure as to what he should do. Soon he was seated on a boulder on the edge of the track on which he found himself, and there he remained in turmoil.

Time slipped past imperceptibly as minutes became hours, until the twelfth hour was approaching. He had spent his time weeping, raging and weeping again. He had never known a time in his life where he had actually felt completely lost until now. And even after so much time, he was no closer to a resolution in any direction.

The sun was setting now, and he had not moved in hours. He was startled when he felt a hand on his shoulder, the owner of which he had not even heard coming. He jumped up to his left ready to defend himself, when he realised Arlett had found him.

"You are struggling with life I see," she said, as she too sat down.

Dysmas did not reply. He had been overwhelmed by emotions and was quite drained.

"I so wish Petmar could be here to guide you through this sadness," she continued. "He would know how to explain the nuance of life to you, man to man. I may try, but I cannot know what you have suffered, what your expectations are. The ways of a woman are not those of a man. I can only tell you how much you are loved. Remember, Dysmas, though you struggle to understand how difficult these things are for you, spare a thought for your mother. I simply can't imagine how she will react to the news that you live."

"How did you find me?" asked Dysmas still staring into nothing.

"Your companion came seeking you. Gestus is it?" Dysmas nodded. "He is at the homestead," she continued. "You will stay with us this night. You and Gestus." She reached out and took his hand as she stood. "It has been a big day, Dysmas, for everyone. Let's go home."

Dysmas got up with tears in his eyes once more and allowed himself to be led back to the house of Petmar. Arlett, a prudent woman, said nothing on the return journey. Gestus too recognised immediately this was not a time for flippancy, and simply told Dysmas that he had brought the horses. "We stay here this night," was the only reply.

They were shown to the guest house on the outskirts of what was a small compound of sorts, and invited to the evening meal that would soon be served.

Dysmas lay briefly on the bunk that was to be his for the night, and fell asleep in moments, leaving Gestus to make apologies for him.

The meal was a humble but filling one, as it was want to be in the house of Petmar. There were numerous strange faces at the table that clearly did not live on the property.

"I didn't know there were so many people staying here," Gestus remarked to Balsar.

"They don't live here, Gestus, but they are welcome at table. Just as they were when Petmar was alive. Little has changed thanks be to God."

The mood at the table was light and the conversation sparse. It was obvious to Gestus that this was more than an occasional event. Those present, although not close friends as such, were genuinely cherished by their hosts and made to feel most welcome.

The meal over, those present one by one thanked their host and left discreetly, until Gestus found himself alone at the table with Arlett.

"I remember you," he said at last.

"You do?" she replied with the hint of a smile.

"Yes. When I was a little boy, I remember you would visit Hebron from time to time with your husband. I was very young, but I remember."

"I remember you also, always following Dysmas about."

"Yes, and look at me now," smiled Gestus, "still following him about. Well, we have a long way to go tomorrow," he continued, rising. "I'd better get some sleep. Thank you for your hospitality."

"You are welcome to stay as you will," said Arlett.

Gestus smiled, nodded and left.

Self-Deception

There was a heavy storm closing in as Dysmas and Gestus approached Nain about the sixth hour on the following day. They had risen early and bid their host a fond farewell. Little more had been said, but Arlett had told Dysmas that she was always home, and he was always welcome. He had smiled and hugged her. He had stopped at the top of the ridge to look once more over this peaceful hamlet, as if to burn it into his memory. A memory to be visited with fondness. A treasure for a dark night, when all was cold and bleak.

It had occurred to Gestus that Dysmas was lacking in his customary urgency, though he kept the thought to himself.

"We will find shelter in Nain," Dysmas cried over the rising wind and the noise that came with it. He had slept remarkably well the night before, better than he had slept in a very long time. He was at a loss to understand why, but knew he had felt very much at home while at the house of Petmar. He had always loved Petmar, and it was as if he were still close during their short stay.

They took shelter at the first inn they came to, as the wind whipped up dust, only to be pounded back to the earth by unseasonably heavy rain.

Dysmas hadn't said much since leaving Nazareth, content with trying to process the new information and insights provided by the visit. He was sad to have missed his mother, yet somehow relieved he had. He wasn't yet ready to face the possibility that his mother was kindly disposed to his greatest enemy.

"Dysmas, Dysmas," he heard again. The voice of Gestus disturbed him then. "What is it?" he replied.

"Where have you been?"

"What do you mean?" replied Dysmas?

"I mean I have been talking to you for some time and even calling your name for the past few minutes. Have you not heard?"

Dysmas was startled. "Really?" he asked.

"Yes, really," was the reply. "You have a lot on your mind!"

"Yes, Gestus, sorry, I do. I think it best we return to the camp rather than going on to Jerusalem. My mission is done. I have found my new recruit. I just hope everyone else has been successful also."

"If that's what you think best, then that's fine with me."

"In the morning we will set out for Sychor and stay with Hazmar once more, and then perhaps take our time returning to the cave. The men won't be returning until after Passover anyway. We can start your training immediately if you would like. There is no reason we shouldn't."

"So be it," replied Gestus with a broad smile. Gestus was a gregarious and extraverted man compared to his quieter companion. Dysmas thought him a good foil for his own introverted eccentricities, and had enjoyed his company on this journey.

The following morning presented a clear sky and a brisk bright new day, puddles of muddy water the only evidence of the one just past. The journey to Sychor was an uneventful one, which allowed Dysmas the luxury of being alone with his thoughts.

Gestus was as comfortable with silence as with banter, and simply occupied himself sightseeing and observing the lay of the land. This was in fact a habit he had been in for many years, and indeed a habit that would prove itself a most beneficial tool in the future, in his new role as a freedom fighter for Barabbas.

Just as before upon their arrival in Sychor, Dysmas was treated with such high esteem by his hosts that Gestus again found himself quite puzzled. They had arrived in the early evening about the eleventh hour, just as the evening meal was being served. All was left to spoil at the announcement of the arrival of Dysmas, as children and adults alike spilled from the dwelling. There was great excitement that Dysmas had honoured their humble home with another visit, and they would not hear of him and his companion staying at any inn but their own.

Much was added to the meal that had already been served, almost transforming it into a banquet. The banter was light as before, and Hazmar in particular sought to sit near to Dysmas, obviously very much delighted by his presence. Dysmas by contrast seemed entirely unaware of his status, which only added to the perplexity of Gestus.

As the evening became night and the night began to age, children first, followed soon by the women, started to take their leave for their night's rest. They had had a wonderful night of stories and laughter, time alone closing their eyes. This was true also for Dysmas, who had been struggling to stay awake for the past hour.

"Hazmar," he said at last. "I am very tired, perhaps I will sleep now."

"Of course, Dysmas, of course. Your room is prepared, come." Hazmar led him to his own room which had been prepared by his wife while dinner was being enjoyed. "You will sleep here tonight."

"Oh, Hazmar," began Dysmas, but Hazmar pushed him into the room. "Go to sleep," he said as he shut the door and laughed to himself.

Gestus had found himself a fresh skin of wine and Hazmar soon joined him outdoors to assist with its consumption.

Alone at last with Hazmar, Gestus found his curiosity had the better of him, and began seeking some answers. "How long have you known Dysmas?" he asked.

"I met him, in a manner of speaking, the day his father died. I have known Dysmas for many years."

"You would be one of the higher ranked soldiers with Barabbas then?"

Hazmar laughed. "No, Gestus, not I. I am a good soldier. I take orders well, that is true, but next to Barabbas and Eleazar, there is Dysmas!"

This took Gestus completely by surprise. "Dysmas?"

"He has not told you?" said Hazmar turning to look at Gestus with some surprise.

"No," replied Gestus. "I thought he was a young trainee. Someone to look after the horses."

Hazmar roared laughing. "We wouldn't even have horses if it weren't for Dysmas," he said trying to contain himself. "I assure you, Dysmas is not only our most fearsome fighter, he is also a tactical genius. His tactics have saved us on more than one occasion. Much of what you will see with regard our living arrangements were in fact designed and built by Dysmas. His stature among the men is second only to Barabbas. Eleazar himself would admit this. He may be the youngest of us but we look to him, as does Barabbas at times."

Gestus spent the rest of the evening with Hazmar, who proceeded to tell stories of Dysmas and his many feats far into the night. Gestus had found it a most surprising and enlightening discussion.

As he and Dysmas were leaving Sychor the following morning Gestus remarked again, "You have indeed made an impression."

"They are far too kind," was the simple response once more, as he rode on in silence leaving a thoughtful Gestus behind.

Muriam had arrived in Jerusalem two days before the Passover as was her custom. She first went to the marketplace to purchase two small gifts as had also become her practice. One was for Gaius which would be given him upon her departure, a thank you message for his kindness. The other was for Jelrah his elderly servant, of whom she had become very fond. His birth date occurred at this time, and in fact this year, on this very day.

Muriam had been of late a little more on edge than in previous years, as she had for the first time consciously realised how much she was looking forward to her visit, and in particular the time she could spend with Gaius and Jelrah.

She had come to understand this on her last visit when she had realised that the selection process for the gifts she was seeking had imperceptibly changed. Where once she would select a gift in the passing of but a few minutes, she now found herself inspecting quality, and scrutinising its value and meaning. It had frightened her when she had come to realise she was now seeking a gift for a man she cared about in a manner she had not known for many years. A friendship forbidden her by not only place and culture, but by the very nature of their first encounter.

These many years had been an emotional ride from precipice to plateau and back again. There were times she was at a complete loss to know what was the right response, or if indeed there was a correct response. Without so much as a single action on anyone's part it seemed, life had all at once become complicated.

Two hours later she had made her selections and was delighted to be finally making her way to the house of Gaius. A beaming Jelrah opened the entry door to admit her. "How wonderful to see you once more," he said as he bowed low to greet her. "The master will be pleased to hear you have arrived safely."

"Hello, Jelrah, it is a special day is it not?" she said smiling.

"You have remembered once more," he said. "How kind to make an old man happy. Come out of the heat, I will arrange to have your belongings taken to your room."

"I thought you might like this little thing," she said as she presented him with her gift. She had purchased a woollen cloak that would wrap his shoulders and protect him from the cold. He was delighted upon opening it. "At my age," he said, "I am truly feeling the cold so much, you have been far too kind as always. Thank you."

"You are very welcome, Jelrah."

"Muriam, how wonderful to see you again," said Gaius entering just then. "You look well."

"Thank you, Gaius," she said. "So do you."

"Harum," called Gaius. "Harum. Jelrah," he continued, "Put those things down, Harum will take care of that."

"Harum?" asked Muriam just as a young man appeared to gather her possessions.

"Take those to the guest room prepared," said Gaius. "Muriam," he continued with a smile, "meet Harum."

Harum bowed low dropping a bag and, nervously gathering it quickly, promptly disappeared in the direction of the guest wing, with all three smiling after him.

"I will arrange refreshments master," said Jelrah and he left smiling.

"Come," said Gaius as he began to walk to the rear porch. "Harum is with us now," he said as he walked. "Jelrah is still getting used to it I'm afraid."

"So he is replacing Jelrah?" asked Muriam.

"Oh, no, none could replace Jelrah, but he is older now. I thought it best that he have someone to assist him. He oversees Harum, ensures all is as it should be. He is really a guest here these days."

"You are good to him," said Muriam smiling.

"He has earned his rest, my trust and indeed my love," replied Gaius. "He will live out his final years in peace. He deserves that."

Just then Jelrah returned with refreshments and placed them on the table. "I will be about arranging the evening meal," he said and left them once more.

"So tell me," said Gaius after he left. "What news of Arlett. How is she coping?"

"She is very well, considering. They were very close. Losing Petmar has been devastating for her, but she is a woman of great faith."

"As was Petmar," mused Gaius thoughtfully.

"Do I sense disapproval?" asked Muriam a little surprised.

"Heavens no, quite the opposite. If anything, a little envy. I have pondered long on so many discussions with Petmar over many years regarding his faith in the Hebrew God. I admit at first great skepticism. Even disapproval would have been an understatement, but now? Well, the wisdom is evident though the proof is elusive."

"I have come to appreciate how difficult it must be for your people to understand," said Gaius, "a Roman's disillusionment with the idea of a one true God. After all, we have so many, none of which have been credited with providing a single tangible benefit to any Roman that I know of who has sought one."

"Your emperor is a god, is he not? Surely he provides benefits," said Muriam smiling.

"Ah, you taunt me Muriam," he continued, still solemn. "Your point is not lost on me, but I dare not speak, or even think of it. I have been troubled since losing Petmar. Such a fine man, a close confidant, a dear friend. I have longed for our talks and to hear his wisdom once more. Your visits are my only link now to your God."

"Yet you reside in Jerusalem the great city wherein is the temple of God, surrounded by His priests?"

"Surrounded by something. It has occurred to me that their god is not the God of Petmar, or the one you know. Their god is as sterile as any in Rome. There is no peace in them, no love."

"You sound troubled," said Muriam, now a little concerned.

"I have been troubled for some time, Muriam. As a Roman I thought I had life pretty much figured out and under control. It is clear to me now that I control very little indeed."

"And that disturbs you?"

"Yes and no. It is at once disturbing and yet comforting."

"What makes you think those in Jerusalem worship another god?" asked Muriam somewhat puzzled.

"Not all, but certainly most. They have no peace or love in their hearts. Their hatred is almost palpable. This is not the God I have come to understand from either Petmar or you. The God that you worship could change the world. Theirs would destroy it, if only to be the last one standing."

"The misunderstanding that people have of God does not alter Him, just their perception of Him," she replied.

"I understand so much more now, yet the more I know the more paradoxical it becomes. For example, if God is all knowing, powerful, merciful and just, why would He create us at all?" asked Gaius.

"I don't understand," replied Muriam. "Us?"

"The gentiles. If only the Hebrews are chosen, what is to become of us? Are we doomed to Gehenna? There seems neither mercy nor justice there. This is the god the Pharisees and scribes speak of."

"How have you come to learn so much?" asked Muriam.

"Aside from all Petmar taught me in our many discussions, I have been studying Hebrew for some time now," replied Gaius. "Reading the Torah and the Prophets. It is difficult to understand. If the prefect found out he would ship me back to Rome on the first garbage scow he could find," he smiled.

"I'm sorry I don't have an answer for you, Gaius, but that doesn't mean there isn't one. I too cannot believe that the Most High would condemn the gentiles. I know when the Messiah comes, He will reveal truths hidden from the ages."

Just then Jelrah entered holding a small scroll and handed it to Gaius, who read it immediately. "I must go," he said simply. "Jelrah will see to your needs. I am so pleased you have come to visit us once again," he said smiling and left.

"Well, I hope you will be joining me for the evening meal," she said to Jelrah.

"It would be my great pleasure," he replied, "and it is ready now." Soon they were seated at table and talking about the past twelve months, and what had happened both in Jerusalem and Nazareth.

"Gaius seems thoughtful," Muriam said at last.

"He is a very complex man, my master, and certainly a paradox."

"How so?"

"Well, he is an astute soldier, a fearless leader and combatant, yet compassionate and gentle. He is surrounded by brutes within the barracks, and yet he is refined. I would have no education but for my master. He believed it necessary and so saw to it many years ago that I was instructed. First rudimentarily, and then classically when I showed promise. He has been kind to me to a fault. With my knowledge and latitude I could have escaped many times, and I know I would never be found, but I do not serve him because I have to, but because I believe it a privilege. So it has been these many years."

"How long have you been with him?" asked Muriam.

"He claimed me in my fifty-second year, when he was in his very early twenties. He was an impressive young soldier, devastating really. I was the slave of a wealthy merchant in Egypt. There was an uprising that amounted to nothing, organised by my former master. He was a tyrant, and fancied himself a station beyond his mettle. He and his movement were crushed by Rome the moment it was visible. Gaius was a rising star in the Roman legion, and was instrumental in the routing of this enemy of Rome with little apparent effort.

"Those who led the conspiracy were gathered together with their households. The Roman soldiers in charge of the group were treating those gathered as one would not treat animals. Gaius happened by as one soldier tried to club an elderly woman. I leapt in front of her and took the full brunt of the blow. The blow broke my arm, but I leapt back to my feet and covered her once more as he drew back to strike again.

"'Hold!' I heard. It was Gaius. The soldier turned and recognised him immediately and became docile. Gaius approached me then. 'You,' he said. 'You are a slave, are you not?'

"'Yes,' I replied.

"'This then is your mistress?'

"'No, sir,' I replied, 'I do not know this woman.'

"He looked at me for a moment and smiled to himself. 'Come with me,' he said, and the soldier released me into his care. I have been with him ever since. He has been most kind to me over those years, and to many others."

"He is indeed a paradox as you say, Jelrah," Muriam said thoughtfully.

Brothers in Arms

"He trains like Dysmas," said Eleazar, as Dysmas flung Gestus over his shoulder once more.

"He does indeed," replied Barabbas. "These two make me feel old."

"You and me both," said Eleazar laughing.

They had been watching the new recruits training for much of the day under the rigorous hand of Dysmas. Gestus in particular stood out as the one to watch.

It had been three months since Gestus had arrived at camp, many of the other new recruits arriving sporadically over the following couple of weeks, though not everyone was successful in their recruiting effort. Barabbas was delighted to welcome another fourteen men. Though his enthusiasm had dimmed slightly as he came to understand that only half of them would ever make up numbers. Dysmas however had other ideas.

"Archers, Barabbas," he had said.

"Archers?"

"Yes, it is true they are not combatant soldiers, but perhaps that is our opportunity to train them as archers. The Romans always have the advantage of cover for their soldiers, and it's effective. If these are not up to hand-to-hand combat, they can cover those who are," he had said.

Barabbas immediately saw the wisdom. "I have a friend who is well trained in archery. I will send for him. It is a wonderful idea, Dysmas!" he had said walking away, his enthusiasm returning more with each step. Now he not only had seven new soldiers but a new battle strategy.

Within days Baalsar had arrived and seven men began their training as archers. Two of these were already proficient with a bow and excelled quickly, while the five remaining improved more slowly, but improve they did with each passing day.

In addition, Gestus had already shown himself an excellent mapper. After surveying the surrounding countryside of the encampment, he had mapped the area with such precision, that as Barabbas, Eleazar and Dysmas inspected his work, they all immediately saw the possible weaknesses of their hidden compound, should it ever come under attack. They could also devise escape routes and plans of attack that had hitherto remained unknown. Barabbas was delighted.

These mapping skills were soon put to further use. Barabbas had sent him out with Dysmas on a two-week reconnaissance of various passes and supply routes the Romans were known to use. It was a very fruitful fortnight as their return provided detailed information on distance, escape routes, hiding and attack points, even success probabilities with regard to combatant numbers. The combined knowledge of Dysmas and Gestus was proving to be an invaluable resource, as the future skirmishes would prove the accuracy of their estimates.

Dysmas had for the first time in many years all but forgotten Gaius as he revelled in the genuine challenge presented by Gestus. Just as had been true of their childhood years, so today their friendship was deeply rooted in a mutual respect and genuine affection. Even though competition was fierce, it never overshadowed their friendship.

Gestus soon endeared himself to both Barabbas and Eleazar, as they too soon fell under the spell of his gregarious nature and willing work ethic. He, like Dysmas before him, had carved himself a place in this group founded on ability and respect, notwithstanding his comparative age and recent arrival. All this apart from being the resident source of jokes and tricks that would inevitably provide levity to a group of men that sorely needed it. Time would also reveal him tenaciously loyal, securing him as a valued and admired member of this small band of fighters.

Using the plans provided by Gestus and Dysmas, the first attack was scheduled a week later. "Time to test the theory," Barabbas had said with a wry smile.

A Roman transport was known to enter the Khorvat pass each week carting supplies. So Barabbas and his men arrived laying in wait. Yet as it turned out, it was not a long wait. Though they had carried supplies for two days, it was less than an hour later that the scout reported the heavily guarded transport approaching. The plan was set in motion instantly, as everyone already had their position pre-determined. Archers to the high ground, and swordsmen hidden so close to the road's edge, as to take the Romans completely by surprise when the archers' work was done.

The plan was a simple one. The two archers were stationed one at each end of the short pass. The one to the rear was to wait for the last soldier to pass his position before firing upon that soldier. He was to continue firing while progressing forward from those at the rear. His first arrow was the signal for the archer at the front to fire upon the leading soldier, progressing from the front and moving back. The other five were to simply fire at will at the main body of the convoy. At worst they were a distraction, while any hit would be a bonus.

The Romans were in disarray in moments. When Dysmas considered it opportune, he gave the signal and the swordsmen were upon the Roman soldiers quickly, taking them completely by surprise. It was a crushing defeat and over in minutes without the loss of a single life from the men of Barabbas, though two were injured. An acceptable outcome when twenty-seven Romans lay dead or dying.

The entire attack had been organised and executed by Dysmas and Gestus, while Barabbas and Eleazar remained atop the ridge observing, ready to spring into action, though it proved unnecessary. It was an uncomfortable decision to make, but Dysmas had insisted that all was in hand. They looked at each other now smiling. A whole new chapter had opened for their group, and it was clearly evident.

"Looks like the children wish to take us to school," said Eleazar. Barabbas just shook his head smiling.

"Load the bodies onto the wagons," cried Dysmas. "We can't leave them here." After the bodies had been loaded, scouts were dispatched to warn of Roman approach. Men were ordered to clear the site of any trace of a battle, while the wagons were driven some five miles to the east.

"What are you doing?" asked Barabbas as he rode up beside Dysmas.

"When they come looking for the convoy, I don't want them to know it was ambushed there. With luck they will not change their routes, and at some time in the future they will be an easy target again."

"Brilliant," said Eleazar laughing and shaking his head.

"You are right Eleazar," said Barabbas. "Back to school."

All that was useful or could be sold without trace was removed from the wagons, which were themselves burned once the bodies were placed upon them once more. The men were left to themselves to make their way back to the cave in twos and threes, some as wealthy merchants and others as poor Jews on pilgrimage. None would draw a connection between them.

Dysmas travelled with Barabbas, Eleazar and Gestus. As a group atop their horses, they looked every inch a group of merchants.

"This changes everything," said Eleazar when they had been riding for some minutes. "We have an entirely new and effective attack strategy. They didn't see it coming!"

"And archers," laughed Barabbas, shaking his head. "Who would have thought we would have archers?"

"They were very effective," joined Eleazar once more. "Considering their training is in its infancy, we can look forward to them becoming increasingly more valuable."

"I think we should consider practice and more practice," said Dysmas. "I have to say we were a little lucky that the Romans were so few. However that would not be such a problem if our archers were more accurate."

"Agreed," said Barabbas. "We have supplies and time," he continued, "and Baalsar has already told me he is at our service. So when we get back, practice it is."

So it was for the next three months all the swordsmen were drilled by both Dysmas and now Gestus, who had proven himself a proficient swordsman in his own right. Baalsar continued the training of the archers as before with two new recruits, much to the delight of Barabbas. He and Eleazar found themselves with little to do with regard the training of the men, and so turned their attention to planning where best they could strike at the Romans, while inflicting the greatest damage with the least amount of risk. It wasn't long before a number of outposts and supply routes were targeted as excellent prospects.

Dysmas, accompanied by Gestus, set out on two more occasions, once to the north and once to the east, mapping and planning. Within four months there were ten new prospective locations flagged as frequented by Roman convoys, with excellent ambush possibilities. Added to those they already had, eighteen locations were now available and mapped all through Judea. As these were being discussed, Dysmas made the point that they should hit various locations separated by distance, to provide cover against the Romans linking the disappearances of their convoys to a single group, at least in the first instance, until they had time to grow. "As we become more successful and show we are a force, more will join us," he had assured them.

Attack plans were drawn up for numerous targets at seemingly impossible distances. Again the plans were simple yet effective. As before they would disguise their identities and attack a convoy, remove the bodies and clean up the site. This time however they would take everything five miles in the direction of their next target, separate what was to be kept and hide it to be collected later, burning the rest. The moment the fire was started they would ride hard for their next target. It was conceded three quick strikes would be all the men would have in them, and the most dangerous time would be when they were together riding from one location to the next. A separation plan on the run was devised, and arrangements made to put the great plan into action.

The men were drilled with regard all three possible locations on the menu, and made familiar with their various individual topographies, places of concealment and those to avoid. Riding instructions and separation protocols in place, they had set out early the first day of their five-day plan.

The first and second ambush were executed without a single injury, with quick and decisive victories. The third however was an entirely different affair, the Romans were almost ready. Even with so little time between attacks, they had joined the dots and sent a garrison after each of the three convoys they had dispatched, following news that two were late in arriving at their destinations and had not been heard from.

The attack had been executed as the others and was in its infancy, when to the great surprise of Barabbas and his men, fourteen Roman cavalry arrived with swords drawn. Though some were taken down by the archers, the now foot-bound soldiers of Barabbas found themselves no match for the well-trained horses and riders who cut a swathe through their ranks in moments.

Eleazar himself was the first to fall beneath a horse. It caught him a savage blow at a gallop as he was turning to the noise he had heard, bearing down upon him from behind. The blow rendered him unconscious, and he fell limp beside Dimmicus, who himself had been seriously injured.

The signal was given and the retreat plan executed immediately, yet too late for six of their number, four of whom were killed instantly. As they all quickly made their way up the boulder-laden mountain to reach the other side, their advantage increased as their wake became impassable for the horses in pursuit.

The centurion in charge of the small garrison immediately called a halt to the pursuit. Realising he had two prisoners from which to extract information, he saw no reason to lose another man pursuing those he was certain he would round up soon enough with that information.

Dysmas had evaluated immediately the battle lost and wasted no time sounding the retreat. The men had responded as they had been trained to, and had made high ground quickly. They briefly surveyed the carnage below them to the watchful eye of Maximus, who was observing them. He was impressed with their discipline, and would be reporting that these were no longer an insignificant presence, but must now be taken seriously. They must be found and destroyed.

Dysmas too had understood that he had been too ambitious. The men were sluggish by the time the third strike had begun, and he should have given more credit to the Roman line of communication. It was no accident that this small band of cavalry had shown up when they did. His forces had been hurt badly this day. Six men to the Romans would not be missed, but six men to this small band was a substantial blow, and the Romans would know that.

They set out quickly riding hard for the two previous locations gathering up the booty they had hidden, and proceeded at speed to the cave undetected.

In the meantime Rome was searching the territory seeking their quarry, but were looking entirely in the wrong direction. They found nothing whatever bespeaking of either their lost convoys, or those that had attacked them.

The mood at the cave was sombre indeed. They had lost Eleazar. The rest were missed to be sure, but Eleazar was a founding father of the group, and it hit everyone hard, none more than Barabbas. What made matters worse, they had taken him alive. None were concerned that he would give them up, but that he would be tortured and executed. It was clear there was nothing they could do to stop it.

Maximus had arranged for the burial of the Roman dead, leaving the Jews as feed for the birds and beasts. After the convoy had resumed its journey flanked by ten of his cavalry, he returned to Jerusalem with the four remaining, Eleazar and Dimmicus strapped to their horses awaiting their fate.

"We must at least go to Jerusalem and see if anything can be done," said Dysmas.

"What could be done? "cried Barabbas. "Would you have us attack the garrison in their beds?"

"We should at least try to find out something. Be close in case some opportunity presents itself."

Barabbas was thoughtful. "He is my closest friend, Dysmas," he said walking away, "but he would caution me to stay away."

"Let me go then. Alone if necessary. If only to give him some comfort."

Barabbas stopped then and turned to Dysmas, "He loves you as a son."

"I know. Let me go to him. Please."

Barabbas rubbed his chin and bit his bottom lip. Much was at stake for he too loved Dysmas as a son. The last thing he wanted was for him to fall foul of the Romans while alone in Jerusalem.

"Take Gestus with you," he said at last. "But under no circumstances are you to engage the Romans or call any attention to yourselves. Is that perfectly clear?"

"Yes," said Dysmas, "I promise." He turned then and called to Gestus, "Get your things, we leave at once."

They were gone within the hour and rode hard for Jerusalem, arriving the following evening. Dysmas had been given a contact by Barabbas within the city walls and so two nights later, found himself knocking at the door of this trusted contact.

An elderly woman answered the door, a coarse and hardened woman without the glint of a smile. Her eyes bespoke much bitterness and little laughter. "Who are you?" she said abruptly.

"My name is Dysmas," he replied, "and this is Gestus."

"Dysmas," she said inspecting him now. "So you are Dysmas."

"You have heard of me?" asked Dysmas, a little surprised.

"I have heard of you," was the cold response. "Enter."

"How do you know of me?" asked Dysmas as the door was closed behind him.

"You have come from Barabbas, have you not? Barabbas is my son. He would not trust Jerusalem with you, only I am here. He trusts me. You are safe here. Now tell me why you have come, and tell me of my son."

Dysmas explained the circumstance that brought them to Jerusalem, and as much as he could about how Barabbas was coping with the loss of Eleazar. The old woman showed some emotion at the news of Eleazar's capture. "He is a fine man," she said, with a single tear escaping her knowing eyes.

"What do you plan to do?" she said at last.

"I am not entirely sure. Be here, I suppose. See if any opportunity presents itself to free him. Comfort him. I don't know." Clearly the gravity of the circumstance was weighing heavily upon the shoulders of Dysmas.

"Have you eaten?" she asked.

"Yes, but we could do with some sleep."

She showed them to two rooms in the loft of the little house. "They are always kept ready," she said as she opened the first door to reveal a tidy room with the bed already made. No encouragement was needed as they were both exhausted, and so they went to bed and slept immediately.

Morning was upon them all too swiftly. Dysmas was up with the first light of morning and was met in the small dining area of the house by the mother of Barabbas holding a bowl of figs. "You must eat," she said simply. He took the figs and sat beside the small window surveying his surroundings in the morning light. "How far are we from the garrison?"

"It is a short walk through that small lane over there," she said, motioning to an opening further up the lane.

"Let Gestus sleep," he said. "He needs it. I'll be back."

Dysmas found his way to the lane's end where a large marketplace spread before him. On the opposite side were the walls of the Roman Pretorian.

Makeshift stalls were being stocked by their owners in preparation of the day's trade.

Dysmas walked the entire perimeter of the structure, noting every gate and possible breach, but found none. Soon he found himself back where he had started. The marketplace had become busier in the forty minutes it had taken him to inspect the garrison.

He found his way back to his lodgings to find Gestus enjoying some figs. "What did you find?" he asked.

"There seems no means of breaking in," he replied.

"Breaking in? You were hoping to break in?" replied Gestus, much surprised. "Surely you didn't think this a rescue mission. There will be no way of getting to Eleazar."

"I know," said Dysmas. "But I had to try. Imagine the impact on our cause if we were to stage a daring rescue of one of our own that was successful. I had hoped, but it is not possible."

"You're starting to sound like Barabbas," smiled Gestus. "So what now?"

The old woman showed herself then. "It is the feast of the Tabernacles two days from now. If the Romans remain predictable, they will execute Eleazar by crucifixion on that feast. It is their custom to hold prisoners and insurgents over for the next great feast, to send a message to us that we might be reminded who is in charge. It is good for Eleazar that he was captured so close to the feast, for they will certainly be torturing him for information."

Though Dysmas saw the pragmatism, it broke his heart that he could do little for his beloved Eleazar. "In answer to your question, Gestus, we stay and do what we can."

Some hours passed before Dysmas set out with Gestus to examine the path taken by the Romans to the place of the skull, the place where they crucified their prisoners.

Dysmas was more interested in the surrounding terrain than in the site of the execution, causing Gestus to wonder if he still had escape plans in mind.

"I'll be back in a moment, Gestus," he said.

He went down into the valley to the rear of the small knoll, circling about, climbing here and there, leaving Gestus more puzzled than ever. Some hours passed and the sun was beginning its descent. By the time Dysmas finally called a halt to the day's proceedings, he had inspected every vantage point available to observe the execution.

They returned to their lodgings a little dispirited. It was clear that nothing could be done to extricate Eleazar from his predicament. They ate in silence until Gestus broke it.

"Do we leave in the morning?" he asked.

"No," was the single word reply from Dysmas as he rose and retired in silence.

"Your friend is very loyal," the old woman remarked with genuine admiration as the door closed behind him. "But I fear there is nothing that can be done," and silence fell upon the small room once more.

Morning found Dysmas before dawn in the temple. All that was left to him now was prayer. He had left it behind as an out-dated notion of his beloved father, who he remembered was a deeply prayerful man, though clearly in the eyes of Dysmas, it had done him little good. It had been lost on one so young that God had indeed answered his father's prayer, and spared the light of his heart that fateful day.

So, pray he did until the third hour. Yet this time served more to unsettle and annoy him, as he became accutely aware of the arrogant hypocrisy surrounding him. The money changers were gathering to his left. The Pharisees were pontificating as always, as the poor were maligned and robbed, their foolish faith the cause of their position, he concluded. He pondered briefly their genuine passion and honest attachment to this ancient faith they held, but it seemed only to anger him more. "Fools," he said under his breath when he passed a couple as they were fleeced of what little they had, buying a pair of small doves for an offering.

The marketplace was abuzz now with the day's gathering crowd as he entered the northern most gate. The great doors of the Praetorian were just that moment being opened and the proclamation exclaimed of a judgement to be passed. Many entered to hear the judgement, so it was safe to do so. Dysmas was moving to the centre of the gathered crowd when Eleazar and another he did not know were dragged out to the podium. Dysmas had no way of knowing that Dimmicus had died the day after he had arrived in Jerusalem.

The area in which he was standing formed an amphitheatre surrounded as it was by more than a hundred Roman soldiers standing on the upper level. There were at least thirty stairs leading up to where the procurator took his seat.

Eleazar looked as though he had been beaten senseless many times. He was truly a mess of blood and bruising. Sentence was being passed that both Eleazar and this other would be crucified at the third hour tomorrow, the feast of Tabernacles. They were then without pause pushed from the podium like dogs.

Dysmas became very thoughtful with regard the fact that both prisoners were exposed. Clearly, extraction was out of the question, yet another idea started to take shape. He hurried through the great gate and returned once more to the place of the skull, and began once more to survey the surrounding terrain.

By the time he had returned to his lodgings he had a firm plan in mind, but it would require no little precision.

Gestus was not very happy with him when he entered. "Where have you been? Gone the whole day, I have searched everywhere for you."

"Sorry," said Dysmas. "But I don't have time for this. Get your things together quickly."

"Why?"

"We need to make preparations. Now move."

They were bidding the old woman farewell within the hour, and made their way to the stables. Having strapped all their belongings to their horses, they were soon on their way into the night. Had Dysmas been conscious at the time of his first meeting with Barabbas years ago, his chosen place of hiding would have been more familiar. He stowed the horses and equipment in the same location that Barabbas and his men were desperately trying to reach while carrying his limp body over the vast open plain. Nonetheless he believed it the best escape route, as had Barabbas all those years before.

Once the horses had been secured and they had bedded down for what was left of the night, Gestus could contain himself no longer. "What are we doing here?" he asked.

"We are preparing to steal the prize of the Romans, and spare a good friend a fate worse than death. Get some sleep." Clearly Dysmas had a plan and was much agitated. Gestus had no desire to further antagonise him, and so left further explanations to the fullness of time.

Early morning found them both on the narrow streets of Jerusalem to witness the brutality of a Roman execution. Two men were dragging their crosses through the jostling crowd as they were literally driven to their fate. The first man was not known to Dysmas, but the second, Eleazar, was being shown special treatment indeed by the Romans. They never ceased their brutality, landing blows whenever they were near enough to do so, yet always careful to cause pain without incapacitating their victim. Dysmas was clearly distressed by the treatment dealt Eleazar. At that moment a familiar face rode through the crowd barking orders, and Dysmas was immediately on high alert. It was Gaius.

He reined his horse just as one of the soldiers struck Eleazar a blow to the shoulder. Kicking his mount hard, Gaius knocked the soldier to the ground, eliciting an oath that was as quickly swallowed when the soldier realised who he was dealing with. "He is to be executed for his crimes, is that not enough for you!" cried Gaius over the din of the crowd, and he kicked his horse forward to clear a path for the condemned men.

Dysmas could not hear the comment, but was grudgingly grateful for the intervention. From that moment on, Eleazar and his unknown companion completed their tragic journey unmolested. None would be so foolish as to test Gaius.

Gestus was still somewhat bewildered as to the plan, but a glance at Dysmas and his state of mind told him this was no time to be asking questions.

The progress of the condemned men ran far more smoothly after the arrival of Gaius, and they were upon Golgotha within minutes of his arrival. Dysmas was strangely grateful that their ordeal was almost over.

Dysmas had been careful to position himself as high as he could to provide the best vantage point some sixty feet from where Eleazar and his companion laid their crosses. In moments Gestus was beside him, still puzzled.

"Get ready to run for your life," Dysmas said. "We have only one chance," and with that, took from beneath his tunic the bow he had hidden there. With the confidence of a master archer he loaded his single arrow, aiming quickly so that he would not dally and put off his aim. He let fly. The arrow passed straight through Eleazar's heart, killing him instantly.

The Romans were looking around in all directions as they were throwing themselves to the ground for cover, all but Gaius. He instantly summed up the intent, and looked first in the direction he thought most probable for such a bold endeavour, only to see two men disappearing into the crowd. Clearly these were his quarry. He knew instantly however the crowd would make it near impossible to catch these two on horseback, without possibly killing innocent people in the pursuit, and so he held his place. "On your feet," he barked at some of the soldiers who were still on the ground.

"Should we pursue them?" one asked.

"And who would you pursue?" he responded. "It would be a fruitless waste of time and resources. Get on with it," he said as he wheeled his horse to report back to the prefect.

Beginning and End

Neither Dysmas nor Gestus had any knowledge that Gaius and his Roman soldiers were not in pursuit of them. They fully believed that they were but steps in front of their own crucifixion, and certainly the commotion they left behind and the considerable noise that went with it had them both convinced that they were in imminent danger of capture.

They burst through the growing marketplace crowd and into a presentation of vegetables, knocking all to the ground, drawing the attention of a furious vender, but not stopping to survey the carnage. Making their way out of the marketplace on the opposite side, Dysmas led the way into the small lane that would be their salvation, only to run directly into his mother. Seeing her at the very last moment, he threw his weight to his left while Gestus, reacting just as quickly, went to the right, sprawling on the ground at the feet of Muriam, who was completely shocked.

Dysmas was on his feet in a moment and running once more when it registered with him that he knew that face that he had but glimpsed. Gestus too had regained his feet and was following close behind when Dysmas sought to look back for another glimpse of this woman, who was now staring after them in disbelief, but there was nothing to be done but to run, and so they soon ran out of sight leaving a bewildered Muriam staring dumbstruck in their wake.

Jelrah, who had been following Muriam some steps behind, was now staring also after those two young men so fleet of foot as they disappeared from sight. As he turned now back to Muriam, he realised that something more had taken place than he was aware of. Muriam was ashen-faced and dumbstruck.

"What is it Muriam?" he asked. Yet she could but stare after the two who had now gone from sight. She seemed as if she would faint so Jelrah guided her to be seated on the step of a door well. "What have you seen Muriam?" he asked once more.

"It was my husband," she said at last, completely disorientated now. "I'm sure it was."

Jelrah said nothing and assisted her to her feet. "Best we go home," he said.

"Yes," she said vaguely. "Yes," but her mind was elsewhere.

Dysmas and Gestus meanwhile were bursting through the western gate, intent on covering the open ground as quickly as possible. Minutes later they threw themselves over a large boulder, listening intently while trying to catch their breath, but there was no sign whatever of pursuit.

Minutes passed with still silence in their wake. "We go," said Dysmas, "quickly." Soon they had retrieved their horses and were wasting no time putting as much distance as possible between themselves and Jerusalem.

Meanwhile, the Prefect was furious. "How could you let this happen?" he screamed at Gaius. "If this becomes common knowledge it will look as though we have lost control and are vulnerable."

Gaius explained the execution had been organised and executed precisely as required. "It is clear," he continued, "that these rebels are becoming bolder. We will in the future provide contingencies to address any weakness. I can assure you, sir, it will never happen again."

This seemed to calm his foul mood somewhat, and he moved on to other security issues with regard the barracks. These discussions concluded, Gaius was on his way to his home within ten minutes.

Upon arrival he found Muriam very much distressed. It was not customary for her to be visiting Jerusalem at this time of year. Business in Hebron with regard the house she had shared with Azel had her in the general passing area, so she took the opportunity to visit, much to the delight of Gaius. Her current state however was not foreseen. She was not so robust as she had been in her younger days as grief had taken its toll on her young soul, and the unexpected meeting with 'Azel' was altogether too much. She retired for some rest and to collect her thoughts.

Jelrah, as best he could, tried to answer the questions Gaius was asking. However, he was confused himself regarding exactly what had happened to upset Muriam so.

"Two men, you say," said Gaius when she had gone.

"Yes, sir," replied Jelrah. "They were running as if for their very lives."

"Can you describe them?" asked Gaius.

"Only one, sir, as I didn't get the chance to see the other." He went on to provide a very good description of Gestus, who was the one he had seen.

Gaius was thoughtful. "Harum," he called, "wine."

Moments later wine was being poured for both Gaius and Jelrah. It had become the custom of late that they would share a wine. Indeed Gaius had delighted greatly spending time with his old servant. Jelrah had few if any duties these days, enjoying the genuine trust and friendship of Gaius, so they had been dining together for some months. His most important duty, indeed his only remaining duty (not to mention the one from which he derived his greatest pleasure), was escorting and assisting Muriam whenever she graced their home with her presence.

Even Harum, far from being envious, delighted in this blossoming friendship of Gaius and Jelrah. Jelrah had always treated him with great respect and deference with regard the instruction of his duties. Even ensuring mistakes were explained and corrected between them alone, gaining his respect and gratitude. Harum had long since understood also, that this feared Roman Gaius that he served was a just man, and a fair one. It was a home where peace reigned as a natural consequence.

While Gaius was piecing together a coherent timeline of the day's events, and considering the identities of those involved, Muriam was horrified as she once more considered the dream she had had all those years ago, in light of what she had seen today.

She had many times while Azel was alive considered the dream with terror, but since his death, she had thought little of it, believing instead it little more than a nightmare. Yet now it seemed more real somehow than before.

Arlett had informed her upon her return to Nazareth last year of the visit from Dysmas. Her reaction to the news had shocked her, she was simply numb. She truly had no idea how to react. She had been at once shocked and overjoyed, angry and incredulous, mostly incredulous. She simply found it impossible to believe. If he were indeed alive, why had it taken him so long to seek her out? She had even wondered if Arlett's great age may have her mind playing tricks.

Now, however, she knew with certainty. The son of Azel lives. Why was he running as if his life were endangered? Why had he not come to see her? Was it Gestus she had seen with him? Where has he been, where is he now, and what has he been doing these years? What of her dream that all at once seemed more real and vivid than ever before?

Though she sought sleep, it eluded her. There were no tears. So many years past, she had shed enough tears for two lifetimes, on as many empty nights. There were simply none left to shed, or so it seemed to her just now.

When she emerged from her room two hours later, she found Gaius and Jelrah still seated in the great room talking. Both stood when she entered. Jelrah then excused himself and left, as was his way.

"It appears we have much to speak of," she said.

"If I am correct, it would seem the past has come to visit," replied Gaius. "You are not aware of the happenings of the day," he went on.

"Happenings?" she asked.

Gaius went on to explain to her what his duties were for the morning watch and what had happened. "These two are no doubt the same two that I saw escaping the scene. I have to admit to you sadly, that I did somehow recognise one of them but was unable to place the face, until I heard of your chance meeting."

"There are more questions than answers," she said. "There is something I need to tell you that I have never told anyone but Azel, and then only on the night it happened. I have never repeated it, but have lived in terror of it for many years."

"Please," said Gaius.

Muriam went on to tell him every detail of the dream she had dreamt many years ago, and the fact that this took place on the night of the conception of her son. "Could it be?" she concluded, leaving the sentence unfinished as newfound tears streamed down her cheeks.

Gaius now sat down beside her and put his arm around her shoulders as she sobbed. "It is cruel to think you have carried this all these years alone. I'm so sorry," he said. "We need speak of this no more until you are ready," he continued, "but when you are ready, perhaps we can try and work out some answers to some of the questions at least."

She looked up at him with a tear-streaked face. "Do you think we could work out what the answers are?"

"What are the questions?"

"Where has he been?"

"Perhaps the better question is, who he has been with? His location we may never know, but we know who snatched him up, and no doubt nursed him back to health. So he has been with Barabbas somewhere, for better or worse."

"Why did he not seek me out before this?"

"That is a perplexing question, I admit," replied Gaius. "I have been thinking about that quite a bit since you let me know what Arlett had to say. Why indeed? I suspect initially he thought the search futile. I believe he may well have thought you dead also. He was very young and seriously injured. He would have had only their word as to your fate. I can think of no other reason he would not seek you out before last year. Somehow he discovered news that you were alive and set out to find you, finding Arlett instead."

"He has had all year to find me," she said.

"You told me Arlett said he became enraged when she told him that you were staying with me. I wonder if he thinks you have betrayed his father. Who knows what he has been told of me? Barabbas hates me with passion. I have thwarted many a plan that Barabbas has undertaken. He has reason to hate me."

"What has he been doing all these years then?" she asked.

"Becoming an enemy of Rome, I suspect," replied Gaius sadly. "Through the eyes of a young boy, the loss of his father would have seemed deliberate." Gaius found himself considering now, really for the first time, the consequences of Azel's death in light of the survival of his beloved son.

"So, he hates me too?" asked Muriam.

"No, Muriam, he doesn't hate anyone. One must know all the facts to hate. Hatred is a very specific disease requiring all of the symptoms proper to it. No. He is angry and hurt with both you and me for different reasons, and he has been trained to be so, which makes him dangerous, I'm afraid."

"Dangerous? Really?"

"He is well-trained, Muriam. I have observed him in action. A confused young man who is clearly powerful and well-trained, is a dangerous man indeed."

"What's to be done?" asked Muriam, her heart breaking.

"Well, I have not reported any of this to the prefect, and nothing of it is known outside of this house. I think it best it stay that way."

Muriam threw her arms around his neck before she had time to even consider her action. "Thank you, Gaius," she cried. "Thank you."

Gaius, though thrilled to be able to hold her in his arms at last, held her now at arms length, knowing this affection was from emotional relief rather than the love for which he had always hoped for one day.

"Rome has brought you enough grief, Muriam, and I have no wish to bring you more. I promise you, in so far as it is in my power, I will try to protect him, but I know I cannot find him for you. I have been trying for years with no success, but I will keep trying."

Muriam, aware of his chivalry, embraced him once more. "I know you will, Gaius, I have always known. Thank you."

The following morning found the mother of Barabbas approaching the sentry at the gates of the barracks. "What do you want?" he barked. Roman soldiers had little time for Jews.

"I have come to claim the body of Eleazar bar Eli." He scowled at her for a moment and then called for Gaius who was the centurion on watch. When he arrived the sentry motioned to the woman and conveyed the request.

"And you are?" asked Gaius.

"The only mother he ever knew. He has no kin. He claimed me his mother, I now claim him my son."

Gaius looked closely at this woman who was clearly weathered by hardship, and familiar with suffering. He was so tired of the hardship he had observed over so many years.

"Come," he said. He led her into the courtyard where the body of Eleazar was laid. Gaius was not expecting any show of emotion from this woman. It had become clear that the Jews would not grant the Romans the pleasure of seeing their pain. They apparently had no idea it showed plainly on their faces and in their demeanour.

"Where will you lay him?" asked Gaius.

"There is a family sepulchre awaiting him outside the western gate."

She bent down to the body, intending to wrestle it somehow onto her shoulders. "Wait," said Gaius, a lump forming in his throat. "Stop."

She looked up at him now, and the sadness was gripping her broken heart.

He called four soldiers and they were present at once. "You wait here," he said to the woman, and marched the soldiers to the opposite side of the courtyard, where he believed he was out of ear shot. "You are to assist this woman to take her son to his burial place. You will treat her with respect at all times. If not for the son she grieves, then for the mother who suffers because of the crimes of her son. They were not her crimes, and she has suffered enough. Do I make myself clear?"

"Yes," they answered as one. "Then be about it," concluded Gaius, and marched out of sight.

Unknown to Gaius, the woman had heard the entire address, and was more than a little surprised. She was elderly yes, but she was in no way impaired in her hearing. This was not the Gaius she had heard so much about.

The soldiers returned to her with a stretcher, and were careful in all their dealings with her, handling the body with the care expected of them from Gaius. They bore the burden of Eleazar through the city to the western gate, much to the surprise and respect of the Jews, most of whom stopped to follow the progress of this most unusual little procession.

At first the soldiers themselves were embarrassed by the attention, but one by one they came to understand there was not a judgement being made upon them, but rather a genuine appreciation that they were showing some respect to this woman and her son, and by extension to the Jews in general. Occasionally one would congratulate them as they passed. A couple of others thanked or blessed them. It was truly a different experience of the Jews than any of them had previously experienced.

Their brief journey at an end, they placed the body of Eleazar in the sepulchre and withdrew, leaving his mother to prepare it by her custom.

As they returned, it seemed as if Jerusalem had forgotten their act, and had returned to its normal disinterest in all things Roman, but they had not forgotten. They returned to their barracks in silence, with a different perspective.

As she dressed the body of Eleazar, the old woman was herself lost in her thoughts with regard the kindness of Gaius, and indeed the soldiers in whom she had witnessed change. They had carried out his order, reluctantly at first and yet with genuine docility in the end, going beyond their mandate. Her heart started to soften as she saw what a little genuine respect could accomplish, and wondered if there could be hope after all.

When she had completed her task, she made her way home toward the evening. She had no knowledge she was being followed. Gaius kept a good distance, but never lost sight of her until she closed her door. He had concluded the instant she claimed the body that there was a connection somehow between this woman and Dysmas. If Dysmas would take such a risk as he did, this man must have been important to him for some reason. He was content to know where to find this woman should it ever be necessary.

The mood at the cave was sullen when Dysmas and Gestus arrived back. Their very presence without Eleazar was enough explanation as to his fate. Barabbas was glad to have them back safe, but it was telling in his demeanour that he had been struggling with the loss of his dearest friend. "You are weary," he said to Dysmas. "Get some sleep and we'll talk later."

Sleep, however, as for the last two nights, eluded Dysmas. He found himself wondering how he would tell Barabbas that it was in fact he who had killed Eleazar. It had been weighing on his mind terribly since the actual event had come to pass. Conceiving the plan was one thing. To execute it was quite another.

The early hours passed slowly as had become his new sleeping habit, and he found himself once more considering the woman he had all but knocked over in Jerusalem. Could it truly have been his mother? Yet what was she doing in Jerusalem? What was her relationship with Gaius? Who was the man with her? There were so many questions crowding his thoughts he found himself unable to keep track or keep up. "If only I had had more time to stop," he lamented. Then an unexpected question invaded his thoughts for the first time: did Barabbas know she was alive? This struck him hard as it had not occurred to him previously. How much did Barabbas know, he began to wonder?

The men were stirring, but Dysmas had long since left the cave and was watching the sunrise just outside the entry. Soon the chatter filtered out to him and he knew they were preparing for the day. Barabbas had guessed where he was and soon joined him there.

"How did they kill him?" he asked. "Crucifixion?"

"They didn't kill him. I did," said Dysmas still staring over the plains watching the sun.

"It wasn't your fault," replied Barabbas. "You can't blame yourself."

"No, you don't understand Barabbas," Dysmas replied turning to face him now. "I killed him. They were about to crucify him with another man. I shot him with an arrow before they did."

"You did what?" said Barabbas, truly shocked by the revelation. "How could you?" he screamed.

"What do you think Eleazar would want? To die instantly by the hand of a friend, or to hang for days in agony to finally die at the hands of his enemy, only to give them the prize of his humiliation? It was all I could do to save him. It was the least I could do to save him."

Barabbas digested this for a moment, realising the full gravity of the position Eleazar had found himself in. He knew Dysmas was right, as tears streaked his cheeks. He realised too the enormous risk taken to execute such a bold scheme.

Dysmas had never seen him like this before, he was truly heartbroken and slumped to his knees, his head in his hands, and just cried. Dysmas put his hand on his back for a moment before leaving him to his moment of grief. He returned to the cave and started to organise the men for training exercises. Clearly both discipline and routine had slipped in his absence, with much about the state of the cave vexing him also.

Throughout the day he found himself getting short with the men for little reason, and began to wonder himself as to why. It was very unlike him, yet he found himself somewhat powerless to be more easy-going, until finally he passed the task to Gestus about the ninth hour.

He found himself an hour later perched atop the small mountain that provided secrecy to the cave beneath, thinking once more of his mother and Gaius, together with his life with Barabbas and how it had begun. More and more questions he would prefer not to consider crowded his thoughts and interrupted his peace.

He remained aloft in his silent haven, losing track of the time until the sun had been set a good hour. His thoughts had turned more to his father over the past couple of hours, and he found himself considering his father's passion for his God, in particular the peace he found in this simple faith. He remembered well his gentle-natured father and his undying love for his mother. As a young child he recalled many times laughing with them both as they simply delighted in each other's company. They were very much in love, he thought to himself pensively, smiling absently.

He remembered, too, how gently they would pray together, the delicate esteem and homage they paid to this God they seemed so familiar with. He was at once deeply attracted and yet, uneasy. To him their great love of this God they were devoted to was repaid with sorrow and bitterness. Where was He when his father needed Him? As much as he wanted to honour his father's memory and respect his attachments, he could not get over what he considered betrayal. Why? The question tolled as a bell, asked on so many other occasions, and as before, the answer still eluded him.

Dysmas had not noticed he had become stubbornly set at a young age in his unshakeably narrow world, and the view he had of it. Just now it was indeed starting to occur to him. Life was simple: hate Romans and eject them from Israel. There had been, given his circumstances, little more than this to consider.

As the second in command, both Barabbas and the men respected and loved him. He had never really had to even consider relationships and thought rarely of them. Considerations as those now crowding his thoughts were foreign to him, and though at one level he delighted in memories of his early childhood relationships, at another they forced him to face vexing questions about current relationships that quite frankly, made him uncomfortable.

Neither could he fathom the conduct of Gaius. Why, he wondered, had he been so determined that his men treat Eleazar with respect? He had for many years had a very preconceived idea of Gaius, but his conduct had not fitted well his idea on those occasions of interaction. It seemed to Dysmas that nothing made sense to him, at least with regard any relationship outside the confines of his cave. He simply lacked the tools, perhaps even the etiquette to understand them.

None knew where he was and so he spent much of the evening uninterrupted until, quite late, he was disturbed by footsteps. "Ah, I have found you at last," said Barabbas. He had been concerned that his reaction to the news of the death of Eleazar had been misunderstood, and had determined to put it right.

"It is many years past time, Dysmas, that you and I spoke of matters unspoken."

He sat down opposite Dysmas.

"Did you know?" asked Dysmas.

"That your mother was alive? I suspected."

"And you didn't feel the need to tell me?"

"Tell you what, exactly? Get your hopes up only to perhaps be dashed again? I did try to find out. By the time I discovered she was alive, it was clear she had developed a friendship with Gaius. How exactly does one explain that to a young boy? Your mother is friends with the man that murdered your father? How does one say that to one so close to his heart? I thought of it many times, but believed it best to keep it to myself for your good. I always knew this day would come."

"How could she?" asked Dysmas seemingly of the stars. "I have been trying to understand, but I just can't."

"Neither could I, nor Eleazar. It was he I sent to find her. It was a difficult decision, but I would make it again in the same circumstance."

Silence fell upon them for some time as all that had been spoken was digested.

"I know," said Barabbas at last, "that you will want answers, and I know you deserve them. I can't believe that I am about to say this, but everyone else chose to be here in this band of soldiers but you. You alone were brought here, not so much against your will, but you had little choice. Yet it is not unfair to say that you have contributed more than all the rest. No indeed, much more. I have allowed you more latitude with regard your freedoms as a result, but also because you needed to be prepared for life after you leave us."

Dysmas looked up now somewhat puzzled. "Leave?"

"Oh, don't be surprised Dysmas, I am not asking you to leave, far from it. I am telling you that of all the men, you have earned the right to leave, should you wish it. I have long known that this would be a possibility someday, but it is certainly not my wish. You are a man that needs answers to questions that should be asked. I am a man that has come to care for you as a son. I will not get in your way," he continued, standing now. "These are decisions that only you can make, questions only you can ask."

Barabbas made his way through the darkness in silence, leaving Dysmas to his thoughts. Thoughts that would have him sleepless the entire night.

Surprised by Life

Dysmas discovered over the following months that questions were plentiful and answers few. He also found himself increasingly uncomfortable with regard his limited view of the world as he knew it. Too often was the case in his mind, that the evidence did not align well with the preconceived positions he had taken as his own.

In this little world within the cave he had climbed to the very top, a position he had once coveted as his goal in life. Revered by his peers and loved by all, one would expect him to be delighted by his success, yet to the contrary, he found himself increasingly uneasy.

In truth, much of his memory revolved around his hatred for Gaius. He had little understanding of it at the time, but Gaius had been in fact the driving force behind his very survival. It was his single-minded determination to destroy him that drove the boy Dysmas to become the soldier he was. He thought Gaius was the reason for his pain, the cause of his bitterness. He was slowly coming to understand he was also the means of his survival.

Yet Gaius was a paradox to him. Though his preconceived ideas regarding the man were set in stone, every interaction with him, indeed every word he had ever heard of him, now that he stopped to consider, had painted a very different picture, one that was now beginning to unsettle him. His treatment of Eleazar most of all had touched Dysmas. None of it made sense to him.

Barabbas had indeed had a very great influence on Dysmas, but so had his father. Barabbas, a rough coarse man, who saw the world in black and white, had influenced him greatly to the same narrow view. How could there be more for one who had never known more? He knew not what he did not know.

His father was the exact opposite. A powerful man, yet a profoundly gentle and cultured one. He was a man of faith, who seemed at ease bridging the divide created by Roman occupation. He had had no difficulty, it seemed to Dysmas, reconciling the practice of his faith as a chosen Jew, with the presence of Rome.

Dysmas had spent many hours contemplating this. He knew his father to be neither coward nor fool. So why was he so at peace with God's chosen being governed by this Roman heathen?

This faith once so familiar and obvious had become a stumbling block for Dysmas. He observed too often the hypocrisy of the scribes and Pharisees, his people burdened with Roman occupation and the cruel treatment of many of them by Roman soldiers. They faced hardships from increasing poverty, and yet still they struggled to remain faithful to this fabled God of yesteryear, a god who had clearly abandoned them long past.

Yet resonating through the years was this man of his past, his simplicity, his gentle and clear explanations of God, and His love for those He created.

By the time he had turned twelve, Dysmas had been well schooled by his father. The Law required that he be ready to take his place in the synagogue by age twelve. Yet his father, not content that he recite and know the Torah as required, sought that he should understand it as a love story, a personal love story from a personal God of love.

Though Dysmas had been unaware as a child, there were many men in the village of his childhood who envied the faith of his father, and indeed his young son. The understanding of a God so personal at once concerned and delighted them. Much had been spoken of the God of wrath, and so many approached this

God with apprehension and fear. Yet Azel had understood what they considered wrath as lessons a father might use to instruct a wayward son.

It had never occurred to Azel that this wrath of God was directed to the destruction of His creation. It simply made no sense. Why would God, for example, devote so much attention to ensuring the wellbeing of His chosen people, only to destroy them with His so called wrath?

Azel, from his earliest years, had considered the Torah in its entirety, rather than the individual stories and books. He understood from an early age, as an important lesson, that had Joseph not been betrayed by his brothers to slavery, Israel would not have flourished as it did. Moses would have been unnecessary, and God would not have communicated the Ten Commandments. Even in this he saw joy, where others saw a threat. He considered the commandments a recipe for happiness, rather than an obstruction to joy. A novel approach indeed for a modern Jew.

These formed the whole man, a man at peace with the will of God, a man able to communicate this joy to his son, a son who now, so many years later, struggled with so much contradiction. The years intended by his father to round off his education and culture having been cut short, were instead filled with the very opposite of what his father had hoped and intended. With no proper instruction to guide the boy Dysmas, he had languished, clinging to those physical realities he perceived served him well. He was half a man devoid of his spiritual heritage. Leaving behind the essence and soul of his father's legacy, however, was proving to be difficult. Contrary to all, he was the very antithesis of what he had gained from Barabbas. It was to Dysmas as if his father were calling from beyond time and space, and his voice was now resonating in this great heart, crushed and misled by a world of hatred and violence, yet still pure, seemingly untouched by the pervasiveness of such hatred.

Dysmas was fast beginning to understand that he in fact did not hate anyone. He was angry because he was hurt by the loss of his parents. Though his anger, a child's anger, had been directed toward Gaius, he now found himself weeping quietly on his many lonely visits to the mountain top.

As a child it had never occurred to him that grief had a place in the life of a man. That concept had been dismissed as weakness and thus neglected. In reality, Dysmas had never grieved the loss of his parents, until now.

These were weeks of great introspection, and deep grief. Dysmas was very often absent from his duties, many of which he delegated to Gestus.

Gestus had delighted in his new duties, and was indeed a most capable instructor. What he lacked in talent he more than accommodated for with enthusiasm. As the months passed, Gestus had cemented his place in this group as the best of them, second only to Dysmas. He was an expert tactician and the source of great amusement, and consequently loved by the men.

With the exception of two raids over these six months since the death of Eleazar, there had been little to disturb the natural development of either Dysmas or Gestus.

Barabbas recognised the growing distance of Dysmas, but had concluded it more necessary that he work things out for himself. To this end, apart from a few meals together and a little mirth, little had passed between them.

Two months after the death of Eleazar, word had reached Muriam of the death of Arlett. She had been devastated, as it had been her intention to return to her side immediately. The shock of the chance meeting with Dysmas however, and the hope of seeing him again had made her tarry, but now she made arrangements to depart immediately.

It is fair to say that Gaius had been privately delighted with the change of plan, and had become greatly used to the presence around his home of this woman he now loved so deeply in the secret of his heart.

"I have time available to accompany you to Nazareth," he had said, "if you would permit."

"That would be very gracious Gaius, but it is such a long way," she replied.

"All the more reason to have the company of a familiar face," he had said. And so it was arranged.

They and Jelrah had left two days later with a passing caravan that was headed to Nain. They would complete the last part of the journey alone.

Jelrah had taken much time to instruct Harum as to his duties while they were away, and his expectations were that they would be carried out to the letter.

During the journey, Muriam had for the first time, quite unexpectedly, a chance to observe Gaius without the pressure of his station. It appeared that none travelling with them were aware of his position with the Roman garrison stationed at Jerusalem. Thus he quickly became simply another pilgrim on a journey, much to his own delight. What followed was somewhat unexpected for Muriam.

What she observed was a man of tender heart, a genuine soul who thought nothing of helping various travellers both Gentile and Jew alike. It seemed he drew little if any distinction between them. He was not only quickly popular among his fellow travellers, but was quite unintentionally letting his guard down.

Around Muriam he had always been deeply aware of his role in her tragic life, having ever his uniform to remind him should his memory lapse. And though it was true that he secretly loved her, he had always considered her an untouchable beauty for one such as himself. So he had inadvertently always been stiff around her, a gentleman with a soldier's discipline.

As the days passed however, the soldier was further detached from his duties and the uniform left far behind. A smile was becoming ever more commomplace, and even laughter around the fire at night. Muriam found herself delighting in a side of Gaius she had not seen before. She had known for some time that she had feelings for this Roman, but she found herself now very much attracted to him, and wondering if she should feel guilty because she was. Life could be so complicated, she thought to herself sadly.

For his part, Gaius was seemingly unaware of the change in himself. He found himself more and more interested in the faith of this simple and elegant woman. It seemed to him that she was all but alone in her delightfully simple approach to her faith. Much of what he had observed since his arrival in Jerusalem had left him believing Jews to be mad to follow the duplicitous wretches that were their leaders. There was one exception: the Baptist. That wild man of the desert that had taken him by surprise just a month ago.

He had been sent to investigate this 'madman', as the Jews had called him. He had come away thinking the world could do with a few more mad men, and a new understanding of the jealousy of the Sanhedrin. This man too spoke simply, yet with such power, such conviction, it was impossible to ignore him. Given the encounter, Gaius was more of a mind to take note. A most impressive man, he concluded, powerful and hardened, yet deep and cultured. Uncompromising yet compassionate. A dangerous man indeed, but not to Rome. He understood well why the Sanhedrin were afraid of him.

Yet this chance meeting with the Baptist had lit a fire in Gaius to know more. It seemed to him that none but Muriam could teach him. It had been his experience that she alone approached her God with similar trust and confidence, one could say as a friend, yet far more familiar, while at once with awe and wonder.

He had realised at some point that the quality he had found so attractive in this humble woman was this very faith, but had never understood why until now. She was at once a paradox to him without guile or deception. There was nothing hidden, and yet mystery personified. He had by now fallen very much in love with her, and on this journey it was beginning to show. Though no secret to Jelrah, wise enough to silently delight in his master's joy, it had not been so obvious to Muriam, and even Gaius now found himself surrounded by his own feelings, far stronger than he had imagined them to be.

There was no sign of a Roman uniform, and little by now of the soldier that wore it. So it was not deemed unusual that so many invitations to eat with this family or that were forthcoming. Though Jelrah would always prepare something, it would inevitably be shared at another camp fire with another family. Gaius found himself much attracted to these Jews he was forced to share his days and nights with. It was an experience that very much surprised him. He found too the simple faith of many of these people so far removed from Jerusalem, often much like that of

Muriam. It left him wondering who those Pharisees in Jerusalem were worshipping. Clearly not the same God, he surmised.

Stories of their religious history mixed as simply and as seamlessly with their life and laughter, as if they were one story spanning many centuries and many lives. He found it fascinating.

Gaius had spent much time on this journey talking with an old man from Nain, whose name was Taitum. He found himself now at night's end and all others retired, alone with Taitum and a skin of wine. They had enjoyed many conversations together which may have emboldened Taitum to finally ask, "How long have you loved her?"

Gaius looked up at him with but the hint of a smile. "What do you mean?" he replied.

"I mean, how long have you loved her, and why does she not know yet?"

Gaius looked at him for a long time smiling. "It's complicated," he said finally.

"Oh, Gaius, it's always complicated. It wouldn't be love otherwise. Complications where love is concerned however, almost always lay with ourselves, rather than with the beloved."

"You don't even know who I am," said Gaius smiling. "If you did, you would likely never speak to me again."

"I doubt that," said Taitum. "I know what I need to. The details rarely make any difference."

"So what do you know?"

"I know you are a Roman, but more to the point you are a man of virtue, a good man with good intent, made like me, in the image and likeness of God."

Gaius looked shocked.

"Why so surprised, Gaius?"

"I have never had a Jew consider me with such esteem," he replied. "Isn't that thinking heresy?"

"Only in Jerusalem and among those who would presume to tell God how He should deal with His own creation. Such people would leave out of the Torah those inconvenient passages that remove the stay that supports their prejudice. 'Let us make man in our own image'. Is there any question that you are not a man Gaius? Would even one in the Sanhedrin claim you were not a man? And what, he continued, should we make of, 'God saw all that he had made, and behold it was very good'? Am I to understand that God only made Jewish men? If God made other men, surely God saw them too, and that part of creation too was very good. I don't pretend to understand everything, nor can I explain everything that I understand, but I know truth when I hear it, and love when I see it, getting back to the point," he concluded with a wry grin. "So tell me, who are you, and why is it complicated?"

Gaius was much taken aback by this man's genuine openness and honesty. Finally, he looked up at him squarely in the eye and said without blinking. "I am a Roman centurion, in charge of the Roman garrison at Jerusalem."

Taitum didn't flinch. "Is that it?" he said at last. "I thought you were going to tell me you were a mass murderer or something."

"Many in Judea would consider I am."

"Many in Judea are young and foolish. I hardly think them equipped to judge much at all," replied Taitum.

"So it doesn't concern you?" asked Gaius.

"Of course not, but I won't be making it common knowledge, and I recommend you don't either. People have prejudices, usually galvanised and generalised, born from emotions more often than facts. Sad to say, but human nature is too often a tragedy of ignorance and arrogance that almost inevitably leads to poor judgments. No, this will remain between us," he said with a smile.

Gaius was impressed with this man's wisdom and candour, and found himself reappraising his view of the Jewish people yet again. The more he met with what he believed were the real Jews, the more impressed he became. He was quickly coming to the opinion that many in the Sanhedrin hardly qualified in all justice to claim themselves Jews.

"You have a habit," continued Taitum, more serious now, "of avoiding difficult questions, Gaius. To me that is of no consequence, because I am of no consequence, but to yourself? I fear it will catch up with you. A shame too, as most catastrophes, and indeed broken hearts, are easily avoided by the simple application of truth. Why don't you tell an old man of your problem? See if I have learned anything that may be of some assistance."

Gaius knew well there was no escape, and was greatly relieved this was the case. Finally he felt he had someone he could talk with regarding all that had been, and all he hoped might be. He picked up the skin and poured a pitcher for his companion and himself, as he gathered his thoughts, and was soon recounting all the events that had brought both him and Muriam to this current moment.

When he had recounted all his memory would allow, Taitum leaned back and rubbed his hand through his beard thoughtfully. "Complicated, you say," he said at last. "You have a gift for understatement, Gaius. Complicated indeed, and yet, as simple as two people in love. When all is said and done, what complicates it is the thoughts of others, is it not? What would they make of the two of you given the history? Or more to the point, you are concerned what people would think of Muriam. You should not worry about such things in matters of the heart. It is my experience that people rarely think at all, so more often than not it matters little what they are thinking about."

"If it is to be simple as you say, there need be two people in love."

"Oh, but there are Gaius. I am old but not blind. You do not see it?"

Gaius was a little stunned. "No," he said. "She is most gracious to me, it is true, but love? I think not. I have hoped, yes, but never seriously entertained that hope. Even if you are correct, what now that we know her son lives?"

"Ah, you are in love with her son?" was the glib reply with a raised brow.

"No, but I feel......."

"You feel you owe him something, yes, I guessed. Ask yourself then. Would denying his mother some joy in her life serve somehow to repay this debt? And just what debt is it you believe you owe?"

"He would not understand," replied Gaius.

"There are many that won't understand Gaius, but it's not about them either. Truly I understand your gallantry with regard these matters. However, some clear thinking is in order. If you are bent on denying yourself love, at least be clear as to the reasons."

Gaius became silent and thoughtful. After some minutes Taitum consumed the last of his wine and stood. "We have not spoken long, Gaius, but there is much in what has been said, and a great deal for you to digest. I know you have much to consider. I am at your service should you wish to talk further, but an old man needs his sleep."

Gaius smiled. "Thank you for your insights," he said, rising.

Taitum nodded and smiled as he turned to walk back to his donkeys. After a few steps he paused and turned for a moment to look at Gaius. "Clearly, Muriam is a good woman, Gaius. She deserves a good man, with good intent," and he smiled to himself and continued on his way leaving Gaius with much to consider.

Gaius remained sleepless that night, and the sun rose over his back as various travellers showed themselves, stretching with the dawn as their backdrop. Birds were already seeking out their quarry as some of the donkeys welcomed the day with their usual hee haws, to the disdain of all within earshot.

Muriam was one of the first to exit her tent, and set about preparing a small meal for their little party. Jelrah was in the habit of remaining wrapped in his sleeping linens for an hour or so longer these days, as his poor bones felt the cold more acutely during the winter months. For his part, Gaius was happy to suffer him this small comfort, even at times delivering some tasty morsel to eat in the warm comfort of his bedding.

This morning, however, he had other things on his mind. He found himself more aware of Muriam's actions in her dealings with and around him. He noted for the first time how often she would place her hand on his shoulder. How comfortable her smile was, and how gentle her eyes when they shared some amusement. How she always ensured he was provided for first, with the best of what was on offer. And so many other small, seemingly trivial acts that had until now been entirely lost on him. Could it truly be, he found himself wondering?

The days were pleasant and the nights cool as they made their way north to Nain. Gaius and Taitum each night shared a skin and spoke much of life. Gaius found himself cast back to his many discussions with Petmar, and found himself smiling, as the familiarity of a past joy was enkindled from time to time. At one point he related to Taitum this recollection of Petmar.

"You knew Petmar?" was the somewhat surprised response. "Oh I shouldn't be surprised I suppose," he continued, "Petmar knew everyone," and he laughed as his eyes watered. "Oh, how I miss Petmar."

"How did you know Petmar?" asked Gaius.

"He was my brother by marriage. Petmar met his future wife, Arlett, at my wedding to her sister Bethal. A most memorable meeting it was too." He laughed as Gaius burst out laughing himself, recalling the story Petmar had related to him of his first meeting with Arlett.

"You know the story, Gaius," said Taitum, pleasantly surprised.

"Yes, I do indeed. He had a wonderful way of telling a story. Is it really true?"

"About the wine jars and commotion?" he laughed. "Every word of it. He was a wonderful man, and he loved you very much Gaius."

"How could you know that?" asked Gaius. "You didn't even know we knew each other."

"Because he shared that story with you. His greatest embarrassment became a joy to him of such delight, that he shared it only with those who were his closest friends. Now, Gaius, I know who you are," he said smiling to himself nodding. "You are my brother's brother."

Gaius was touched. "What of Bethal?" he asked.

"Bethal has been dead these past nineteen years."

"Have you remarried?" asked Gaius.

"Who could replace Bethal?" was the wry response. "No, Gaius, there was only one Bethal and none could replace her. She is waiting for me, and I will go to her when time decrees. We will arrive in Nain at the sixth hour tomorrow," he continued. "Will you be my guest and rest before you continue to Nazareth?"

"I would very much like that, but I will see what Muriam has planned. I am simply at her service on this journey."

"Well, there is room for all," said Taitum as he rose. "Consider this Gaius," he continued. "Petmar's greatest moment of humility became the most treasured moment of his life, and indeed his greatest story. It netted him his greatest treasure also, his beloved Arlett. Just when Petmar thought his life was over, it was in fact just beginning, and what a life it was. You see only the impossible with Muriam and yourself. Be careful you don't lose the future to the past. That truly would be a crime. Goodnight," and with that he made his way slowly back to his donkeys in the moonlight, leaving Gaius to ponder his future.

It was decided the following day to push on to Nazareth, as they had made good time and believed they had time to arrive before twilight. Gaius had sought out Taitum to thank him for their many conversations and for his insights. Goodbyes and pleasantries over, they were on the road to Nazareth just after the sixth hour.

The journey was a long and tiring one for Muriam, who had been mourning her dearest friend since the news had reached her. When they finally arrived and made their way to the humble home that held so many happy memories for her, she broke down, really for the first time.

The little home lay before them now, as quiet as the outlying buildings surrounding it. As they approached, the door of the house swung open to reveal a frail old man. "Baslar," said Muriam. "Oh, Baslar," she repeated as she hugged him.

"Muriam, it is you. Praise the Lord you have come." They wept in each other's arms. "Come in and rest yourself; you look exhausted." And so she was.

"Perhaps it best if you rest, Muriam," said Gaius.

"By all means," said Baslar, motioning her to her old room which had been left untouched.

"Honestly," she replied, "I would first like to go to pay my respects to Arlett."

"So be it," said Baslar. "She is entombed with the love of her life."

"Then it is not far. Let us go now," she said, and so they were on their way in moments. Minutes later she found herself standing before a huge boulder, where had been left many flowers and tokens of love.

"Many from Nazareth still visit to pay their respects," Baslar explained to Gaius and Jelrah, whom he had as yet not formally met. "They were very much loved here."

"They were very much loved in many other places also," replied Gaius. "Forgive me, my name is Gaius, and this is Jelrah. We thought it best to escort Muriam on her journey."

"Bless you," said Baslar. "Bless you. You are welcome here. There is plenty of room."

Soon they had returned to the house of Petmar, and Muriam was quickly asleep. Baslar had escorted her companions to one of the many outlying buildings and set about preparing their lodgings.

"We will be fine from here," said Gaius. "Thank you."

Baslar withdrew, leaving Jelrah free to get some sleep, while Gaius walked the area to acquaint himself with the lay of his surroundings. The soldier in him was not yet entirely extinguished.

Unexpected Truth

The days passed at Nazareth peacefully. So much so that Gaius found himself wondering at the nature of his surroundings. The very nature of this peaceful place seemed to permeate all that entered or surrounded it. They had arrived a week ago and he quite simply did not wish to leave.

Each day Muriam would make her way to the tomb of her beloved friends and pray there. Each day Gaius would accompany her, delighted by the opportunity it afforded him to admire once more this loyal soul.

On the morning of the ninth day, they had set out as usual to the tomb after breakfast. When they arrived they found kneeling before the tomb a woman, clothed in pale blue, prostrate in prayer. They had rounded the corner unaware of her presence and unintentionally disturbed her. As she looked up now, Muriam recognised her immediately. "Mary," she gasped as she knelt down now to embrace her.

"Muriam" she said, "I had no idea you were here in Nazareth. When did you arrive?"

"A little more than a week ago."

Mary stood then with Muriam, noticing for the first time Gaius. "Oh Mary, this is my dear friend Gaius. He and his servant have been seeing to my safety," she said with a smile as she turned to him now.

"Bless you, Gaius. I heard about Azel from Arlett," she continued, still looking at Gaius with a gentle smile. Clearly she knew the entire story. Then turning to Muriam she placed her hands on her shoulders. "He awaits the reward of the just in the bosom of Abraham. God is very good, praised be His name."

Gaius had been instantly taken with the simple beauty of this woman before him. She was at once homely and regal, simple yet elegant. Clearly of the poorer class and yet, there was something in her bearing: a strength, with a certain power of sorts. An assurance of self without the least trace of arrogance. She was certainly beautiful, and yet this was eclipsed by that beauty that is the nature of humility.

Gaius had discerned some years before, that humility retained in itself a certain and singular radiance that somehow renders physical beauty secondary, even while making it so much more attractive. Humility then truly created a paradox of beauty that elevated beauty beyond that which is base. This woman before him truly illustrated the theory. He guessed at a glance she was in her mid-thirties, though her eyes, knowing and wise, betrayed a much greater age. She was clearly struck from the same mould as Muriam. Simple, humble and dignified. In Rome, he concluded, either of them would be a singular treasure.

"Have you any word of Dysmas?"

"Of sorts," answered Muriam, and went on to recount her chance meeting in Jerusalem. Mary listened attentively as she took Muriam's hand in her own. Even now this chance meeting with Dysmas clearly had impacted Muriam. Mary held her it seemed with every fibre of her being, and every ounce of her attention.

"Fear not, Muriam," she said at last. "Providence is caring for him as it does us all. Let us together seek the Lord's care for Dysmas." Mary called on the Lord's favour for Dysmas, and at once Muriam's mind was cast back to a time many years past, when this woman once prayed for her son in the little house of Hebron. As before, she prayed like no other. Muriam was once more swept up in the simplicity of this woman's gentle prayer. Just as before, they sat silently for what seemed a few moments but was in fact nearly ten minutes.

Gaius was more than a little impressed. Watching these two together was for him a window to simple beauty.

"How is Joseph?" Muriam asked at last.

Mary smiled to herself such a gentle smile. "He awaits the Christ and his reward. Such a good man Muriam. Such a blessing."

"I'm so sorry, Mary, I didn't know."

"Don't be sorry. He is at peace. Will you visit with me before you return?" asked Mary. "I could perhaps show you some of the hospitality you gave to us those many years past."

"Oh, Mary, I would love to," Muriam replied, wanting to ask after Jesus, but she was afraid to now.

"I will expect you as well Gaius," said Mary, turning to him now.

"Thank you, Mary, I would very much like that."

"I had best take my leave then," she said with a smile, and withdrew to allow Muriam time to pray.

On the return journey to the house of Petmar, they stopped atop the hill overlooking the homestead and the valleys beyond.

"She is a most interesting soul," remarked Gaius at last.

Muriam turned to him. "Gaius, I have not seen Mary for nearly thirty years and yet, it seems to me that she has barely aged a day. I could hardly believe it."

"How did you two meet?"

"Oh, Petmar, of course," laughed Muriam. "Once Azel and I met Petmar, life became surprising almost all of a sudden." She went on then to recount the day Joseph knocked at their humble little door in Hebron. As the tale unfolded, Gaius was ever more interested. He had heard the stories of the children slain at Bethlehem at the order of Herod. He had also heard that the soldiers had been meticulous to ensure they slaughtered every male child.

When Gaius had first heard of it mere weeks after his arrival in Judea, he had cursed the soldiers involved as cowards. Unfortunately for Hasshim, he was present to hear the insult. As the commander of the garrison involved, he was not willing to let it go and had confronted Gaius with his sword. It did not end well for Hasshim, as poetic justice provided him the same end he had overseen for so many children of Bethlehem.

As Muriam's story unfolded of the soldiers passing from town to town in search of the family they believed they had missed, he found himself smiling at the wisdom of Petmar once more. What a man, he thought to himself, and still bringing joy to my heart these years later.

"You're smiling," said Muriam, suddenly waking him from his muse. "Why?"

"Well," said Gaius. "It is always good to hear of the antics of Petmar. What a joy he was, and indeed is. I had the pleasure of meeting the garrison commander who oversaw the slaughter at Bethlehem. As it turned out, we did battle soon after my hearing of this cowardice," he continued more serious now.

"What happened?" asked Muriam.

"I am still here," replied Gaius. "It did not end well for him. The gods were smiling on me."

"The one true God had other plans for you," replied Muriam with a smile.

"Indeed."

As before, the days passed peacefully over the next week, when it was arranged to visit with Mary. The house of Joseph was found on the exact opposite side of Nazareth to that of Petmar. It was quite a walk, and Muriam found herself marvelling at Mary for making the journey so often to the tomb.

The little house of Joseph was a most humble affair from without. It was located at the highest point of the small holding of land upon which it was built, affording it a simple yet beautiful view down the little valley spread before it. At the lowest point was a small orchard and olive grove. The water naturally gathered by the lay of the property, was neatly caught at the very lowest point. This provided a form of rising damp to the trees located just above, ensuring they always had at least a sip of life-giving water.

To the left of the little house was a work area of sorts, covered by a skillion roof off the main structure, which was itself a small outbuilding built hard up against the rock face of the little mountain, that formed the boundary on that side. It all seemed very humble indeed.

As they drew near, a young man of about thirty appeared from the little workshop and approached.

"Jesus?" asked Muriam.

A smile formed immediately upon his tanned features. "Muriam," he said as he took her hands in his own. "How wonderful to meet you at last. So much I have heard."

"How did you...?"

"My mother told me you would be visiting, and I have been much looking forward to it."

"How kind," said Muriam. "This is Gaius," she said turning to him now, "who has been accompanying me on my journey," she continued.

Gaius was greatly interested to meet the sole surviving male child of the Bethlehem slaughter. This young man before him looked as strong as a Lebanon cedar. He was at least six feet in height and broad across the shoulders. He was lean of build, yet clearly strong from years of hard work. Though his appearance could possibly be daunting, his bearing was gentle, his face lined with the evidence of an easy smile.

Jesus then looked at Gaius, with a gentle gaze. "It is a great pleasure to meet you, Gaius," said Jesus. "Please, come," he said leading the way to the little house.

Just as they approached, Mary opened the door to welcome them.

As they entered the little home, it was immediately apparent that all was not as it seemed. The inner walls were inlaid with the most intricate and beautiful timber work Gaius had ever seen. Though there were only three small rooms and space was at a premium, clearly that space had been used in the most practical manner.

The small stone stove was set flush with the outer wall on one side, itself forming part of the wall. To left and right was shelving to the ceiling, while the outer walls themselves had in them alcoves of space for storage, hidden behind some of the timber panelling. Gaius found it quite impossible to detect where a door was or was not, though some were revealed as Mary opened various of them to extract this or that for the entertainment of her guests.

The roof structure had been designed to provide light boxes above, that could be opened or closed by the pull of a rope, so the home itself was well lit. Each door to adjoining rooms finished perfectly to the stonework, where no timber jam could be detected. Rather the stone formed the jam and abutment perfectly.

The furniture also told of a craftsman. Every piece was constructed from olive wood, taking full advantage of the magnificent grains and textures so familiar to this medium. Gaius mused to himself that Caesar has not furnishings so fine as found in this little home of Nazareth. It was at once humble, functional and practical, while displaying especially remarkable tradesmanship in its design and finishes.

Mary had been preparing twisted bread sticks that morning, and had laid out figs and pomegranates. It was indeed the perfect time of the year to take full advantage of the trees that were laden with fruit.

Muriam had been much looking forward to the opportunity of visiting Mary and was unaware that she was chattering far more than usual, much to the delight of Gaius. He had been grateful she had met up with one so like to herself. One that she at least had some knowledge of, and that had known those that she had been so fond of.

Jesus, having seen to his mother's comfort, organised the table to provide generous access to the fare on offer to their guests. He, like Gaius, seemed to delight in Muriam forgetting herself, her beautiful innocence on display. She told them of the happenings of her life since Mary's visit so many years ago. Though the story revealed so much trauma, there was to be found no bitterness in the telling. No self-absorption or self-pity, but a simple acknowledgment of the challenges life often presents, and a trust in providence.

Absent too were the gasps of disbelief and pity from the audience of this sad tale. Muriam completed her tale with this latest trip to her current location.

"Oh, Muriam," said Mary as she took her hands in her own. "You are so blessed. How good the Most High has been to you. What wonders He has wrought in you."

This reaction from Mary puzzled Gaius, though he remained silent as the gaze of Jesus fell upon him once more. Indeed Gaius had never heard Muriam orate an overview of her life before. She had always been a very private woman when it came to her feelings, but much had changed on this journey they had embarked upon together. He had never realised until now, how much he had figured in her story over these many years since the death of Azel. Though hearing this again saddened him, he was more than a little aware that there was no trace of blame directed to himself. It was simply so. Nothing more.

"And what of you, Mary?" asked Muriam. "It appears you are yourself preparing for a trip." There were some travelling satchels beside the entry door.

"You remember Petmar's brother, Taitum?" she replied.

"Oh yes, we travelled with him as far as Nain. Gaius and he were fast friends by the time we arrived," she laughed. "I thought he would abandon me at Nain," she said smiling turning to him, "they spent so much time together."

"His only son Galum is to be wed next week in Cana. He has kindly invited us to attend."

"How wonderful. Weddings are so filled with hope and possibilities. A new Adam. A new Eve."

A short silence followed. Gaius turned to Jesus. "You are a carpenter, I see!"

Jesus stood then. "Come," he said smiling, "I will show you." They left the little house and the women, and made their way outside.

"You have questions, Gaius?" said Jesus as they made their way the short distance across the yard.

Gaius smiled to himself. This young man was very intuitive, he thought. "I was surprised your mother thought Muriam so blessed by your God, for a life so sad."

"Life is not for the faint-hearted, Gaius. Life is never sad, though sadness is an inevitable part of life, and may well prevail, but it need not. If life is lived it is dangerous, but always it is what it is. How we deal with what life presents us, is what is important. Muriam is indeed blessed. She has not allowed bitterness to rob her of the beautiful memory of the life that was, yet perhaps more importantly, the life yet to be. And there is one, Gaius," he said with a knowing smile. "Only they that are blessed learn that lesson. Come," he said as he led the way to the little work shed.

Gaius was struck by the simplicity of that which had not occurred to him, and as always, the very different view of reality often provided by the Jews he had met.

As they entered the workshop, Gaius realised it was as deceptive as the house. Hewn from the rock of the little mountain was a larger work area completely hidden from view within the little shed. It opened up in all directions and was some fifteen feet high. There was a large beam that spanned from one side to the other, and from this hung down a block and tackle with a large hook. Hanging from this was a massive piece of granite suspended just above the ground. To one side were timber tables, with various tools displayed on the wall, all easily accessible. There were various lengths of timber of different width, stacked and packed against the adjoining wall.

The other side had a number of different sized platforms, yet what caught his attention was that two of these had wheels constructed of wood. A most unusual and all but priceless tool of assistance, found here in the most unlikely of places. These were neatly stacked against one part of the wall. The rest of that side and the adjoining wall was covered with many shapes and sizes of granite and sandstone pieces. Both blocks and sheets of masonry no doubt left over from past projects. Over the table on which lay a large slab of granite, water flowed from a fissure in the wall, fed by a cistern overflowing from above. A simple straight sliver of granite placed in a groove in the granite slab, redirected the water at will, providing a simple yet effective means of controlling its flow. This area was perfect for suppressing any dust generated from the cutting of stone, while at once cleaning and enhancing the stone being cut, making it a far easier undertaking. Gaius found it a very impressive workshop, nothing like he had envisioned. In fact, he thought to himself, the same was true for every aspect of this journey he had undertaken with Muriam. It seemed to him that everything he thought was so, was in fact not so, in a most delightful way. The Jews, it seemed to him, even this young man before him, saw what he perceived as black and white, in many different hues.

There were two chairs and a small table to one side of the work bench, and wood shavings could be seen swept into a pile beside the entry. It was windy outside, and just then a gust of wind blew through the entrance to distribute the shavings over the floor from which they had recently been swept. Jesus, without the least annoyance, simply took up the rough broom and began sweeping them up once more.

"Have you lived here all your life?" Gaius asked.

"The greater portion," was the response. "When will you be returning to Jerusalem?"

"The caravan passes through this very night. We have been preparing to join it prior to leaving to visit with you. I'm afraid our time is short."

"Time is always short, Gaius. It is man alone who believes he has time, yet it is he that has least of all." Just then there was a call at the entrance.

"Rabbi?"

"Come, Simon," was the response, and entered in a man of about forty-five years, and a younger man not much more than a boy. The older was of coarse demeanour and suspicious bearing, a weather-hardened and clearly worldly man, who regarded Gaius with a suspicious gaze. The other man was the quintessential opposite, clearly a gentle soul of innocence, with a ready smile and a delightful simplicity. After greeting Jesus, he turned immediately to Gaius. "Hello," he said. "My name is John."

Gaius smiled. "Gaius," he replied.

"And this is Simon the fisherman," chimed in Jesus grinning broadly. All at once Simon felt a little silly. "Pleased to meet you," his meek reply.

"A pleasure," said Gaius who was himself quite expert at discerning men and situations. Clearly Simon was far more at ease hauling in fish with other hardened fishermen, than exercising the social graces. Gaius could deal with that. He found honest folk much more agreeable to him than the duplicitous and the haughty.

"You are a Rabbi also," said Gaius, not in the least surprised.

"Of a manner. Nothing official," replied Jesus smiling. "Simon and John are here for Galum's wedding. A little early," he said turning to them smiling, "but very welcome. And where are the rest?"

"They are coming," laughed John. Simon had found his legs once more and Gaius realised quickly how gracious Simon could be, when he was not expecting an enemy to ambush him, as they settled into an afternoon of delightful banter.

Soon after their exit, Mary had paid compliment to Muriam with regard Gaius. "It was a very fine thing he has done to accompany you on this journey, to see to your safety. He must care for you a great deal."

"He has been generous and kind to me since the accident, truly a gentleman in every respect. He has sought out Dysmas for years without complaint. Truly he and Azel would have been friends, good friends. He is a very good man, and I know that the accident still pains him grievously."

"And what of you?" asked Mary with the gentlest smile.

Muriam looked up at her now. "Does it show?" she asked a little apprehensively.

"Love tends to be infectious," replied Mary smiling. "If we are to fear love Muriam, what is it we would not fear? And yet you are afraid."

"I thought I was alone and Dysmas dead. I was just getting used to that understanding when I met him in Jerusalem. Now I don't know."

"You think yourself a traitor to Azel because of your feelings for Gaius. Who would understand? Probably few indeed, but is that of any consequence? Is not the purity of love its own reward?"

These words put Muriam much at ease, and much more passed between these good women, until Muriam realised the sun was starting to descend in the sky.

"Oh, Mary," she said, "we must be leaving, time has flown past so quickly." Rising they headed into the yard. Mary and Muriam appeared just as Jesus was exiting the workshop with the other men.

"Simon, John, you are already here, how wonderful," said Mary.

"Time has flown," Muriam said to Gaius. "We must be on our way if we are to meet the caravan by dusk."

She turned to Mary then and hugged her. "I can't tell you how good it was to see you once more."

"Have a safe trip back," replied Mary.

Gaius turned to Jesus. "It has been a great pleasure meeting you," he said. "And you, Simon, and you too, John. I hope we meet again."

"We will certainly meet again," replied Jesus with a smile, and placing a hand on the head of both Gaius and Muriam continued. "The Lord bless you and keep you. The Lord make His face to shine upon you. The Lord lift up His countenance upon you, and give you peace."

Though this was an alien custom to Gaius, it seemed to him just at this moment, the most natural act imaginable.

Soon they were on their way, and Gaius felt as if a great weight had lifted from his shoulders. He found himself considering the comments of Jesus in light of the advice of Taitum. There is a future, he thought to himself, an unwritten one of countless possibilities, and time is indeed short. The journey home would be one of great contemplation.

"What are you thinking?" Muriam asked, disturbing his thoughts.

"Oh, just about life, the future and what it might bring," he said with a mischievous smile.

"You should do that more often."

"What?"

"Smile. It suits you," she said.

They continued in silence for a few minutes, until she broke the silence once more.

"It must have been hard for you hearing me babble on earlier. I need you to know that I have never blamed you, Gaius, nor has it occurred to me to do so. Perhaps it is past time that you stop blaming yourself. It was an accident decreed by providence, for reasons known to providence."

Gaius was touched by Muriam's candour. "I know, Muriam, and thank you. I confess that it has stayed with me all these years, but something about this journey has been healing, though I am unsure what exactly."

"Perhaps you had the chance to leave your duties behind for the first time in many years."

"Perhaps. A little over three years and I can leave my duties behind forever." He looked at her now. "For the first time in my career, Muriam, I truly hope that day comes quickly."

They walked for some distance in silence, both pondering their thoughts until they again found themselves stopped atop the hill overlooking the homestead of Petmar and the valleys beyond.

Gaius was the first to speak. It took him some minutes to gather the courage, but at last he said, very gently still looking over the valley, "What of us, Muriam?"

She turned to face him now a little surprised and yet grateful, as his nervous gaze fell upon her.

"I don't know, Gaius. I confess nothing has turned out as might have been expected. Who could have imagined that you and I would…" and her gaze fell again upon the valley below as she found herself realising the truth was exposed on both sides.

Silence fell once more, and Gaius was greatly relieved that their friendship had survived the suggestion, with even an admission of reciprocation. More courage was needed, and a little boldness he concluded.

Finally he said, "I am in love with you, Muriam, and have been for some years. I have never and would never impose upon you, so I have been and remain content simply to admire you from afar, but I have not been honest with you in this regard. I thought it just that I told you the truth."

"Oh, Gaius. Goodness me, I myself for some time misled myself, let alone you. Who could have imagined?"

"I have agonised over it for so long," he said.

"Me, too. What are we to do?" she said smiling at him now. Her hand over her mouth as a tear escaped her and glistened down her cheek. Her eyes were dancing with joy.

Gaius took her in his arms and held her for the first time. He had ached for so many years just to hold her hand in his, and now here she was in his arms at last. He could barely believe it as she lay her head on his chest. Truly a dream that had come to pass.

As they parted, he held her hands in his own at last.

"The answer to your question is I don't know," said Muriam, "Do you?"

"No. I know what I would like, but there are so many complications."

"I know, I know," she said nodding and smiling as another tear escaped.

"Well, what we must do is get moving," he said, "or we will not be going with this caravan."

"Of course," she said smiling, and they made their way down to the house.

Soon they had joined their conveyance and both were heavily burdened by their thoughts through the night that followed. Jelrah could almost feel the atmosphere, yet was unsure whether to be joyful or sad.

A few days later found Gaius sitting atop a boulder as the sun was setting, just thinking. Muriam climbed the little incline to join him, and they both just took it in.

Finally Muriam broke the silence. "I can't let go just yet, Gaius. I'm sorry."

"You have nothing to be sorry about, Muriam. I understand. Does that mean a change of how things are now?"

"What do you want?" she asked.

"Muriam, no matter how small a piece of you I can get, I'll take it and be grateful. It is enough to have you near, I would very much like you to stay as long as you will."

"I would like that also." And so it was that love would take its place in the scheme of life.

Back in the Fray

There had been much discussion between Gestus, Dysmas and Barabbas about a plan Dysmas and Gestus had been hatching with regard a raid on a Roman patrol known to carry the payroll for Jerusalem. They changed the route every time now, given the success of previous raids, but Gestus had secured information that they had six routes in all, and used them indiscriminately. He had further information that the Romans had not used the Magdala route so far this year. This route took the Roman cargo twenty miles south of Magdala, and Gestus was sure that it would be the preferred route.

Barabbas had been concerned that there was no ravine to provide cover, but Dysmas as always had a plan. First, the Romans would not be expecting an attack in open country where they clearly had the advantage. "This," they both assured Barabbas, "would be a great advantage," as Dysmas laid out their plan.

"Visibility in the area stretches for miles. This will provide for us the element of surprise," he said. "Their confidence will be their undoing. By whatever route, the payroll will be delivered in two weeks. That gives us time to get to our location and make the preparations necessary."

"And what if they take another route?" Barabbas had asked.

"Well then, our preparations will be in place for the time they do take the route, and we will use them then."

It was hard to argue with the logic. So it was agreed. Preparations were made immediately to gather the men and equipment, and within twenty-four hours they were under way.

When they arrived at the location, Barabbas was very uncomfortable. As he stood on the road that ran through this open plain he could see in all directions for miles. There was simply nowhere to hide or take any cover whatever. If this goes wrong, he thought, there will be no escape.

The plan was genius in its simplicity and daring. Yokim and Melech were dispatched to a mountain in the distance. The patrol would be coming from that direction. They were to construct a fire, a massive fire that could be seen from the point of attack. Should the Roman patrol be coming in this direction, they were to wait until it was well past their position before lighting the fire. This would be the signal that the plan would be executed.

Meanwhile, the rest started digging holes twelve feet from the road's edge, in a line that would be the best guess of the length of the patrol. Each hole would be big enough for a man to comfortably lie in and be hidden. Dysmas had ordered the hessian he had brought be cut into lengths no more than twelve feet each. The hessian itself was six feet wide.

"Lay the hessian out, even over the place where you will be digging," he had said, "Then roll back six feet of it and dig your hole, throwing the dirt on what is left of the hessian. Cover it with the dirt. It matters not that there will be mounds formed. With so many banking together it will look like a small rise in the terrain, nothing more, but it will serve us well later. Then lay the six feet of hessian that you rolled up back over the mound." The men had seen enough planning from Dysmas and Gestus to know there was a reason, and a good one at that. So they set about their task.

The archers would have the horses, and after the initial attack, which was entirely a distraction, they were to circle around, leading the cavalry that would surely be following them back to the point of the initial attack. If all went to plan there would be no Roman left alive by the time they arrived, leaving the cavalry alone and outnumbered.

To test the plan, Gestus had two men lay in their holes. Pulling the hessian over them and placing sticks across above them, he laid more hessian over the sticks and cast dirt and rocks over that. Both were entirely hidden. He challenged Barabbas to find them from the road atop his horse. Search as he might, he admitted at last that he could not see them at all. "My word," he said, "this just might work."

"It will work, Barabbas," cried Gestus with a grin. "It will work!"

Two days passed after their arrival, and all was in readiness. Dysmas had gone over the plan with the men many times, and everyone well knew his task. Dysmas would lead the archers, while Gestus at one end of the line and Barabbas at the other, would lead the swordsmen.

At the very crack of dawn of the fourth day, a fire could be seen burning in the distance atop the mountain, and all knew at once that the hunch had come to pass.

"They will be here by mid-afternoon," said Gestus. "It is time we prepared." There were thirty-one men to be concealed beside the road, and eight archers on horseback that would ride in from the other side of the road, drawing all attention in that direction. It would take a few moments only for the Romans to assess that there was no threat from anywhere else, turning their backs on the real threat buried just a few feet away.

The trigger would be the commotion. "Count to sixty," Dysmas said, "and then exit your hiding places as quickly and quietly as possible. The cavalry will set out in pursuit of the archers, believing it a foolish attempt to ambush them, while the rest will no doubt be cheering them on, all the while unaware of the danger. Surprise is crucial," he said. "Make sure you have enough water to sustain you for the day, and try and get some sleep. You will be well-rested and fresh for this fight. They have travelled all day."

"We will prevail," said Gestus.

"It's a great plan, Gestus," mused Dysmas.

"It's brilliant," said Barabbas. "Who would suspect?"

Dysmas called for a rider, "I need you to ride toward the Roman patrol at a walk for twenty minutes. Then mark the place with a landmark that we can see clearly. We will ride at a walk for twenty minutes in our direction. We will know then when to ride on the patrol so that they stop where we want them to. We cannot have them stopping either long or short. When they pass that landmark, we will have to gauge well our ride." And so it was done.

"We will assess their strength before we ride in," he told the men. "If they are too great in number we will not attack, and you can remain hidden until they pass. So if we do attack, you will know that the numbers are favourable."

All the men were concealed over the next two hours, and the entire area brushed with branches. At a casual glance, it was impossible to spot any activity had taken place in the area at all. Tired soldiers at an unannounced spot on the journey would pay little or no attention to their immediate surroundings when they could see for miles in all directions. This, Barabbas concluded as he lay quietly in his hiding place, was probably the most ingenious plan Dysmas had ever concocted.

The day passed slowly, and many of the men found themselves dozing from time to time as the hours passed. It was a pleasant day and their places of stealth were comfortable and conducive to a short nap. At about the ninth hour, they sensed what seemed far in the distance, a tiny rumbling sound, perhaps more felt than heard. As each of the men became aware of this vibration, they began straining their ears to hear what would be their target.

As the minutes passed, the vibration became greater, yet the noise began to eclipse it to the senses. To those beneath the ground unsighted, it sounded as if it were a legion of Roman soldiers, and many began to grow uneasy.

Dysmas had lined himself with the backdrop of a distant mountain with regard the place of the mark, as it was not visible to him from this distance. Still, he had a pretty good idea of its exact location by triangulating his position with a more prominent landmark. He became intense now, as he spied the Roman column passing its position.

He was trying to accurately calculate the difference in distance travelled by the column's slow walking pace and what must be an attack pace that he would have to adopt.

The column appeared to him from this distance to be no more than thirty men, and nine mounted cavalry. Though a formidable task, with the surprise that was in their favour, he believed it by no means an overly difficult one. Timing was imperative.

Gathering his men, he began his own walking pace to the position of his comrades keeping a watchful eye on the column's position. "They will be watching us as we approach," he told the men. "They should stop pretty much immediately when we break into a gallop straight at them firing arrows, so we need to wait until they are where we want them before we start our run. Wait for my signal."

So the game of cat and mouse had begun in earnest, and tensions had risen the closer the moment approached until, all at once, a cry was heard from Dysmas to attack.

He had deliberately ensured his voice carried across the dry vastness as they broke into a gallop directly at the column before them, and as expected the column stopped immediately, exactly where they were supposed to.

The Romans on foot climbed the wagons to obtain a better view, greatly enthused that there was a break in the monotony. The cavalry set off at once to intercept this seemingly insignificant force approaching, much to the delight of those left behind, who were themselves whooping and laughing at the prospect of the sport before them. Not a single one noticed, a few moments later, the men appearing behind them, literally from beneath the ground. The first many of them knew of their folly, was the cold blade of their attacker, as it snuffed out their lives.

Only a few had time to draw their sword, but it was all too little, far too late. They were overcome in moments, with little in the manner of a fight. The entire affair had been eerily quiet. The plan had in fact worked far better than anyone could have imagined.

The cavalry, still unaware of the outcome behind them, continued to pursue the horsemen that had engaged them, who were themselves wielding their horses to keep their attention. Meanwhile the rest of the men were dressing themselves in the Roman uniforms of the dead, while the bodies of these were being dragged into the holes that had concealed their assailants. With helmets and chest plates in place, at a glance, all seemed as it should be. It was hoped the returning cavalry would be too concerned with their quarry to notice anything was amiss until they were in the midst of their enemy.

Dysmas and his men had kept the Romans busy for almost ten minutes by the time they headed directly for the position of the column. Aside from a single arrow that had struck the flank of one of the Roman horses, more by luck than aim, little damage had been done to either side.

As they neared the position of the column, Valens, the leader of the cavalry unit, was dismayed. "What are they doing?" he called to the rider beside him who was equally puzzled. "Making our job easy," he replied shrugging.

Valens had by now convinced himself that this band of riders were mad. Nothing they did made any sense, from the initial attack on the column to this tactic which could only be described as suicide. The other men too were puzzling as to the reason for the entire attack.

 As Dysmas approached the cheering 'Romans', he turned his horse to ride parallel with the column and rode at a gallop past the 'Romans' position. Valens and his men followed immediately. Valens wondered now why the archers had not fired on his quarry as they passed. This thought was all he had time for, before the rider beside him fell from his horse, an arrow through his heart. All too late he realised some deception had tricked him. Two others fell immediately after the first, throwing the unit into disarray. They broke off the chase looking in all directions wondering what was happening.

Dysmas had turned with his men and were now engaging those left, given their numbers were now even. One cavalryman headed to the column hoping to find some protection, having not yet understood that this was the danger, and was killed as he approached. The rest then knew that somehow their enemy had supplanted their companions. This knowledge provided little more than further confusion, leaving them at a loss as to what to do. Even their Roman training had not prepared them for this. They were in complete disorder, and were being now picked off one by one with ease.

Valens was the only one to have the presence of mind to flee, and set out in a vain effort to escape. Even as he was riding, he was wondering how he would explain to his superiors what had happened, when he himself had no idea. This would not be necessary however, as Dysmas had his measure, and ran him to ground before he had covered a mile's distance.

The entire operation was a resounding success. As Dysmas returned with Valens slumped over his horse, there was much cheering. What was left of the cavalry lay dead around the wagons, or were being dragged into the makeshift graves with their fellow Romans.

"I would never have believed it," said Barabbas, taking hold of the reins, as Dysmas reined his horse in. "Oh, I wish Eleazar had seen this; he wouldn't have believed it either." Barabbas could hardly contain himself. "That was the most amazing thing I have ever seen."

"It really was a great plan," chimed in Gestus, as Dysmas smiled for the first time.

"Who would have thought, in the middle of totally flat country, we could ambush a Roman column so easily?" continued Barabbas. "This calls for a celebration. We will feast tonight."

"There is much to do before we feast," replied Dysmas, becoming serious once more. "The job is not yet finished. Let's finish it properly, then we can talk about celebrations."

"Alright," replied Barabbas laughing. "You are right, of course." Turning to the men who were unloading and sorting cargo, he said, "Burn the bodies."

"No," said Dysmas, "not this time. Take their armour and uniforms, they will be useful. Put the bodies in the holes, they are graves now." When all the Romans were entirely in the holes, he told the men to find the edges of the hessian they had covered and start pulling it back.

With very little effort they found the dirt simply pouring back into the hole from which it had been dug, nearly covering its contents. There was little digging required as the bodies simply disappeared under the fresh sand and dirt. "Cut the hessian hanging out of the grave and fold it up; we'll take that with us. Now cover it all with dirt."

Yokim and Melech had returned with the closed wagon they had been told to retrieve, and the men immediately started loading everything into it. This raid had provided a literal gold mine of weapons and funds. The uniforms alone would be worth their weight in gold at some point.

"Aren't you worried that the graves will be found?" asked Barabbas.

"Not this time," was the confident answer. "The Romans will send out a search party within a week. The bodies won't start noticeably decomposing for a couple of months. They will ride past this place no wiser than when they rode past it just now. It is unlikely those here will ever be found. So long as we burn everything else somewhere else, the Romans will discover nothing more than an empty road. It will not even occur to them to look here. After all," he laughed, "who in their right mind would try to ambush them here?"

Barabbas smiled and shook his head. "I have to give it to you," he said. "My word, who would have thought?"

Everything surplus to their needs was loaded into the Roman wagons, as Harcrum and Jelek were dispatched to return to the mountain from which they had come, to burn it there. "When the Romans find it, they will pull their hair out trying to figure how the column was ambushed," laughed Gestus. "I would love to be there to watch!"

Nathan and Solane were given the task of transporting the wagon containing the reward of their endeavours back to the cave, and were underway as soon as loading was complete.

"They should be arriving," said Barabbas with a hardy grin, "about the time the Romans will send out a search party. That being said, we cannot all go into Magdala. It would be too suspicious, thirty-odd men riding into a town. We will split up into groups of seven or eight. Our group will be going to Magdala. Each group can decide where they want to go, and we will all meet back in the cave a week from now." So it was agreed.

Three groups headed off almost immediately, while Dysmas again surveyed the site. "We need to brush it again," he said. "The wind will do its job, but it just doesn't look quite right."

"Alright," said Barabbas sighing, "but quickly now. The faster we get done here, the faster we get to Magdala." A final brush and they were underway.

Gestus couldn't remember a time when he had seen Barabbas so buoyed.

They reached Magdala six hours later, and many skins of wine were purchased. There would be much celebration this night as Barabbas had announced.

Dysmas Meets Magdalene

"What are you going to do, you coward?" screamed Eden. "What do you think we pay you for, can you not hear her screaming? Get in there and stop this animal from killing her."

As she finished speaking, Kalil and Rachel arrived.

"So this is what we can expect for what we pay you. If you don't get in there right now there will be no more," said Rachel.

"Damn," he said as he started for the door.

Kiman was a big man, though by nature a quiet soul, yet few would guess it. Truly he was a fearsome sight, and up until now there had been little trouble owing more to perception than reality.

Kiman had been approached some two years before this night by five women with an unusual proposal. Rachel had known Kiman for three years already, and had come to realise during that time the true nature of the man, not withstanding the fact that his appearance was overwhelming by any standard.

He was approaching seven feet in height with a larger physical build thrown into the bargain, though in truth this made him a little clumsy. As a young man he had been gored by the horn of a bull he had taken for granted once too often. As a result, a massive scar dominated the entire left side of his face. He had been most fortunate to survive his injuries which upon healing, had greatly contributed to the instant respect he commanded from those around him.

It had been Rachel's idea to approach Kiman to become the guard of this ill-reputed group of women. She had invited Kiman to her home for the evening meal. Kiman had been most surprised, it is true, though completely flabbergasted when upon his arrival, four other women were seated at table. After initial introductions over a skin of wine, they got right to the point.

"Many is the time," Eden had explained to Kiman, "we have been beaten and abused. It doesn't happen often, but far too often. We are publicly frowned upon and denounced by those who privately avail themselves of our services. Perhaps it is their guilt and self-loathing, or perhaps because we are alone and considered helpless, maybe both. Whatever it is, they seem to feel it their right to bash and abuse us, as if money makes it alright."

"We believe we have a solution to our dilemma," they had told Kiman. "It is our intention to join together in a single location so that we are all living together. To this end we have already rented a large house. We want to pay you to live there, to be permanently present. No one would dare bash us knowing they would have to deal with you," Mary had said.

Kiman was completely taken aback. He had had no idea this was the purpose of the invitation. He was very hesitant. "I don't know," he had started when Eden cried. "We will pay you very well. You would have the best job in the village. Think of it, we would pay you to stand around and look dangerous, room and board included."

After further discussion, the proposal had seemed ever more attractive, and finally Kiman had agreed.

Arrangements had been made the next morning to move Kiman to his new abode. He had been allotted the first room, right of the only entry door. None could enter or leave but by the good grace of Kiman the protector.

In truth it had been a remarkably uneventful and profitable couple of years for Kiman and the women. Indeed all involved were more than happy with the arrangement. The intuition of the women with regard to Kiman had itself been found to be most accurate. Kiman was not only greatly feared by their seemingly endless line of customers, but soon demonstrated himself to be a most caring and decent man.

On the very rare occasion now when a client had become unruly, it was enough that Kiman show himself to silence the reprobate. There was occasionally an uneasy moment when a drunken fool would consider taking offence to the clearly threatening presence of Kiman, but it was inevitably a momentary lapse of judgement, and the problem was quickly solved via a sheepish exit.

When Mary had become ill with the fever while the other four women were with the caravan, it had been Kiman who had nursed her back to health from delirium. He had found her late one morning after becoming concerned that he had not seen her up. Having no response to his knocking, he entered her room to find her in the grip of the fever. He was aware that four people in the village had died in the past week alone, yet abandoning her never entered his mind. In no time he had carted water from the well to the house. After making her comfortable, he had spent hours sponging her with a soft cloth in the hope of getting her temperature to drop. He had seen to it that a local woman, the nearest thing to a doctor the village had, called on her every few hours, while he himself had never left her side.

When she had finally come to her senses, she realised what he had done, and the woman he had engaged to bring herbs and medicines was glowing in her praise for him.

Mary was so touched, when she was fully recuperated, that she had invited him to her room.

Tears welled in Kiman's eyes as he ran his hand over her beautiful hair and kissed her on the forehead. He turned then and left for the village, leaving a very surprised and confused Mary staring after him.

Some hours later upon his return, she had knocked at his door. "Come in," he said.

"I hope I didn't offend you, Kiman, I just wanted you to know how grateful I am to you. I would not have survived had it not been for you," she said. "Quite apart from the fact that you could have contracted it yourself."

"You didn't offend me, Mary, I realise that is your way. I didn't help you for any other reason but that you are so worthy."

Mary was stunned.

"You are the most beautiful woman I have ever seen in my lifetime, and any man would be tempted. Yet since I have been here with you, I have come to see the beauty on the outside is as nothing to what is on the inside. You are beautiful in ways I have never understood before. I want to be more than a brute, and I have come to love you women for who you are, not what you are or what I can get from you."

Tears welled in Mary's eyes and she knelt down at his feet sobbing in his lap for almost an hour. He was at a total loss to understand what he had said to hurt her so, but did not want to make things worse.

Finally, Mary looked up at him and said, "Thank you, Kiman. I feel like a woman again for the first time in many years."

When the other women had returned, they came to hear of all of the events in their absence. A real bond had been forged between this giant of a man and these delicate women, whose real beauty was treasured by that one least expected.

One night at dinner Kiman had admitted to them his fear of conflict, not withstanding his fearsome demeanour. "In truth," he had said, "I am a coward. Perhaps it is best if you engaged another."

"But," they had said, "look at the history; these men just see you and they are too afraid to even challenge you. And what if we did seek another? How would we know that he himself wouldn't harm us? Would we be able to trust him as we do you? No, indeed," they had assured him, "we have the right man for the job!"

From then to now it had been so, but Kiman had had a very bad feeling about this man now with Mary, and had tried to convince her to send him on his way, to no avail.

Now these women whom he had grown to admire and love were screaming at him to do something. He feared the time of bluff was at an end.

He kicked the door with all his might, smashing it from its hinges, sending the splintered mass across the room. The scene he beheld infuriated him. Mary was on the floor on her knees, her beautiful hair held in the fist of this brute before him, his other fist pulled back ready to strike again. There was blood on the wall and the floor. Mary's face was a mess and severe bruising was already evident.

"Get out," he screamed at Kiman.

Kiman lunged at him, but he threw Mary into his path by her hair, tearing out a mass of bloody hair, forcing Kiman to catch her in order to stay on his feet. Kiman turned to push Mary toward the other women at the door. As he was turning back to face the brute, he felt the cold steel of a blade pierce his side. It passed through his stomach, thrusting down and through his kidney. Kiman swung his right elbow with all his might catching the man on the side of his head, flinging him across the room, head first into the wall. Still clinging to his sword, the man collapsed to the floor in a daze trying desperately to gather himself, blindly flaying his sword about through the air to ward off another attack.

Kiman collapsed to one knee, bleeding profusely.

The women had half-dragged, half-carried Mary to another room in the hope of hiding her from this animal who had attacked her so brutally. They were sure Kiman would prevail.

Kiman struggled to get to his feet, but his head was spinning. He located the other and made for him with what strength he could muster.

By now the man had gathered himself and lunged once more at the wounded Kiman, finding his mark again, this time to the right lower chest piercing his lung.

Kiman instinctively grabbed him by the hair, and with every ounce of strength left in him, smashed his head so violently into the wall he dislodged two bricks, knocking the man senseless, while tearing a great gash down the right side of his face.

Kiman fell back then to the corner of the bed and rolled off onto the floor gasping for air, for his lung was filling with his blood.

Eden ran in then and surveyed the scene. She ran to Kiman and lifted his head to her lap. His eyes were already starting to glaze over.

"Mary?" he asked. "Is she?" and he coughed up blood.

"She's safe Kiman, she's alright," said Eden.

"Good," he sighed, and his body was limp as he stared up at Eden with lifeless eyes.

Just then a crash was heard from the other side of the room as the other man dragged himself to his feet, covered in blood and moving on instinct more than deliberation.

He blindly ran through the door still clutching his sword. His senses in disarray from concussion were deceiving him. His sight all but darkened by the blood pouring into his eyes from his wounds, he slammed into the walls of the small hall many times before he finally found the entry door. Pulling it open at last, he staggered into the darkened lane, making his way as best he could toward the noise of the crowd where he had left his companions. Shortly he burst forth into their midst and immediately collapsed unconscious.

Dysmas leapt to his feet, "Barabbas!" he cried, just as Gestus broke through the crowd with new skins of wine, ready for more amusement. "What happened, Dysmas?" he yelled. "Who did this?"

"I don't know, Gestus, he has just arrived in this state."

"Where has he been?" asked another.

"I don't know," said Dysmas. "Kovel, Aziel come with me. Gestus, get Barabbas to safety while we get to the bottom of this."

Dysmas ran to the mouth of the only lane Barabbas could have exited from. Sword drawn, flanked by Kovel and Aziel, he stopped at the mouth of the lane to allow his eyes to adjust. He could hear in the distance women wailing and much commotion. "Come," he said at last entering the lane.

There was nothing to be found in the lane, yet screams and wailing could be heard from the house he knew well to be of ill repute.

Barabbas and Gestus had sought him to enter on a previous occasion, but he had refused.

He noted the entrance door was open and unattended. "What has happened here?" he said to his companions.

Slowly he started up the stairs, his sword drawn only to realise that none were guarding the door, even from within.

He entered then, wary of any movements as he made his way to the commotion ahead.

Finally, he was at the door where three women were crying in utter despair for the lifeless body they cradled in their arms.

"What has happened here?" demanded Dysmas.

"A butcher, an animal was here," cried Eden. "When Kiman tried to save Mary, he murdered him."

"Lies," yelled Dysmas.

"Well, go down the hall and see the lie," screamed Eden, gesturing to the body of Kiman. "Does this look like a lie?"

Dysmas looked up the hall and saw the last door was illuminated by a light. As he drew closer, he could hear heart-wrenching sobbing. He looked in then and immediately pulled back. "Kovel, Aziel," he commanded. "Go back and tell the men we have found the man who attacked Barabbas, and he is dead."

"But," they began.

"Go now," he demanded.

When they had gone, he entered the room to find one woman unconscious, bleeding and brutally wounded, wrapped in some linen, while another was kneeling beside her battered body sobbing, her head buried in the bed clothes.

He was overcome at the state of the unconscious woman. Even in her current state her great beauty was still evident. He sheathed his sword then and knelt down beside the sobbing woman, putting his arm around her shoulder. She turned then and threw her arms around his neck crying bitterly.

He was taken aback but could do little more than comfort her.

When she had regained her composure, he asked her gently, "Tell me what has happened here."

She looked at him at last and gave him an account of the evening's events. While she was speaking, he was examining the battered body of Mary, and he became deeply disturbed. How could Barabbas have done this, he asked himself. He could hardly believe a man could do such a thing.

Just then Gestus burst through the door, "Where is the body?" he yelled.

Dysmas stood then and squared up to Gestus, "That is not your concern. He is dead. Leave."

Gestus hesitated.

"Now!"

Gestus had seen that look before and knew well not to push his luck. Without a word he turned on his heel and left.

When Dysmas turned around, the woman on the bed had regained conciousness and was surveying him through swollen eyes.

"I am Rachel, and this is Mary. Thank you."

"My name is Dysmas. I am deeply sorry for what has happened here tonight, really I am," he said, still shocked.

"Why would you be sorry?" asked Rachel, curiously.

"I just am." He was clearly troubled. He opened Rachel's hand and placed in it two coins. "This will help with the burial," he said. He nodded to Mary and left them.

Dysmas walked down the narrow hall in turmoil as he made his way back to Barabbas, yet could not bring himself to rejoin the others. He returned to the house then, securing the door for the women inside, and soon after made for the well on the opposite side of the small town to douse his head and think.

How could Barabbas have done this, he kept asking himself. What has he become? Dysmas had always been aware that Barabbas hated the Romans even more than he. There was a viciousness about this hatred that had always troubled Dysmas, but up until now he had considered it just a zeal for Israel. He had realised long ago that Barabbas did not seek just to kill Romans; he wanted to watch them suffer. He had bloodlust in his eyes in battle.

"Is it possible that I too may become the same, should I continue on my current path?" asked Dysmas of the night.

Hours passed and, watching the sun rise, Dysmas found himself as troubled as when he had first sat down.

"Hiding from something?" he heard from behind and leapt to his feet. Rachel was holding a water jar and looking very much the worse for wear after her night of crying. "Who are you, really?" she asked.

"I am Dysmas, I told you."

"You know what I mean," she said. "We know now of Barabbas. We had only heard of him until last night, but we know the truth of him now."

He lowered his eyes then, "I am his second," he said as he looked up at her now with tears in his eyes.

She filled her jar and placed it on the well's edge. "It is a sad thing to be a second to one such as that. I know men, Dysmas," she continued as she placed her hand on his forearm. "Do not allow yourself to become like that," and she swept up her jar and started to return home.

Dysmas watched her go without a word and stared after her long after she had left.

"Dysmas at last," he heard now, and he turned to see Gestus running toward him.

"You had us all worried, where have you been?"

"I have been here," replied Dysmas. "Just here."

"What's wrong?" asked Gestus.

"Nothing," Dysmas replied.

"Dysmas, we have been friends since we were children. What's wrong?"

"I cannot get over the brutality of Barabbas against a helpless woman. It troubles me greatly. It angers me."

"Dysmas, it was a whore, are you going to be in disarray over a whore?"

"It was another human being, Gestus, a most vulnerable and fragile one, quite apart from the fact that she too is a Jew. Remember, they're the ones we are apparently fighting for. Are we to save them from the Romans so that we can kill them ourselves?"

Gestus was silent then; he knew Dysmas was right.

"How is Barabbas?" asked Dysmas.

"He is in a bad way. There will be no raids for some time. It will be a week at least before he is able to get up, I expect."

"Come with me," said Dysmas rising.

They made their way back to the camp site and found Barabbas still unconscious.

Dysmas gave Kovel the order to return Barabbas to the cave until he was strong enough to walk. "The rest of you go with them."

"Where are you going?" Kovel asked.

"I am going to Jericho."

"I'm coming with you," said Gestus. "Just you and me like old times."

"Alright," said Dysmas, still very troubled. They helped the others get on their way, and then headed in the opposite direction.

The next couple of days were days of turmoil for Dysmas. He was deeply absorbed in thought, and Gestus very much worried about him. He had never seen him like this before. He was normally the light-hearted one of the group. There was clearly much on his mind, and he was struggling with a decision of great importance.

Destiny Calls

"**D**ysmas! Dysmas!"

"Who's that calling, Gestus?"

"I don't know, I can't see, there's too many people."

"Dysmas!" he heard again, as Thomas finally breached the marketplace crowd.

"Oh, it's Thomas, I haven't seen you in an age," said Dysmas, hugging his old friend.

"Where have you been hiding yourself?"

"Well, for a long time I was at the Jordan river with the Baptist."

"He exists?"

"Oh, yes, he most certainly exists."

"You of all people, with the Baptist! I hear he's mad!"

"Well, you hear wrong, he's amazing."

"What happened then, you've left him have you?"

"Oh, it's a long story."

"Great! Gestus and I have all afternoon, we were just discussing how we were going to fill it and providence has sent you to us. Come; we eat, you tell us of your travels, we laugh... It'll be like old times."

Soon they were buying grapes and pomegranates at one of the stalls. Dysmas was in fine form bartering.

"I see you still get the best prices," remarked Thomas with a knowing grin.

"Best prices?" returned Gestus. "He's all but a thief," and they all laughed.

Soon they were beneath an olive tree joking about old times.

"Alright," said Dysmas at last. "It must be three years since I've seen you, Thomas; let's have the story. How did a wayward rebel like you get interested in a religious outcast like the Baptist?"

Thomas became serious now and his eyes softened as he stared off and smiled to himself, remembering how it all had come to pass. "Remember," he said at last, "how as children we spoke always of the coming of the Messiah? What he would be like?"

"Of course, it took up a lot of our time."

"Well, when I moved to Bethany it took up all of mine."

"Really? Sounds boring," said Gestus.

"Oh, it was anything but boring."

Dysmas thought to himself how strange this old friend of his appeared to him. He and Gestus were poking fun at him and his great prophet, with not so much as a terse reply. The Thomas he knew would have long past lost his temper. He became most interested in this story to be told.

"It started on a very hot day, and I was sitting under a tree not unlike this one, when I heard coming toward me a crowd. Above the din was a single voice shouting about repentance and penance, and I scoffed to myself, here comes another one," and he laughed to himself as if to chide himself. "Just another one he was not! He was fearless, really fearless. The Pharisees and scribes were well within earshot as he was pointing out their sins. He denounced even Herod and Herodious that all might hear. I had up to this point not even heard of him and yet here he was.

"He was as hard and rough a man as I have ever seen, yet there was something about him that just drew me to him. So much of what he was saying, Dysmas, was not unlike what we used to talk of, and it still made a lot of sense.

"One scribe asked him a question with so much of the puffed up pride we have come to expect, yet he simply answered bluntly. He pointed out not only where he was wrong but his evil intent in asking the question in the first place. The scribe went away without another word. None could best him, yet he was not proud or haughty. His answers were simple and easy to understand, his gentleness with those who had nothing… Well, you could touch it. You could feel it. I know how strange that might sound but it is true.

"I found myself walking with the crowd just listening to his words and being astounded by his courage and simplicity. He feared nothing and no one. It is God and God alone that we should fear, not man, he said. We should have no fear of God at all if we are His. He taught us all as we walked and I hung on every word. What manner of man is this? I found myself asking. Nothing was too much. His patience seemed endless for those with open hearts, yet none was granted to the proud and the haughty. The more they esteemed themselves, the less interested he was in them."

Dysmas and Gestus were by now engrossed in this strange tale.

"We came to the Jordan where he waded to the middle and sought the people to come to be baptised, so they did, in their hundreds, Dysmas. Many were crying and beating their breasts, such was the sorrow they had for their sins, but he took them gently one by one and encouraged them. 'Be not afraid, but repent,' he said, 'and receive the baptism of water, the gift that the Most High God provides for you as a foretaste of what is to come.'

"There were three Pharisees there who had been watching, and they started to enter the water, but he denounced them even as they were pushing past those who had been waiting their turn. 'You!' he cried out, 'You think you can escape the punishment that is your right, go, do the penance required for your sins. Be humbled for the evil that you claim you have eluded. The dead have no place among the living.'

"'Who do you claim to be with such insults,' they replied.

"'I am one crying in the wilderness, make straight the path, level the mountains, prepare the way for the Lord.'

"'So you're the Messiah,' they said?

"'I am not,' he said, 'but there is one who stands among you whom you know not, for blinded are you by your pride, and I am not fit to loose the strap of His sandal. He has in His hand His winnowing tool, slash He will the darnel and wheat together. The wheat will be gathered while the darnel yet cast to the fire. Repent, you, and do not think you can escape the wrath upon you with outward signs. Purify your hearts with penance before you claim place with those that have.'"

"You're joking," said Dysmas. "What did they do?"

"They were furious and ground their teeth at him, but he gave them no more of his time and turned his back to them and went on baptising as they left. There was not much else they could do even with their guards. The people would have rioted, I think, had they seized him.

"As the sun was going down many of the people who had been baptised started to disperse and return to their homes, and there were but a few left. He had now been in the water for many hours, and I was overcome with the desire to receive his baptism, so I waded to him with tears in my eyes. He looked into my eyes and seemed to see to a place beyond me, like he was looking right through me. He baptised me. Then, when I had come up from the water, he asked me where I lived. When I told him, he replied, 'No longer, in a short time I will be finished here, wait for me on the bank, I would speak with you.'"

"Just like that?" said Gestus. "Why pick you from so many?"

"I still do not know," he replied very pensively. "There was another also he called, Andrew. When he came up from the river he motioned us to follow him. Without a sound or question we did. He took us up into the foothills where we found a fire with bread on it and some food. We looked and looked but saw no one. 'Eat,' he said. I have to tell you I was starving so I did not have to be encouraged, but I noted that he did not eat. He wrapped a makeshift blanket about himself, laid down and slept. To be honest, it was only then that I realised how exhausting the day had been, and as soon as our meagre meal was over, we both slept also."

"You weren't worried at all that this wild man might hurt you in any way while you slept?"

"No, I have never in my life felt so at peace, so safe. I slept like a baby. The next morning, just as the first light was at the horizon, I woke, and woke Andrew when I could not see the Baptist anywhere. I looked around but he was gone. I stood up and could not make too much out; however, as the sun rose higher the light soon spilled over the land and I saw him then, further up the hill sitting beside a boulder, his head bent. It seemed he was talking with himself, wrestling with a problem perhaps, I thought. Soon he returned to our makeshift camp and sat before us.

"He told us that the world had been waiting for truth to rise, but in its wait had become immersed in trivialities, such was the inconstancy of men. He said that this could not continue as the Master was coming and all must be made ready. 'You two will assist me to prepare His way. It is for you both, for you have been called. Eat now, we return to the people soon,' and he returned to his boulder and sat.

"Well, you could imagine our surprise. We looked at each other dumbfounded. 'What just happened?' I asked Andrew. 'I have no idea,' he replied. We were both speechless and yet both looking forward to where this adventure would lead us.

"After about an hour he returned. As he walked by he said simply, 'Come', so we did. As we walked along he taught us many things, in a manner I have not been taught before. He told us of the glory of God in terms I had never imagined, in ways you and I had never even touched on, Dysmas."

"What do you mean?" asked Dysmas.

"Well, it was so personal, yet so completely all-encompassing. The total power of our mighty God in the tender embrace of our Father, yet nothing was lost. No stone unturned. No mysteries and yet nothing but mysteries."

"You, of all people," said Dysmas. "You question everything more than anyone I have ever met," he said frowning, truly perplexed, yet deeply drawn to this extraordinary revelation.

"That makes no sense, Thomas," said Gestus.

"I know, trust me I know, yet it does somehow?"

They sat there for some time, seemingly digesting this remarkable tale while eating the grapes they had acquired when finally, completely absorbed, Dysmas said, "So what happened next?"

"Well, that day went much as the one before and like so many after. He taught us so much of God I could hardly begin to know where to start. The Scriptures just unfolded and made sense in light of all we were doing, and yet remained completely contradictory to all I had previously believed. Yet, I found myself at peace, overcome with a profound love of God I had never before known.

"There was no turmoil, no desire to argue against these new truths that yet seemed old, just a peace formed somehow from an inner knowledge that I had stumbled upon truth itself. Each day I learned more, and each day my joy was complete. Complete, did you hear? And yet, the day that followed would add to my joy that was itself complete. How is that even possible? I hear myself at odds with reason and yet it is truth itself."

Dysmas had been watching Thomas closely and was amazed not only by what was said, but with the gentleness with which he said it. He had known Thomas for much of his life and yet this man before him was a stranger to all intents and purposes. He was at once at peace and yet anxious for more of this joyful paradox. He remembered Thomas as one of the most disbelieving of souls, and yet here he was before him discussing mysteries with a matter of fact clarity, that bore no resemblance of the friend he remembered so well. Dysmas was at once puzzled and intrigued.

"Please continue," he said at last.

"My days from that time on were taken up with listening to the Baptist. Every waking hour I spent listening and watching. Nothing did I see of self within him. Nothing of self did the Baptist possess, neither of goods nor dignity, of fear or even truth, none were his. It was as if the single burning passion, the only preoccupation, was the will of God and his duty to that will. He was no more concerned for the traps of the Pharisees than for the accolades of his followers. He dealt with them both with disinterest and yet compassion. Even his enemies recognised his care for them. It no doubt annoyed them greatly.

"Even Roman soldiers sent from Jerusalem to assess the threat were themselves dismayed by what they found. One day a centurion approached him even in the water. Andrew and I were up in a moment expecting trouble. We were ready to die to protect him, but he held us paralysed with a glance, an amazingly gentle glance.

"To everyone's surprise the centurion stopped before him and asked, 'What hope have I as a soldier, how should I live?'"

"You must be joking," said Gestus. "A Roman soldier?"

"Not just a soldier, but a Centurion. I assure you, I am not lying."

"What did he say?" asked Dysmas, just as surprised.

"He looked him straight in the eye and stretched out his hand and placed it on his shoulder and then he said, 'Be neither afraid nor vengeful. Orders too can be carried out with justice and compassion. Don't bear false witness against even your enemy. Demand no money that is not your just right, be content with your wages. You too are of God's creation, as are those you serve.'

"I tell you, Dysmas, I have never before known such utter silence as I heard at that moment."

"It's hard to believe," said Dysmas.

"I assure you, every word is true," replied Thomas.

"The soldier smiled and nodded and looked around at those gathered with a gaze of real peace. He nodded again as if to himself and left the water, joined up with his companions and they left without a word. When they had gone, the Baptist said, 'Do not imagine that God's love is restricted to Israel. As Scripture says, 'God saw all that He had made and behold, it was very good.' Let not your hearts be troubled by worldly pettiness, for the kingdom of heaven is at hand.'"

"So he does not discriminate between Jew and Gentile," said Gestus with suspicion.

"Not in the way we were taught to, no."

"Yet we are the chosen people, are we not?" continued Gestus. "What part can the Gentiles have? Does he stand with Israel or Rome?"

"He stands with God, I think," replied Thomas with a smile.

"God stands with Israel," returned Gestus.

"Apart from the fact that the Baptist has not said He doesn't, I for one would not be so bold as to claim I knew what was in the mind of God," replied Thomas simply. "As Scripture does indeed say, 'God saw all that He had made and behold it was very good.' The Gentiles did not create themselves, Gestus. Foreign lands did not create themselves. I don't pretend to claim I know what these things mean in practical terms, but I can claim my own ignorance. I can claim a newfound trust in God's will and providence for me. What God has ordained I freely submit to as his most grateful and unworthy servant." And opening his arms and smiling, "I am at peace in all things."

Dysmas was astounded. Who is this man before me, he asked himself. "What happened next?" he said at last.

"Well the people kept coming, the Baptist kept teaching. For Andrew and I it was ever more instructive. We were just fortunate that we were hearing him each day. The layers of his discourse were having a great impact on our lives as they deepened our understanding of what the prophets were eluding to. It was different for the others as they would be there for a day or two before having to return to their homes and work, but for us it was constant illumination. As we ate our meagre meals each night he would explain some aspect of Scripture, or something that had taken place during the day.

"One morning when we arrived at the river's edge he took the hand of a little girl who had greeted him and walked but a few paces before stopping. He turned to us and said, 'It is to you my brethren, to baptise the lost and forgotten children in my stead while I teach them here.'

"I don't know how to explain it to you, but it seemed like the most natural thing in the world for us both. What a privilege. We smiled at one another as we entered the water and the people came, and they kept coming. He sent them and they came. I tell you I had tears in my eyes many times as I saw the simple faith and real joy of those that came. What a privilege", he said again.

"So you were baptising?"

"Yes, indeed. We listened as we did. We learned as we did. We found peace as we did. Oh Gestus, it was many things, but it was never boring. By way of explaining, I think, he said that the children of the kingdom must serve the children of the kingdom, that the King may find the whole household in accord when He comes."

"What does that even mean?" asked Gestus.

"As I heard him, Gestus, so you have heard me. What I give is a just and true account of what is come to pass. It is my service to you, you in turn will hopefully tell others in service to them.

"About a year passed in this way. Many times the Pharisees and scribes sought to trick him to denounce him, yet each time they were sent away as fools.

"Many soldiers came and went. It was strange but they always seemed to understand him more than the Pharisees. Some, it is true, were scoffers, yet they always left respectful and pensive. He had a real impact on them for the most part. The same was true for so many foreigners. The Pharisees by comparison seemed never to get it. They were so caught up in themselves, they had no vision for anything else. It was a great shame.

"I am here today to purchase some supplies before returning. You are both very welcome to accompany me if you would like."

"We are heading for Syria," replied Gestus, "but we will most likely see you again soon."

Dysmas hugged his old friend, deep in thought as they parted, and wondered briefly if he should not consider changing his plans, but Gestus assured him that they would return soon enough to visit with the Baptist.

Change of Direction

For the year following their chance meeting with Thomas, Dysmas and Gestus had become little more than nomads. They had travelled first through Egypt then Macedonia, circling back through Mesopotamia and Syria, always living by their wits. Opposites in almost every respect, Dysmas always awe struck and thoughtful by what they discovered, Gestus ever flippant and dismissive.

Dysmas had once pointed out the enormity of the statement being made by the very existence of the pyramids, their timeless lesson and singular design. Gestus considered them little more than an egotistical eccentricity of a long dead Pharaoh. "Didn't do him much good," he had quipped with a smile as he returned to his gambling. This gambling was not an altogether bad thing, Dysmas had thought to himself with a smile. He usually won, and they needed the money.

However, finding themselves now back in their homeland over the past month, prospects had been anything but promising, and Jericho was proving no exception. Having arrived the previous night, Gestus found himself at the end of yet another bleak losing streak, as they were down now to their last few coins.

Over the course of the game, there had been many questions from one of the players that were off subject entirely. It was clear to this man that this stranger before him was either a soldier, or mercenary of some kind. He had enquired of Gestus in an off-handed manner, as to his travels and origins. He seemed greatly interested in the answers and, the game having concluded for the evening, had invited Gestus back to his home where he wished to discuss a proposition.

He believed he had found the right man for the job he had in mind, and indeed he had. "There is a man in Jericho who has been a terrible thorn in the side of the local inhabitants for many years," he had said, "a Jew, yet a traitor to his people. We in the town are enraged by his very presence, and there is no recourse to the injustice perpetrated against us."

As the conversation had progressed over a skin of wine, it was clear that Gestus had no qualms dealing with reprobates such as this. This man had dealings with the Romans, which was more than enough for Gestus.

"If you agree to kill this man," Roboam had said, "I will return to you your losses of this night, in addition to the purse that has been acquired by the offerings of many in Jericho." This was indeed a very favourable offer.

Having heard the tale, Gestus had replied in the affirmative. "For myself," he had said, "I will accept the offer. However, I have a partner that we will need to convince." So they had made their way to the campsite outside the town where Dysmas was trying unsuccessfully to get some sleep. He had been much surprised to see Gestus had brought company at this late hour.

Gestus set out the offer as he understood it, with Dysmas growing more incredulous with every word.

"Gestus, really? Are we assassins now?"

"Look, just hear him out. We need the money, and as I see it, it's no different from killing the Romans."

"How does that follow? He's a Jew."

Roboam chimed in then. "He is a Jew by birth only. He is a traitor to our people. It is a small matter."

"It is no small matter," said Dysmas. "You want us to kill this man. Why?"

"He is a demon," said Roboam. "He has been stealing from us for years and is now fat on our labours, and those of our children. Many have been pleased to contribute to this purse. He is a Jew and yet collects taxes for our enemy, and for himself. Fleecing his fellow Jews while hiding behind his Roman guard, he is hated as no other in Jericho. He is a Roman first, a traitor." There was genuine passion and the ring of truth to this man's story.

Dysmas looked at Gestus. "What do you think?"

"He assists the Romans in oppressing our people. Is he any better than the Romans we have killed in the past?"

This was a bit of a new venture for Dysmas and Gestus, but funds were running low and it appeared a worthy cause.

"What is his name?" asked Dysmas.

"Zacchaeus. He is a small man. You will find him at the gates of the city from the third hour collecting taxes. When will you do it?"

"That's not your concern," he said as Gestus took up the purse on the makeshift table with a grin.

"Consider it done," said Gestus.

So it was that they found themselves two days later watching their prey from the other side of the square, just after the sixth hour.

"Let's not get into a battle with his Roman guard," said Dysmas. "Better to follow him home and do it there." As they watched they could hear a growing commotion as a crowd of people could be heard approaching. People started spreading word that Jesus the prophet was coming. Soon all in the marketplace were as one scrambling to get a good view, lining the small dusty pathways by which he would have to pass.

Zacchaeus too was curious to see this prophet, but could not get through the crowd, and was too short to see over them. He ran ahead then to a sycamore tree that provided a branch low enough to climb, and yet spreading above the heads of the crowd as they passed.

Dysmas turned to Gestus, "This might be the perfect opportunity," he said. "Come on." He led the way toward Zacchaeus, who was now halfway up the tree. They took up position at its base. "When he comes down we will assist him," said Dysmas.

"And we get to see the prophet," Gestus smiled.

The commotion approached surrounding the tall, lean figure of Jesus, the carpenter of Nazareth. Some people were proclaiming him a prophet. Word had it some even believed him to be the Messiah. Dysmas had long since given up hope of Israel being saved by the God of his ancestors. This God had abandoned his father who was always devout and faithful. 'What manner of God must he be?' Dysmas had surmised in the end. Still, his chance meeting with Thomas a year earlier had touched something in Dysmas. It had rekindled a hope. Yet the Baptist himself was in Herod's dungeon now and he had spoken of this man Jesus. 'I wonder how he's feeling now?' he pondered.

No matter, he thought. He looked up to check on Zacchaeus just as Jesus appeared through the crowd, and walked right beneath the branch on which Zacchaeus had perched himself. At that moment a man leapt from the crowd screaming obscenities and throwing himself to the ground. His father burst through the crowd a second behind him and tried to calm him down, but he was agitated beyond being calmed.

People moved quickly out of his way for fear of injury while his father sought in vain to control him. "I'm sorry Rabbi; he is not normally so aggressive. He has been like this for two years, I know not why."

Gestus looked at Dysmas and up at Zacchaeus, as if to say now might be a good time with all the distraction, but Dysmas was unmoved.

Jesus reached out to the man who was now bleeding from two wounds to his head and touched his shoulder. The man tried to move back but found himself unable to do so. Then a deep voice screamed more obscenities before Jesus said simply, "Silence. Be gone," and the man immediately became calm. His father looking up to Jesus took hold of his son's shoulders and raised him to his feet.

"Thank you," he said. "Thank you," and he moved away with his son to take him back home. The people were amazed, and the commotion began anew.

Jesus did not move, but rather looked up into the sycamore tree. "Zacchaeus," he said. "I would be honoured if you would share your table with me this day." Zacchaeus was dumbstruck.

"You know me, Lord?" he asked.

Jesus just smiled. "Come down," he said, and so he did with haste.

"Please, Lord," he said when he was before Jesus. "Please, follow me," and he led the way overjoyed in the direction of his palatial home.

Jesus glanced over to Dysmas then. "And what of you, Dysmas?" he said simply with a smile. "Will you not join us also?"

Both Dysmas and Gestus were stunned completely. "Yes, of course," he stuttered. "Of course." Jesus turned then to follow Zacchaeus, leaving Dysmas and Gestus looking one to the other to follow sheepishly behind in disbelief.

When Zacchaeus arrived home, he immediately instructed his servants to provide additional seating for whomever the Rabbi wanted to join them, and there were many indeed. Given his lonely state in Jericho, there were few that would associate with Zacchaeus other than fellow outcasts. These were invited to dine with the Rabbi mostly for numbers' sake, as Zacchaeus was afraid his popularity, or lack of it, would be on display.

There were another two tax collectors who were visiting, along with various people who had dealings with the Romans and were considered unpalatable. Two Pharisees who would not normally sully themselves by crossing the threshold of such as Zacchaeus invited themselves also, as did many others who despised him, even some who had contributed to the assassin's purse still held by Gestus.

For his part, Zacchaeus was overjoyed just to have his home filled with people for the first time in his life, even those he knew to be his enemies he accepted without regard to his pride. He had longed to be accepted as one of them but it had never been the case. Food and wine were plentiful, and people found his hospitality both willing and generous.

The twelve were with Jesus, but sat at different places among those gathered. "There's Thomas," said Gestus motioning to Dysmas, as Thomas waved him over to sit next to him.

"So, you did join him," Dysmas said as he hugged his old friend.

"Of course," he responded. "Please sit," he said.

Jesus was seated beside Zacchaeus, smiling as he listened to an animated Zacchaeus tell him of the lavish surroundings of his home.

The meal eaten, Jesus could tell that there was talk of his presence here in the house of a known sinner. One of the Pharisees asked him for a lesson, to which he responded.

"Let us take the lesson from the cup," and he held his aloft. "See how shiny it is. So clean that we see our faces reflected. Yet when we look within, it appears spoiled by the wine that has been left. Who among you would drink of it, having found it so? We concern ourselves generously with what matters little, with what others perceive from without, while we ourselves would not drink from a dirty cup. The truth is, we know instinctively that what is within is what really matters. Be careful you are not spoiled within, providing a show for the opinions of others that bears you no good, while your Father in heaven sees the truth of who you are.

"Thou shalt not steal nor bear false witness, thou shalt not covet," he continued as he set his gaze upon Dysmas now, "and thou shalt not kill." Dysmas was instantly uneasy under the gentle piercing gaze that seemed to see right through him. "These are given not only for reason of their own value, but to make us understand the value of our neighbour. He too is priceless before God. Who among you has the power to give life?" Releasing Dysmas from his gaze he then looked over those gathered. "Who among you would therefore dare take it?

"Man is ever at work with his own interests, ever seeking his own comfort, yet judges his brother, often less guilty than himself, for coveting the same aspirations. Who here would deny it? Many, it is true, seek their interest by way of honest labour, while they blaspheme, or are covetous of their neighbour's goods, envious that God did not provide so well for them. Still others are not so honest, and soon lose those precious virtues they were once much attached to," and his gaze fell upon Zacchaeus, "foregone for mere trinkets. Yet do not imagine such virtue, though still deep within, will not yet rise. Trust in God," and his gaze returned once more to those present.

"Be careful not to turn a harsh glare to your brother because his sins are more visible, though perhaps less than your own. Your Father in heaven sees all. Forget not he is your brother. Be grateful for what you have, for many have less. Be grateful that your Father has given you many brothers to love. That Caesar claims what is his by tax, in no way releases you from your duty before God. It is far better to clean the cup within, that as brothers you abide in truth.

"Our Father is in heaven. Where our Father is, we hope to be, home with our brothers and sisters. Let not your judgement condemn your brother. Let not the trinkets of the world endanger our family ties.

Dysmas felt a little sick. He realised he had been about to take his brother's life, a far greater sin than taking his money. Many present were troubled by their conscience immediately, yet it was Zacchaeus who was most touched. Silence fell among them as they digested these things as Jesus sipped from his cup.

A few moments passed when Zacchaeus stood in the midst of them, and addressed all those present. "Brothers, though I know that there are some who would not call me brother, please hear me. Rabbi, I have wronged my brother, some here present and others beside." He looked around the room with tears in his eyes. "I was angry, yet now I know it was not with you I was angry, but myself. Hear me and spread it abroad. I pledge here and now that I will make right every wrong that I have been guilty of. Where I have left short those who have dealt with me, I will pay them back four times the amount and beg their pardon. From this day forward I will seek to be the Jew my father raised me to be." Stunned silence was the result of so honest an appraisal of self.

Jesus said simply, "Salvation has found this house tonight," after which the room erupted with applause, and Roboam himself went to Zacchaeus and embraced him.

Dysmas found himself smiling as he turned to Gestus, "Looks like we give the purse back!" Gestus could only smile in return, shaking his head.

Festivities continued well into the night. Jesus excused himself just after dark and was soon lost to the night, while Zacchaeus found lodgings for the twelve, and a few stragglers, including by chance Dysmas and Gestus.

As Roboam was leaving, bidding farewell to Zacchaeus, Dysmas caught his eye and met him by the gate of the house. "I expect you will be wanting this back," he said as he handed him the purse.

"I confess I would not know what to do with it, and I dare say, all who contributed to it are ashamed. Use it as you will," he said with a sad smile. "That will be the punishment of our folly. We are sorry that we have brought this shame upon ourselves. Forgive us," he said bowing as he took his leave.

"We keep the money?" said Gestus in disbelief, his eyes wide with glee. Dysmas threw the purse to him, very deep in thought. Gestus headed back inside for more wine, while Dysmas found himself admiring the outcome of the carpenter's work.

An hour later, Gestus appeared once more to find Dysmas deep in thought. "What are you thinking about?" he asked.

"For years, Gestus, I have burned with the desire to free Israel. I have sought the best for my brother Jew. I have slayed our enemy and taken up the sword to defend our lands, yet all that is left in my wake is bloodshed and discord. In truth I have achieved nothing."

"That is not true," said Gestus.

"I have resolved nothing and therefore I have achieved nothing. Yet this carpenter from Nazareth walks into Jericho today defenceless, no ire to scold the people, no judgement to play on their guilt. He claims no high moral place, nor concedes it. He justly condemns injustice leaving the unjust man a means of redemption. In his wake is resolution wherever one looks.

"The little man of Jericho has been taught and redeemed. Those who planned his assassination are taught and redeemed. His assassins themselves are not only taught and redeemed, but rewarded with the purse for being so. Did you see Gamilael the Pharisee? His gentleness with regard Zacchaeus was touching given his aversion to him earlier. Even the Pharisees see, Gestus! Even the Pharisees," he said again now a little distant, lost in his thoughts.

Gestus didn't quite understand the depth of thought, but knew it was pointless trying to keep up. "I will be inside with our money," he said grinning after a few minutes of silence, leaving Dysmas to his thoughts, who had not even heard him.

Hours passed, but the festivities showed no fatigue. Dysmas was absorbed in the stars of the night when he sensed someone approaching from behind. "Be still, Dysmas," were the gentle words of Jesus, seemingly aware that his presence had been discovered. "You have nothing to fear," he said as he now sat beside Dysmas.

"What will Zacchaeus do now?" asked Dysmas.

"I expect as he has always done, only now with the integrity and honesty that were lost to him for a time, yet will be lost no more."

"You mean he will still collect taxes for the Romans?"

"What is wealth, Dysmas, when compared to what God provides? Taxes are not an evil in themselves. Yet even should Rome seek to steal money with tax, this would be of little consequence, if the people have already surrendered their hearts to bitterness, and found reason to ignore the commandments God gave them to secure their joy?"

"Are we not told thou shalt not steal?"

"Yes, indeed we are. We are also Jews who have been told. They are Romans who have not. Yet even had they the commandments, is it permissible, do you think, that having been wronged, we perpetrate a greater wrong on our neighbour?"

"Of course not."

"Then you have solved your own riddle," Jesus said smiling. "The wrongs of which Zacchaeus spoke were not his collecting of tax. This must be done, if not by Zacchaeus then by another. The children of God now have an honest man who will watch over their interests with care and integrity."

Dysmas was thoughtful and knew well that all this was true.

"The real question is, what will Dysmas do now?"

Dysmas smiled to himself. "You are right of course, but I do not have an answer to that question."

"Perhaps while you consider an answer, you might consider joining us on our travels."

"Join you?" Dysmas said startled. "Why me?"

"Why not you?" Jesus asked. "We will be leaving for Bethany at dawn," he continued as he rose. "If nothing is going right, Dysmas, perhaps it's time you went left," he said with a wry grin, causing Dsymas to smile at last. Simon called Jesus then. "We might see you in the morning then," he said, "I'd best go and find out why Simon is calling," and he left having caught Dysmas completely off guard.

Gestus rejoined Dysmas soon after, and they found their way to their lodgings for the night. Dysmas realised there was little point in telling Gestus of his offer from Jesus in the state he was in. He simply said with a smile, "We will be leaving early," as Gestus threw himself on his bed.

The following morning as the sun was cresting the horizon, Dysmas was up and ready to go, while Gestus demanded, "Why the rush?" He was nursing a well-earned headache.

"We have been invited to join Jesus on his journey," replied Dysmas grinning to himself. Gestus nearly had a fit. "What? Who invited us?" he said rising to his feet holding his head.

"Jesus," replied Dysmas.

"Why us?" asked Gestus in disbelief.

"Why not us?" replied Dysmas enjoying himself now.

"You're toying with me," said Gestus.

"I may be," said Dysmas, "but I'm also leaving, right now. Get your things," and he threw his pack over his back and left.

Gestus was stuffing his clothes into his own pouch while on the move to catch up with Dysmas, who was outside scanning the area for Jesus and his disciples. Jesus was at the gate of the house bidding a fond farewell to Zacchaeus, who had gratefully supplied all that would be necessary for his journey, and that of his companions. "I am so grateful to you," he told Jesus.

Jesus smiled at him and hugged him for a long moment, then held him at arm's length.

"You lost yourself for a little while, but your Father has found you once more. Lose yourself now in Him alone, that you may never be lost again. You have been born now as if a second time, be sure to live in the freedom of your Father." Placing his hand upon his head then, he gave him the threefold blessing of his ancestors, and left his brother with tears in his eyes.

Dysmas caught up to him then.

"So, you have decided to join us after all," Jesus said with a smile. "Good, and your companion?"

"He'll be along. Eventually," smiled Dysmas.

Soon they had joined up with the twelve and a handful of other disciples who were also travelling with them on the road. They had not travelled far before Gestus had caught them, and Thomas was now walking beside Dysmas.

"Here you are," said Thomas.

Dysmas shook his head. "I'm not sure I believe it."

"Well, I know I don't," Gestus interjected, somewhere between incredulous and annoyed.

"So, how did you get him to invite us along?" Dysmas asked Thomas.

"What?"

"You must have said something to him to get him to invite us."

"Not a single word, Dysmas, I assure you."

"You haven't spoken to him about us at all?"

"Not a single word. As far as I am aware, he doesn't know we even know each other."

"Then how did he know who I was?" asked Dysmas.

"You had better ask him that," replied Thomas smiling, "but you had better get used to things happening around you that you can't explain or understand."

"What do you mean?" asked Gestus.

"I mean exactly what I say. The time I spent with the Baptist was awe-inspiring. This past year I have spent with Jesus however. I would not dare try to find the words to describe it. You have stepped out of known reality, and into something that you need to experience to understand. There truly is nothing I could say that would assist you to understand. I could tell the story of the Baptist, and in doing so convey to you who he is, but this man? I could tell you of his words and miracles, yet who he is would remain a mystery. You will see."

"Miracles?" said Gestus smiling.

Thomas just smiled back, "You are little different from all of us not so long ago. We were ever expectant of the next moment. You will come to realise the next moment is not so important as the present one. You will see."

Dysmas was admiring the banter that seemed so familiar to this group of men he was now walking amongst. They were clearly very close. It appeared Simon the fisherman was the leader of the twelve. He was also the oldest of them, and very often the target of their humour, though very good-natured about it.

As he watched them, he could not help but compare the camaraderie existent among this group, and that of the group in the cave he had left behind a little over a year ago.

He had grown into his formative years in a very harsh environment indeed. Men were hard and exchanges more often coarse. Concerns for the welfare of the other were driven mostly by the welfare of self. The stronger the force, the more chance each member had of survival. While Dysmas often found himself contemplating mysteries beyond him, he had never held a single conversation with any one of Barabbas' men who shared the value he placed in those mysteries, nor indeed the least interest in understanding anything outside their immediate surrounds. The general atmosphere had always lent itself to the concupiscible and irascible appetites. Passions raged, often with no regard for restraint. This all too often had resulted in an environment of factions, tensions, arguments and on the rare occasion, even death.

This group by contrast was a very different story. There appeared to be no factions or tension whatever. Though they had been together now for well over a year, they were clearly of one mind and heart, happily giving way one to the other. It appeared there was no rivalry between them, but much good humour, and they followed their master because they seemed genuinely to love him. Where Barabbas was by any definition a profoundly simple man,

Jesus by contrast was a profoundly complicated one. Yet this, rather than confusing the group, formed the foundation somehow of its pleasant genre.

When he spoke, all would listen intently and with good reason, Dysmas surmised. This man had something to say that seemed to ring with truth and it reached into the depth of one's being. As they stopped now on the way to eat he began again to teach them.

"Fear not the world and the flesh which has so little to offer. Waste not your effort with them either in thought or deed. Concern yourself with those things of the spirit that lift you to your Father in heaven, and conform you to His likeness. That you defer one to the other because you wish to contribute to the group's wellbeing is in itself good. Also, should you wish to humble yourself as a penance for your sins, this too is good in itself. Yet that you defer one another, foregoing your just rights even to injustice with joy, to freely desire your Father's will for you over your own; this is perfection. So then, the greatest of you will be the least, and the servant of all."

"And what when others take advantage of our weakness?" asked Gestus.

"Humility and obedience, Gestus, is hardly a weakness. These are only for the very strong. Who else could bear such a burden? Humanity tied so deftly as it is to its own perceptions of truth will almost always take advantage. This just increases your merit before your Father, for your Father sees all. Do you imagine that your Father who sees your act of virtue, does not see also your brother's error? Yet His just judgement in no way releases you from your duty, any more than your brother's abuse of justice excuses you from exercising virtue. Is not virtue that much more meritorious when it is practised within the furnace?"

Though those around him were nodding, Gestus was greatly unconvinced, that being somebody's willing servant held any merit whatever. "I'm sorry," he said at last, "I don't understand. That I defer to another, foregoing my just rights even to injustice with joy, to freely desire my Father's will over my own, how is this perfection?"

"You can do nothing of yourself, and yet man clings to self as if he and he alone were master of his destiny. But there is another,

One who watches over His creation with such tender care, that not even a sparrow falls without His knowledge. His will for man is so much more than man's will for himself. When a man's will is one with His, so disinterested in the world that he cares not for the clothes on his back, the abode of his body, his rights or even his reputation, then and only then is he a free man. He has chosen freedom when so few do. Do not be seduced by what appears to be. In truth, the only time a man truly owns anything is when he gives it away. At that moment he knows with certainty that it was truly his, because he has freed himself from its burden."

This was to be the first of many lessons that found Gestus bewildered, and Dysmas deep in thought.

As the days became weeks, the prediction of Thomas was born out day after day. Both Dysmas and Gestus found themselves in a constant state of wonder, just to behold the simplicity of the complex. Nothing it appeared, was beyond this man before them. Difficult questions were answered simply, yet the wisdom was astounding. Each answer found Dysmas reflecting how obvious it had been, and yet he had not even considered it before.

Pharisees often sought to trap him into saying something to charge him with, and yet, the ease with which they were corrected and dismissed was poetry to the ears of Dysmas.

A group of Pharisees had approached Jesus at Caesarea Philippi, and watched as he and his disciples began eating. After some time one of them, Eleazar bar Hedon, stood and addressed Jesus, making a show of the scandal he was addressing with a smirk. "Why is it, Master, that your disciples do not observe the washing rituals of our fathers? They eat with unclean hands."

"And yet you stood by and watched as they did so," Jesus replied, "without seeking to stop the scandal you claim offends you." Eleazar's smirk disappeared. "These fathers you follow, who by your own admission killed the prophets the Most High sent them, it is these you follow not just in deed, but in your heart's desire. We must return to the lesson of the cup," he sighed. And so he did; however, this time without the gentle manner of the last.

"You concern yourselves with outward signs of virtue, while that which lay within is corrupt through and through. Hypocrites!" he said, slowly shaking his head with the saddest expression. "How right was Isaiah when prophesying of you, 'These people honour me with their lips while their hearts are far from me'. What does it profit a man concerned with everything entering the body that will soon pass from it, while the heart of that man's body is corrupt? That others perceive not the corruption while a show is made for their benefit matters not at all. Your Father in heaven sees the corruption within you. Hypocrites! Make clean your hearts before your Father who is in heaven. Do not think you will escape His wrath with outward signs and trinkets.

"You burden the children with onerous obligations, not given you by your Father, and yet change those obligations that were. When He tells you to honour your mother and your father, you claim 'corban'. Do you think by offering your money to God you are free from your obligation to use it to assist your parents? What need has God of money? Hypocrites! Washing your hands to brush away a grain of dust, while you are corrupt through and through.

"The doctrines you teach are the sterile doctrines of men. They serve you, not your heavenly Father, and it is you who rely on them."

The Pharisees were much angered by the reprimand but managed to hold their place, even as Jesus turned from them to continue conversing with young John, who had been sitting beside him the whole time, effectively ignoring them.

Finally, Eleazar, as composed as he could manage, replied, "We are of the Sanhedrin chosen by God to lead His people, and you insult not only us, but those who went before us."

When Jesus turned again to face Eleazar, his genuine sadness was clear for all to see. "Worldly men of worldly vision," he said, "perceiving only worldly goods. It is because you claim you see that your sin remains. You claim yourselves offended by truth." Jesus laid his eyes now directly upon Eleazar, "If a man be offended by truth, that man should know that the God of his ancestors is near, and has provided the truth he is in need of that he might repent of his many sins. All of creation is ever solicitous for his salvation, yet none more than He who loves him in truth. It is not possible that I offend you, only that you are offended. Hear, then, if you have ears," he concluded.

The mere stare of Jesus had paralysed Eleazar, who became thoughtful now. Though he found himself much embarrassed for the first time in the presence of his brother Pharisees, he cared little. He was absorbed with this message of Jesus. It had astounded Dysmas when he had stood after a few moments and bowed. "Thank you, Master," he had said simply, prompting all the Pharisees to stand. The arrogance so evident when he had first addressed Jesus was noticeably absent. The other Pharisees were looking one to the other, wondering at the strategy of Eleazar, but there apparently was none. He simply left in silence and remained so, while his brother Pharisees discussed at length the insolence of this carpenter of Nazareth as they returned to Jerusalem.

Dysmas had realised also the charity of Jesus toward Eleazar now. Though Eleazar's intent had been duplicitous, Jesus had not sought to antagonise him. Although his correction was brutal and targeted, it was also instructive and enlightening. Clearly this had not been lost on Eleazar either. Jesus was building the man, while tearing down the lie.

Sent

Six months had passed since Dysmas and Gestus had joined the other disciples of Jesus, much to the surprise of Gestus, who had predicted their early departure soon after their arrival. He too however, had been swept up in the happenings since then, and very much indeed had happened.

Countless were those possessed of evil spirits made free by the hand of their Master. It seemed little more than a parlour trick at times, given the ease with which the spirits were cast out. Many times these demons were silenced by Jesus before they spoke further; yet, the little they did scream was much more than disturbing; it was positively instructive. They were clearly afraid of Jesus.

The miracles spoken of by Thomas and scoffed at by Gestus, were all too frequent, a little too frequent for Gestus. He had been skeptical from the start, and was always going to be hard to convince. Even though he was present when four men lowered a paralytic through the roof where Jesus was teaching, who later was able to rise and walk, he still held many doubts. It had annoyed him that by contrast Dysmas had been taken in so easily. He had argued that neither he nor Dysmas knew this man, or the men who lowered him. "How do we know he was really paralysed?" he had asked.

When they were passing through Nain, and came upon the funeral procession of a young man who had died, Jesus had apparently raised the man from the dead. This too was far too much for Gestus to take on face value. "How do we know that he was truly dead? I have no doubt everyone believed him to be dead," he had argued, "but was he?" Both he and Dysmas had known a man in Hebron who had apparently died in his sleep. As the funeral procession had progressed, he had woken from his deep sleep. Dysmas, though convinced of the miracle of Jesus, could not argue with Gestus on this count, as he himself had been present as a young boy.

However, one day early in spring had changed everything for Gestus. They had been for some days tarrying around the shores of the lake near Gennesaret, surrounded by thousands of people as Jesus taught them and answered their questions.

Judas had pointed out that their supplies were by now running very low, and the twelve were planning to send the people home as they themselves needed to replenish even their water skins. Word had been passed about throughout the disciples that they would soon be moving on for this purpose and to be ready. Jesus however, had had other plans.

Phillip had approached him to tell him that they had run out of supplies and would need to get more, suggesting they send the people away to get their own supplies in order.

"Phillip, they have not eaten well for days, surely they will faint on the journey from fatigue," was the response. "We should give them to eat," Jesus had continued.

Phillip was a little stunned, "But Master," he had replied, "we have no supplies ourselves."

"Fear not Phillip," Jesus said smiling. "Move among the people and see what you can find. Man does what little he can; faith will suffice for the rest."

Phillip shrugged and smiled apologetically, "Yes, Master," he replied, and was soon off instructing the others to move among the crowd to see what they could gather.

It wasn't long before Phillip had returned with seven loaves and a few small fish. "Some people had these that they have offered to us," he said to Jesus, "but what are these among so many?" he continued.

"They are a generous gift, Phillip, from those who had little to give. Beautiful," he said smiling as if to himself. "Ask the people to sit down in large groups where they are comfortable."

So the twelve and the other disciples had moved among the crowd, arranging them in large groups. Jesus caught the arm of Gestus. "I see some of these people have baskets that are now empty. Ask if they could spare them to us to use for a time. We will need a few".

Gestus had complied, but was more than a little confused as to any possible use they could be.

The people having settled, the disciples seated themselves on the grass just below Jesus in front of the crowd. Jesus took the loaves and placed them in one of the larger baskets, placing the fish in another large basket. "Father in heaven, I give You thanks for the generosity of Your children who have given of the little they had. Bless this their gift, and make it Thine own."

There were many baskets now lined up before Jesus, and as they watched seated below him, he picked up that one in which he had placed the loaves and then made as to pour its contents into another basket, then another and yet another. He repeated this action with the basket in which he had placed the fish. From their position below it was not immediately clear what was happening.

Though the twelve were seemingly at ease, some of the disciples were looking at each other puzzled. Gestus shot a look at Dysmas rolling his eyes smiling as if to say that Jesus had lost his mind.

When Jesus had finished, he called the twelve to himself. These were clearly shocked when they stood before the baskets, looking from one to the other in great surprise. The smile vanished from the face of Gestus as he now wondered what was happening. He would soon know. Jesus had instructed the twelve to continue filling what baskets were left from the two he had originally chosen, and to distribute those already filled to the disciples, to distribute to the many seated on the grass around the lake. They were to return the empty baskets for refilling after distribution. So it was done.

When Gestus had arrived at the place where the baskets were lined up as he himself had spread them, he could barely believe his eyes. He had stood motionless as he beheld dozens of baskets filled with loaves and fish to overflowing, where only a moment ago they had stood empty. These were being swept up by two disciples per basket, and whisked away to be distributed to a bewildered crowd, that were clearly in need of their contents. A moment later, Dysmas had Gestus on one side of one of the baskets, and they were making their way through the crowd doing the same.

As they moved among the crowds of people over the next hour or so, it was clear that people were becoming more and more aware of what had just taken place. Certainly Gestus had been astounded.

When Jesus observed that those seated before him were talking among themselves signalling the meal had ended, he called a few disciples to himself. "Move among the people and gather the scraps," he had told them. "Let us not waste what the Lord has provided."

Gestus, now very enthusiastic, had been the most diligent in his efforts to collect those scraps not consumed. He himself had managed to collect three baskets of scraps on his own.

As he had returned with his third basket full, Jesus had enquired of him how many he had gathered.

"This is the third, Master," he had answered.

"Who'd have thought, Gestus?" Jesus said with a wry smile.

Gestus had smiled to himself, then to Jesus as he returned to gather more scraps. For the first time in his life he had been overwhelmed with joy, and was most animated in his praise of Jesus to the benevolent ear of Dysmas, assuring him that he had never really doubted. Not really.

The people were overwhelmed now by what they had just experienced. Some were beginning to claim that Jesus should be made king. "There are so many of us," they said. "We are at least five thousand men strong! We could install him as king in Jerusalem. We outnumber the Roman guard there by thousands! Surely it is time Israel had a king as of old," and so they continued to murmur.

Jesus, aware of what was being said, called the twelve to himself and gave them instructions. They in turn called the disciples together, giving them instructions to send the crowds home, and where to meet again when all was done. Gestus noticed that Jesus was nowhere to be seen, and wondered where he might have gone, as the twelve boarded the boat that was awaiting them at the shore line to be put out onto the lake.

Many of the people still remaining were excited by their experience of the day. There was much discussion between them and the disciples of Jesus with regard the events of the day. Many questions were asked of them all. One man asked Gestus if he had ever seen anything like this before. "All the time," was the reply, providing Dysmas with a broad smile, as he could not help but laugh for the briefest moment before he caught himself.

As the hours passed, the people grew fewer and fewer, until the disciples were alone. As the fires began to burn, they sat about cooking some of the fish that had been held over, talking about the day's events. So many were still overwhelmed by what they had experienced earlier, and there was much animated discussion about how it could have happened.

"Clearly, it was a miracle," said Dysmas smiling at last. "That any of you are even trying to work out how it could be anything else is perhaps another one. Did we ourselves not see that from nothing came enough to feed five thousand men at least? From nothing came twelve baskets of scraps," he continued laughing. "That any of you could believe there is even the possibility of another explanation other than a miracle is simply irrational."

"Are you saying that we should just accept everything as a miracle without question?" asked Natan.

"No, of course not. I'm saying that faith must be rational. If faith is irrational it cannot be truth. However, listening to you discuss what happened today is insightful because you are leaving rationality out of the discussion. We know with certainty that there was no food. We know with certainty the baskets were empty. I could go on but we know all these things with certainty. The problem with some of you and your discussion is that you choose to leave out of it facts that you know with certainty, while you speculate another possibility. If there were another possibility, it would conform to the facts that you know to be true. Leaving those facts out of the discussion while you seek to plumb the truth, will provide you only with the 'truth' you seek. To deny the obvious miracle is in itself irrational, when you need deny the evidence before you to find that conclusion."

"So you have no problem whatever with all those supposed miracles we see?" Natan asked.

"Without making a statement on 'all those miracles', I have to confess since joining Jesus and the twelve, I have not seen or heard anything that I would not consider rational."

They all immediately burst into laughter, some slapping Dysmas on the back causing him to laugh at himself. "Oh, come," Natan said at last laughing. "Rational? Really? Have you been sleeping?"

"What is and isn't rational depends largely on the prevailing circumstances, don't you think?" replied Dysmas.

"What do you mean?" asked Natan.

"Well, if Jesus is a man, I agree, irrational."

"Are you suggesting he's not a man?" laughed Natan, incredulous.

"I'm not sure what I'm suggesting, but he's like no man I've ever met in either word or deed. If you were to multiply loaves and fish, that would make no sense at all. People would be looking instinctively for the trick, but with Jesus? Let's face it, even though we still don't believe it, we more or less expect it. How could that be? You are quite right it is irrational for any of us, but in his case? I don't think so." This caused the rest to stop and consider the wisdom of the observation.

They camped where they were for the very windy night that followed, and at first light were on their way to the other side of the lake, where they had previously arranged to rejoin the twelve. They arrived the next day, and although the twelve were waiting, Jesus was nowhere to be seen. Yet there were stories of events on the lake the night they were being blown about on the shore after their conversation about the miracle. Apparently the boat the apostles were in was being blown about uncontrollably when Jesus came to them walking upon the water.

Gestus just smiled and shook his head. "You're not serious?" he said. Oh, but they were, and the story was told in detail. "Who is this man?" asked Natan looking now at Dysmas, who himself shrugged his shoulders and smiled.

"Where is he now?"

"He has gone to pray," was the reply. "He said he would return before dusk."

True to his word he returned to them just as the sun was touching the horizon. He found there waiting the twelve, and sixty other disciples, most of whom had been with him for six months or more.

As they all gathered around him now he began to speak. "You have seen the terrible need of the children of Israel, how they suffer the attacks of the evil one who has no regard for them. The fields are wide and heavy with crop, yet the workers are few. Pray to the Father that He will send more workers, as I am sending you now.

"Go in pairs as of old into all of Israel. Seek out the lost and forgotten, the discarded and despised. Bring to them the good news; their redemption is at hand. I give you authority to drive out the evil one and to heal the sick in my name. Pay him no heed for he has no power over you. You have been witnesses to the means of banishing the coward. Do the same. Stay where hospitality welcomes you, and be grateful for what providence provides.

"Do not judge your brethren, lest you be judged. Nor be solicitous for your needs. Your Father in heaven knows well your needs and will provide. The worker deserves his wages. Make plans now as to each pair, and where each will travel, that all of Israel may hear the Father's voice, as one brother to another.

"We will meet again forty days hence, at Caesarea Philippi, that we might rejoice as one, for I know well how deep is the need of the children, and what marvels can be worked through the hand of man by the will of the Father. Be solicitous only that His will be done, and all else will be granted you. Never forget, when man does the little he can, his Father is well pleased and will provide whatever may be lacking. I bid you farewell until you return."

With that Jesus called the twelve to himself and walked a short distance, apparently giving them further instructions. As they returned Jesus continued on his way, and was soon covered by the closing light of the day.

Simon and John began organising the routes each pair would take, while the others paired those who would travel together. Each of the apostles then, had charge of three pairs, preparing the supplies they would need initially.

The evening was charged with apprehension and expectation, as discussion was plentiful with regards the task at hand. All had their partners, destinations and supplies in order by the time they had retired.

At first light, they bade each other farewell, to begin their adventure into the unknown, many filled with apprehension and misgivings. It had never occurred to any of them that they would be sent out even to teach, let alone drive out evil spirits, essentially performing miracles. Was not that the sole domain of God? Even this thought had many of them asking themselves more seriously now, who this man Jesus really was. None of this was lost on Dysmas.

Faith and Reason

The route laid out for Dysmas and Gestus, who seemed naturally always paired, took them down the main trade route through Pella, Alexandrium, and Jericho. Branching off then they were to visit Qumran and follow the Dead Sea down as far as Masada. They would return via their home village of Hebron and Herodium, before making their way directly to Caesarea Philippi.

"You know our path takes us near the cave?" said Gestus at last.

Dysmas smiled. "Yes, I know."

"Well, should we go and preach to Barabbas?" smiled Gestus.

"It's probably about time we paid him a visit," was the response.

They had not travelled a day before they came upon a crippled beggar sitting under an outcrop of an enormous boulder a little off the road, who was literally arrayed in rags. Dysmas asked him if he was in need of food, prompting Gestus to remind him of just how little they had themselves. "We'll find more," replied Dysmas as he pulled a loaf and some salted beef from his satchel. "It looks like he needs it more than us," he continued sadly.

Many times he had encountered the destitute of Israel, and it always had an impact on him. Though life had been harsh, he had come to realise from examples such as this poor soul, how truly fortunate he was.

The man took the food gratefully and yet, though obviously hungry, did not eat any of it. "Thank you a thousand times," he said. He sought to move from his place, stumbling a little as he made his way to a small cave behind the boulder that came into view when they moved slowly past it. He was clutching the food as if gold. He climbed the small grade to the opening. A woman appeared, just as poor as he, yet unlike him, showing very definite signs of leprosy. This seemed of little interest to the man, as he put his arm around the woman and guided her back into the cave, showing her the food.

"Jesus is right, Gestus," Dysmas said thoughtfully. "There is great good in the world. It is we who choose to focus on the evil."

"A pity he's not here to heal her," Gestus replied sadly as they continued on. A few steps more and Dysmas stopped suddenly.

"What?" asked Gestus.

"I was just thinking," replied Dysmas, "I wonder..."

"What?" asked Gestus again.

"Wait here," said Dysmas at last as he started up the rock toward the cave.

"What are you doing?" cried Gestus. "Do you want to be a leper yourself?"

"Just wait there," replied Dysmas. He made his way to the cave's opening then, but the man had heard him coming and met him at the entrance.

"You can go no further," he said. "She is a leper. You know what could happen."

"You are with her," replied Dysmas.

The man smiled. "I can be nowhere else. She is my wife and I am where I belong."

"I have been sent on a quest by my master. Trust and bring her forth." The man hesitated.

"Bring her forth," said Dysmas again. Even though he was scared himself, something in him told him this was what he should do.

The woman came out then with her husband with tears streaming down her cheeks. "Please don't touch me. It is enough that my dear husband is no doubt infected; let no others become so on account of me."

"Fear not," said Dysmas. All at once now in her presence, he was calm and knew exactly what he must do. He stepped forward but she pulled back, yet he stepped forward once more. He took her hand in his left, her husband's in his right, and they were both amazed at his bravery. "In the name of Jesus the Nazarene, I order you, be clean. You will be cleansed of leprosy," he said to the woman, and turning to the man. "For the sake of your faithfulness and love, you will be protected from its grip."

He took them to himself then and put his arms around them both. "Trust in God, for it will surely be done for you."

At once the woman looked to her husband. "All at once," she said a little confused, "I feel well. I cannot explain, but I feel as I have not for many months," and tears were welling in her eyes. As her husband turned to her now, he saw that her features had been restored, as had the fingers that had previously been wasted away by the disease. Tears started streaming down his face as he hugged his wife now, and realised the strength pulsing through her body as she held him now with all her might. They were both overcome, weeping with joy.

Dysmas smiled to himself and quietly withdrew leaving them to their moment of joy. It would be some time before they even realised he had left them, and though they immediately went seeking him in gratitude, he and Gestus were well on their way to Pella.

Even so they did not have to travel far before they found another poor soul in need of food. However this time it was Gestus who cleared out his satchel, and gave its contents with a smile.

As before, the man was truly grateful. Gestus turned to Dysmas with a smile and said simply, "We can get more." Dysmas smiled. He had always loved Gestus, because he really did have a big heart. His drawback was the frequency with which he blocked its movement to generosity by thoughts of self.

No sooner had this man left than two more appeared, followed closely by another. Dysmas looked at Gestus, now smiling broadly. "We are well fed, Gestus, we can go without for a couple of days until we reach Pella." Gestus agreed, and the rest of their supplies were soon distributed among those in need.

They continued on their way and made camp along the river's edge just after dusk. As Dysmas was pulling out his blanket, he noticed two loaves still in his satchel. "Gestus," he said as he held them up, "did we not give them all our supplies?" he enquired a little bewildered.

"I thought we did," he replied. "I'm certain we did." He then looked in his own satchel and found two more loaves. "Could we have missed these?" he asked.

"Well, let's not look a gift horse in the mouth," said Dysmas as he enjoyed his first bite of the afternoon, as did Gestus.

As Dysmas lay beneath the stars an hour later considering the day's events, he found himself greatly at peace, delighted he could do something for these poor souls who sought his charity. This then engendered in him questions as to the place of the poor in the plan of God. It was a question that had plagued him for many years, just as he had never reconciled God's abandonment of his father in his moment of need. One so faithful. One so chaste. Reconciling suffering to God's mercy was proving just as difficult to understand.

As he fell asleep considering these things, his dreams took him to the edge of the sea of Galilee, where he found Jesus alone looking over the still waters, enjoying the sun's climb to its place of supremacy.

He sat now beside him in silence within this dream that seemed so real.

Jesus spoke then. "You have questions, Dysmas?"

"Why does God allow so much poverty, that they must beg the charity of others?"

"It is not poverty that is an evil, Dysmas, but destitution. The poor will always be with you. Yet they recognise their need of others and are often humble as a result. Community is therefore built on charity and love of neighbour. They, more often than the wealthy, know their need of God and their place before Him. This is a great blessing. Yet know this: it is man, not God, who allows so much poverty, while the destitute seek not charity so much as justice."

"Justice? I don't understand," answered Dysmas.

"When God created Adam, He did so exclusively for Himself. All the array that Adam could and could not see, He created for Adam. All of creation is rich in the abundance of your Father in heaven. He has provided in superabundance for all men to be fed from the fruits of his creation. There is more than enough for all men to be fed and clothed from the abundance of creation.

"It is man who stores up for himself far more than is his due. It is the lust of man for riches Dysmas, that has him store up the wealth that is provided for his brother, out of his brother's reach. By commerce and greed he gathers to himself more and more wealth unto his own death, to be passed on to one he has well formed in like thinking. As time has passed, the abundance of wealth provided by your Father to His beloved Adam, and so to his children, is held in ever greater measure by fewer, to the detriment of an ever growing number of poor, many destitute.

"This is the greed of man Dysmas, not the will of God. Thus, when one shares of what he has with one who has nothing, is he not providing justice to that one who is without? Is not the share of this destitute soul held ransom by the greed of another? Each man has a God-given right to the goods of life itself. That he is provided those goods is justice. What makes your act one of charity, is that you are not the one who is storing up his just share, and thus from the little you have, you are willing to seek to right a wrong.

"Yet, does not God allow it? So much suffering I see. Could not our Father put right these wrongs?

"Should God withdraw man's free will? Is not that more than anything else what sets man apart from beast? It is man alone who has reason. It is man alone who has the power to act contrary to his nature. This is the profound gift given to Adam and his descendants. As with all promises from God, it will never be revoked. Fear not, Dysmas, the flesh has nothing to offer.

"The man without food or shelter is without justice; therefore justice itself will hear his cry. When justice is absent, a void is created that shines like a beacon unto Justice itself, who will not close His ear to the cry of the poor."

"Yet still they suffer so," replied Dysmas.

"Do you imagine suffering to be alien to the human condition, Dysmas?" Jesus asked with a sad smile. "You, so much more than others, know it forms the very essence of man's reality. Yet you know well that your sufferings are little when seen in the light of what others suffer.

"It is not suffering that man should fear Dysmas, it is how he deals with it that steers his course, both his own sufferings and those of his neighbour.

"If he is enraged by his own, he has neither joy nor peace. If he is indifferent to the suffering of his brother, he is similarly afflicted. If on the other hand he perceives his trials, whatever they be, as a means of knowing his Father's will for him, and suffers them gladly, the burden becomes a joy and peace will reign in his heart. Those brothers of his who suffer any affliction are the dearest of his brothers, for they are the means given him by the very hand of his Father in heaven, to show his love for God through them. In this he will know joy and peace.

"Whether a man stubs his toe or suffers disease, loses a loved one or loses a limb, all men will know suffering of some kind. Yet man can always trust that his Father in heaven will not burden him with a load greater than his strength. Suffering then either transforms a man, or crushes him.

"It is an evil only if man allows it so. Could you imagine the mediocrity if there was no suffering? How would man appreciate joy? Indeed, how would men appreciate each other? As the air he breathes provides man with life, Dysmas, his dispositions to suffering determine its worth." Jesus turned to him now and smiled that gentle peaceful smile that Dysmas had come to know so well over these past few months. "Fear not the providence your Father provides," he said. "He knows well what is best for you. Go now and be at peace."

"Dysmas, Dysmas," called Gestus shaking him from his sleep. His eyes opened to find the sun already risen, and the broad smile of Gestus as the welcome to the new day. "I've never known you to sleep past sunrise," said Gestus.

Dysmas was stunned himself. He had slept through the entire night which seemed to pass in an instant, and yet his dream was as vivid as a memory just gathered.

Gestus saw clearly the look in his eyes and asked if he was alright.

"Yes," replied Dysmas blinking. "Just dreaming when you woke me, that's all," he said. "We'd best be on our way," he continued as he got to his feet.

Their bedding and belongings gathered, they were soon on their way once more. Dysmas was entirely engrossed in his thoughts, and Gestus, knowing well the moods of his confrère, knew it best to leave him to them.

Just after the sixth hour they took shelter in the shade of a great tree by the side of the river to rest. They had no sooner sat down than a man ran toward them screaming abuse. Dysmas was first to his feet in time to grasp the man by the front of his tunic, and fling him over onto his back with a great thud as he slammed into the hard ground. Much to the surprise of Dysmas he was back on his feet in an instant still screaming abuse. Dysmas prepared himself for a fight as Gestus was flanking the man, who seemed to have all his attention on Dysmas. As they circled this man now, Dysmas collected himself as he realised in that moment what was happening.

"Wait, Gestus," he said now raising his hand. He stood upright then. The man seeing his opportunity, prepared to lunge when Dysmas held up his hand before him and cried "Halt!" The man was instantly still.

"Who are you to order me?" screamed the man in a fearful voice.

"I am one come in the name of Jesus. In his name I order you to be gone from my brother. Be gone," he repeated, and the man immediately fell to his knees and wept great tears of relief. Gestus was stunned as Dysmas went to him, placing his hand on his shoulder. The man looked up at him now, tears making lines through the dirt on his face. "Thank you," he said as he once more bent to the ground to weep.

They tarried there for some time then, and shared what food they had left with him. They discovered that his name was Keplar, and he was from Jerusalem. He could not tell them how long it had been since he had left his home, only that he had left the practice of his faith for some time before falling victim to the demon that had possessed him. "I have been unfaithful to my holy faith," he had said with tears. "It will never be so again," he affirmed.

They talked together for some time before Dysmas said finally, "You are a long way from home, and we had best continue our mission." Standing now, he gave the man some coins from that which he carried to assist him on his journey home, and some fresh clothing since he was of a similar height and build to Dysmas.

Keplar, having now gathered himself, thanked them with such genuine gratitude that they were a little embarrassed. Soon, however, he was on his way, and they were free to continue their journey.

After their departure, Dysmas was considering his initial reaction to Keplar. He had immediately prepared to injure him, having not only taken personal offence at the insults, but being all too ready to deal out punishment. He realised now that he had been angry with the wrong one. Keplar, a brother, was not himself. How often, he mused, had he been angry with the wrong one in the past? How often had that anger resulted in injustice and retaliatory self-gratification? He found himself ashamed of many past acts of aggression now, as the truth of man's frailty became ever more obvious to him.

The following afternoon found them arriving in Pella at the ninth hour. A sleepy village lay before them, the only activity around the well, located at the centre of the village. They made their way toward two men they saw sitting beside the well, gesticulating animatedly as they discussed what was no doubt an important question.

"Shalom," said Gestus as these men turned now to face the strangers who had just arrived in their village. "Shalom," they replied. One turned to the other then and said simply, "We will see who is right with an independent view."

Gestus shot a puzzled look to Dysmas who just raised his brow.

"I am Rushcal," said one, "and this my dear friend Pishca, who is trying to convince me that his understanding of the Law is correct while my own is not." He spread his arms wide and a great smile appeared on his weathered face as he continued. "Clearly he is wrong, and you may tell him so when you hear our debate. Please sit, take wine and join us."

All became clear at once, and the two travellers introduced themselves and took their place, smiling at the playful banter of these two friends, to hear the dilemma as it unfolded.

"We both recognise poverty is a part of the human condition. Our disagreement lay in how best to deal with it in charity. Should we provide the sustenance itself, or the means of purchase?"

Dysmas smiled to himself as he leaned down to pick up a stick and began scribbling lines on the ground, as Gestus immediately replied to the question. "Should you provide the means of purchase, could that money then not be spent on frivolous pleasure instead of the goods required to feed those who are hungry?"

"My point, exactly," replied Rushcal slapping him on the back. "You have it!"

Dysmas realised instantly the lesson of the dream was for this moment. "You are all wrong," he said now looking up at them.

"How can we all be wrong?" replied Gestus smiling, as he looked now to a puzzled Rushcal.

"You are all wrong, because your understanding of the poor is wrong, therefore the conclusions are wrong!"

"Please?" said Pishca.

"Poverty is not a part of the human condition, it is a result of man's greed. God provided for all in abundance from His creation. Yet there are those who store up wealth to the point where others have not even the essentials of life. Did not God provide for them? Has not their rightful share been stolen from them? It is therefore not charity but justice you exercise in assisting the poor, by giving them back that which was theirs by right."

There was a great pause then. "Amazing," said Pishca as he looked now to Rushcal. "Have you ever heard such as this? Clearly he is right."

"I agree," said Rushcal. "He is certainly right. Do you have a place to stay this night?" he continued.

"No," replied Dysmas.

"Then it is settled, you will stay in the house of Rushcal and share with us your wisdom."

"It is not my wisdom," replied Dysmas, "it is the teaching of Jesus."

"We have had word of him. So he truly exists?" asked Pishca.

"Oh, yes indeed, he truly exists, and has sent us out with many others to all of Israel to bring good news to the children of Israel."

"Then we will hear you this night if you would grant us your time," said Rushcal as he stood now. "Come," he said, and led the way for them to his home on the edge of the village.

As they walked, Dysmas was thinking about his answer, and the mysterious means by which he had attained it.

It was not long before they were entering the compound that surrounded one of the more palatial homes within the precincts of Pella. Rushcal was a merchant of means. He ordered two of his servants to show his new guests to their sleeping quarters for the night, while the rest prepared a meal and brought wine for their return.

Neither Dysmas nor Gestus had been accommodated with such finery in their lives. Each were shown to their own room on the upper floor, each of which were lavishly furnished. They placed their few belongings upon their beds, and returned with the servants to the great hall where their benefactor awaited them.

Wine was poured for all when they were seated. "Tell us now," said Rushcal, "of this Jesus we hear so much about. How long have you been a follower?"

"We have been with him for about seven months now," said Dysmas, "and I assure you he is most certainly real."

"The stories we have heard are, well, not to place too fine a point on it, unbelievable."

Both Dysmas and Gestus smiled to each other then. Dysmas looked at Rushcal. "We have been travelling with Jesus for seven months, being ourselves present with him for much of that time, and I assure you sir, unbelievable in no way does it justice. But tell us, what have you heard?"

"Well, for example just yesterday two travellers passing through on their way to Masada told the most fantastic tale of any we have heard of him to date."

"Please stop before you say another word. I suspect I know of what they spoke. A couple of days ago you say?"

"Yes."

"They were perhaps travelling from the region of Gennesaret?"

"Yes."

"They were among five thousand other men who were present when loaves and fish were provided to feed them all from nothing?"

"It's true?" asked Rushcal visibly shocked.

"It is most certainly true," said Gestus. "Jesus even asked me to gather some empty baskets from the people present. I seriously had no idea why, but I did so anyhow. I am not lying to you when I tell you, and Dysmas saw me himself. I personally lined up the empty baskets as he instructed. There was nothing in them. Phillip, one of his apostles, gathered from the people present a few loaves and fish; when next I saw the baskets, they were all full to overflowing with loaves and fish."

"How is this possible?" asked Pishca as he looked now to Rushcal shaking his head, bewildered.

"We have two witnesses," said Rushcal. "We did not even lead the second to suspect the story from the first, and yet they recount it accurately."

"We are blessed that you have come," said Rushcal now. "There are others in Pella who will wish to hear you. Would you mind if we made known your presence among us?"

"No," replied Gestus much to the consternation of Dysmas. Dysmas really didn't want to place himself so much in the limelight, but Gestus had a story to tell and he wanted to tell it. So it was arranged.

Servants were sent out to gather those who were interested in hearing of Jesus. Soon the great hall was filled with many from Pella, eager to hear firsthand of this Jesus they had only rumour of until now.

Because both Dysmas and Gestus looked to them to be warriors of some sort, the people found it paradoxical, mainly with Dysmas, that culture seemed to eclipse his more obvious persona.

Soon Gestus was explaining the events of Gennesaret over the past few days in great detail, beginning with the days leading up to the event. He was speaking loudly to accommodate those who found themselves to the back of the hall, and had arranged that Dysmas would stand at the back to signal him if he could not hear.

As the attention of those present was entirely directed to Gestus, Dysmas found himself released from public duties, and wandered out through the doors to the rear into the courtyard. There was a wall that circled the compound that was only waist high, and he noticed something moving behind it. Soon he found eight men and three women sat down on the opposite side, listening intently to the story of his companion unfold. They were clearly not of the class of those within. They looked up, now frightened that they had been discovered. Dysmas just raised his hand to put them at ease.

There were servants standing at the rear of the hall. He approached and called them together. "Please gather some food for me, I am very hungry still." As they started to move off he took one by the arm. "I will need quite a lot." The servant nodded and was gone. A few minutes passed and they returned with four trays of meats and fruits with two skins of wine. "Will this be enough?" one asked. "Just about," smiled Dysmas. "Follow me," and he led them to the wall where he instructed them to place the trays upon it. As they did so they saw those hiding behind it and looked back to Dysmas smiling. Soon they were gone and a feast begun for those who had not seen so much food for a very long time.

As the great hall had filled earlier, Rushcal, after introducing his guests, and not being one for crowds of people, had retired to the room directly above, to listen in peace. As he stood now on his balcony listening, he was well placed to observe the obscure events taking place in secret behind his home.

Those who had occupied the lesser seats out the back were now well fed, and Gestus, drawing near the end of his story, was now beginning to struggle to hold the attention of his audience.

Improvisation was not Gestus' strong suit. Dysmas moved now to the great hall in a bid to relieve him.

Rushcal had himself returned to the hall, as Dysmas took his place beside Gestus.

"Who is this man Jesus?" asked one man.

"He must be a prophet!" another joined.

"If he is a prophet, what message does he bring?" another asked.

Just as Rushcal raised his hand to bring order, there was a commotion at the side of the room where the main door was located. The servants of the house having let their guard down, and being engrossed hearing the extraordinary story told by Gestus, had not noticed the entry of Palar son of Pishca. Palar had been quite mad for some years, so long so that his father had stopped grieving for his dearly lost son, for it was killing him. He lived in the caves outside the village. His father each day would see to it that food and drink were left where he might discover it.

News of the arrival of these strangers to the village had found its way to his attention via the interest it had generated around the well, as word spread around Pella of the meeting in the great hall of Rushcal.

He entered in now with his usual temperament, screaming obscenities and denouncing those present as evil. The servants ran from everywhere, as they knew from experience many would be needed to restrain him. Pishca was greatly agitated when he realised his son was again making a terrible scene and was seeking to leave the room of his closest friend when Dysmas stood upon the table at the end of the hall. He had asked the name of the man and could hear the words from his mouth. Familiar words to him, he knew well what was happening.

"Silence," he called and the room quietened a little. "I said be silent," he cried in a louder voice now, and all complied but Palar, now forcing his way through a crowd who, though remaining silent, were trying desperately to stop him.

"Do not stop him," said Dysmas. "Let him through." People started to part then as Palar made his way toward Dysmas, though he was now hesitating. Though his abuse and obscenities continued unchecked, he started to move from side to side and coming toward Dysmas in an erratic manner, sometimes hiding behind this one or that, a far different approach from the initial method of a direct line. He was not used to being invited or even tolerated in company, so he was all at once suspicious of this stranger. Pishca stopped also and prayed that his son might just leave.

As Palar neared Dysmas still standing on top of the table, all the room held its breath. They were well used to the antics of Palar, though there was something about this stranger that had them wondering at his bravado with an obvious wild man of which he knew nothing.

Palar, still screaming, was now only a short distance from Dysmas, when the latter raised his hand as with Keplar, and demanded he be silent.

"Who is it dare silence me?" was the response of the guttural voice that answered.

"In the name of Jesus I command your silence. You will speak only to answer," and at once Palar fell silent. All in the room were stunned and began looking one to the other. Dysmas came down from the table top to stand immediately in front of Palar. Remembering how Jesus had dealt with the demons he asked Palar, "Who are you?"

"Legion," was the response.

"Why are you here?"

"This house was empty, so we took it for ourselves."

"This house was not yours to take," replied Dysmas, "I banish you from this house, be gone."

"You have neither the power nor authority to banish me," he laughed.

"I have all the power and authority I need, given me by Jesus the Nazarene. You have no place here, be gone. Now!" Without another word being spoken Palar dropped to the ground like a dead man.

None moved to raise him, unsure of what would happen next. Dysmas bent down now and lifted Palar to his feet. He was calm and, although a little disorientated, smiled for the first time in many years. His father was overcome and slumped to the ground in tears, as he suddenly recognised the son he loved so dearly had been returned to him once more.

Palar soon recognised his father, and went to him and held him close as they wept together. The room erupted in cheers and applause and many were seeking to speak now with either Dysmas or Gestus about what had just happened. Rushcal went to his dear friend Pishca and held both him and his son, overjoyed that they had been reunited at last.

Local people realised the miracle they had just witnessed, as Palar was one of their own, and immediately started praising Dysmas. He stood and spoke now.

"Brothers," he began and the room fell silent. "Your brother has been returned to you not by my hand, but by the hand of the one who sent me, Jesus the Nazarene. Be sure to know the meaning of this gift. He sent us to tell Israel their redemption is at hand, and the kingdom of God is very near to you.

"Take care that you judge not your brother, for we know not our brother's burden. Palar was dead, even to himself, prisoner of the evil one. Let those who judged him harshly from fear be once more united to him. He that was judged harshly, let him be grateful and forgive, lest he himself judge his brother and be himself guilty." The room erupted once more. Dysmas turned now to face Pishca and Palar in time to see Rushcal leading eleven people into the great hall: eight men and three women. He ordered food and wine for all present as he stopped now before Dysmas. "I am my brother's keeper," he said with a smile. "They will be well cared for, Dysmas. Thank you."

From an impromptu gathering called at the last moment, grew great rejoicing and excitement that did not cease the entire night. Every member of the village approached Palar and his father, welcoming Palar home, some apologising for their sentiments toward him, others just weeping in his arms. He received them all with great joy and humility, while Pishca thought at one point he would die of sheer joy.

As Dysmas scanned the scene before him he smiled to himself as he saw resolution in every place. "That's more like it," he said to Gestus now, "and we didn't have to kill anyone."

As the sun began its ascent, people were starting to take their leave to go about their various daily duties. "Pella will be a tired village today," commented Rushcal to Pishca with a smile.

"Ah, yes," he replied, "but far happier nonetheless."

Rushcal sought out Dysmas and Gestus now. He thought they were probably ready for a well-earned rest. He showed them to their rooms himself this time. As Dysmas entered his room Rushcal took hold of his arm. "You have brought great joy to our little world here. Thank you," he said.

Dysmas was thinking of the events just past as he dressed for bed; however, he had no sooner laid his head to rest than he was fast asleep. He knew not how weary he truly was.

They both slept for much of the day, waking just after the ninth hour.

Rushcal besought them to stay, but they reminded him they had been sent on a mission and needed to continue on their way.

Rushcal ordered that all they needed for their journey should be provided, and so the servants hurried to pack supplies, while Dysmas and Gestus washed and prepared their belongings. As they came down now, they were greeted by Rushcal and Pishca, who hugged Dysmas with tears in his eyes. "Palar would have been here but I could not bring myself to wake him. These many years have drained his strength."

Dysmas just smiled. "No doubt," he replied.

"Come," said Rushcal leading the way to the courtyard beyond the entry. There they found a young donkey, laden with supplies. Dysmas was taken aback.

"It is the least we can do to assist you for the blessings you have brought to our little world," said Rushcal. "Pishca had a young donkey, and I the supplies that he could carry for you," smiled Rushcal. "You are most welcome to it all and more besides, should you have need. You are always welcome here, both of you," and he embraced first Dysmas and then Gestus, as did Pishca.

"We are grateful to you," replied Dysmas. "There is more than enough here to sustain our journey," he said smiling as he turned to Gestus.

The servants too had turned out to bid farewell to the two strangers who had had such an impact on their master's house in so short a time. They had not only rejoiced at their master's joy, but had been greatly attracted to the message of these strangers, and yet more at their dispositions, in particular to those less fortunate.

Walking now beside their donkey an hour later, Gestus smiled and mused, "I told you we could get more, did I not?"

"Look at us," Dysmas said. He was aware that they were now moving with optimism and a spring in their step. "Who would have thought, Gestus, that we of all people would be teaching others, let alone saving them. Feeding the hungry. Performing miracles no less."

Even Gestus had been overwhelmed by the past few days. "I have to say," he said, "this was not at all what I expected. Jesus said that our Father would provide. We give what little we have away, and it is replaced immediately in abundance. Even I have to admit, it is truly extraordinary."

The weeks that followed were no less so. As they moved from village to towns and small communities of outcasts, they often found sorrow, yet left at least peace in their wake, if not always something miraculous. They shared what they had with the poor more freely now, and found always that their heavenly Father could not be outdone in generosity.

They found no place in their travels that did not welcome them, and in fact, at times there had been those who had gone ahead of them to the next village to announce their pending arrival. It was somewhat overwhelming to Dysmas, who was greatly delighting in the opportunity this journey gave him to relieve the sufferings of his fellow Jews. The entire journey seemed to him a balm that soothed his own bitterness, and gave him a more realistic perspective.

He had been delighted also in the progress of Gestus who was now ever ready to assist the poor by whatever means. Dysmas had smiled with tears in his eyes when Gestus had given a poor soul his sandals, having found the size of his foot was similar to his own. At the very next village however, a merchant who noticed the unshod feet of the shoeless Gestus, being greatly impressed with what these strangers had to say, generously provided him with the finest sandals he had ever owned.

"It just never stops," Gestus had said with a smile, still somewhat bewildered by it all.

The weeks passed all too quickly for them, and they found their journey so engrossing that they both forgot entirely about visiting with Barabbas. So many were seeking their counsel and assistance that the intention was simply lost somewhere, and was never found again. Before they knew it, the day of the reunion was upon them, and they in fact had to hurry to keep their pre-arranged appointment at Caesarea Philippi. As it was, they would be arriving in the late afternoon.

Barabbas, it seemed, would have to wait.

Enlightenment

One by one the pairs sent forth from Gennesaret arrived at Caesarea Philippi. Over the course of the entire day they straggled in, overwhelmed with joy and stories of wonders that had happened to them over the past few weeks since going their separate ways.

Natan and Caden were among the first to arrive. It was as if Natan were a different man entirely. He was greatly animated, telling stories of wild men calmed in an instant with a single order in the name of Jesus. Caden was glowing in his praise of Natan who had apparently taken charge of 'exorcism' duties, leaving him to preach. Natan for his part claimed himself overwhelmed by the oration of Caden. "It was as if you were there, Jesus; when he spoke, all in earshot listened intently. Me included," he laughed.

In truth, the choosing of the pairs had proved insightful, as each of them provided individual talents that had complimented one another beautifully.

As each pair arrived, they were greeted with such genuine affection and familiarity that it was clear for all to see that the group as a whole had formed a deeper bond, even while apart.

For his part Jesus remained largely silent, smiling as he welcomed each one back with an embrace of genuine affection.

As evening fell and the last of them arrived, they found fires burning and three fat lambs almost cooked through. The deliciously aromatic smell of what was to be their feast flooded their midst and surroundings. Jesus and some of the apostles had apparently ensured a special dinner to celebrate the reuniting of the disciples.

Spirits were high as they all shared stories of their adventures, and although it was true that they all had many stories of their own, they were no less astounded when hearing so many stories of the travels of their confrères.

Stories of healing, and people freed from demons, could not but elicit from others stunned silence. Though they had all shared similar experiences, nonetheless, it had been a breathtaking introduction to a world not dreamed of by any of them, who had set out only forty days previously.

Many stories also included the kindness of so many people, who had welcomed and assisted them. There were invitations to return, and indeed two proposals of marriage, and they all laughed.

As the night deepened now and the stories waned, Dysmas, who had been quiet for some time, looked up to Jesus. "I had a dream," he said as they all turned now for another story.

"What kind of dream?" asked Natan as the gaze of Jesus rested upon Dysmas now, the hint of a smile upon his face.

"One that seemed so real that I retain it as a memory. One that told me what to say when the time was right."

Alon joined then, admitting he too had had such a dream, as had Elemar and others. A pause followed. "Was it real?" Dysmas asked now of Jesus.

"The dream?" asked Jesus. "Clearly so," he said smiling. "Do not imagine that I would leave you orphaned, a rudderless ship blown by the whim of chance. Trust in me, and trust in the one who sent me. I share your joy, for I saw Satan fall as lightning from heaven, defeated by the good will of mere creatures. Yet do not rejoice because the demons obey you, take joy rather that your names are written in heaven."

Quiet fell upon them now as they considered these things, when Jesus spoke again, "Who do people say I am?"

"A prophet as of old," said Natan.

"I have heard them claim you are John back from the dead," said Phillip.

"And you," said Jesus at last. "Who do you say I am?"

They looked around one to the other for a few moments when all at once Simon stood up. "You are the Christ," he said. "The Son of the living God!"

"Good for you, Simon-bar-Jonah, for flesh and blood has not revealed this to you but my Father in heaven. So I say to you; you are Peter, and on this rock I will build my church, and not even the gates of hell shall prevail against it. And I give unto you the keys to the kingdom of Heaven. What you bind on earth will be bound in heaven, and what you loose on earth will be loosed in heaven."

Simon stood dumbstruck, as the rest were silent, wondering what such a statement might mean. It was clear to them all that a statement of profound importance had just been made, though none understood it.

"From this moment forward," Jesus continued, "you shall be known as Peter. Hear me, all of you. I bind you all to silence as to what has just been said here. As you are my brothers, you must not repeat it abroad. What is given to you is for you, and you alone."

Jesus stood then. "I tell you most solemnly, the time approaches when the chief priests and scribes will seek to destroy the Son of Man. They will hand him over to be put to death. I make this known to you now, before it takes place, that you may not be scandalised."

Simon Peter who was still standing, motioned Jesus that he might follow him. They moved a short distance out of hearing when Natan said to the group, smiling. "He doesn't seem to know that the people want to make him king."

Elemar just shook his head, smiling. "It is because he is so humble, but they will surely make him king at some point. You are right though, he doesn't seem to understand at all."

When Peter returned, he seemed upset, but took his place with the others as before. Though many were wondering what had been said, none would dare ask.

"It is late," said Jesus upon his return, standing now beside Peter. "It is best you all get your rest; we will be leaving early for Joppa." While he was still speaking, an approaching noise could be heard as two figures emerged from the darkness into the light of the fires. The first to enter was Joseph of Arimathaea. Peter leapt to his feet recognising immediately the two as Pharisees. "Lord," he said. But Jesus simply smiled, "Calm yourself, Peter," he replied. "It is my uncle," and he stepped forward to embrace the much-loved Joseph, whom he had not seen for some years.

"It is good to see you, Jesus," said Joseph. "Your mother told me where I might find you. There is much word of your travels in Jerusalem, and I fear much misinformation." He turned now and placed his hand on the shoulder of his old friend Nicodemus, who was now standing beside him. "This is Nicodemus. We have been friends since before you were born. After what has been said within the walls of the Sanhedrin regarding your ministry, I thought it well past time Nicodemus met his brother. I know you both well, and you are indeed brothers."

"Welcome, Nicodemus, please sit, there is still lamb to be found, I'm sure."

"All these men," said Nicodemus. "Your disciples?"

"Yes," replied Jesus. "My hardworking and very tired disciples. They were about to retire," he continued as he looked about them now. He smiled then as he said once more, "They were about to retire."

At once they were moving, collecting their various cups and utensils, and stowing them back into their satchels as each of them made their way back to the patch they had earlier staked out for themselves as their bed for the night.

The area Dysmas had his bedding in was just out of the fire glow and behind a tree, quite near where Jesus and his visitors were talking. He was straining to hear and could make out the gist of what was being said.

Nicodemus was greatly impressed as he found himself now alone with Jesus and Joseph. "So many," he said. "How do you provide for so many?" he asked.

"Does not our Father in heaven provide for the birds of the air and the beasts of the field? It is a small matter. What brings you here, Nicodemus?"

"I know in my heart that you have been sent by God. You could not do the things I know with certainty you have done, if it were not so. Yet I have studied the holy word of our fathers all my life and find myself unable to understand or reconcile some of your teachings."

"It is because you place value upon the flesh, which has nothing to offer other than a means to serve the spirit. Truly I say to you: none will see heaven but that he be born again."

"How can one be born again when he is old?" asked Nicodemus.

"Truly, I tell you Nicodemus, no one can see heaven unless he is born of water and the Spirit. Flesh is born of flesh, the spirit of the spirit. You should not be surprised of these things. You are a great teacher in Israel and yet you know not these things. The wind blows where it will. You hear its sound, yet you know not from whence it comes or to whither it goes. The same is true of those born again of the Spirit."

"How can this be?" asked Nicodemus.

"I speak to you of earthly things, Nicodemus, and you do not believe. How then would I speak to you of heavenly things? Hear me, Nicodemus," Jesus said lowering his voice a little, causing Dysmas to strain greatly to hear the rest of what was said.

"No one has gone into heaven except that one who came from heaven, the Son of Man. Just as Moses lifted up the snake in the wilderness, so the Son of Man must be lifted up, that everyone who believes in Him might have eternal life.

"For God loves the world so much Nicodemus, that He sent His only Son, so that whomsoever believes in Him may not perish, but have life eternal. For God did not send His Son into the world to condemn the world, but that it might be saved through Him."

Nicodemus was greatly puzzled by these words, though his training immediately called to mind all the related Scriptures surrounding Moses and his people's experience in the wilderness. "I am grateful to you for your insights," he said at last. "I confess that I do not understand them as I probably should, but I will study these things you have shared with me, that I might learn their meaning."

"You are a great teacher in Israel precisely because you have not closed your mind and heart to the action of the Spirit. Those who do, are lost by their own hand. Led by their pride, they hear not the Spirit. A great ransom must be paid that He may dwell with them also."

"I am troubled by the anger I sense building among the Sanhedrin," said Nicodemus.

"Do not let your heart be troubled, Nicodemus. Your Father in heaven knows all. The machinations of man are man's own folly and of little interest. All of creation is consumed with the task of man's salvation, tirelessly labouring through man's history that it may be realised, time the measure, providence the means. There is nothing to fear from the Sanhedrin," he concluded smiling.

The next thing Dysmas knew it was morning, the sky just starting to blue. He had dozed off to sleep after that comment, and the visitors of the night before were now gone. As he lay now quietly watching the smoke from the smouldering fires rise through the early morning mists, he puzzled over what Jesus had said. Must he always speak in riddles, he mused?

There was no one stirring when he rose, so he put more wood on the fires and prodded them back to life. He saw now someone in the distance sitting by the water. Jesus, he thought. Given he was alone, Dysmas thought it an opportune time to speak with him, so made his way to him before any of the others awoke. As he neared him now he could not help but wonder if he ever slept. Although he had seen him lay down on occasion, he had never actually seen him asleep.

"You're an early riser Dysmas," said Jesus without turning.

"How did you know it was me?" he asked.

"Well," he said, "many won't approach me, you will. Some move apprehensively, you don't. Others approach me timidly, careful to remain quiet. It is you and Peter alone who are rightly sure of my ear." Jesus turned to him now smiling. "Unless Caesar is atop his chariot riding though our camp site with a Roman legion, I may safely assume Peter is still sleeping. It is not such a mystery, Dysmas."

Dysmas smiled and nodded to himself.

"You found in your journey with Gestus great peace, I feel," Jesus continued.

"Yes," replied Dysmas, "but in the midst of great suffering."

"And where was suffering greatest, Dysmas, the flesh or the spirit?"

Dysmas realised he had not considered there to be a difference. Yet now he stopped to think of it, the question was a valid one when he considered the hunger of some with the possession of others.

"The hungry are fed and they are hungry no more," said Jesus, anticipating his thoughts. "But with those afflicted in spirit, a healing is needed. There is much to be healed in every soul Dysmas. Do not feel yourself alone. The life of man is such that suffering is as much a part of each man's soul as is his heartbeat. Man seeks with all his will to avoid suffering, and yet it is inevitable. From simple inconvenience, to the death of a loved one. How can one avoid it? And if suffering cannot be avoided, what is to be done? Is bitterness truly the only answer? Must man really need to become so agitated that the seeking of peace becomes itself burdensome and necessary? Do not let suffering disturb you."

"How can one be indifferent to suffering?" asked Dysmas.

"I did not say be indifferent to it. I said don't let it disturb you. A world of indifference is one of omission that only serves to increase suffering. That you even notice it is a first step. Caring is the second. Yet you can do little of consequence until you understand what it is, and why your Father allows it."

"The suffering of those I see has always disturbed me, but I confess I neither understand what it is, or why our Father allows it."

"Your own suffering has in great degree charted your course, has it not?"

"Yes, I suppose so, but it was anger that got me through."

"Not only anger, Dysmas. Had it been anger alone, it would have consumed you and made you indifferent to suffering. Would you not have demanded others endure, given you had endured? No, you have as yet not understood that you were prepared for suffering in greater measure than others by a father who himself understood these things, one who prepared his son well to endure them. Much has been given you, Dysmas, far more than you know. Yet suffering not only has its place in the formation of a man in this life, but eternal merit for him when he is called to give account. Suffering has not only purpose, but merit."

Dysmas was thoughtful.

"People are prepared well or poorly. If they are prepared well as you were, they will grow much when they endure hardship, as you have. So suffering is about growth, Dysmas. That is precisely why your Father in heaven allows it. Yet it was never originally His plan for Adam and his sons. It was Adam that sought out suffering; your heavenly Father simply uses what is evil to bring about the best outcome for Adam and his sons."

Dysmas remembered his many reflective moments atop his little mountain considering his father's instruction as a child, and saw immediately the truth of the observations.

"Anger may well have been the initial means of survival, Dysmas, but what drives you now? Do you not now see the world through different eyes? Would you say that you have grown or regressed? Have you not lived a life of adventure so many claim to crave? And as great as you perceive your sufferings to have been, have you not come to know them to be more inconvenience, when viewed in the light of others you have met in your travels?"

"My father's murder was not an inconvenience."

"Murder is a strong word Dysmas. One needs to be careful it is used wisely. Inconvenience is as much a perception as suffering itself. If your father waits expectantly in the bosom of Abraham for the redemption he knows to be sure, would he consider it an inconvenience, or a joy? Is he not precisely where he hoped he would be? Indeed where every man would want to be? Would you not wish it for him? Is your sorrow for your father or yourself?"

Dysmas was suddenly angry. "How could you understand?" he said, rising, and returned to the rest of the group who were all stirring now.

Gestus was up wrestling with Natan and laughing when Dysmas brushed past him abruptly. "What's the matter, Dysmas?" he asked, but he kept walking without a word. He was intent on being alone.

He found his way an hour later to the top of the great rock formation overlooking the lagoon formed by the spring that ran there. From here, he could see the entire area below, including the bustle of the camp of his confrères, but his thoughts were elsewhere.

Dysmas had always been blessed with clear thinking, an attribute his father had deliberately fostered in him. Yet he was also a victim of the fall of Adam, and the perceived slight from Jesus forced itself harshly upon his pride. He knew in an instant that Jesus had been correct, yet this served little to placate either his pride or conscience. Fallen man often finds there are some subjects far too taboo to broach with the inconvenience of truth. For Dysmas, the death of his father was one such subject.

He had pondered many times that day and its outcome. Yet more to the point, he had pondered his own contribution. Though he yet blamed Gaius for murdering his father, the passing years had reminded him that his father's presence in that place, at that time, had been entirely his own doing. Try as he might to reconcile this truth, the pain of accepting his part in his father's death, and the subsequent loss of his mother and the life he had loved so dearly, was just too much to accept, and had been all these long sad years. He found himself in all too familiar tears once more.

The day passed slowly as he considered these things when Gestus arrived some hours later. "We are leaving," he said simply.

Dysmas hesitated, but a moment later was on his feet and following Gestus down to the group below. Soon they were underway, headed for Capernaum, Dysmas giving Jesus a wider berth.

Forgiveness and Redemption

They travelled for many days and stayed two nights in Tiberias, before continuing to Capernaum. Half a day out of Tiberias they made camp beside the Sea of Galilee. As was his custom of late, Dysmas found himself once more leaving the group for the caves he could see not too far in the distance. He had been spending a great deal of time alone on this journey.

Having reached a large overhang, he inadvertently startled a woman who was all but naked. She clearly was living in this deserted place, and had not expected visitors. Caught now with little to cover herself, she sought to hide behind a large boulder at the entrance to the cave. "What are you doing here?" she said clearly afraid.

"I mean no harm," replied Dysmas, "I was just trying to be alone."

"So am I, so what are you doing here?"

From the moment Dysmas had laid eyes on this woman, it seemed to him that he had met her before, and he was combing the recesses of his memory trying to locate that one needed to identify her. A most extraordinarily beautiful woman.

"Go," she said again. He sought her pardon and turned to leave but stopped suddenly. He turned back to her then. "Mary?" he said now.

A look of horror formed on her face as she screamed at him, "I don't do that anymore. Go. Just go."

Dysmas suddenly understood what was happening, and the reason for her reaction. Even the terrible beating she endured could not hide such beauty.

"It's alright Mary, you need have no fear of me. You would likely not remember me for I saw you only once, and we never actually met."

She stared at him now as she calmed herself. "You were there, weren't you? That night you were there!" she repeated as tears started streaming down her cheeks. "I saw you the night Kiman was murdered. That was you!"

"Yes, Mary, that was me. My name is Dysmas. You are here now. Why are you here?" he asked a little confused.

"I could not stay," she said through tears. "Not after that night. Dear Kiman, he should not have died for me," and she broke down sobbing as if it had happened yesterday. Clearly she was greatly burdened by the events of that night.

Dysmas approached her now and threw his cloak around her. "Come," he said, and led her into the cave where her meagre possessions were kept.

"It seems it was a night of change for both of us," said Dysmas as she found her clothing and a private place to adorn herself with it.

"What do you mean?"

"Your assailant was a man called Barabbas. He raised me after the death of my father. I left him that night and haven't been back yet," he said.

Mary replied, "I have heard of him. I left as soon as I was well enough."

"How long have you been here?" asked Dysmas.

"Ever since."

"That was eighteen months ago. What have you been doing?"

"Fighting myself mostly. Repenting of what I had become, or what something inside me drove me to be." Mary looked at him now puzzled. "How did you come to be here is a better question."

"Ah, yes, that is a long story."

"Perhaps you have a short version."

"My travels from that night led me eventually into the company of Jesus of Nazareth."

"You know Jesus the Nazarene?"

"I am one of his disciples," replied Dysmas.

Mary leapt to her feet, now very focused. "Where is he now?" she asked.

"I suspect by now he will be on his way to Magdala with the rest of the disciples. I will catch up to them. We are headed for Capernaum."

"We will catch up to them," she said, as she quickly began gathering what little she had. "I am coming with you. Hurry."

Dysmas was stunned. "What do you mean 'we'?"

"I mean 'we', I must see him. I have longed to see him since I first heard of him. Since first hearing his name, I have been driven to see him in person. I must answer the call. Come!" And with that she was gone.

There was little more for a shocked Dysmas to do than follow. When they arrived at the place where he had left the rest of the group some hours before, they were already gone.

"Where will they go?" Mary asked, a hint of desperation in her voice.

"He has been invited to the house of Simon the Pharisee. He will eat there this night."

"I know where he lives," said Mary. "Come," she said as she started on the road. "It will be after dark before we reach Magdala."

They made haste and while still some way off from Magdala they could see a large group of men in the distance approaching the town. She began to run, calling the name of Jesus, with Dysmas, somewhat bemused being left behind. She was closing the distance between them and herself when one of the disciples heard her calling and signalled to the rest to stop. Jesus moved to the back of the group and watched as she ran down the hill to him, by now completely out of breath.

Even though there were so many men she knew somehow exactly who Jesus was, and fell down on her knees in front of him catching her breath. "Please help me," she cried.

"Who are you?" asked Jesus.

Mary threw herself down on her back and screamed, "You have brought me here."

"Who are you?" repeated Jesus.

"I am Legion," she screamed. "I am pestilence and lust, this is your doing, I know who you are."

"Silence," said Jesus raising his hand. "Come out from her," and Mary tried to rise but then screamed and threw herself to the ground violently and was still. A moment later she stirred and looked up at Jesus, a shocked look of bewilderment, as Dysmas arrived to a show that was already over.

Jesus lifted her to her feet. "Everything will be alright now, Mary," he said. "Your faith has set you free. Be at peace."

"Ah, Dysmas," he continued smiling. "You have joined us once more. Good. I feared we'd lost you," and he started to move once more to the front of the group, leaving Mary staring after him. The group began now to cover the last few hundred metres to the outskirts of Magdala.

The sun was almost set when they reached the house of Simon, who welcomed them himself at the gate, and guided them into the large courtyard that had been arranged to house their number.

Lamb had been roasting for some hours and a genuine feast arranged for their arrival. Jesus was guided to his place among various dignitaries of the town, while the twelve and the other disciples were left to fend for themselves, taking various places around the courtyard area.

They had no sooner said the blessing when a woman of extraordinary beauty, eyes filled with tears, entered the courtyard.

Those of the town recognised her immediately, though they had not seen her for many months, but none said a word. She made her way directly to Jesus and knelt at his feet behind him. She had with her a small alabaster vial, and from it she took some perfumed ointment and anointed his feet. Silent tears streamed down her face as she smiled up at him now. She noticed that her tears were falling upon his feet, and so leant down then, and with her golden red hair, wiped them away.

Simon was a little taken aback, wondering if Jesus knew her for the sinner she was. Surely, if he is truly a prophet he would know, he thought.

Jesus looked now at the woman with such compassion that it caused her to lower her eyes and hug his feet as she kissed them.

"Simon?" asked Jesus.

"Yes, Master?" he replied.

"Two people owed money to a lender. One owed five hundred denari, the other fifty. Neither had the means to pay him back, and so he forgave both debts. Who do you believe would love him more?"

Simon thought for a moment, "The one who was forgiven more, I suspect."

"And you would be right.

"When I arrived, Simon, I was touched that you took care to meet me yourself, and care personally for my needs. You are a good and upright man, and have always been so." Jesus turned then to Mary as he continued. "Yet, you did not provide me water with which to wash my feet, while this woman has washed them with the tears of a repentant heart, and wiped them dry with the veil of her hair. You did not greet me with a kiss, yet still she kisses my feet. You did not anoint my head, and yet she has provided perfume for my feet. I tell you solemnly Simon, she loves much, because she has been forgiven much. And that of which she has been forgiven, has been cast aside never to be recalled." He raised her up then. "Your sins are forgiven, go in peace and sin no more."

Some of the other guests wondered who Jesus was, even forgiving sins, but he continued. "Go now and have no fear, your faith has saved you." Mary was overwhelmed with an inexplicable feeling of peace, as if a weight that had crushed her for much of her life had been finally lifted. She rose then and nodded humbly to Jesus smiling, before going to Simon who was sitting beside

Jesus, where she stopped and knelt before him with silent tears in her eyes. "Thank you," she said as she looked up into his eyes. "I am so grateful to you that you have allowed my presence in your home this night. I truly thank you," and she bowed her head, rose to her feet and left quietly.

Simon was greatly touched by her genuine humility, as the look in her eyes somehow pierced into his very heart. He turned to Jesus then. "Master," he said, "I have much to learn, but I hope that I am willing to learn."

"You will, Simon, have no fear," Jesus said.

What followed was a delightful evening, as Simon began to see the wisdom of the gentle hand, the forgiving heart. It was as if to him the Scriptures were unfolding in an entirely unexpected way, in a delightfully practical way. He considered these things all night as the evening bubbled along fermenting, with the yeast of joy.

Many of the disciples retired soon after the meal, tired from their long journey. Jesus walked with Simon for a time, while Dysmas found himself at the edge of Magdala, close to where he had been on the last night he had spent there. In the moonlight now he could make out a tiny form, seated almost precisely where he had been when Gestus had found him on the night he had left Barabbas.

He sat now beside Mary as she was admiring the crescent moon and the stars of the night. "Are you alright?" he asked.

She turned to him, her face all but glowing with joy. "I have never been better in my life," she said. "Never. It's as if I'm seeing the wonder of creation for the first time. I am free," she said, "truly free. And you?"

"You are perceptive, aren't you!"

"A captive can always recognise another captive, Dysmas."

"I'm still working on it."

"Stop working on it and open your heart. He will make up for what is lacking, and you will be free."

"Did you not work on it for many months?"

"No. I endured it for many months, waiting for him who would heal me. In a dream I was told he would come, and I never gave up hope that it would be so. And here I am. We must learn to trust, Dysmas, and I have to say with all honesty that I never doubted; but then, if we do not trust, is there any alternative?"

Quiet fell upon them now as they entertained their own thoughts, until Dysmas announced finally that he was going to retire, and with that bid Mary goodnight.

Morning found the group packed early and soon underway for Capernaum. It wasn't long before Dysmas noticed some distance behind, a tiny figure following. When they stopped at about the sixth hour and the fires were lit, she came into the camp and began arranging the food before cooking some mutton for Jesus and the twelve. For the most part, it had been the case that the other disciples organised their own needs.

At these stopovers, Jesus always took the opportunity of instructing the disciples with regard the virtues or on sin and its perversity. Today as he began to speak, he glanced up and noted that the camp had a visitor, busying herself with its needs. He simply smiled to himself and continued his discussion.

From that time on, Mary became a familiar sight around the group, and a greatly popular one. Like little boys they would bring her their torn garments to mend, their problems and fears, but mostly their thanks. Like Kiman before them, they found in Mary over the weeks and months that followed, a woman far more beautiful than the stunning beauty that had been in many ways, her cross.

Their time in Capernaum was brief and they headed then to Chorazin and through Bethsaida to Gennesaret, where they stayed for some days. Dysmas, as always, was dismayed that the reaction to Jesus varied so greatly. The closer their travels took them to the place of his childhood, the less he was welcomed. Dysmas found it a most extraordinary phenomenon.

Leaving Gennesaret, they made their way to Pella, and the days slowly unfolded. Dysmas had not engaged Jesus in conversation after their last discussion at Caesarea Philippi, and for his part, Jesus had left Dysmas alone to ponder what had been said there. And ponder he had. At times he found himself angry with Jesus that he considered the death of his father an 'inconvenience'. And at others that he suggested it had not been murder. Yet other times he struggled in tears at the thought that he was the reason his father had been killed. Had it not been for his actions, the events of that day would never have come to pass. These things plagued his thoughts as they had always done. He knew well he had spent much of his life fixated upon the events of that day.

"And ruined it as a result," he heard from behind.

He turned then to find Jesus behind him.

"Meaning?"

"Meaning providence blazes the path that mortal men must walk, Dysmas. The journey is a waste if the destination is not reached. All of creation conspires to assist man to reach his destination. Creation has no interest when he reaches it, only that he does. Having done so, he is an eternal success without regret, without sorrow. To mourn one for having achieved his goal, is more than a lack of trust or faith. It is a selfishness that clouds one's own life, making his own journey more perilous, as not only the destination he seeks becomes hidden, but the path itself. Be careful you don't lose yourself to the past, Dysmas."

"Well, if providence is so concerned for my welfare, I'm sure it will work that out also," he replied sarcastically.

Jesus smiled to himself. "Be that as it may, Dysmas," he said, placing his hand on his shoulder, "for my part, I will walk the path with you to the bitter end. You are and have always been my brother, and I will always be near you, no matter what." Jesus left him then to his thoughts and made his way back to his disciples.

Dysmas was angry with himself that he had been disrespectful to Jesus. Truly there had never been a man in his life, with the exception of his father, that he respected more than Jesus, yet his blunt honesty so often angered him. The fact that he was inevitably correct, made it that much more irritating.

Over the next couple of days Dysmas again became a little reclusive, again giving Jesus a wide berth, but as they now entered Pella, two familiar faces caught sight of him at the well. Rushcal was on his feet in an instant with the older Pishca, a few moments behind. Dysmas moved through the group and hugged Rushcal, who threw his arms around Dysmas in return, as did Pishca with genuine love.

"You have returned to us at last," said Rushcal. "You and your friends will be our guests tonight, yes?"

"Yes," said Dysmas, smiling, as Gestus himself broke through the group to greet the two men. Dysmas looked about and saw Jesus standing behind Peter, admiring the welcome his two disciples had just received.

"Come, Rushcal, Pishca, let me introduce you to Jesus of Nazareth," he said as he led them over to Jesus now. They both bowed to Jesus. "If you are master to such as these men, you are most welcome here."

In no time at all Rushcal had very willing servants arranging a feast for his friends and their master, the servants themselves joy-filled that Dysmas and Gestus had returned to them once more.

Though the story of Pella had been told along with the many others from various of the disciples upon their return to Caesarea Philippi, all were delighting now to be reliving the animated version from Pishca, whose son was now somewhere between Pella and Jerusalem travelling there to offer a sacrifice of thanksgiving for having been released from the grip of the demon.

This was to be a most light-hearted visit for Jesus and his disciples, for Pella was indeed a most happy and changed village. Much had happened since Dysmas and Gestus left. The wealthy of the village and surrounds, recognising the plight that had been Palar's, and also the temporal state of the homeless and poor, had met to devise a plan on how they could assist their fellow Jews.

There was, not far from Pella, a large field that had not been worked for some years. Bela, its owner, had offered it to the project. Others had oxen they could spare while Pishca had seed, Rushcal ploughs and so on. Rushcal had also provided some of his servants to properly teach methods of planting and harvesting. Between them all they had provided the poor and homeless of the village and surrounds, the means to provide a living for themselves as a group.

It had not only been greatly appreciated, but was working very well at many levels. Those without work now felt useful. People, both poor and wealthy, saw hope and were helping each other. The harmony in this little village was almost tangible. Dysmas was thrilled listening to the excitement of Pishca and Rushcal, who thanked him for the idea. He protested that it had not been his idea, but they wouldn't hear of it.

Jesus was quiet for much of their short visit, preferring instead to listen to the praise given to his now embarrassed disciples. Even the rest of the disciples were greatly impressed, and it became the talking point on the road the following morning as they left for Salim, a day and a half walk south west, where they stayed for an uneventful three days of well-earned rest.

They then made their way for a little over a week to Jericho, where Zacchaeus met them with a very warm welcome. Much had changed in Jericho also, clearly a far happier town. When they arrived just after the sixth hour, they found Zacchaeus at his table in the square, without his Roman guard, laughing with Roboam over how his brother had taken a tumble off his horse that morning. It was difficult to know who was more pleased to see Jesus of the two of them. They had put their differences well behind, and had discovered a friend in each other, that they had both nearly missed entirely.

Many of the town's people found their way to the house of Zacchaeus that night, to hear Jesus and to simply enjoy each other's company. It was a night that held not the least tension, as Pharisee sat now beside his Jewish brothers, one in mind and spirit. For though it was true that many in the Sanhedrin despised Jesus, and from time to time in their travels they would run into those, it was true also that some Pharisees saw the works of Jesus and were attracted by them, seeing in them the answers to many questions.

The night's festivities over, and almost all of the visitors home in their beds, Dysmas found himself now seated around one of the fires with Peter, James, Phillip and Judas. Jesus, having bid Zacchaeus good night, soon joined them watching the flames and embers. "It is good to come back," said Peter at last.

"It is always good to retrace your steps from time to time," said Jesus. "Hope is enkindled when the fruit is on display."

"Is that why we came back?" asked Peter.

"There were many reasons, but that was certainly one of them. Also, man is fallen; it is wise to care for his interests, in case he has neglected to care for his own. We will be leaving early," continued

Jesus, "I have already bid Zacchaeus goodbye. We will travel to Jerusalem, Lydda, Joppa and then north back to Capernaum."

At first light they continued their journey. After leaving Jerusalem, it was notable that various of the Pharisees from Jerusalem began following the group, always out of sight, but notable for their presence in each town, seemingly seeking to trap Jesus.

It began in Emmaus when Reuben asked Jesus if it was licit to pay the tax to Caesar. "Please," replied Jesus, "do you have a coin with which you pay these taxes that I might see?"

"Of course," smiled Reuben as he immediately produced one and gave it to Jesus. He inspected it briefly before asking, "Whose image is this on the coin?"

"It is Caesar's," replied Reuben with a smirk, to which Jesus replied, "Then clearly it is his, is it not? Give then to Caesar what belongs to Caesar, and to God what belongs to God."

This had left Reuben with his mouth opened staring at Jesus with nothing further to say.

They had been in Lydda for less than a day before Zebulon the Sadducee posed a question about marriage. "Master," he said. "A woman married a man who had six brothers, and he died leaving her childless. Another brother married her and he too died leaving her childless. So it was with all the rest. When the woman dies herself, whose wife will she be?"

"It is because you have not understood the Scriptures that you ask this question. In heaven, men and women do not marry according to what God has provided for the earth, but are like angels residing in the heights, in the presence of their Father in heaven."

Seff the scribe approached Jesus in Joppa. He, unlike some of the others, was very respectful. "Master," he said. "Which is the greatest of the commandments?" When Jesus looked up at him, there was the hint of a smile upon his features as he answered, "You must love the Lord your God with all your heart, with all your soul and with all your mind. This is the first and greatest commandment. The second is like it. Love your neighbour as yourself. On these two are built all the law and the prophets, as one virtue sustains another."

"You are right, Master," he replied. "To love our Lord with all our being and our neighbour as ourselves, these are far more important than holocausts and sacrifice."

Jesus gazed upon Seff then and his smile grew wider, "You are not far from the Kingdom of God," he said.

"Master, if I may," replied Seff, "I do not understand your instruction of the virtues sustaining each other. As a young boy I was instructed that the greatest virtue was temperance, that the passions might be brought to heel."

"Apart from the great and necessary virtues of faith, hope and charity," began Jesus, "which exist to support the lower faculties, the virtues are many. Yet in truth can be claimed as seven, each subordinate one to the other. Faith, hope and charity together form the mortar that binds the lower virtues together as one.

"The greatest of these is humility, for it forms the foundation upon which all others stand firm. Man would not perceive the passions as an issue, unless he understood he were in need of saving? Humility therefore assists him to see the truth of who he is, in light of the reality in which he exists before his heavenly Father. He assesses honestly and truthfully therefore, that he must bring his passions to heel for the good of his soul. Man would not even bother unless he perceived accurately his station. This requires that he perceive reality in truth, this in fact is true humility, the true assessment of man's place before his Father.

"Humility then, assisted by charity, leads the soul to seek that which is best for it. Charity is not only a commission for others. Each man is made in the image of God. It is incumbent upon each then to be charitable to himself. In so doing, he recognises his Father's claim not only to his purity, but his joy. It is the proper and just love of self for the glory of our heavenly Father that drives men to subdue their passions, that they might be better men. So the practice of temperance brings forth fruit to the glory of your Father who is in heaven, but it does so because humility has first revealed the truth, as charity then seeks its exercise. In like manner the virtues are sustained as a cohesive truth supported one by another. Humility is ever the foundation. Faith, hope and charity, is ever the mortar that binds them together."

Even though these answers and more were greatly appreciated by some of the teachers, who now began to leave rather than pursue what they had concluded to be a just man, there were some still asking questions to trap him. This had continued in Antipatris and Sebaste, all answered kindly and simply, yet so decisively that there could be no rebuttal.

As they had continued, the soldier in Dysmas was at times visible as his patience was tested by these "jackals," as he referred to them.

When they finally arrived in Capernaum, the collectors of the temple tax came to Peter and asked him if his master pays the tax. "Of course," was his response. When Peter came into the house, Jesus asked him simply, "From whom do the kings of the earth collect taxes, from their children or from others?"

"From others," replied Peter. "So the children are exempt," said Jesus. "Yet, lest we cause offence," continued Jesus, "go to the lake and cast for a fish. The first you catch, open its mouth and you will find the temple tax for both you and me."

Dysmas being present for this exchange could not help but accompany Peter as he made his way to the lake as instructed. He cast his line which almost immediately hooked a large fish and, just as predicted, two coins lay in its mouth. Peter smiled at Dysmas as he threw them into the air a little, snatching them again in his fist with a laugh as he rose and made his way back to the temple.

Many of the disciples had spent the day between the temple, listening to Jesus speaking with the Pharisees and scribes, and shopping for their various needs in the marketplace. Much of the day had been their own. They met up again as a group at the back of the house where Peter lived, which opened into a small field surrounded by a low wall as was the building custom of the area. There was more than enough room to accommodate all of them there.

The sun was almost gone when a Roman centurion stood looking over this same wall seeking an audience with Jesus. As Dysmas looked up now he recognised him immediately: Gaius. "What's he doing here?" he said to Gestus, who had as yet not realised his presence. Gestus was stunned when he realised who it was, and one of the disciples knelt down now beside Jesus, to inform him that an audience had been requested.

Jesus rose then and went to the wall standing face to face with Gaius, surrounded by the rest who were unsure of his motives. Dysmas in particular was ready to pounce, but Jesus smiled and shook his head. "Welcome, Gaius," he said.

"You remember me," he replied.

"Certainly. It is good to see you again."

"I heard you might be in Capernaum. My servant Jelrah, he is very ill and I fear he will die unless he is made well. He is more a dear friend, really. I have come to ask it of you."

"I will come at once."

"No," said Gaius, "I did not bring him with me; he is too ill to travel; he is still in Jerusalem, and I am unworthy that you should enter under my roof. I have men under me and I say to this one 'go,' and he goes. To another I give a task and I know that it will be carried out. Say but the word and I know he will be healed."

Jesus turned to those gathered. "I have not found faith such as this in all of Israel, and I tell you solemnly, many will come from the east and the west to the joy of the kingdom, while those for whom it was intended, will be forbidden from entering."

He turned back now to Gaius, "Go in peace. What you believe has been done for you."

"Thank you, I am very grateful." As he started to turn to leave, one among the disciples caught his eye, stopping him briefly as he glanced again. Dysmas glared at him knowing he had been recognised, but Gaius left then without a word to find his lodgings in the town.

"He recognised me," Dysmas said to Jesus quietly. "He will be back with a Roman guard."

"He will not be back with a Roman guard, Dysmas."

"You don't know him as I do," Dysmas said. "Why would you help him, a Roman? Do you not know who he is, what he's done?" Dysmas was angry and his blood was boiling.

"Yes, Dysmas," replied Jesus calmly, "I know exactly who he is, and precisely what he has done!" Dysmas stormed off then furious, believing Jesus had been flattered because he had found a Roman who now believed in him. He had thought more of him than that.

As he stormed angrily through the town now, he came upon the area that ordinarily housed the marketplace, now empty, marching straight into the path of Gaius, who himself had been strolling through the town considering whether to return to talk with Dysmas or not.

At last Dysmas was face to face with the enemy of his childhood, and yet all he could do was stand as a man frozen. He was unarmed, while Gaius, as always, bore his sword on his hip. Dysmas knew well he was completely vulnerable.

"We meet at last, Dysmas," said Gaius.

Dysmas stood statue still.

"You need not concern yourself, Dysmas, you have nothing to fear from me. I have spent much of my life looking for you, that I might return you to your mother. I have no intention of harming you now."

"What of my mother?"

"She is well, though heartbroken, and has been for far too long. You can hate me, Dysmas, but don't hate her. She has no fault in all that has been. Adoring her husband and her son is her only crime."

"And what are we to you?"

"Well, she is one who has taught me not to give up. She has relentlessly searched for you, had me searching for you. She has never given up on you. Don't give up on her, she deserves better.

"You are one who has had his life snatched away, a disillusioned boy grown into a confused man. I know you hate me, and given what you have likely been told, I don't blame you. Yet I have seen how hate consumes a man, Dysmas, many times. I'm done with it. I'm glad to see you with the Nazarene. You will find peace with him if you allow it. You deserve that." He turned then and made his way out of sight on the other side of the square, leaving Dysmas amazed to consider their short exchange.

Over the days that followed, Jesus remained at Capernaum, so the disciples were able to visit loved ones and had some time to themselves to take care of their personal needs. Dysmas found himself considering Gaius and his comments, even during some of the discussions Jesus was having with various people who sought him out with questions. It was as always, difficult to reconcile the Gaius of his imagination to that one in the flesh.

Having been sent with Gestus on an errand to Chorazin by Peter, he had much time to consider his plans regarding his future, and had come to the realisation that he had never been more at peace than during his time with Jesus. Gestus was of like mind. Clearly it is where they were meant to be, they had concluded.

When they entered Chorazin marketplace now just after the sixth hour, they could not believe their eyes. There eating a pomegranate was Barabbas, large as life. He saw them at the same time and leapt up to greet them with great excitement, introducing them to some of those who had joined him since their departure. They were legends within this group of men, so all were eager to meet them.

Soon they were alone with Barabbas who was greatly interested in the story of their travels, and in particular their time spent with Jesus, in whom he had been taking far greater interest for some months.

"You should come and hear him speak," said Gestus.

"Yes, you should," chimed Dysmas. "He teaches with authority, and what he teaches resonates with truth. It is impossible to argue against his teachings. You really must come."

"Where is he now?" asked Barabbas.

"He is still in Capernaum. He will be speaking again this night in the synagogue. Why don't you come back with us? We will be leaving soon."

"I can't just at this moment, but I may try to get away later. We will see."

"It is good to see you again," said Dysmas as he hugged him once more. "Hopefully we will see you later, but we must pick up our errand and return."

"Peace be with you," added Dysmas quite by reflex, surprising Barabbas a little and causing him to smile. It seemed to him that this was a very different young man.

Crossroads

"**B**arabbas," cried Dysmas, smiling. "You came, great to see you."

"Well, here I am at Capernaum no less. Could there be a deeper backwater?"

"You won't be disappointed. Will he, Gestus?" said Dysmas.

"Truly, Barabbas, you won't be disappointed. He is a prophet of God."

"Yes, so I keep hearing, Gestus, but I have heard that many times before."

"Ah, but not from us, come quickly."

In no time Barabbas was ushered into the midst of the synagogue just as Jesus began to speak.

"You have not sought me here because of the signs that are before you, but because you had all you could eat. Foolish guides of the blind. You perceive a miracle as many were fed from so little on the shores of the lake. Amen I say to you, it is a far greater miracle that wheat grow in abundance from dirt to feed multitudes. Yet you ignore this, like so many other miracles around you. Your senses are dulled by familiarity, leading you to a perception of reality that bears little resemblance to reality at all. You seek food that does not last, work rather for food that endures unto eternal life."

A Pharisee cried out, "And what must we do that is pleasing to God?"

"Believe in the one He sent!"

"And what sign do you give that we should believe? What work will you do? Our fathers had manna to eat in the desert; as Scripture says, 'He gave them bread from heaven.'"

"It was not Moses that gave your fathers bread from heaven but my Father who is in heaven. The bread of God is that which comes down from heaven and gives life to the world."

"Give us this bread."

"I am the bread of life. He who comes to me shall never hunger. He who believes in me shall never thirst."

A scribe shouted, "Never hunger, never thirst. What are you saying?"

"You see me, yet you believe not, but those who believe are given me by the Father, and none shall be lost that He has given me. Yes, it is the will of my Father that whosoever sees the Son and believes in Him, shall have eternal life, and I shall raise him up on the last day."

"You? The son of the carpenter? Did you hear him? We know who he is, how can he say he comes down from heaven?"

"Never heard so much nonsense in my life," said another.

"Looks like your great prophet is sinking fast, Dysmas," said Barabbas smiling. "If nothing else, he's entertaining."

"No one can come to me unless he is drawn by the Father, and I will raise him up on the last day. It is written in the prophets, 'they will be taught by God'. To hear the teaching of the Father and to learn from it is to come to me."

"He is claiming to be God!" shouted a Pharisee.

"I tell you most solemnly, everyone who believes has eternal life. I am the bread of life. Your fathers ate manna in the desert and they are dead, but this is the bread that comes down from heaven, so that a man may eat it and not die. I am the living bread come down from heaven, anyone who eats this bread will live forever, and the bread that I shall give is my flesh for the life of the world."

"He's mad!" said another Pharisee, "and here we have thought him a threat when he is simply mad. How can he give us his flesh to eat? And if we ate, Scripture says we will be cut off from our kinsmen."

Barabbas was much amused by what he heard and saw. "Really, Dysmas," he said now smiling broadly, "I had no idea your prophet was a comic. Wonderful!"

"I tell you I have never heard him speak so," replied Dysmas, dismayed as he watched people leaving.

"I tell you most solemnly, if you don't eat the flesh of the Son of man and drink his blood, you will not have life in you."

People were jostling each other now as some were trying to push their way free from the crowd while shouting, "This man is a fool, who could listen to this outrage?"

Yet he continued, "My flesh is real food, my blood real drink. He who eats my flesh and drinks my blood lives in me and I in him. As I who am sent from the Father draw life from the Father, so he who eats of me draws life from me, this is the bread come down from heaven."

"This is intolerable," screamed a Pharisee blocking his ears as the synagogue collapsed into uproar.

"Who are you claiming to be?" yelled another as he pushed his way to the door in disgust.

"You thought he would lead Israel to freedom?" asked Barabbas. "This prophet? He's mad, Dysmas, and you're a dreamer."

"He has never said anything like that before, Barabbas, truly."

"He's right," joined Gestus. "He has never said anything like this before."

"Well, he has said it now," laughed Barabbas, "I'm leaving before they stone him," and he turned and started to bustle his way through the crowd toward the door. He stopped then and turned to Dysmas as the roar of the crowd increased.

"Dysmas, you're a fine soldier and a leader of men, come with me and do some good. You're wasted here, can you not see that?"

Dysmas looked at Gestus, unsure of himself for the first time in many months. "I was so sure, Gestus, that he was the one," he said with tears welling in his eyes.

"So was I, Dysmas, so was I, but well, I hear Israel crying out to me, and I have to answer. I'm going with Barabbas."

Dysmas looked at Barabbas and back to Gestus as they both started to move through the crowd who were now screaming obscenities at Jesus. Finally, he looked at Jesus through the uproar. At that moment Jesus, as if he knew somehow, looked straight at him. His look was at once serene and yet piercing, as if reaching into his very heart.

Dysmas looked away as he heard Gestus call over the roar of the crowd, "Come on, Dysmas." He felt his arm being pulled and he followed obediently. He was thinking to himself how serene he had looked, how always at peace he was. What manner of man was this, he thought? Did he not know they intended to stone him? Was he a fool? So many words of wisdom flashed across his mind, confusing him. How could such wisdom be from a fool?

Just at that moment they finally breached the crowd that had spilled outside, and started for the road. "There is nothing we can do here," said Barabbas. "He has started something he won't finish I think, but there is no pleasure for me in the outcome other than the return of my two best men," and he smiled broadly as he threw his arms about their shoulders.

They could still hear the crowd some way down the road. Barabbas looked back, "Looks like they're all leaving," prompting Dysmas and Gestus to turn around.

It did indeed appear that they were all leaving, still gesticulating and shouting.

"Well, it would appear his movement has fizzled out," said Barabbas.

"I feel like a fool. Almost a year I have been following him, believing in him, only to find out he is mad," said Gestus. "How could I be so stupid?"

"Don't worry," said Barabbas. "It hasn't been a complete waste if he survives this day, though I doubt he will."

"What do you mean?"

"Well, what you have learned of his movement may be useful yet," replied Barabbas. "You know his habits and movements, how he thinks, where he goes. If, and that's a big if, he recovers from this, there may be opportunities to coordinate our operations."

"He would never agree to a frontal assault, or to assist in helping one," said Dysmas.

"Oh, I don't know," replied Barabbas. "What if we should make him king? Would he refuse to rule Israel? Does he not claim to be our king? And even if he would not help, just knowing where he will be with his followers would swell our numbers and perhaps even goad some of them into taking up arms with us. No indeed, the time was not wasted Gestus. This is a long way from over. The question is, will he survive this night?"

"So, what now?" asked Gestus.

"You are both fine soldiers and leaders," replied Barabbas. "Since you left, much has happened. We have new moulds for swords, melting vats for steel and many more men than you remember, but we need men to lead and train them. They are not so easy to come by. You, Dysmas, will be my right hand, my second in command. You will see to the combat training of our new recruits, and oversee the production and procurement of weapons once more.

"You, Gestus, will be my left. You will be in charge of infiltrating the Roman ranks with spies and raising funds for our army. Use your new connections to find out who our friends are. Both of you will help me plan the best targets and times to strike as before, though I have a plan already underway, a bold plan that will surprise even you two. We together will free Israel from Roman tyranny, and if this prophet of yours can be of any assistance, so be it. If not, it makes no difference, we will prevail. The road is long. We will sleep in the foothills tonight."

As they walked in silence, Dysmas was a conflicted man. He was at once hurt and angry, yet greatly disturbed at the events of the day. He had had so much hope. He had been so sure that Jesus the Nazarene was a genuine prophet from God.

They found themselves at the base of an outcrop of boulders surrounded by grass.

"This looks as good a place as any," said Gestus, "I have some bread and grapes, what have you got, Dysmas?"

"I'm not sure, ah yes, figs and grapes."

"You two have truly lost your way," said Barabbas laughing. "At least I came prepared," and he produced a full skin of wine. They all smiled to one another and all at once the tension was gone and it seemed like old times.

Captured

Barabbas' plan was bold and made Dysmas uneasy. It was an attack directly on the Roman garrison in Jerusalem itself, under cover of the Feast of the Tabernacles, when there would be thousands of pilgrims in the city. Barabbas wanted to show the Jews of Jerusalem that they could strike back at Rome. He believed it long past time that they made a public statement, and given they were at their greatest strength now, why not? Especially as his two finest soldiers had returned.

Dysmas was very much unconvinced as to either the wisdom of the intent, or the plan itself. Gestus too was less than enthusiastic.

Barabbas had believed it a good plan until Dysmas started pointing out the many flaws. It would not be possible from the position the men had been allocated to reach deeply enough into the Praetorian to make any real inroad, or inflict any real damage. And if it were to be a spectacle, then real damage was necessary. Further, if they put themselves in a position where they could inflict heavy casualties on the Romans, the chance of escape should there be a single mishap would be highly unlikely, given the extra ground they would have to cover to lose themselves among the crowds.

These were the two main sticking points, though there were many other logistical considerations.

"What is the answer, then?" enquired Barabbas.

"You still wish to go ahead with this attack?" asked Dysmas.

"Yes," was the confident reply. "Imagine if we brought our cause into the heart of Jerusalem. Imagine the new recruits that could be the result. If we could garner enough men, an army perhaps, we could push the Romans out of Judea entirely. We are never going to get the men we need with small raids in the middle of nowhere. Israel has to see that we are a force to be reckoned with. How are they going to see that if we don't show them?" he asked.

Dysmas had to concede the logic behind the intent, but it would not be easy. "In order for this to have any chance of success," he said, "we will need to strike from within the temple. There is no other way. That would require the cooperation of the Sanhedrin. That means we would have to trust the snakes of the temple."

"They are Jews like us," Barabbas had urged.

"Like us, you say?" retorted Dysmas. "They cannot be trusted."

"Leave the Sanhedrin to me," said Barabbas, "I have strong contacts with people I can trust. You two work out a credible plan. Between us we can make this happen," he said buoyed now, as he left to contact some of those 'strong contacts'.

"I don't like it," said Gestus, "I don't like it at all."

Dysmas was very skeptical. Any possible plan would require that at least some in the Sanhedrin, if not all, were aware of its detail. Revealing their plans to the jackals in the Sanhedrin was not his first choice.

As the planning proceeded, much discussion was had about revealing one thing while planning another, using decoys to execute the fake. However, at every turn it was made impossible by the complexity of the entire operation. "It is impossible without clear access to the temple courtyard," said Dysmas finally. "And that is not possible without people on the inside granting that access. There is nothing for it but to reveal the plan as it is," he had conceded finally.

That decision having been taken begrudgingly, they had set about forgetting their reservations and concentrating entirely on designing their plan. Two days later they had one that bore no resemblance to the original plan of Barabbas.

"Brilliant, brilliant," said Barabbas now as he surveyed their plan. There was perfect use made of the inner courtyard of the temple, giving them clear access into the heart of the garrison precincts. From this point they could inflict quick and heavy casualties, almost with immunity. It was proposed that they bind and gag all of the Sanhedrin present, to ensure their safety from scrutiny. With the seventy-two men that now made up their band of freedom fighters within the garrison precincts undetected, it was not out of the question that they could vanquish the entire Roman garrison within the walls of the city from that position.

"That would certainly make a statement," concluded Barabbas with a wide grin.

"The plan hinges upon the silence of the Sanhedrin," Dysmas said as he looked gravely at Barabbas.

"Leave the Sanhedrin to me," he replied. "It has been arranged. Prepare the men," he said. "I will be back in two days, the feast is in eight. We don't have much time."

For the next six days both Dysmas and Gestus drilled the men with both arrow and sword. All of them had to be proficient with both, should they be needed. This was to be the boldest venture yet, every detail had to be perfect.

Two days from the feast found their entire number on the road for Jerusalem. They had no way of knowing that only one would return.

The plan had been executed to the letter. As they scaled the wall under cover of the noise coming from outside the fortress, lowering themselves into what was an empty garrison courtyard, many couldn't believe their luck. Ten men at a time scaled the wall and hid themselves where they could, as the rest kept coming. At this time they believed the Romans to be unaware, perhaps still in their beds, given no one appeared to have had detected their presence. When Dysmas landed however he immediately called for retreat, but all too late.

Arrows rained down from all sides. The Romans had deliberately been awaiting the last of their number. All knew Barabbas, and so no arrow would find him as its mark. However the Romans were watching for any of the rebels giving orders, and they too were left unharmed. Bigger plans were awaiting them.

All the gates had been secured, there was to be no escape by that means. Some tried to scale the wall again, but it was an impossible task. Shot with arrows as they ascended, many were dead before they hit the ground. It was a massacre, well organised and planned. The Romans had been waiting. Clearly they had forewarning of the entire plan. "The jackals," Dysmas thought to himself.

Much of the battle was over in minutes, with every archer's bow aimed at the only three that remained standing. Barabbas and Gestus had laid down their swords, but Dysmas knew what awaited him should he be captured. Better to die here, and quickly, he surmised. However Maximus had anticipated such an action and had his best archer ready. Dysmas, before he could move, took an arrow through his shoulder, as the Romans opened the gates and came flooding into the courtyard.

Both Barabbas and Gestus were bound and dragged more than led away, while Dysmas lay in agony on the ground. Maximus pointed at Dysmas. "Leave none alive save that one," was the order, and the Romans passed among those that had survived, and put them to death by the sword.

"Get that arrow out of him," ordered Maximus, and two men raised Dysmas to his feet. Another unceremoniously pushed the arrow through his body, taking hold of the arrow head, then simply pulled it through without heed of the screams of his victim.

"Plug that bleeding up, we don't want to lose him yet," said Maximus very pleased with himself now.

Dysmas heard him order eight men to the temple to untie those there. "The jackals," he thought. He had known it all along.

Barabbas and Gestus were dragged to the dungeons below the garrison, while Dysmas was taken to the infirmary, where his wounds were attended to. The Romans were intent that he survive his wounds. So for the next couple of weeks at least, he was treated with some attention. The food provided him was high quality, and his body healed well. The moment it was clear, however, that he was out of danger, he was cast with the others into the cells below. Dragged out as the others had so often been from time to time for questioning, he would be beaten before being returned to his cell.

It was a living nightmare. After what seemed an eternity, but was in fact only two weeks, they stopped coming for them and left them to more or less rot. Time was soon of little consequence as there was no light to guide their senses, and only occasional groans and tears, as it seemed to them that they were slowly going mad.

Dysmas had been captured while Gaius was to the north escorting the payroll for the garrison. He had been chosen in case the information they had received from the Sanhedrin was itself a diversion. Pilate wanted to leave nothing to chance. The news of his capture had reached Muriam through Gaius upon his arrival back in Jerusalem, a few days after the event.

"I have already asked Pilate for an audience," he told Muriam. "I will seek his pleasure for you to visit Dysmas, but you shouldn't anticipate that he will allow it. I doubt he will in this case, but I will do what I can," he promised.

Muriam had begun praying from that moment that God would be merciful.

The following day, Gaius met with Pilate and sought a meeting between mother and son. The request was met instantly with a denial. "Prefect," continued Gaius boldly, "I know you are a just man. If you will hear me, I believe there is more in this case than you are aware of." Pilate sighed but had never known Gaius to be a man of folly. "Continue," he said at last.

Gaius explained the circumstances of how Dysmas came to be in the hands of Barabbas so young, and how his mother had searched for him since that day. "It is a tragic story, my lord, and though his father's death was entirely accidental, it was an accident at the end of my blade, a Roman blade. I plead Rome now show compassion, if not for the man, then for the mother who has suffered his loss undeservedly for so many years."

It was a compelling case, but Pilate had heard many compelling cases. After deliberating for a time as Gaius stood silently, finally he said, "What is this woman to you?" Gaius looked at the two guards at the door and back to Pilate. Pilate understood immediately. "Leave us," he commanded and they both left the room and sealed the door.

"Well?" he asked again.

"I am in love with her, my lord. I have been for many years."

"So you are in a relationship with her then?"

"No, my lord, there is nothing more to it. I have watched her for many years, admired her courage and strength. She is important to me, but there is no relationship as such other than that. Given the circumstance of our first meeting, how could there be?"

Pilate saw at once that there had indeed been many years of suffering, on both sides. "I will consider your request," he said at last.

"There is one other request I would have you consider, my lord, if I may be so bold."

"What is it?"

"Given I was the instrument that took her husband from her, I beg of you to allow me to stand down at the execution of her son. I could not bear to think myself the instrument that took her son as well."

Pilate was thoughtful. "I will consider this as well," he replied.

"Thank you, my lord," replied Gaius.

When he had left, it occurred to Pilate that this man was a man of great virtue, a true Roman in the ancient mould. If only I had a few more like him, he mused.

A week went by and nothing was heard from Pilate. Muriam had all but given up hope, but Gaius had encouraged her. "It is a good sign," he had said. "He is considering it. Trust me, he will summon me when he has made his decision."

That very evening a Roman soldier knocked at the door. Harum escorted the soldier to Gaius. "The prefect would see you this evening."

"Thank you," he responded, "I will accompany you back."

All business had been concluded by the time he arrived, and he was escorted immediately to Pilate, who ordered all but Gaius from the room. "Wine?" asked Pilate lifting the skin.

"Thank you, my lord."

Passing Gaius his cup, he continued, "I have considered both of your requests. Let it not be known that Rome is ungrateful to her faithful servants, or unjust to her subjects. For both of these reasons, I have granted both of your requests."

"Thank you, my lord," said Gaius, inwardly relieved but showing little of it.

"There will be one visit Gaius. Only one. She will have to make the most of it. Of all prisoners, I cannot be seen to be gracious to these, the enemies of Rome."

"I understand, my lord. I am grateful."

Pilate sitting now continued. "And what of you, Gaius?" he asked. "You have barely two months left to your commission. There are so many who don't live long enough to see the end of their commission. You are somewhat the exception. What will you do?"

"I honestly don't know, my lord. I have considered returning to Rome, but I have been gone so long now, there is none that I have known that still live. My parents are dead, and both my brothers have fallen in battle many years ago. I came through the ranks, so there is no property or fortune awaiting my return."

"There is the senate," replied Pilate. "It needs good men, Gaius."

"I am a soldier, my lord," he smiled. "The senate would be no place for the likes of me."

"I wonder," said Pilate. "I think the senate could do with a few more like you. In any case," he continued, "if you remain in Jerusalem, I believe I would have a position for you should you be interested. It would be a non-combatant position of course, more advisory."

"Thank you, my lord," said Gaius, a little surprised.

"Well, consider it, Gaius, and in the meantime you may organise the meeting with the prisoner, at a time best suited to his mother. Keep it low key."

"I understand, my lord, thank you again."

Upon his return the door opened before he even got to it, and an anxious Muriam stood before him. He just smiled and nodded. This was enough to have her jump up and down like an excited little girl. "Wait, Muriam," he said as she caught herself expecting bad news. "He has allowed only one meeting. There can be no others." This did little to dampen her spirits, as one meeting was one more than the past thirty years had allowed her.

"When?" she asked.

"Whenever you're ready," he replied, "but think about it. You have only one meeting. It is a meeting you should prepare for. The questions you want to ask. The things you want to say. This is the only chance you will have to ask what you will. Say what you will. You want to make the best of it."

"I understand," she said sobering a little now. "Of course, yes I see," she said to herself thoughtfully, as the gravity of her position now weighed on her.

She turned as if in her own world talking to herself, working out already those things she wished to say, making her way back to her rooms when she stopped suddenly and faced Gaius. Her eyes were filled with tears. "I am so grateful, Gaius. Truly I am. Thank you." Then she made her way back to her rooms to start the preparations she knew now she must make, for this once in a lifetime meeting.

Very early the following morning found Gaius ordering the prisoner Dysmas to be brought to him for interrogation, in a dimly lit room only a few steps from the one in which he was being held. Two guards dragged him into the room. "That will be all," said Gaius. They looked at each other, puzzled for a moment, but left immediately.

Dysmas was trying to adjust to the light. Though it was quite dim, it was still more than he had seen in weeks. Gaius said nothing, but slowly Dysmas could make him out. There they sat for a time across from one another. Finally Gaius spoke. "I have arranged with the prefect that you might have a visit from your mother."

"Why?" was the cold response.

"Because she deserves it. She has earned it with the heartache she has endured." Dysmas had no retort for such an answer.

"When?" he asked.

"The prefect has allowed her only one visit, so she is taking time to consider everything she wishes to say to you. The two of you have lost a lifetime. I cannot change that, but I have done what I could. I will see that you get as much time as I can. I am here now to let you know in advance of this meeting, so that you might prepare. You must have questions."

"Yes, I have a question. What is she to you?"

Gaius paused and sighed. "A woman I have admired for many years. A woman who inadvertently I think may have developed feelings for me that will never see the light of day, because of what happened so long ago to her beloved husband. Because of what will soon come to pass with her beloved son. She will never allow herself to live again, and I love her too much to ask it of her. You needn't worry Dysmas, in truth she is heartache to me. A woman I love, that I can never have.

"Prepare yourself," he continued. "It will be the only leniency Pilate will grant. She is so excited to be able to see you; treasure this time with her. I will let you know when it is to be. Make no mention of this to anyone.

"Guards," he called loudly. The door burst open then, and Dysmas was escorted back to his cell in silence. He was both angry and bitter to be so helplessly in the hands of Gaius, yet found himself once again begrudgingly grateful to this nemesis that had been such an integral part of his life. Dysmas, as always when considering Gaius, found little if anything aligned with his preconceived ideas of this Roman soldier.

Only a few days passed when Dysmas was disturbed once more, and delivered once more to Gaius. The guards having been dismissed, Gaius was surprised to find that he seemed in better spirits. Being a good soldier, this put him on his guard. Bitter experience had taught him that very often what seemed so, was not. However, in this case there were no deceptions. Dysmas had been very much looking forward to finally seeing his mother once more. So many years of longing for what he believed was impossible, yet now the day had arrived.

"How is my mother?" asked Dysmas.

"She is well," replied Gaius.

"Spare me the platitudes, Gaius, how is she?"

Gaius sat back, very melancholic now. "She is healthy, physically," he said, "but she still bears the scars of that day when we met for the first time. It never leaves her. It seems her heart was so offended by that moment that she never moved on. She has never really seemed to be rid of it. I think it hurts her especially as a person, because she has such a deep capacity to love, and yet she has not let herself love for so many years. It has left an emptiness in her, I fear, that injures her. Yet, with those around her she is ever a delight. Smiles are left in her wake wherever she goes, but I see. It never leaves her."

They both sat in silence for a time. "What else do you see?" asked Dysmas.

"I see you, Dysmas," said Gaius very serious now. "I see your father."

"What could you know of my father?" retorted Dysmas suddenly angry.

Gaius smiled.

"Ah, you mock me," said Dysmas.

"No, not at all. I understand your anger, I do. I spent so much time with Petmar bragging about your father, such joyful times, it was impossible for me not to know your father. A truly great man. A simple man it is true but great in his simplicity. A wise, cultured and gentle man. Make no mistake, Dysmas, I know well your father. I have known his like before. They in fact make up many of my friends, who are, I am sad to say, almost entirely Jews."

Dysmas scoffed. "Why would that make you sad?"

"Oh, Dysmas, always looking for the worst. It makes me sad not because they are Jews, but because I am Roman, and I believe in Rome. Yet those qualities that Rome embodied and held in such esteem I find now not in Rome but here, among your people, not your leaders," he laughed. "Your people. Sadly Rome no longer embodies the virtues that started our march across the world. Rome was not so much seeking glory as spreading truth. It breaks my heart that we seem now to have lost our way."

Against all his instincts, Dysmas found himself overwhelmed by the genuine honesty of this Roman.

Gaius continued, "Dysmas, I am not important at this moment. You and I can talk as you will if that is your wish, I owe you that much. However, the meeting you are to have with your mother is tomorrow. There can only be one. I don't wish to distract you in any way. Please be ready, if only for her. Pilate has allotted to her only one day and that day is tomorrow. He has however made no reference to the period allowed. It is my intention to bring your mother here at first light tomorrow. As long as it fits to the hours of the day, I am in no way compelled to cut short your visit before midnight." He threw a bag to Dysmas. "Clean clothes for you. The guards have been ordered to take you to the ablutions block before dawn tomorrow. Clean up and be presentable for her. Try not to break her heart. I can only do what I can do, Dysmas, it's up to you to make the most of it. Guards!" he called and they again entered abruptly to escort Dysmas back to his cell.

True to his word, the guards woke Dysmas well before the change of the morning watch the next day, and escorted him to the ablutions block, where a number of water jets were available for washing. It certainly felt good to be clean once more. From there he was taken to a room somewhere above, considerably more pleasant than he had been used to of late.

He did not have long to wait. Muriam hadn't slept, as anticipation had the best of her all night. She arrived just before the change of the guard. Gaius showed her to the room where Dysmas was waiting. Two guards were stationed at the door. When he opened it, Dysmas snapped to his feet. "Your mother is here," he said. "Are you ready?"

"Yes," he said. "Oh, and Gaius. Thank you." Gaius nodded and stepped back to allow Muriam through the door.

She stopped in an instant. She could hardly believe her eyes. Standing before her was Azel, just as she remembered him. "My goodness," she said aloud before she could stop herself and tears began to fall. Dysmas was a little confused when she went to him suddenly and took him into her arms with tears now flooding from her eyes. She held him for a time and simply wept, yet she knew not the reason. So overjoyed to be at last holding her beautiful little boy who had become a man, and yet so devastated to know that her greatest dread would soon be realised.

Dysmas himself, overwhelmed in this embrace of such power and emotion, found himself weeping uncontrollably. "Mother," he said at last, "how I've longed to be with you again," and he held her tightly to himself. After some minutes, he held her at arm's length, to behold this woman of sacrifice and virtue. She was as he remembered, a beautiful soul.

"You must have many questions," she said at last drying her tears.

"And you," he replied. "I have been thinking much about you these past few days. I never realised before how I have dwelt on myself over these years, taken up entirely with how these events have impacted me. It hardly occurred to me since I realised you were still alive, what it must have been like for you."

She smiled and wept again.

"I saw Arlett a while ago. She told me some of the news. I was so sad to hear Uncle Petmar had died."

"Arlett has gone to join him now," said Muriam smiling. "They are at peace. Petmar loved you as the son they had lost, and your father as the son he wished he'd had."

Dysmas bit his bottom lip as he remembered these people that had been such a large part of his young life.

"What happened, Dysmas?" Muriam said at last.

"Life, mother, swept me along in the torrent. At first I knew not how to escape, then anger and hatred taught me how to survive, as I have done so ever since. I learned how to be what I was not, never realising life was for living, not surviving."

"Tell me," she said.

He leaned back then and began to unfold the events of his life as best he could recall them. From time to time, Muriam felt a stabbing sadness, as the horror befalling her son's young life was revealed. How he had used his wits, and the skills he had learned from his father, to rise in stature among a group of thugs and brutes it seemed to her, that had used him in his innocence. He explained to her how he had come to leave, and re-join Barabbas, the year he had spent walking and listening to Jesus, the carpenter of Nazareth. "A happy year," he reflected now wistfully.

Muriam sat quietly as the years unfolded and washed over her, numbing her. When Dysmas had finished a full hour later, she realised it had been an exhausting tale.

"And what of you?" asked Dysmas.

"That day remains a blur to me. I know what happened, but remembering it in detail has never been possible for me. I know that Gaius sought to find you immediately after you were snatched up, while Petmar assisted me."

"Gaius," said Dysmas shaking his head.

"Yes, Gaius," replied Muriam. "If you knew how much trouble he was in from the prefect. I found out from Petmar that Roman soldiers were killed looking for you on his orders. Had the prefect known that he kept looking for you in the years that followed he would likely have had him demoted, but he didn't give up." These were surprising facts that Dysmas had never known or considered.

"I hear you are living with him."

"Who tells you that?" asked Muriam. "I stay in his home from time to time, I am not living with him. There is a difference." She told him how she would visit Jerusalem each year to honour her husband and son, and how each year Gaius had treated her with great kindness. "When your father was killed, it was Gaius who assisted us more than any other. He asked nothing in return, and has never done so at any time over all the years since then."

Patiently Muriam told him of the efforts to locate him and return him to her. "The fact that he couldn't had us all believing you were dead," she said crying. "When I returned to Jerusalem the following year, Gaius moved into the garrison, and left his house and servants to my pleasure. I have stayed there every year since, honouring my husband's memory, and hoping to see my son one day. If it weren't for Gaius, I would never have seen you again."

"He loves you. You know that?"

"Yes, I know."

"And you?"

"He has been nothing but a gentleman, and a friend. Somewhere, somehow in the last few years, I admit I have feelings for him. It's been thirty years, Dysmas," she had said a little annoyed now. "I thought you dead until three years ago. Why did you not seek me out? Sitting there judging me now because I see the good in what I know to be a good man doesn't help. It doesn't matter anyhow. It can never be."

Dysmas was at a loss for words. He knew full well that he had felt betrayed and had jumped to conclusions. "Gaius said he knew Petmar," he said at last.

"He did, and well. They became great friends for many years. Petmar would visit with Gaius each time he was in Jerusalem."

"Why?" asked Dysmas astonished.

"Because he didn't see Gaius through the distorted view of a boy who believed he killed his father."

"He did kill my father," he said a little agitated now.

"No, Dysmas," said Muriam sadly. "A terrible accident killed your father, whether you choose to believe it or not. I have watched Gaius suffer for many years over that day. I have no doubt you see it as you do honestly, but that is not how it was. Petmar was right behind your father that day. He knew well it was an accident beyond the control of Gaius, or anyone else. Was it the fault of Barabbas who attacked him that day? Was it the fault of the son that innocently ran off that day? Was it the fault of a father that chased the son he loved blindly? Who should we blame, Dysmas?"

Silence fell upon them for a time as they both silently wept. "How did Petmar die?" asked Dysmas at last.

"In his sleep, peacefully."

Dysmas smiled. "He was such a good man, I loved him very much."

"And he you. He was always seeking the latest news of the search for you whenever he was in Jerusalem. Gaius always welcomed him with whatever news he had."

There was a knock at the door then. Two soldiers brought fresh figs and drink, leaving immediately after placing them on the table.

"So you were with Jesus of Nazareth?"

"For a year."

"Why did you leave?"

"I left when he lost his mind, telling us to eat his body and drink his blood."

"He doesn't seem like the kind of man to lose his mind," said Muriam a little surprised. "Are you sure you understood him correctly?" she asked.

"It was pretty clear. You know him?"

"I have known him since he was a little boy. His parents brought him to our home when you were about nine. You were very ill. They were fleeing Bethlehem."

"Bethlehem. He survived the slaying at Bethlehem?"

"He was the only survivor," she said. "You did not know?"

"No, I did not," said Dysmas now thoughtfully. "Does Gaius know this?"

"Of course. We both met him about three years ago when we visited Arlett's grave. He and his mother were living in Nazareth. Gaius was most impressed by him. Now, something that you perhaps don't know; Gaius killed the commander of the soldiers that were responsible for the attack on Bethlehem. Gaius called him out as a coward. His response ended in his death. The secret of Jesus is safe with Gaius, as would be any other secret. I believe your father and Gaius would have been friends had they had the opportunity. I believe that in other circumstances you would see him in a different light."

"He has always been a paradox to me," Dysmas had to admit. "So what have you been doing all these years?" he continued.

Muriam went on to tell him of the many visits to Petmar's home and the time spent with Arlett, her visits to Hebron and Jerusalem, her work taking food to the leper's rock, and her many hours at the tomb of Azel, interceding for him. The hours slipped away so quickly, as often they found themselves just looking at each other. Their lives laid bare one to another, it was clear to both how much each had suffered. Now here they were, all but at the end.

They laughed and cried over so many memories shared and explained, without the slightest idea of the passage of time until there was a knock at the door when Gaius entered. "It is not long to midnight," he said simply, closing the door.

"So," said Dysmas. "So little time," as he stood and held his mother with deep affection. "I have always loved you, mother, and I always will. I really am so grateful for this time." Nothing further was said, as they held each other for what they both knew would be the last time.

Muriam with tears in her eyes knocked twice at the door and it swung open. She stole a final glance at her son as Gaius escorted her into the corridor that led to the great gates.

Soon after her leaving, the guards returned to take Dysmas back to his cell below. It was immediately clear to him that they had not approved of this luxury that had been provided to him, and made their disapproval known as soon as Gaius was out of sight.

They need not have bothered. In truth, the visit of his mother was itself another punishment, as it pained Dysmas so much to think how his life had been paralysed so profoundly by a single event. When she had left with her heart breaking, it occurred to Dysmas at that moment that he had never known such heartache in his tragic life. He had lost so much to bitterness and hatred, that he wept bitterly for many hours in the solitude of what was now his little world of agony.

Awakenings

L ight burned into their eyes as they found themselves thrust into the courtyard with little pomp. It had been five months since their capture, and almost two since Gestus or Barabbas had seen any light, let alone the sun, and weeks for Dysmas. They had been held in the dungeons below the Praetorian almost exclusively since their capture at the Feast of the Tabernacles. Blinded now by the sudden brightness, they could hear only mayhem around them. Orders were being barked, women were screaming and crying. Neither one knew he was standing next to the others.

As the minutes passed, they kept opening their eyes and testing them, in the hope that they had acclimatised to their new environment. Slowly they could make out figures as they were pushed in the direction of what they would soon find to be the instruments of their deaths. As their vision returned, each of them soon made out the crosses leaning against the wall before them, standing on their edge.

Both Dysmas and Barabbas seemed resigned to their fate, but Gestus was hyperventilating and collapsed at the sight, only to receive four lashes for the inconvenience he provided the soldiers, who had to make him stand.

Though the straps that bound their hands behind their backs had been cut as they entered the courtyard, leg irons still bound their feet one to the other, joined by a chain that provided enough movement for walking at an impeded pace. There was nothing for it but to comply with the demands made of them, lest the lash be laid upon their backs once more.

As they regained their full sight, they all soon became aware that the commotion they were hearing was not emanating from the courtyard in which they stood. There were but eight Roman soldiers with them. The noise was coming from the other side of the wall that separated their courtyard from the main Praetorian courtyard, where the prefect would hear cases of importance before the Jews. They were at a loss to know what was going on, but clearly the crowd were in an uproar.

"Choose a cross, you dogs," the centurion barked, but none of them moved, frozen as inevitability and realisation collided. One of the soldiers kicked Gestus in the back of the knee sending him sprawling, as another struck Dysmas across the face with the lash. Barabbas moved quickly to gather his cross before a similar punishment was his.

Soon all three had the instrument of their death upon their shoulders. "That's better," barked the centurion. "This can be easy or hard, it's up to you. We don't care." He arranged them in order of their rank. Barabbas at the lead and Dysmas immediately behind, Gestus behind him. "Now get moving," was the order, and they set off toward the huge gates before them, which were at that moment swinging open.

They had taken only a few steps when Gaius burst through a side door. "Halt!" he ordered. Barabbas however, his head swimming didn't hear the order and kept walking, only to have one of the soldiers kick the cross he was carrying, sending Barabbas sprawling on the ground with the huge cross pinning him there. "Stop when you're told to stop," the soldier barked.

"Bring Barabbas," yelled Gaius, "and wait here until I return." Barabbas was hauled to his feet then and delivered to Gaius, who was inspecting the state of the other two under their crosses. "They can put those down until I return," he barked as he started to turn to leave, but stopped suddenly, turning back to the soldiers. "I see these men," he said. "I see their wounds. If I detect a single mark on them that is not there now when I return, I will want to know who inflicted it. Should that information not be forthcoming you will all suffer my wrath. Do I make myself very clear?" They were all quick to respond with a hardy, "Yes centurion." From that moment on, both Dysmas and Gestus were left unmolested as they laid their crosses on the ground once more, grateful for a reprieve.

Barabbas was dragged to the adjoining courtyard, where much to his surprise he was the figure of interest. Though the Pharisees had sold him and his men out at the Feast of the Tabernacles, here they were now shouting for his release. Barabbas was totally confused as he was led to stand at the right side of Pilate, who was seated in the judgement chair. He could hear the people yelling, "Release Barabbas!" and observed the Pharisees moving through the crowd, encouraging them to yell louder.

Just then he saw to his left a man being pushed through the soldiers, but could barely recognise him as the carpenter of Nazareth. When Pilate saw him enter in the state he was in, he seemed a little startled, and was instantly uneasy at the sight of this man who had been reduced to raw flesh on bone. Barabbas himself sucked in his breath. He had never seen the like of a man still living, as this one before him.

Pilate stood then and addressed the crowd. "Behold the man," he said, and a silence fell upon them for a moment. They too were shocked by the sight. Then one of the Pharisees yelled, "Crucify him!" He was immediately joined by others screaming the same.

Quieting the crowd momentarily Pilate continued, "You have a custom that a prisoner be released to you on your great feast. Who would you have me release for you: Barabbas or Jesus?"

All at once the realisation of what was happening hit Barabbas, and he understood. As he looked around, the crowd erupted. "Barabbas, Barabbas," they cried. Those who were shouting "Jesus," were being pushed over and trampled by the crowd, encouraged by the Pharisees. For the first time in months Barabbas had hope of escape.

Gaius leaned over the shoulder of Pilate. "My lord, surely we cannot release Barabbas!" Normally Pilate would have snapped at him for his insolence, but not this time. Pilate himself understood the ramifications of releasing Barabbas. He had placed himself in an impossible position and he knew it.

He silenced the crowd once more. "What am I to do with Jesus called the king of the Jews?"

"Crucify him, crucify him," they yelled.

"You want me to crucify your king?" he replied, almost pleading.

"We have no king but Caesar," they screamed.

Pilate thought for a moment before he called for a bowl of water. He stood then washing his hands before the people and said. "I find no case against this just man. His blood be on your hands." With that he motioned the soldiers to release Barabbas, who pushed him toward the steps.

Seeing a chance that may never again present itself, he immediately rushed to the bottom, surprised to be ignored with disdain by all those who had just saved his life. They pushed him out of their way when he sought to thank them, and in the emaciated state his confinement had left him, he was in no condition to argue. It was clear that he disgusted them.

Pilate called Gaius to him now, and ordered Jesus be taken to the adjoining courtyard to take up his cross. "You are in charge of this detail now. I know one of them is the son of your friend. I know I agreed to let you stand down for his execution on compassionate grounds, but that cannot be helped now. This could erupt into a full-scale uprising, and your personal issues are secondary to the needs of Rome. I want every centurion on station around the city. I want you to ensure this task is completed without incident, by whatever means necessary, without delay. Get it over with," he snapped as he hurried away.

"Yes, my lord," answered Gaius obediently. He realised there was no point in arguing. Providence had set his path and he must trudge it.

Dysmas and Gestus had been listening in disbelief from the adjoining courtyard and realised that Barabbas had been freed. Moments later Jesus appeared. They could hardly believe their eyes at the state he was in. He was pushed to the position where Barabbas had left his cross on the ground, and ordered to take it up.

"You will be their new leader," laughed the soldier who pushed him over, until he sprawled over the cross upon the ground. "Now you dogs have another leader," he continued to the others. "A king no less."

"Oh yes," said Dysmas, "and you were going to save Israel."

Gestus laughed for the first time in weeks, "King of the Jews," he chimed in. "You saved others, why not save us now?" he continued. "We need a real king," said Gestus, "not a dreamer."

"Enough," said Gaius as he came into their presence. "Get those men walking," he snapped. "Now!" All at once the scene was returned to the cold regimented Roman exhibition that had become a more or less familiar spectacle in Jerusalem. Soldiers hurried to assist the prisoners to their feet, and even helped Gestus when the cross fell to the ground slipping from his hands. Clearly this was not the day to displease Gaius.

They had no sooner exited the courtyard when Jesus stumbled and fell, the cross crushing him to the ground. Gaius had ridden ahead to ensure the way clear, so the soldiers were free to vent their frustrations, lashing him again and again. Both Dysmas and Gestus too were angry at the delay. Apart from Dysmas nearly himself falling over Jesus as he fell, it meant he was stalled with this cross on his back yet longer. There was no pity to be found for this poor carpenter of Nazareth, even among those who would share his fate. Gestus yelled obscenities at him while Dysmas, himself angry, coldly demanded he get up.

Jesus found his feet once more and stumbled forward.

Dysmas was dragging his cross which seemed to weigh far more than he had thought. During their incarceration they were the most hated of prisoners. They were credited with killing many Roman soldiers, fellow soldiers of their captors. Consequently they had been kept alive, nothing more. They had no bedding provided them but the stone floor, no exercise periods. No comforts of any sort save one; Muriam's visit with Dysmas. They had been given enough food to keep them alive for one reason only, the delight of crucifying them. As a result Dysmas had become far weaker than he knew. The burden of his cross was excruciating. He was in no mood to tolerate some would-be king who he believed had misled him, and indeed all of Israel.

Just then a woman he recognised from many years past, burst through the crowd to kneel before Jesus. He remembered her immediately as that one he had helped escape with her husband and child so many years ago, so little had she changed in these many years. Surely Jesus is not the boy, he thought to himself. This mother and son exchanged not a single word. It was simply a look that passed between them, an agonising look that Dysmas could not help but feel pity for, remembering his own mother.

Jesus struggled past her then and her gaze fell on Dysmas, as she placed her left hand on his shoulder and smiled at him, a gentle confident smile. Her touch and compassion seemed to reach deep into his heart. For the first time in a very long time, he was genuinely comforted. She nodded, a sad smile as he passed and continued on his way.

Jesus was by now becoming very unsteady and was beginning to look as though he would give out. Gaius noticed immediately and ordered one of the soldiers to commandeer someone to help carry his cross. A Cyrenian was promptly plucked from the crowd that was hemming them in on every side and given the task, much to his outrage. The threat of the sword was enough to convince him he should reconsider, so he wrapped his right arm over the shoulder of Jesus and at once the weight became bearable.

It was a mystery to Dysmas what was holding Jesus up at all, while Gestus was indignant that he was being treated with favouritism and continued voicing profanities at both Jesus and the Roman guards, one of which lashed the whip across his face once more, knocking out a tooth. This brought Gestus under control in short order.

Dysmas noted that every time Gaius rode ahead to clear the way, the soldiers would again lash out at Jesus, either striking him with their fists, or lashing him again and again. Their hatred for him seemed insatiable. Given all that he had experienced of Jesus, his genuine kindness and concern for people, he was at a loss to understand why they hated him so, and why he and Gestus were in the main being left alone. It had been made known to them in no uncertain terms during their incarceration, that they were the most hated of any prisoner that had ever been held in Jerusalem. Yet it was Jesus they were attacking. The more they were driven through the streets of Jerusalem like dogs, the more baffled he became as to everything he was observing.

Gestus had taken offence at a man in the crowd who was laughing at him, and with all the strength he could muster, had rammed him with his cross, knocking the man to the ground, the weight of the cross providing means. Gestus found himself pinned under this heavy weight with his victim, taking the opportunity to bite his ear off. The man screamed in pain as the soldiers tried to separate them to get the deadly march started once more.

A woman in the crowd rushed forward during this small reprieve, removing her veil and splashing it into the well as she passed. Kneeling before Jesus she wiped the blood from his face and thanked him for healing her husband, before one of the soldiers, realising what she was doing, threw her roughly back into the crowd.

Just as they were passing the city wall, five women were weeping and calling out the name of Jesus, but he turned to them as he was passing. "Weep not for me but for your children. If this is for the wood when it is green, what when it is dry?" A soldier hearing flogged him across the back for his insolence, causing Jesus to fall for a second time. Gaius, however, was close by for this one, and slammed his horse into the soldier knocking him to the ground, dislocating his shoulder. From that moment on, the others were most careful to curb their conduct, and even more careful to know the whereabouts of Gaius at all times.

The rest of the journey from this point to the place of the skull was relatively uneventful. What had started out as a cloudless day, was fast becoming overcast, as thick black clouds were starting to form, and the wind was beginning to pick up.

As they were making their way up the final stretch of rocky hill, Jesus stumbled again and slammed into the ground, the heavy cross landing on top of him, opening his wounds that had once again sealed themselves with congealed blood. Yet still not a sound of discontent or anger escaped his lips.

Dysmas found himself, even in his own perilous position, feeling compassion for Jesus, and wondering what manner of man he was. Remembering now everything he had learned from him with regard loving and forgiving enemies. Everything about the exercise of virtue, was truly before him in action. This was without doubt the personification of the many lessons he had received while travelling with Jesus, and slowly it was sinking in.

The last part of this tragic march was the hardest, as they dragged their crosses up the stony incline that brought them to Golgotha. Gestus slipped and fell also, swearing under his breath at one of the soldiers for his mishap. He was becoming more enraged with every step he took. The soldier just laughed, ignoring him. He would have satisfaction soon enough.

Gaius had gone ahead to see if the holes were deep enough to support the crosses, and that there would be no impediments to their work. Muriam was standing at the edge of the mount to the left of the area where her son's life was to end. Gaius saw her and he steeled himself for what he must do, but his big heart was breaking for this woman he loved so dearly.

He had been in charge of so many crucifixions, yet this one, his last, was somehow very different at so many levels. He was lamenting the fact to himself that his commission finished at the end of this very day. Could it not have finished days ago? He had no doubt that this would be the end of any hope he had of a life with Muriam. She would leave after this day and never return. And who could blame her, he thought. Though he was the picture of Roman supremacy, Gaius was at breaking point as tears were welling in his eyes and his body was cramping with heartache. All his life he had dreamed of a relationship with a woman such as Muriam, and now that he had found her, circumstances beyond his control were about to rip her from his grasp.

For her part, Muriam had seen him approaching, mounted upon his horse, and could not bear to think of what he was about to do. She was numb, at a loss to understand her feelings just now. She well understood the position he was in, yet this man she had such deep feelings for, had been, and was about to be the instrument of the deaths of all those she had loved. Tears ran down her cheeks unchecked, as the full realisation of the horror unfolding before her revealed itself, just as it had all those years ago in a vivid nightmare that plagued her still.

She had determined, the previous night, to return to Nazareth after the body of Dysmas had been laid to rest with that of his father. After that, she would see Gaius no more, and this too was a source of terrible guilt as the thought of it broke her heart even more. How dare I feel love for this man in the face of the destruction of all I have cherished at his hand, and she shrank to the ground, weeping as she had never wept before. Never had she been so torn and broken.

Jesus was the first to reach the summit and the great cross fell to the ground as the soldiers roughly pushed him over to lay exhausted beside it on the stony ground.

Dysmas was the next to arrive, the only one who had not fallen on the ascent. He had been very thoughtful for much of the second half of the journey and had said precious little. The same could not be said of Gestus, as all in earshot heard his wrath, as his anger with his lot reached a crescendo when he arrived at the top, throwing his cross to the ground. What he had not realised was that he had inadvertently thrown it on the ground in such a way that the base of the cross landed right beside one of the holes. Given how easy it would be for the soldiers to simply lift the cross so that it slipped into the hole, Gestus was immediately chosen as their first victim.

The brutality of the crucifixion was somewhat lessened by the economy of movement of the soldiers who carried it out. Truly the Romans had perfected this form of execution, and went about their various tasks with precision and diligence. No sooner had Gestus thrown his cross on the ground than his clothes were torn from his body. He was in an instant stretched out across the wooden beam. An agonising scream was heard, as the first great nail was driven through the base of his left hand with a single blow, finding the pre-drilled holes provided for its entry. This terrible blow caused his fingers to cramp and clutch at nothing but air. A moment later and the act was repeated on his right hand. He was crying out in pain, waking Dysmas from his thoughts. His hands secured now to the cross, the soldiers removed the leg irons and tied his legs to its base, all the while Gestus alternating between obscenities and howling in pain. Four soldiers began lifting the cross, and its base finding its mark, slid into the hole stopping with a terrible jolt, eliciting heart-wrenching screams and moans from the poor soul that was now nailed to its structure.

Great wedges were driven into the ground around the base of the cross to stabilise it, and a plinth secured just within reach of the now hanging feet, to grant the poor wretch a means of lifting himself a fraction to breathe. However, then the agony was rekindled as the man's feet were themselves nailed to the plinth.

Pain exploded through the body of Gestus, as this final indignity brought blood-curdling screams from him. He had little choice but to raise himself to breathe, yet the placement of the plinth provided very little freedom to lift himself. He quietened now as he turned his efforts to breathing, which was already becoming difficult. He needed to press on the plinth on which his feet rested to raise himself up even the little he could. This released the pressure from his airways provided by his shoulders, which by the weight of his body was crushing his esophagus, and in turn his windpipe. The agonising pain stabbing through his feet when he did so, made him wish he could just suffocate. Human instinct however was guaranteed to keep him alive until every ounce of strength was exhausted. If the excruciating agony of the crucifixion was not bad enough, the torture of the slow death by suffocation that followed was inhuman.

These soldiers had many times experienced such executions and had no sympathy for what they considered the murderer of their fellow Romans. It was clear from the beginning that this would be a particularly callous execution, and so it began with smirks and smiles from what appeared a heartless group of men.

The gathered crowd that was now getting too close, were pushed back by Gaius and another horseman. This spectacle, though expected, was disturbing to many spectators present, as many of their number began to feel greatly uneasy about both their presence and their part in all of it. Though they had come here to witness the crucifixion of Jesus, and though Jesus himself had not yet been nailed to the cross, many of their number had already lost the stomach for what they had demanded of Pilate earlier. They were leaving.

The soldiers next turned their attention to Dysmas, as one of their number dragged his cross to the nearest hole from where he had dropped it. The procedure was as before, diligent and ruthless. Dysmas screamed in agony as the great nails were driven through his limbs. His leg irons removed and feet tied, the cross was raised until it too fell into the hole chosen for it with a thud. Dysmas had never before known such agony, as tears ran down his cheeks, and his life's blood ran down his upstretched arms.

As with Gestus, his cross was secured with wedges and a plinth attached at the most inconvenient position, before his feet were nailed to it.

Muriam was inconsolable as she witnessed this outrage perpetrated upon her son. The detail was so exact to the memory of her nightmare years before, that she was bewildered as now she lived the graphic terror of that night in reality.

Gaius was trying desperately not to look at the terrible scene behind him. He could not bear to see Muriam so devastated, or this gentle carpenter brutalised. Then he heard the hammer blow behind him, yet no piercing scream followed. He stopped his horse immediately and turned to face the execution of Jesus.

The soldiers had, as for the others, dragged his cross to the hole that would receive it, and stripped Jesus with no accommodation to either his dignity or comfort. The congealed blood had bound his clothing to his flayed body and, as they tore the clothes from him, whole portions of his body were left raw and bleeding, as they tore away also what little of his open wounds his body had been able to heal.

They had pushed him onto the cross and driven the first nail through, yet this had not elicited other than a groan from him. This seemed to anger the soldiers as they stretched out his other arm and secured it, also in silence. Now indeed silence fell upon the scene, and those attending.

Gaius had never before seen such a thing and had initially turned, expecting that Jesus was already dead. Conceivably, that would be the only explanation for the silence. He was stunned when he realised that Jesus was very much alive. As the cross was raised and slid into the hole, even the soldiers were noticeably more subdued in their bravado and arrogance, in the face of the silence that seemed very loud indeed. It was not lost on anyone present.

The wedges placed and the feet secured with nails, they were glad to have this execution behind them. They were about to turn their backs on him when he cried out, "Father forgive them, they know not what they do." They found themselves looking up at him perplexed.

"Well, then, we have been forgiven by the king. Give him something to drink," one said to another. "It might shut him up." They offered him a vinegar-filled sponge on a pole, but he refused it.

"Alright then, be ungrateful," the soldier said with a smile. Turning to his comrades he continued, "Let's get down to business." They set about then gambling for the seamless cloak they had taken from him.

One Pharisee yelled, "Come down from the cross now and we will believe you," as others hurled abuse at him. All the while he remained silent.

To the degree they could, both Dysmas and Gestus were now beginning to acclimatise themselves to the terrible pain they were suffering, trying to find as best they could the position of least discomfort.

Gestus was soon gravitating back to his anger but by now found it so difficult just to breathe, that hurling insults and obscenities were reserved for when he could muster the strength.

Dysmas, though very much in agony, was still bewildered by all he had observed and was now angry with himself for his earlier callous treatment of Jesus. Tears ran down his cheeks as he began to understand so many lessons he had learned from Jesus. He had understood so little because he had let his pride and anger direct his path. Now before him, was this great final lesson being taught by his old master. Thus far his only response had been to insult him.

Some in the crowd were yelling abuse at Jesus, and Gestus was getting worked up himself. "If you're a god," he said with some difficulty, "save yourself and us," but Dysmas raised himself and chided Gestus, "Have you no fear of God? We are getting what we deserve, but this man has done nothing wrong," he said as he slumped back in tears, as the effort needed was so great.

Gaius had allowed those relatives that wished to approach their loved ones access, and Mary approached with John and Mary of Magdala, as Muriam remained alone at a distance. Mary was clearly heartbroken and yet so very dignified, as John put his arm around her for support, while Mary of Magdala slumped at the base of the cross of Jesus, weeping inconsolably.

Silence fell upon the scene for some minutes as Dysmas struggled with the guilt and the sheer selfishness of what he wanted to say. Yet, it was neither fear nor selfishness that determined what he said next, as finally he understood so much of what his father had taught him, Petmar's words, and the words and works of this man before him. He was proud and honoured to be counted with him. Raising himself once more with terrible effort, he turned his head to face Jesus whose head was slumped almost to his chest.

"Lord," he said at last, "remember me when you come into your kingdom," and he slumped once more exhausted.

For a moment Jesus did not move, but Mary looked up at Dysmas with her sad smile, yet with eyes that seemed joyful, while still filled with tears. Jesus slowly turned to Dysmas then. "I promise you, this day, you will be with me in paradise."

Dysmas was overcome with joy, the burden of his sufferings seemed to lighten greatly, as momentarily he was lost in love. Mary was still smiling up at him when Jesus said at length. "Woman, behold thy son," and again, "behold thy mother."

At the ninth hour, black clouds covered the land and the sun was darkened until it was barely visible. Jesus cried out, "Father, into your hands I commend my spirit."

A moment later, though his breathing was shallow, a mighty cry that stunned those present was heard. "It is finished!" His head fell forward, and his lifeless body hung, a gruesome reminder of the terrible evil that had taken place.

Gaius was standing before Jesus' cross. Slowly shaking his head he said to himself out loud, "Surely, this was indeed the son of God."

Those who had remained were deeply affected by what they had seen and heard. They returned to their homes beating their breasts and repenting their part in the evil they had just witnessed.

As people were leaving, more of the surrounding landscape became visible and Dysmas could see, slumped on the ground, a woman broken by grief. He began to consider how much suffering his mother had endured, as silent tears flowed freely once more.

The death of Jesus and the dispersal of the crowd meant that silence fell upon the surrounds. Gaius stood before the cross of Jesus while the rest of the soldiers, no longer needed for crowd control, were gambling some distance away, tired as they had become of squealing women.

The centurion Maximus and his men arrived then, having been sent by Pilate to strengthen the contingent at Golgotha, but it was clearly unnecessary. His men simply joined the others gambling, while Maximus assessed the surrounding area.

"Gaius," was the rasping call of Dysmas. Gaius looked up to him. "Please," he gasped, "my mother."

Gaius thought for a moment and at last turned to see poor Muriam so broken a short distance away. His heart went out to her, yet he was not supposed to... No, he thought. He had been a pillar of Roman detachment, but not this time, he decided. He went to her and raising her up, assisted her to the foot of her son's cross.

"Mother," Dysmas said at length. She raised her eyes to him, tears streaming down her cheeks. "There has been enough suffering. My Lord has called me to paradise and I go with joy. I am at peace at last." He struggled with all his might to catch his breath. "You have found love once more. Do not lose it on my account," he said weeping. "We will be together in time. Be good to her, Gaius."

Gaius nodded to him solemnly.

"Leave me now, mother, to my moment before God. Please don't stay. Gaius," he said, pleading in his voice. Gaius looked up and nodded. He steered Muriam away toward Jerusalem taking a last opportunity to look upon Jesus once more.

Maximus was in his line as he walked. "Could you...?" enquired Gaius as he half-carried Muriam off the mount. Maximus nodded. He understood entirely, as he and Gaius were good friends. "Bring him home to us," he said simply to Maximus, who nodded that he had understood. He took charge of the sad scene from that moment, leaving Gaius to assist his love.

Life Anew

Walking now beside Gaius, Muriam found herself with mixed feelings. The last few weeks since her meeting with Dysmas had been ones of great introspection. She had been and remained very grateful to Gaius that he had ensured that she could at least see Dysmas. She knew well that it would simply not have happened had he not interceded for her. Yet, it was also true that Dysmas had been held, and in fact executed, by the same occupying army that Gaius was a part of.

Now as she walked along she found herself steadier than she thought she would be. The attitude of Dysmas had buoyed her greatly. Gaius had been in great part holding her up, yet now she felt strong enough to support herself as they neared his house. She stopped, turned to him and realised he had tears in his eyes. She squeezed his arm, a reassuring touch. "He seemed at peace," she said.

Gaius knew by now that those on the cross would be dead. It had been arranged earlier that their legs were to be broken to accommodate the Passover.

"He was at peace," he replied very thoughtfully. "So many people never find it, yet he found it on the cross of all places, next to that one I feel has the power to grant it. I didn't want to be there, Muriam, but now I'm glad I was. I confess I don't know whether to be happy for him or sad. In one way I'm crushed, yet I sense hope. I have no idea why, but somehow I feel there is. I can't help but wonder what he would have achieved had circumstances been different. Then there is Jesus. What has Rome done?" he said shaking his head. "What has she become?" and tears started to run freely.

"Come," said Muriam as she took his arm and led him to the door of his home. Jelrah was waiting, anticipating their arrival. He already knew his master to be a man of deep feelings, so was little surprised by his emotion after what he knew would be a gravely troubling day for him.

Gaius took a little time to compose himself before asking Jelrah to see if Simon could assist once more with the burial arrangements at this, the inconvenient time of Passover. As always, Simon was most gracious. He liked Gaius very much. He had already arranged for his nurse to stay in case Muriam needed her, yet to his surprise, she seemed to be coping well, considering.

An hour later the body of Dysmas was being carried into the house and laid out, just as his father had been before him so many years ago. This time, however, there was not the luxury of so much time before the Passover began. There was time only for the body to be embalmed and dressed. Dysmas was then carried to his father's tomb, where the stone had been previously rolled back in readiness.

Muriam accompanied the little gathering to the tomb in a state of numbness. There were so many emotions; it was simply too much to process. Gaius was always near in case he was needed, though he made a point of staying in the background as much as possible. As the body was now placed upon the slab within the tomb, all withdrew save Muriam. She looked about her now and saw she was alone. She went to the opening and called to a despondent Gaius. "Please," she said, "join me."

As he came into the tomb now, she took his hand and led him to the body of her son, laying at last beside the decomposed body of his father. They both stood with tears in their eyes. Without taking her eyes off her son, she said at last, "He bore you no grudge, Gaius, and he was right, there has been enough suffering, don't you think?" as she turned and looked into his eyes. He cried then as he had not done for many years, holding her as she too let her tears cleanse the countless wounds of a life of sorrow and solitude. Together, for nearly ten minutes, they washed away the years with their tears.

Finally, it was time to close the tomb. Jelrah was on hand to take Muriam back to the house, while Gaius would remain to assist in rolling the boulder back to its seat.

When she had left, Gaius found himself kneeling beside the slab on which the body of Dysmas lay. "I have much to say to you before I bid you farewell, Dysmas," he began. "How sorry I am I could not find you so long ago. How sorry I am for your father's death, and your mother's pain. How sorry I am that I never really got to know you, I would have very much liked to have known you. How truly sorry I am that Rome has become so corrupt, that she failed you. I want you to know how grateful I am to you for your forgiveness. I so wish we could have met under different circumstances. I don't know what will happen with your mother; that is for her to decide, but I think she can now live once more thanks to you. I am grateful most of all for this. Be at peace."

He found himself looking at Dysmas for some minutes before leaving, and assisting the men outside to roll the stone back to its place. It was at once a relief and a burden. It had been a tragic day that would not be quickly forgotten.

As he was leaving, he saw a short distance away some people at another tomb. He recognised Mary as one of those standing outside while the great stone was rolled into place. He could not imagine what she must be feeling.

The two paths each of them had to walk would join just before the exit gate, so Gaius deliberately stalled his walk so as to delay his arrival at that point. He felt distressed that he had had any involvement in the events of this day, and could not bear the just anger of a woman he respected so much as Mary. It was to no avail however; as Mary reached the fork in the paths, instead of exiting, she left the group and came toward Gaius. He tried to steel his heart for the anger he felt he deserved and was sure would come.

However, Mary stopped in front of him and took his hands in her own. The pain in her features was so obvious and great that tears welled again in the eyes of Gaius.

"Trust in God, Gaius," she said quietly and gently. "Do not fear this day now past, but trust in Him. Hope is nearer to you now than ever," managing a sad smile as she turned and walked away, leaving Gaius marvelling after her.

She was no sooner out of sight when two soldiers came running up to him disturbing his thoughts. "Jerusalem is in uproar," they said. "You have been ordered to the Praetorian to take command of the garrison."

Gaius reached across his chest and removed his chest plate and sword, as they watched, wondering what he was doing. He gave them both to one of them saying, "Tell the prefect my commission is ended, as is my allegiance to Rome." He walked between them then as they stared after him in disbelief, and went home.

He entered now wearing only his tunic, having discarded the rest of his vesture on the journey. Gaius had determined in that moment that the world was going to be a very different place for him from this day forward. It would no longer be one of regret and guilt, but one of hope and peace.

Muriam was surprised to see him arrive dressed only in his tunic. He went to her and held her hands in his own saying simply, "I am done with regret and guilt too great to bear, and I am done with Rome, Muriam. I understand that you will want to leave, but I will remain here in case you should ever return. You are the keeper of my heart, and there is nothing I can do that can change that."

"I will never again return to Jerusalem," said Muriam, "but you would not have me travel alone would you?" she continued with a smile as she put her arms around him and her head to his chest. Although the people of Jerusalem were wailing from fear and guilt, the house of Gaius was very much at peace that night.

Two days had passed since the death of Dysmas, when a lone figure walked through the opening of a silent and empty cave.

Barabbas, not really knowing what to do, headed instinctively for familiar surroundings and immediately wished he had not.

The full gravity and magnitude of his position, as well as his failure, weighed heavily upon him now. He fell to his knees weeping, utterly alone and dispirited.

He could not bear to stay and witness the crucifixion, so had fled the city moments after his release and not looked back. Now the weight of regret for this and so much more was crushing him, as this vast domain that had been his kingdom lay desolate before him.

When word reached Pilate of the response of Gaius, he was at first angry that he was left with inferiors to command, then envious that he too could not simply walk away and leave Rome behind, as his dear wife had begged him to do the night before. "I should have listened to her," he said to himself, as men ran here and there a hive of activity, around a pensive and thoughtful Pilate, whose mind was occupied by greater considerations than the state of Jerusalem just now.

Gaius related to Muriam his meeting with Mary. "She is an extraordinary woman," he concluded.

"She is a woman of faith and hope," replied Muriam, "of a line long past I feel." So dignified, she thought to herself. For the first time since her terrible dream, she knew where she had seen Mary before; in a dream of all places. The irony of it stunned her as she now told the only person who knew of her dream. "Now I remember her, Gaius," she said, "as clearly as I see you. Do you know what that means?"

"I don't understand," he replied.

"Petmar once told Azel and I something that I didn't fully understand until now. The one guarantee we all have as a certainty, is one from whence every peace comes. God has ordained all creation to conspire for our greater good, and that of our families. God knew this day would come, Gaius; he even told me of it all those years ago in a dream, so that when it did, I could have confidence in His providence. What I have long thought a burden, was all this time a gift," she said smiling as tears began again.

"Oh, Gaius," she said, "how he has cared for me and those I love. I was so busy with regret that I have not been aware of His delicate touch within my life. I see now. I understand now. Thank God," she said as she hugged him. "Thank God."

Lightning Source UK Ltd.
Milton Keynes UK
UKHW021347150221
378811UK00012B/2795